THE DEATH OF ENDENBOUGH WOOD

JACY RITCHIE

ISBN: 979-8-9905400-0-2 (Paperback)

ISBN: 979-8-9905400-1-9 (eBook)

Library of Congress Control Number: 2024911354

Any references to historical events, real people, or real places are used fictitiously. All characters, incidents, and dialogue are drawn from the author's imagination and are not to be construed as real.

Cover Design by Eric Labacz

Editing & Proofreading by Erika's Editing

For Victoria Dice,
who was the first to tell me to follow this dream
that's finally come true.

PROLOGUE

The first person I saw die at Abraham Gallander's hands wasn't a Lucian.

I should've thought that strange at the time.

Or maybe I did, but was too terrified of the Commander to protest when I saw his powerful hands around the kid's neck. Every soldier in the Barracks feared Gallander.

The kid was a few years younger than me, maybe nine or ten. Bone called him Walker, ever since the first night when the boy arrived in Barracks Six and wandered in his sleep all the way to the canteen. I didn't want him in my squadron, but I had little say in the matter when the Aces showed up with him in tow. His terrified eyes shifted from one side of the room to the other, searching for a friendly face.

I turned my head away. He was the kind of kid who latched, like a nursing kitten, onto anyone who looked remotely amiable. I didn't want anything to do with him. The word was he'd been in trouble before, charges mostly relating to cowardice. Apparently, the higher-ups thought a real squadron might toughen him up and set him straight.

They were wrong. Two weeks later, Walker ran. Fear made him foolish, and he fled in the middle of his first mock battle, pushing through the trees of the training grounds as though his fight suit were on fire.

I thought I was the only one who saw him go. I followed him, yelling for him to stop. But Gallander got there first. Gallander would always get there first.

There were four other Boquan training bases under his command, bases he himself had founded years ago. He visited each one often, never letting his soldiers out of his sight. Today he was at ours, sizing up our progress and watching our mock battles. Watching Walker.

The boy froze, horrified as the Commander stepped out of the trees and into his path. Gallander himself, slayer of a thousand Lucians, hero of Boqua. Rumor had it he was well into his two-hundredth year and nothing in the world could kill him. The man who'd instated the draft, who swore to mold the best and brightest Boquan children into soldiers. A necessary sacrifice. Saving our nation from the Lucian plague required no less. We belonged to him.

Walker's gaze followed the Commander's towering frame upward. Gallander glared at him with dark eyes from beneath a cap bearing the national insignia. The rest of his spotless uniform barely moved—even the rise and fall of his breathing betrayed only the slightest flutter of the tan fabric. His brass buttons gleamed in the sunlight like flaring matches.

I tried not to blink against the brightness, my back as straight as I could force it to be as I saluted.

"Sir."

Gallander, trained on Walker, ignored me. The boy's shoulders trembled with fear, his fight suit stained with sweat. He struggled to remain still, knowing he couldn't run this time. I felt my breath hitch in my throat when I caught the fury in the Commander's hard eyes. The *C*-shaped scar extending downward from his left temple seemed to etch itself deeper into his cheek with each passing second.

"Is this how you plan to fight the Lucians, boy?" Walker flinched as Gallander's voice grated like crunching gravel. I bit the inside of my lip, afraid to move. Afraid to breathe. Gallander's presence filled the air like a choking fog, enveloping everything in sight.

Walker tried to speak, his mouth opening and closing like a fish, and I fought the urge to clamp my eyes shut as the Commander's hand shot forward. The boy let out a terrified squawk that was abruptly cut off when the man's muscled fingers grabbed his neck. Barely pausing, Gallander lifted the boy from the forest floor, holding him at his own eye level, while Walker gurgled and grunted, legs flailing.

I held back a gasp. The rumors were true. No ordinary man could hope to hold a boy like that with one arm, and yet Gallander stood firm, his victim seeming no heavier than a newborn. And just as vulnerable.

I struggled to keep my composure, unable to block out the pained sounds of Walker's writhing. He clawed at the Commander's wrists, his eyes wide with terror. He gagged, fighting for air. Gallander's face twisted into a snarl, his teeth visible from between stretched lips. The forest itself went still, contrasting Walker's spasms. Gallander's grip only tightened.

"You're a disgrace to the Boquan army," he growled. "I've been lenient with your cowardice since day one, but this . . . " The Commander's teeth gnashed together, a hissing noise passing through them. "This is treason!"

The child squeaked. Begging, even without a voice. Gallander pulled him closer, his free hand joining the other around the boy's neck. "Everyone knows what happens to traitors."

My mouth went dry, my chest constricted. A quick twist of Gallander's hands. A cracking of bones. The body suddenly limp.

Walker fell to the dusty earth like a grungy laundry sack, his eyes lifeless and frozen in horror. My heart flew into my throat and stuck there, pounding out its frantic rhythm.

Dead. Walker was dead, his life taken from him so easily. I was sure Gallander would come for me next, but when he turned, his snarl had vanished. He took several steps toward me, his thick black boots pounding against the ground and sending waves of terror through my trembling legs.

He bent to my level, close enough that I could see the individual strands of gray in his cropped hair. "I know you wanted to do that," he said, his voice now soft, almost kind. The tone made my stomach roll. "And you will. When I see you're ready."

I kept very still, standing at attention as if clinging to my life. The chill in my bones threatened to cause my teeth to start knocking together. What did he think I "wanted" to do? Did he mean kill one of our own?

Gallander walked away, leaving me alone with Walker's body. I listened as his footsteps retreated into the woods, then I turned into a bush and retched.

From then on, I knew he was watching me, studying me. Evaluating me. His steely eyes bore into me long after the mock battle was over, his face haunting me at night. He made it his mission to find something within me that he could pull to the surface. Something he'd already found in himself.

A killer.

ONE

THE WORST PARTS OF MY DREAMS ARE THE EYES. Always staring, never blinking. Sometimes they belong to a young boy waiting for my blade to descend and take his life. Sometimes they're Gallander's eyes burning into me, his outstretched hand aiming for my neck. Fingers tightening until I can't breathe.

I jerk myself awake, my body shaking so violently I'm convinced the cave will collapse. My heart leaps, and I press my palms into the hard, rocky ground, scanning the stone ceiling. I'm safe. No dust or rock-flakes crumble onto me. No spiderweb-like cracks growing in the walls.

I squeeze my eyes shut, draw in a lungful of air, and will myself to be still. When I open my lids, Inari regards me with deep brown eyes that evidence an understanding a dog should not possess. She lowers her head and nuzzles it against the paw she's resting on my leg.

I stroke the black fur between her ears, and she tilts her head, pressing against my touch. Her tranquility floods into my fingertips, slowing my heartbeat and spreading warmth through my bones. She takes a deep breath, and I run my hand down the side of her long face. Somehow, she can sense my turmoil, the memories that haunt me.

Tossing my blankets onto the sleeping mat, I push off from the ground. Inari wags her long tail. For breakfast there are leftover hawkberries in a cracked ceramic bowl and a strip of dried rabbit. My dented canteen holds only a few mouthfuls of water, and the other containers, stored in the rocky niches toward the back of the cave, have run dry.

We have work to do today. Inari looks longingly at the rabbit meat, and I grin as she pricks her ears at me. I slide the hawkberries into my mouth, toss her the meat, then begin collecting the empty water jugs.

Outside, the late summer sunlight streams through leafy trees and bathes my skin in oddly shaped patches. I stretch the stiffness from my muscles, letting the scent of the forest flow over me. Wood and moss and grass and dirt. The other soldiers would've laughed if I told them it comforted me. I don't see them anymore. I don't see anybody anymore.

Inari trots faithfully by my side, her head down as she takes in the world through her nose. I glide through the trees with trained silence, eyes sweeping from one leaf to another. Occasionally I glance at Inari to check if anything has sparked her interest. To check if anyone has ventured into my Wood. Ventured too close for comfort.

The stream is my first stop. I kneel and take a gulp of the crisp water before splashing a handful across my face. The silver pendant hanging on a leather strap around my neck slips free from inside my jacket. The medallion glints in the sunlight, and the lump in my throat grows as I watch it twirl. I swallow and tuck it safely inside my shirt.

I fill the water jugs and sling the strap of my satchel over my shoulder. Following the stream, I collect my bounty from the hawkberry bushes that grow in clumps by the water's edge. Now and then, I throw a few more berries into my mouth, as I step carefully through the trees, alert and watchful.

I press further, past the small clearing and my garden where yesterday I collected the potatoes and carrots. The buckgorn isn't ready for harvesting yet, but it will store for nearly the entire winter. I gently pick off a few of the round green kernels, cracking them between my teeth. Sweet milk bursts across my tongue, filling my mouth with flavor.

But my true prize lies ahead, although I won't be collecting it this morning. My snares are arranged in spirals around my cave, spreading outward from my camp. Inari doesn't seem to notice when I skip the first three traps and delve further toward the edge of the Wood. I break away from the South Stream where it meets its western sister. The two will soon join the North Stream. The three, flowing together, will become the Lux River.

Treading gingerly, I cross the last snare-line, my boots barely crunching on the sandy earth. I keep one eye trained on Inari as my heart begins pounding a tense rhythm. I'm getting dangerously close to Boqua.

Every movement draws my gaze. Birds flying from their nests. A chipmunk dashing into the underbrush. Leaves stirring in the breeze. Every hint of every shadow. My eyes move like butterfly wings, my nostrils inhaling the deep, fresh scent of the air. All of my senses, damaged or not, are searching for something that doesn't belong.

Searching for them.

They come in groups of three or four, but their faces are never the same. They bring papers and markers and measuring tapes, and I watch them examine trees and squint at blades of grass as they scribble notes. They put samples of fur and leaves and soil into plastic zip-top bags that disappear into square containers which they carry away draped over their shoulders. Sometimes they snare small animals in complicated traps and poke them with sharp and twisted devices until the creatures cry out in pain. But what they seem most interested in is Vitmor. A stiff, broad-leafed plant with streaks of yellow in its leaves and a single yellow-and-red flower protruding from its center. It's rare here in the Wood, but I know it's dangerous—as a child, my father warned me not to touch it on the camping trips we took together. The memory is murky, but his meaning is not: stay away. Yet the strangers take every scrap of it they can find.

I first detected them six months ago. I didn't see them then, only what they left behind. Strange marks on the trees, lines drawn in the dirt. A twitching rabbit on its side, cowering in the dust.

Two weeks later, when I was checking the outer ring of my traps, I found them. There they stood, staring at a slash they'd made in a tree. Four strangers, surrounded by strange metal boxes containing even stranger equipment, a tangle of wires and lights. They stayed for hours, cataloging species and dripping testing-liquids onto rocks, until they finally nailed a white square to a tree, packed away their gear, and tromped away.

Crashing through the underbrush like a herd of mindless cattle, they never noticed me tailing them. They crossed the Lux River toward Boqua and complained loudly of wet socks and mosquitoes as they sloshed through the last half of their journey. They tumbled out of the forest near the town of Gesher and disappeared into hovercabs. From the safety of the trees, I watched them speed away.

Whatever these strangers are doing, they care nothing for the Wood.

I leap across the stepping-stones of the North Stream, leading Inari to where I found them last week. Her keen ears flick; they have detected something mine cannot. The strangers' visits are drawing closer together. Closer to my camp, buried in the center of the Wood. No one has ever ventured that close, but the uneasy twisting of my gut warns me that they might.

Inari growls, but I shush her as I crouch. Her ears are pinned forward, pointing toward a clump of bushes. I inch closer, stepping silently until I'm close enough to pull back a branch and peer through.

Three of them, kneeling in the dirt with their noses buried in logbooks and soil samples. They wear dark shirts and pants, thin jackets draped over their shoulders. If I squint, I can make out letters sewn into the fabric: RAMIUS.

Two men and a woman, all with dark hair; the older man bears streaks of gray in his. I press my back against a tree, slide myself upward, and turn my head to watch their lips, reading in their movements words my ears would never be able to hear, even though they call to each other without care. Without the slightest fear of someone close by.

"Say that number again?"

"Three point four eight."

"Results are certainly better than at the last site." A stirring of excitement. "We may have found the sweet spot here."

"At least he'll be off our necks for a few weeks."

"That's enough for today. Let's finish up and get out of here."

Inari looks at me anxiously. She wants to hunt. To chase. To drive these intruders away. She whines, and my heart pitches. One of the strangers throws his head up at the sound.

"What is it?" the woman asks. My body freezes.

"Thought I heard something out there."

They pause, scanning the edges of the clearing with their hard eyes. A few seconds pass before the woman relaxes her shoulders. "Probably just a bird or a squirrel."

The man adjusts his collar. "This place gives me the creeps," he mutters, and I have to angle my head to hear him at all. "You know the stories. People coming here and never coming back. And that soldier who's supposed to be living like a caveman up in the hills."

The older man barely lifts his gaze from the clump of mud in his tweezers. "Nothing but rumors, Frenam. Stories to scare children. We've been here a dozen times and we've never seen a thing."

"Yeah, but what if—"

Inari whines too loudly again, cutting off Frenam's worried speech. The trio bolts upright as one.

"I know you heard that!" Frenam shouts.

"It sounded like an animal," the woman says.

"Can we all calm down, please?" the older man says. "Grena's probably right."

"But what if she isn't?" Frenam's eyes bulge. I watch with sparked curiosity, his face filled with fear. What tales *have* been told about the wild man in the Wood? I'm certain no one has ever seen my camp, yet the rumor is surprisingly accurate.

"It came from over there," Grena points in my direction, and my stomach flips.

"You know what could happen if the Lucians ever found out—"

Inari growls deep from her throat. They panic, shouting and stumbling over each other, unsure of whether to investigate or flee. The older man points his stern face in my direction and pulls a gun, ignoring the others as he marches toward me.

I hold in a curse, peeling away from the tree and ducking into the cover of the deeper Wood. I hear nothing more, but Inari does. She flings her head back several times before accepting that we're not going after them today.

The gun is new and alarming information. The strangers are clearly scientists, collecting data for some reason I can't even begin to imagine. Why do they have weapons? What will I do if they find my camp? I could never let them leave it again, but if they didn't return, more would come looking for them. Maybe not just scientists, either.

I follow the North Stream, slapping at branches and leaves in my path, hacking away at vines and bushes with my hunting knife. I should be heading back to camp, but anger roils within me. All I want is to live in peace, away from everything. Away from them. Alone—just me and Inari. Sooner or later, they'll come, take it all away, and I'll have to run again. Find somewhere else to hide.

I whack a loose branch, and it shudders before crashing to the forest floor. I stab my knife into the fallen branch and let out a sigh. Inari whines. I move down to the stream's cool water and wash the sweat from my forehead.

And this is where I see the first signs.

Blackened earth, disintegrating logs crumbling to dust. A campfire burned here. And there, the grass is matted, flattened where somebody has slept. The scientists never overnight in the Wood. Never light fires.

A glinting in the grass catches my attention. Between the blades, I find a silver coin resting in the dirt. I pinch it between two fingers, frowning at the strange design. My eyebrows pull together, touching. This is unlike any currency I've seen. The coin is too large, and the face portrayed on the front is unrecognizable, utterly foreign. The reverse shows a flourishing tree with sprawling roots.

Inari sniffs the ground and growls. I blink at the makeshift campsite. I can't make out footprints, but flattened patches of trampled grass or bits of upturned soil are all the trail I need.

I travel slowly, my hand at the hilt of the blade sheathed at my thigh. I watch Inari closely, reading the twitch of her ears and the shift and tilt of her head. All is well. For now.

Tracking them, I follow the trail as it curves, hugging the border of the forest. They crossed the West Stream here not too long ago. Impressions left in the softer earth, broken twigs snapped beneath heavy work boots. They moved quickly through the underbrush here, not attempting to conceal themselves.

I leap from the last stepping-stone as I cross the bubbling water. Inari's ears are on the alert, her head held high. I follow her gaze and hear a faint rustle of leaves in the bushes ahead. My adrenaline spikes. If the sound is close enough for me to hear, it's likely too late.

Black fabric and tanned skin emerge from the trees. My stomach shrinks in dread, my throat dry as sand. Too close to Boqua. I've ventured too close. Inari's warning growl fills my right ear.

The figure pauses as he lays eyes on me. Wide, unbelieving eyes. His blond hair hangs down past his ears, his sweat-stained shirt drooping from his belt. Four golden stars embellish his shoulders, signifying his rank. A Boquan soldier. And he's found me.

His face drops in surprise and recognition, then hardens in anger. "You!"

The blood freezes in my veins as I take in his familiar features. The thin face, the curve of the nose, the blond hair, the crooked lips. The gleam in his eye. I know them all. Too well.

"Link?"

He snarls. "Oh, I'm going to enjoy this."

I swallow. Link's mouth opens, a blur of a shout passing through his lips as he lunges forward. I dart away from his outstretched arms, and he whirls around, glaring at me like a feral dog. My choices are clear: fight or flight. He's much stronger than I am, but I'm faster. His eyes sparkle with power and strength, his large fists ready to break bones. His gun remains holstered at his hip—he's not after a quick kill. He's itching to fight. To fight me.

I am hungry. I am tired. I choose to run.

I give a brisk nod to Inari, and she takes off into the brush, my feet kicking up earth and leaves behind her as I pump my legs, fleeing through the trees and ducking branches. I know the Wood's every dip and ridge. I know its brambles and quagmires. I think I can lose him without too much effort, but my chest jolts in shock when his hand clamps onto my shoulder.

"Is running all you know how to do now, coward?" Link snarls, shoving me forward. I gag as the leather cord of my pendant snags my throat. Link has caught it, and the pressure only gets worse as he yanks back. I choke, grasping for the cord, but I'm off balance and tumble down with a painful thud, the leather snapping from the strain.

I draw in air through my bruised windpipe and clutch my neck. I roll over and find Link staring at the silver pendant in his palm. His eyes rake across the intricate design: three spheres arranged in a triangle with intertwining vines connecting them. Tiny leaves curl from the vines.

He squeezes his fist around the metal, the leather strap dangling from his fingers. His eyes move to mine, hatred flashing in the dark pools. "I oughta gut you right where you lay," he growls, hovering over me with clenched fists. "Traitor." He spits the word as though it were poison on his tongue.

My two choices are now narrowed to one. "Are you sure you want to try me?" I snap. Link may have the upper hand, but I still know how to provoke him.

He sneers. "I always said I'd be the one to bring you down. Even *you* can't run forever."

I can't make out much else of his speech, the muffled words sticking in my damaged ear, but I don't need to. He's distracted, gloating, and wide open. I narrow my eyes, my muscles tightening. He should have let me run. He should've fled the other way, out of my Wood as fast as his strong legs could carry him.

He doesn't notice when I tense my muscles, and it's only when a spark flickers in his eyes that I know he's realized his mistake. By now, it's too late. I launch myself forward and plow into his knees.

He howls as he falls, but his muscles tighten instinctively. He flings my weight from him, but not before my punch leaves his nose badly bloodied. He wipes the crimson stream with the back of his hand and stares down at the red.

"Always were quick on the attack, weren't you?"

"You were never quick at anything," I retort. I take his body in. His stance, the tension in his arm. He's going to lunge. He's also going to miss.

Before he can shoot forward, I fling a fist at his jaw. He blocks it with his forearm and pounds his own punch into my side. I grunt, doubling over in pain. He lands a gut-kick that sends me to the ground, ache screaming in my stomach. Before I know it, he's on top of me, fists pounding my face, over and over. Pain explodes in my head and blurs my vision. His blood drips onto my cheek.

I clench my teeth and jerk my hips upward, throwing him off balance. The pummeling stops, and before he can try it again, I've grabbed his arm and flipped him onto his back. With one hand, I yank his hair, pinning him. With the other, I form a fist and smash it into his face. More blood spurts from his broken nose as he screeches.

Red streaks down his shirt, but he still manages to clip my chin with a punch that sends me reeling. He easily pulls his legs free and aims a kick at my sternum. The air flies from my lungs, and I fall to the earth, groaning.

"You think you can beat me?" he grunts, pulling himself to his feet. "You've been hiding in a hole for years. You're soft and weak."

My jaw clenches, but he's right.

Link snickers. Blood lines his teeth. He shakes his head, and droplets spatter on the ground. "You're lucky Gallander wants you alive. Otherwise, I'd tear you apart."

I push myself to my feet, staggering on shaking legs. "Gallander?"

Link knows he's found a pressure point and grins. "He says the first soldier to bring you in gets an automatic promotion, plus enough money to buy half the country." He wipes at his nose again. "You're actually worth quite a lot for a traitor."

My fingers tremble. Gallander wants me alive. Boquans never bring traitors in. Never let them breathe any longer than is necessary. Betray them and they'll drop you where you stand, not one second of mercy. There aren't many explanations for Gallander's wanting me alive, and none of them involve any kind of clemency.

I know what I have to do. Link spits out a glob of blood and glares at me with more hatred than I've ever seen in him. He's not the soldier I knew. When I look at him, I see bitter rage and insatiable hunger.

Worse, I see me.

My voice threatens to break. "I thought you had better things to do than wander the woods pretending to be a soldier."

His lip curls. "You have no idea how far I've come since you betrayed us," he snarls. "Everyone always thought you were the best, but once I bring you in, they'll see who really had it all along."

"Well done, Link," I reply, cocking my chin at the now-bloodied stars on his shoulder. "It only took you an extra two and a half years to reach my old rank. I'm sure Gallander thinks you're an excellent replacement for me."

It's just enough. My goading drives him past his breaking point, and his insatiable anger flares. He shoots forward, a wild howl flying from his lips. But I'm already drawing my blade. It cuts off his growl in mid-lunge as the steel slices deep into him. Blood from the new wound covers my arm as I twist the blade.

Even more blood burbles from his mouth, and he freezes with his arms outstretched, too weak to take hold of me although his body is mere inches from mine. With a jerk, I withdraw the blade, stepping away. Link crumples to the ground.

I stare at him, grateful for the familiar silence of the Wood. I break it only to bid him goodbye in a whisper I barely hear. "Say hello to her for me."

His body stirs one last time—a quick spasm as life leaves him. Regret pricks inside of me, but I fight it back as I bend down and pluck my pendant from the grass. I stuff it into the safety of my jacket pocket. Regret won't help anything now. Link left me no other choice.

Inari's chilling growl bursts through the quiet. She's returned to me, her tongue lolling from her mouth with every pant, her eyes focused on the trees ahead. Cursing my damned ears, I scan the brush through the one eye not swelling shut.

A loud voice soon follows.

"Don't move!" Another soldier steps from the undergrowth, a rifle gripped in both hands, barrel pointed at me. He takes aim, but his gaze falls to Link's motionless body. His face drops in shock.

"What . . . have you done?!" he cries, his face flooding with anguish. Inari snarls, but she stands firm, waiting for me to tell her what to do.

I rip another knife from my belt, and before the soldier can take another step, I launch it with all the strength I have left. I watch as the blade sinks into his chest with a dull thwack. His mouth agape, he collapses without a sound reaching my ears.

Inari's growls trail off, her hackles again flat against her neck, but I'm still tense. Still waiting. Still searching. Because the tracks I followed here were not made by two Boquan soldiers.

They were made by one single man.

Meaning there is someone else still out there.

One more intruder in Endenbough Wood.

TWO

I NEVER LIKED TRAINS. THE DEEP RUMBLING TERRIFIED me, as did the screeching and grating of metal as they wound their way down the tracks. My father told me that sometimes we had to deal with things we didn't like, and so I learned to summon my bravery in the face of the long, black, metallic snakes.

On the day Gallander's men came for me, it only seemed natural that they stuck me on a train, testing me from the start. I was one of the chosen eight-year-old kids from my hometown. They hauled us to the train station, tossing us inside the freight cars like bags of flour or cans of beans. Immediately, I scrambled to a corner of the car and huddled there, the hollow in my chest growing when the engine roared to life. Through the slats, all I could see were my parents' shattered faces as we pulled away.

There weren't many of us in the car—a dozen or so, boys and girls alike. Some of the kids clustered together and leaned on each other's shoulders, while others sat alone with their backs pressed against the walls. Some wiped at their pale, stunned faces and pretended they had dust in their eyes. We were supposed to be strong. We were the chosen.

Sinking to the cold floor and pulling my knees to my chin, I gripped my jacket and inhaled the familiar scent of my mother's laundry soap. The jacket was a gift for my eighth birthday, only a month past. I had asked for a pocketknife with three blades and a built-in screwdriver, but now my jacket became the most precious gift I'd ever received.

I buried my face in the soft fabric. I smelled home there. I felt my mother's arms embracing me when I awoke from a nightmare. I heard my father's reassuring voice, the constant promise of protection and warmth. I gripped the silver pendant that he'd tied around my neck before they marched me away, and I squeezed my eyes shut, willing back time. When I opened my lids, I would find myself in my room, waking from another nightmare. She would be there. He would be there. As it always was.

But the train continued without pause. The lights overhead flickered out, and startled gasps squeezed from already-terrified throats as the car plunged into darkness, then flooded with light again. No one spoke. Nervous eyes flitted from one face to another, all dropping to the floor before locking with any others.

A boy slid down beside me and smiled grimly. "Hi," he whispered. I started at his voice. His mouth hung crooked on his thin face, his lips deformed by his uneven smile. He brushed stringy blond hair across his brow and lifted his head toward the ceiling. "Which base you think we're going to? North or south?"

I shrugged my shoulders and turned away before he could get me in trouble. We were headed north, of course, but I wasn't about to volunteer that information. He'd have to figure that out for himself, which would have taken a single look at the angle of the sun through the roof's vent. They told us not to talk to each other, not even to exchange names. Besides, his question was pointless. Our direction revealed nothing—we could be going to the moon for all I knew. All that mattered was we were going away from home. Away from everything we'd known.

Fear settled in the pit of my stomach, squirming like restless leeches in my gut. They crawled up and suctioned onto my heart until tears gathered in my eyes. I blinked the moisture away before the blond-haired boy could see. How could he sit there, a smile stretched on his face as if his dream-come-true awaited him at the end of these tracks?

Hours passed. The train never stopped. The hissing of the engine and rocking of the car rolled together as one continuous sound buzzing in our ears. Some of the kids shifted onto their sides and gripped their stomachs, hunger gnawing away at them. Others tried to hide the wet stains seeping through their pants.

I balled my jacket into a makeshift pillow and rested my head on my knees. I stayed that way, barely moving, even when my muscles began aching. The blond-haired boy wouldn't leave. Occasionally he would say something I ignored, but when he licked his cracked lips, I noticed his resolve beginning to waver.

"You don't talk much, do you?" he finally said. I shot a glare at him as the train finally jerked to a stop. The boy lost his balance and flopped onto me. I grunted and shifted away from him, gripping my jacket tighter. The car door slid open with a painful screech, the bright sunlight blinding us.

A man's face appeared in the opening and smirked. The rest of his body followed, climbing aboard in a flash. "New shipment of Greens, ready and waitin'!" he shouted over his shoulder. He lowered his voice slightly, addressing us. "Alright, out! Find a place on the green line— and no talking!"

Nobody moved. A lump formed in my throat. His dark eyes glinting in the sunlight, the man leaned forward. His black T-shirt stretched across his tight muscles, his fingers clenched into fists. "I said *move!*"

We sprung as one at his thundering voice, pushing past one another and forming a line at the door. I was shoved toward the back, with only the blond-haired boy behind me. Still, I could tell we were high up, much too high for eight-year-old kids, and I saw no ladder or platform. The man shouted again, and the kids ahead of me began leaping from the train. Crushing thuds and cries of pain followed, sending my stomach to my shoes.

When my turn came, my eyes surveyed the area as quickly as I could. In the distance, a tall, barbed-wire fence curved in front of several gray buildings. It extended even further beyond, past a glistening lake and around a sandy obstacle course. Small people navigated through the ropes and barriers as though their lives depended on how fast they could traverse the course.

I looked at the paved ground. The fall was further than I'd anticipated; the train had stopped at the top of a ravine. Several of the kids were crawling away, their faces twisted in anguish from their swelling ankles.

The man scowled at me viciously. "Come on, Green. You're holdin' up traffic."

When I'd got on the train, a soldier had practically thrown me aboard—even three or four feet was too high to manage without steps. Now, the pitch below added two meters to the distance. The only person who could save me from a twisted ankle stood with his arms folded across his chest, watching me like prey.

I glanced behind me at the blond-haired boy's colorless face. Taking a deep breath, I bent my knees and lowered myself to the car's floor. My eyes caught on the metal handle of the sliding door, and I paused. I pulled my jacket free of my body and looped one sleeve around the metal bar, tying the fabric tightly into a knot. Tugging to check its strength, I eased one leg from the car. The other followed, and I inched myself down with both hands, keeping my legs tucked under me for balance. The fabric strained, a popping coming from the seams. Another deep breath. I let go.

My feet hit the ground, and the impact forced my hands to the pavement, but I felt no pain except a slight sting. I moved away and took one last look at my jacket, which dangled loosely from the car. My eyes shot back to the man in the black T-shirt. Hard-faced, he stared at my makeshift rope, arms still crossed. But one corner of his mouth curved upward, and his eyes sparkled for an instant before he pointed to the blond-haired boy still on the train.

"Hurry up!" he barked. He turned to me with another order. "The line, now!"

I took the next open spot on the line, my toes touching the green paint on the cracked concrete. The blond-haired boy slid down my jacket and hurried to join me.

The man dismounted from the train, hitting the ground with a practiced landing that left him unfazed by the impact. He scrutinized us as we shifted nervously. Some tried to stifle whimpers, others stood with a sore foot cocked. I watched him closely. His T-shirt had two stars embroidered on each shoulder, and he wore forest-green cargo pants with a black belt. A better look at his face told me he was a teenager. Old, but still not an adult.

"They call me Bone," he shouted to the line. "Last long enough here and you might find out why." His eyes narrowed, dark brows casting shadows over them. "I'm the Ace of the Greens. From now on, until you've completed your basic training, your orders come from me."

He tapped at his shoulder. "These stars signify my rank. Anyone with two stars is an Ace. Leader of their barracks. One star is a UL—a Unit Leader. Every Ace has four ULs under their command. Both Aces and ULs are able to give you orders, and you're expected to carry them out to the letter. Understand?"

We nodded. Bone was not satisfied. He leaned into the face of one kid. "*Understand*?" he shouted.

"Yes!" we cried.

"Yes, what?"

"Yes, sir!"

He relaxed slightly. He pointed behind us. "Beyond that fence is your new home, where you'll learn to become the soldiers you're destined to be."

Destined? No part of me felt destined to become a soldier, no more than I was destined to sprout wings and morph into a hawk. If I had a choice, I would've picked the hawk—at least then I could fly out of this place. I nervously eyed the other recruits. Most of them wore the same sick expression I knew I did.

"Bone!" The shout pulsed through the air, and Bone turned his head as another young man approached from inside the fence. One star adorned each shoulder of his sweat-stained shirt. A UL, whatever that was. He looked us over menacingly and asked, "How many this time?"

"Fifteen," Bone replied. The second man scoffed.

"Number goes down with every roundup."

Bone shrugged. "It's not like you can order people to have more children—Gallander can only select from that. I'm not sure many of this lot are gonna be worth keeping, anyway." His sweeping eyes landed on me for an instant. He folded his arms again. "Alright, Greens! Once around!"

We stared at him blankly. He leaned forward; we cringed. What did he want us to do?

"Turn around!" he shouted. We obeyed. He stepped in front of us and pointed to a building with the Boquan flag flying on its roof. "That's the induction building, where you'll have your physical and get your uniforms, haircuts, and standard-issue supplies. Once you're finished, I want you all in Barracks Ten. Understand?"

One girl tested her luck. "Where is Barracks—"

"—Anyone who can't find it sleeps in the dirt!" Bone shouted. "Now move!"

The blond-haired boy sneaked a worried glance at me before we took off. I hurried along behind the limping recruits, heart thudding in my ribcage. The induction building seemed miles away, a speck in my vision.

Home was even further.

The broad double-doors swallowed us and dropped us into an octagonal room with white walls streaked with gray stripes. Three women clad in white looked up as we entered. A large desk sat directly in front of us, a looming door taking up most of the wall behind it. Fake potted plants stood in every corner, a pathetic attempt to cheer up the dismal place. As if plastic foliage could calm our nerves.

"Alright, everybody," the first woman said, her voice not exactly welcoming but kinder than Bone's. "We have a lot to get through in a short time, so to make things go faster, we're splitting you into three groups." The second woman counted us off into groups of five; the third, holding a clipboard, sized us up as she scribbled her notes.

The first woman led my group, the blond-haired boy included, into a white hallway with closed doors lining both sides. Her eyes twinkled as her head tilted down toward us. "If your Ace didn't make it clear, induction includes your aptitude test."

"What's that?" the blond-haired boy asked. Her smile grew, her pale hair falling in sagging curls around her pasty face. "All in good time, dear." She addressed the five of us again. "Now, we have a limited number of rooms for each part of the induction, so you'll go through the stages in different orders." She turned and pulled a skinny girl from the line, guiding her toward a door. "You'll be issued your uniform and supplies here." The girl nodded obediently and walked through the door, the lock clicking behind her.

Another girl was selected for another door. "You'll have your exam with Dr. Grear."

A boy. "You'll take your aptitude test." He hesitated by the door, almost shaking in fear, as the woman turned to the blond-haired boy and me.

"And you two will both get your haircuts, here." She motioned to the next door down, swiping a hand across the boy's locks. A small giggle pressed up from her throat. "Won't have those for much longer."

She focused on the other boy still waiting before the aptitude test door, his large eyes staring up at her. A sickly sweet smile spread across her face, and she pushed the door open, her sleeve sliding back to reveal her oatmeal-like skin. "Go on, dear, there's nothing to be frightened of." He hung his head and slowly moved over the threshold, giving her one last look as the door closed behind him.

The blond-haired boy blinked at me cluelessly, then ducked into our assigned room. I followed, the door shutting with a click. Inside sat a single chair; a man holding electric clippers stood behind it. He waved the device at the two of us, his bright white teeth made sinister by the harsh fluorescent lighting.

"Alright. Who's first?"

The blond-haired boy clearly wasn't volunteering. I bit my lip and stepped forward, turning to slide into the stiff chair. The man shot me a smile and slipped a white sheet around my neck.

"Here we go. It's not that bad." He thumbed a button on the side of the clippers, and they hummed to life beside my ear. "Trust me."

He placed a hand on top of my head to steady it. The clippers grated against my skin.

I squeezed my eyes shut and prayed to Elorai above for it to be over, the buzzing of the clippers almost drowning out the screams of the boy in the next room.

THREE

THE STRANGER DOESN'T KNOW HIS WAY AROUND THE forest. I've followed his trail for several miles now, his footprints clear in muddy spots, flattened grass and broken twigs leading the way everywhere else. He's traveled through areas I hardly ever venture into, and he's crossed his own trail several times. He's clearly lost, but his wanderings have brought him closer to the center of the Wood. And to my camp.

The strap on my satchel digs into my shoulder, and I know I'll soon need to empty my bag. I went back for my harvest, after the encounter with Link. Food is too scarce to waste.

Three hollow trees up ahead each contain a metal bin inside, each buried to the lid in the cool soil—I had to chop away at the trees' stubborn roots to create these hiding places. To insulate my food, I've filled the bins with dried sand from the stream beds. Thirteen of these food-stores surround my camp in the same spiral pattern as my snares; one is always nearby when I need to empty my satchel.

As I kneel beside one of the hollow trees and reach for the bin's latch, Inari pricks her ears forward, her fur rising—whatever she's detected, it's not an animal's sound or smell. I take a breath to steady my heart, and I hold up a hand to quiet her before she growls. Warning blares in her eyes. I give her head a soft pat of reassurance, telling her I'll handle this my way. Danger is close, but it's not time to strike. Not yet, not now. But soon enough.

I put half the hawkberries into the bin, pushing them beneath the sand with the other fruit, and close the lid. The intruder is watching me, I can feel it now, just as Inari can. I stroke her and guide her away from the tree. Hoping my performance fools the intruder, I keep my shoulders slack, my steps easy. I push on as though continuing on my way, but as soon as I'm clear of his vision I duck behind a nearby clump of bushes and peer through the leaves. The intruder makes horrid noises as he tramps through the forest—twigs snapping, leaves crunching, and, when a skinny branch slaps him on the side of his head, he mutters something unintelligible. My eyes follow him as he makes his way toward my food-store. He knows a secret of mine now, and that makes him twice as dangerous.

He falls to his knees at the tree, his hands disappearing into the hollow. I move.

My feet press silently into the soil, the earth spongy beneath my boots. My arms are high, my body poised. The muscles in my legs quiver, taut and ready to give chase if he bolts.

I close the distance between us while his back remains turned. In an instant, I'm on him, my grip sinking into his bony shoulders. I pull him from his knees and fling him sideways. Startled, he cries out as the force of my throw shoves him fully into the dirt. His arms flail for a second, but he freezes when he sees me.

Wide, terror-filled eyes. Smooth, thin face. Young, no more than eighteen. Still a kid in many ways.

My fist hovers above his chest, my knife's tip aimed at his neck. My other hand grasps the collar of his shirt, choking him with his own clothing. His gaze darts from me to the blade, then to me again. He sags in defeat and holds up his palms.

"Okay, okay," he breathes, his face pale. "Look, I'm sorry. I just wanted some food, that's all!" He risks a glance at the hollow. "I promise! I'm just hungry."

I stare. Thin muscles make no struggle against my hold. His dark blue eyes are set deep, and the fear in them blares louder than a bugle's horn. He stares warily at my poised hand. My fingers twitch around my knife's hilt, my jaw clenching.

This intruder is no threat. Not an immediate one. My arm slowly lowers, my other hand releasing the hold on his shirt. I watch him as his eyes follow me. I straighten my legs, still gripping my knife tightly. Inari, now at my side again, mirrors me, easing up slightly but still on alert. The teen doesn't move as I step toward the tree and reach inside. When I pull my arm from the hollow, I toss a sandbear in his direction.

He catches it, looking from me to the fruit."Hey, thanks," he says, bringing it to his lips and tearing into it. He eats like he's forgotten how to do it properly, and when he finally notices my revulsion, he slows his chomping and sheepishly wipes the juice from his chin.

"My name's Lukas," he says, chewing the skin of the wild fruit. With his mouth full, I can't read his lips, and I can barely make out his words. "What's yours?"

I hesitate. "Fiver," I say, and he scrunches up his nose, pulling the sandbear from his lips.

"Fiver?" The food in his stomach must be making him sloppy; he doesn't remember that moments ago his life was at my mercy. Still is, for that matter.

"What kind of name is that?" he asks. "It's a number."

I frown. "It's my name."

He shrugs, throwing away the chewed core. "If you say so." He licks the stickiness from his fingers before gesturing to my blade. "What are you doing out here with that giant potato peeler?" He gives a slight, lopsided grin. "You could kill a moose with that thing."

"It does its job," I grunt. Inari barks, as if confirming my words.

He shrugs again, the grin still on his face."If I ever need a moose killed, I'll know who to come to. Hey, what happened to your face anyway? Did a moose attack you?"

I don't reply. His pathetic attempt to show me he's not afraid is useless; I can see the fear he's harboring. In the way his fingers tremble, the way his skinny arms quake. My eyes rake over his torn clothes: a brown T-shirt with a ragged hem, faded jeans that have a hole in one knee and are wearing thin in the other. Mud cakes his shoes, which are black and thin-soled. Terribly worn. Nothing about him is ready for combat.

"You're not a Boquan soldier," I say.

A mixture of disgust and shock flashes across his face. "No, of course not. What made you think that?"

I don't answer. Fool that he is, his words have just confirmed what I suspected. Heat rises within me, crawling up my spine and pulsing inside my skull. My heart begins pounding faster than I can count the beats, so fast I'm sure Lukas can see it hammering through my shirt. My lips purse in a thin line, the muscles in my neck throbbing. I ball both fists.

He's a Lucian.

Fifteen years of training flood to the forefront of my mind, all screaming one thought: They are the enemy. From the smallest child to the greatest soldier, all Lucians deserve to die.

Lukas notices the change in my stance. His face falls, the blood draining from his cheeks like water dribbling through cupped hands. He pushes to his feet slowly, swallowing nervously as his brain tries to work out what to do.

"You . . . " Terror pools in his pupils. He takes a shuddering step backward, stumbling over a root. "You're . . . you're a Boquan." He steadies his footing, and his eyes widen, fighting the disbelief. He steps back again, and his eyes transform into almost-pity. "You're one of the stolen children."

Lukas shakes uncontrollably, trying to keep himself still. He knows what I am, knows he cannot fight me and win. Perhaps feeling the strength of my arms when I flung him into the dirt wasn't enough, but now he's certain. He's too slow, too weak, and too clumsy to escape. He's up against a soldier, and he knows it.

A bead of sweat rolls down my back. The Lucian deserves to die. Conflicting emotions play tug-of-war in my gut, but in the end I slip my knife into its sheath. I'm no soldier, not now.

"I was, not anymore," I tell him. "And you're lucky. I could've dropped you where you stood." I turn away, flexing my fingers to discharge their remaining tension. "But that would've been a waste of a perfectly good sandbear."

FOUR

"YOU GOTTA GO DOWN THIS HALLWAY, THEN TAKE A right."

The boy towered over us, wiping grease from his face while chewing the last bite of his sandwich. One of the Greens in my group had stopped him and his buddies in the hall outside of the canteen, nearly begging for directions to Barracks Ten. The rest of us had piled around him, listening as though Elorai himself were speaking from a cloud up above.

"Follow that hall until you get to the second door on your left. That's where Greens belong."

The two boys behind him snickered into their hands. I furrowed my brow, but the rest of the Greens nodded gratefully before shooting off like a spray of bullets. The blond-haired boy, his locks now reduced to a pale fuzz across his scalp, started to follow the Greens, but he paused when I didn't.

His face screwed up in confusion. I shook my head, glancing at the three older boys. They were turning into a corridor across from the one they'd pointed out. Their sinister laughs echoed back to me.

I made for the older boys' corridor, the blond-haired boy hissing his protests behind me. He wasn't thinking; no one else had been willing to help us, so why should we believe the older kids had told us anything other than a bald-faced lie?

I ignored him, rounding the corner just as the older kids turned a second corner. Despite his protests, the blond-haired boy followed me as I followed them. Down one hallway, into another, staying far enough behind that they wouldn't notice. Eventually, we found ourselves in a long hallway with five doors on each side, a number painted in black on each one. At the end: number ten.

The older boys disappeared, laughing, into a door marked with a three. The blond-haired boy sucked in a breath. "Bastards!"

I walked down the empty hallway and pushed open the last door.

On the other side, Bone stared at me. He stood in the center of the huge room, its white walls streaked with angled gray stripes. Single beds lined the room; a metal dresser separated each. Nearly half of the beds were occupied, and from them, heads turned to size up us newcomers. Pairs upon pairs of eager, consuming eyes. I fought back a flinch.

"Well, well," Bone murmured, unfolding his arms. He reached for the stack of manila folders piled on one of the beds, and he rifled through a few files before finding the one he wanted. He gazed at its contents with vivid curiosity, his brows arching in astonishment. "Aren't you full of surprises, Green?"

I stood frozen, watching his sweeping eyes. My file. That was my file. A streak of nausea shot through my gut. Bone looked up at me again. "You scored a five on your aptitude test."

I swallowed. Was that bad? I'd always been scolded in class if I received a low mark, but this wasn't school. An entirely different world. What would they do to me here? Would they prick my arms with needles again, tape wires to my head once more, force me to face those terrible pictures over and over until I did better?

"That's a record, Green," Bone said. "Highest I've ever seen is a three and a half."

A record? The dark images of the aptitude test flashed in my mind. Swirling masses of terror and teeth and blood, visible even when I closed my eyes. Horrors that growled menacingly and nipped at my skin until I all but begged for them to stop. Pleaded for someone to take them away.

The blond-haired boy, still behind me, snorted. The other kids in the room broke into restless chatter, a murmuring that spread the apparently impossible news through the room. The kids who'd been inducted previously stood up from their bunks. I shrank beneath their gazes.

Bone folded his arms over his chest again and sauntered closer, half-mocking, half-astonished. "A fiver, huh? Who'd have believed it?"

§

The rest of the Greens found their way to Barracks Ten, each of them red-faced after figuring out the older boys' directions had led them straight to the men's toilet.

In the bunk next to mine, the blond-haired boy shot up and declared the news across the room. "He scored a *five*!" he shouted, pointing at me.

"A five?" a tall, stocky boy said. "You're lying!"

"Ask Bone! He said it!"

The Greens' eyes boggled, and the room again filled with surprised whispers. The stocky boy who'd challenged the blond-haired boy's announcement glared at me, and I could feel the hatred radiating from him.

New fear wriggled its way down my spine. I didn't know this boy's score, but clearly he'd thought he'd beaten the rest of us. I'd seen that look before, in those who didn't get their way or had lost at their favorite game to the one person nobody thought could win.

But this boy harbored something deeper than mere jealousy or embarrassment. He stood favoring one leg after his jump from the train, and I knew I'd shown him up twice now. His resentment wouldn't be forgotten anytime soon, and he would make damn sure I'd pay.

I swallowed and looked away, reaching up to clutch my father's pendant. But it wasn't there anymore—they'd taken it from me at induction. Taken my father even further away from me.

FIVE

HE'S FOLLOWING ME. HE'S BEEN BACK THERE FOR OVER an hour now, traipsing through the Wood with all the grace of a wounded elephant. Keeping his distance in a pathetic attempt to hide from me.

I can't really blame him. He's so hungry his cheeks are slightly sunken in. He hasn't had much more than that sandbear in a long time.

I may be one of the most dangerous things he's faced in Endenbough Wood, but apparently, I'm also the only source of food he's been able to find. How he's survived this long is beyond me.

Inari surges forward at a sound, and I follow her around a tree. A rabbit thrashes in one of my snares. It jumps frantically, attempting to get away, but the twine digging into its hind leg has sealed its fate. Bending, I plant a foot on its back, grab the animal by the ears, and pull its head back. With my hunting knife, I slit its neck smoothly.

Lukas watches. I can feel his eyes behind me, staring and probably horror-stricken. I scoff, wiping my bloodied blade on a patch of grass. Lucians know nothing about surviving in a place like this. What does he expect me to do? Bottle-feed him?

I finish cleaning the rabbit, wrap the meat in a cloth, and shove the bundle into my satchel. I walk on, not looking back. Another cleaned rabbit joins the first in my bag as I circle the traps, deliberately keeping my distance from my camp, my cave.

The sun is setting behind the trees. I need a place to spend the night, and I begin searching for a natural shelter. We're not far from my cave, but I won't reveal its location to Lukas. For now, I find a tree stump with a fallen trunk alongside it. This is a good spot—high on a hill, where I can see everything around me throughout the night. It's close to fresh water, with the North Stream nearby, and the surrounding bush offers protection from the wind. Or other things.

I gather some dry rot from inside the tree stump, along with twigs and dead leaves, then scrape my knife against a piece of flint. Sparks. Tiny flames hungrily begin lapping at the tinder. I feed the fire with more twigs, then move up to larger sticks until I have a decent fire. It crackles and pops, sending smoke billowing into the darkening sky. I skewer one of the rabbits with a sharpened stick and hold it over the flames.

Now, to wait. He'll show himself soon enough.

The rabbit is almost ready when Inari lifts her head, ears pointing into the shadows. He is close now. Still, Lukas holds back, torn between his empty stomach and the possibility that I might spring on him the instant I see his face.

"Make up your mind before I do it for you," I call, biting off a chunk of meat and savoring it between my teeth. The tip of his shoe crosses into the firelight before withdrawing again. I sigh. "Last chance."

He hesitates for a moment longer before the smell of food is too much for him. He moves into the light, inching closer. I fight the urge to strike, reminding myself I invited him. Inari rises into an attack stance, but she too holds back. Lukas's eyes shift from side to side before he folds his legs, sits himself by the fire, and begins warming the evening chill out of his fingers.

I toss a handful of hawkberries into my mouth and chew, silently watching him.

"So." He clears his throat. "You live here? In the woods?"

I pull off another chunk of meat. He wants me to reveal something—anything—to put him at ease. To assure him that I'm not his enemy. It's not going to work. "What are you doing in my Wood?"

He blinks. "Your Wood? This is the Crosswoods, neutral territory. Nobody owns it." I chew on a rabbit leg without a word, and he looks away with a huff.

Inari lifts her head and gives a low growl. Lukas shoots her an anxious glance, and I toss my now-stripped rabbit leg at her paws. She crunches down on the bone. Lukas relaxes, plants his hands behind him, and straightens himself out.

"Alright, I live in a city called Dekkan," he volunteers, not knowing enough to hold his tongue. "It's next to the Crosswoods, on the Lucian side. I went for a walk in the forest and got lost."

I narrow my eyes at his feeble lie, but he only licks his lips hungrily. At least he's smart enough to attempt deception—to guard his reason for being where he doesn't belong. After a moment, I reach forward and offer him the rest of the rabbit. He takes it with a grateful smile and tears into it.

"So what about you?" he presses after his first few mouthfuls. "You don't exactly . . . look like a Boquan soldier."

Somehow, the comment pleases me. I hide it, tossing another bone to Inari. Lukas raises his eyebrows at me, still waiting for my answer.

"I'm not anything. Not anymore."

The expression that spreads across his face is a strange one. Studying me for some hidden meaning, he examines me as though trying to figure me out using only his eyes. I don't know what he hopes to discover, but he'll have to work harder than that if he's to learn my secrets.

"Elorai didn't put you on this planet without a reason," he says finally.

Irritation ripples through me, the bristling that always accompanies a statement ingrained in me as false. Yet sometimes I can't tell the difference between my own beliefs and those told to me for years. I've been away from people for too long, the memories all swirl together in my mind.

He shrugs. "But you don't believe in him, do you? Probably don't even know who Elorai is."

My mouth clenches shut. Lukas is still too hungry to notice the fire behind my eyes, and he turns back to his food. I bristle again: I do know Elorai, I remember him well.

Elorai, the god who forsook the child I once was.

The day the letter came, my father read it silently, his half-moon glasses perched on his nose. He was still wearing his white lab coat; pencils stuck out of the breast pocket. I watched as he brought the letter from his face slowly, trying not to meet my mother's anxious gaze.

Her hand covering her mouth, she whimpered, "Oh, Matthew!"

My father crumpled the paper and stuffed it in his pocket. He reached for my mother. "Calm down, Anna."

"Matthew, he's been selected!" she cried, her fists balling as he gripped her arms. She looked over her shoulder at me, her head twisting at an awkward angle. She kneeled, grasping me in her arms. "They can't take him. They can't!"

"Anna, it'll be alright." My father took her by the shoulders. His eyes moved to me, his face forming a small smile of reassurance, but I knew better. Something bad had happened, something horrible was written on that letter in his pocket.

"We should've run as soon as we knew we were going to have him!" I didn't think it possible, but my mother pulled me against her even more tightly, covering one of my ears and pressing the other into the crook of her neck.

"To where? It's not like we could've marched into Lucia and—"

"—To anywhere! To the states across the sea, all the way to Mijora if that's what it took!"

"Anna, we can't run forever!" Sorrow pooled in my father's eyes, and when he continued, his voice cracked. "Elorai will keep our son safe. He'll watch over him."

My mother hadn't been a believer, and neither was anyone in my Barracks. Very few soldiers on base ever spoke of Elorai, and fewer claimed to believe in him, but the name still remained, buried in the back of my mind along with my parents.

But my father had been wrong. Elorai didn't watch over me. Not then, not now.

Inari growls. Lukas has inched forward to offer her his rabbit bone. I've let my guard down, and I rebuke myself silently. My penance is my aching hand, throbbing from having gripped my pendant so tightly. I shove it inside my jacket before Lukas can see, holding up my free hand to quiet Inari. Lukas smiles timidly as he waves the bone, tossing it to her. Inari questions me with her eyes. The bone falls untouched between her paws.

"I guess he's not hungry, huh?" Lukas says as he flops onto his side.

"She," I correct him.

"Oh. What's her name?"

I set my jaw. What am I doing? If this boy had walked in on the bivouac of any other Boquan warrior, he'd have been torn limb from limb in a matter of seconds. That's what is expected of a soldier, what was expected of me. But they don't own me anymore. No one does.

"Inari," I say.

An eerie silence follows. His gaze slips downward, and he reaches for a stick to stir the fire. "So, Fiver, right? How'd you get a name like that?"

They don't own me, but I still use the name they gave me.

"I earned it," I reply. Lukas pauses with his hand still holding the stick, curiosity on his face. Yet he says nothing more.

"You can sleep here," I growl a moment later. I don't like it, but I'm resigned to it. There's no better option: if he finds my camp, if he makes it home and tells others, they'll force me to leave the Wood. My Wood.

Lukas curls in a ball near the fire, but some time passes before I notice his shoulders trembling. His back is to me, but his arm reaches and swipes at his face, and I think I hear him sniffling. I wait, and soon his breaths slow, his body relaxing. He can sleep peacefully, knowing I won't lay a finger on him. That he'll wake up in the morning without a single drop of blood spilled.

He's right about that, but he won't find me again.

Inari lifts her head from her paws as I silently push to my feet. My things don't take long to pack, and Lukas never stirs. As I step over his prone body, one last thought makes me pause, and I pull out what's left of the hawkberries. I leave them wrapped in a cloth by his head and hope he has enough sense to make it out of the forest alive.

There's nothing more I can do for him. I've spared his life, yet the voice in the back of my mind screams that I'm making a mistake. That I should protect my camp at all costs. That I should just kill him and be done with it. It's what Gallander would do. It's what any soldier would do. It's what I was trained to do.

Which is why I turn my back and walk away, silently disappearing into the trees, leaving Lukas breathing deeply beside the fire.

They don't own me.

SIX

THE FIRST THREE DAYS WERE FILLED WITH NOTHING
but schedules, books, and finding ourselves in strange hallways with no idea how we got there as we learned to navigate the base. Our building was only two floors but full of countless corridors, the doors marked with black letters and numbers. At least all the classes for Greens seemed to be in the same general area, but with no windows anywhere, it was difficult to orient ourselves. We were given electro-badges with large green stripes across their bottoms, and Bone had inscribed our names on each. Our new names.

"These badges let you through any door where Greens are allowed," he told us the morning we lined up outside Barracks Ten, all of us staring at the strange words on the pieces of plastic in our hands. Our Ace continued. "Your old names are left behind with your old life. This is your new life, so you get a new name. Learn it. Learn everyone else's."

I studied my badge, "Fiver" written across it in blocky black letters. I frowned. My name wasn't Fiver. Such a strange thing to call a person. All the badges were like that. The blond-haired boy's read, "Link." Others had even stranger names. Bloom. Turtle. Twitch. Star. All seemed to stem from a physical attribute, an article of clothing we'd arrived in, or a defining habit or action.

I squinted at the boy now called Link. Where had the inspiration for his name come from? And the tall girl deemed Shrimp. Why'd they choose such an odd name for her?

"Today," Bone's voice broke through my thoughts, "you're gonna spend most of your time in the gym."

Excited murmurs broke out among us, heads turning with anticipation. Bone growled at us to shut up and marched us down the back stairs. We followed him through hallway after hallway until he stopped before the first door of three on the left side of a corridor. He slipped a clear card from his pocket and swiped it in front of the scanner. The square beeped and changed to green, the lock clicked its release, and Bone pushed the heavy door open.

The boy who'd hated me from day one, his badge reading "Scourge," gave a hard smile as the room unfolded before us. At least a hundred meters square, the brightly lit gym made my head spin. Much of the room was covered in thick blue padding, the rest a simple carpet. There was a track along the perimeter with heaving kids trotting in single file around it. In one corner stood weight-lifting devices; in another, knotted ropes hung from the high ceiling, with some of the older children racing to the top. To the right, three pairs of Greens threw weak punches at each other and grappled for control on the blue mats.

Half of one wall was covered in a series of black lumps; kids clung to them, struggling up to a ledge where two girls, jeering at the others below, had already seated themselves. Punching bags in the nearest corner bounced back and forth as fists flew against them. Instructors paced at every station, giving advice, adjusting stances, and demonstrating moves.

A grunting tangle of arms and legs whirled past us, the two boys trying to pin each other to the floor. An instructor followed, shouting as he watched their progress. Scourge laughed, and he excitedly shoved further into the room, knocking me over with his arm.

A collective murmur escaped the other kids' throats as they pushed past me to follow him. Pulling my hands up, I protected my face from the batting arms and scratching nails.

A hand brushed my shoulder and planted itself there, and I opened my eyes to see Link smiling. "Come on, let's go!" he urged, tugging on my arm. "They're gonna teach us how to fight Lucians!"

Link pulled me along to the area where the other Greens had spread out in front of Bone, who stood in his usual pose with his arms folded.

"This is Training Room One," he announced. "It's the Greens' gym, although younger squadron members come here to practice their moves on their own. Here you'll learn basic defense and attack while building up your strength. You don't start on mock battles until you're placed in a squadron."

He turned and gestured broadly at the equipment. "Each of these stations is self-explanatory. Before you're promoted to a squadron, you'll have to prove your skill at each one to me." He paused, becoming grave. "And to the lead Commander."

Nervous whispers floated through the gasping Greens. Only two words surfaced from their mouths. "Abraham Gallander!"

A shudder of contagious fear shot through me, and I knew this Abraham Gallander was not one to be contended with. From the expressions on the Greens' faces, Bone must've seemed as threatening as a housefly in comparison.

Bone continued. "Commander Gallander expects everything you've got. You earn your keep here, or you're out. Permanently." He eyed us to let his point sink in, then raised his voice. "It's my job to keep you from that fate. I'm the one who makes sure you're each ready for your testing. You'll spend four hours in here with me every day, learning basics. You'll also have to keep your grades up in all your classes. Military history, science, math, the works. Learn how to balance your time, otherwise . . . " He shrugged his shoulders and lifted his hands as if to rid himself of all guilt.

A collective groan. We'd started classes yesterday, joining with Greens brought to the base earlier in the year. For the next two weeks, extra classes to catch us up were mandatory.

"Alright, enough dull speeches. Let's get those heart rates up!" Bone clapped his hands at us. "Two laps around the room, go!"

As one, we jumped into action. Scourge's arm swiped across my chest, knocking the wind out of me and sending me crashing to my backside. The others left me heaving for breath, some throwing me glares of disgust—I'd fallen twice now. I tilted my head up and saw Bone's hard face staring at me. He leaned forward; my throat went dry.

"I said move!" Bone hissed, his voice low. I scrambled to my feet and rushed to catch up with the others.

Ten minutes later we collapsed to the gym floor, red-faced and sweating. Bone took pity on our sorry bodies and let us catch our breath.

"Bone!" a voice called from across the room. Our Ace turned his head as a teen with one star on each shoulder jogged toward us. I recognized him as the same UL we saw by the train three days ago. A lifetime ago.

"Ridge?" Bone replied, returning his attention to us.

Ridge inhaled. "Commander Gallander wants to see you. He said it was important."

Bone's attention snapped to the UL with a new interest. "What is it?" We muffled our heavy breathing, watching with barely suppressed curiosity.

Ridge shook his head. "Dunno, he wouldn't say. But he wants to talk to you. Now."

Bone's gaze flicked to me. "You Greens," he commanded, "on the ground for twenty pushups, then around the track for two more laps." He nodded at Ridge. "Let's see what all the fuss is about."

The two walked briskly toward the exit, and I felt my stomach flip again. The door had barely shut when Scourge's hand clamped on my shoulder. "You're awful small, *Fiver*," he growled. All thoughts of pushups and laps cleared from the group. "How'd you get that score, anyway?"

The aptitude test. I'd hoped they'd all forget about that. Bone said the test was a measure of our potential, but that it was only a guess at best.

None of that mattered to Scourge. I shrugged myself free of his hold and turned to face a line of boys and girls with arms folded, all daring me to try walking past them. Scourge's newly found friends. Likely, he'd been looking for an opportunity like this ever since he'd laid eyes on me.

"*Fiver*," Scourge spat, his voice enormous for a kid. "What a joke.

You're just a lunk with wet pants."

I looked away, my insides tightening. My father had always told me to ignore such jabs, to never raise a fist unless absolutely necessary. What good could come of punching someone in the nose just to prove them wrong?

Link hung on the corner of the group, itching for action. He wanted to fight, but there was more fear in his eyes than anything else. No help would come from him. Not now.

"You hear me?" Scourge jabbed my back with a finger. "You deaf? I'm talking to you!" When I still refused to answer him, he spun me around hard. "I said, I'm talking to you! What's the matter? Cat got your tongue?"

Scourge was muscular, big-boned, and at least four inches taller than me. Large for an eight-year-old. I wasn't necessarily small, but he outweighed me by twenty pounds. Increasingly desperate, I scanned the room, looking for shoulders embellished with gold stars. Someone with authority, someone in charge. Anyone.

"So how'd you do it, huh?" Scourge sneered. "Must think you're so much better than all of us."

The others laughed briskly, and I fought to keep from panicking at the spur this gave to Scourge's ego. "Oh, yeah, so much smarter than us, aren't you?" he jeered. He leaned close, his stale breath putrid. My teeth clenched together in barely suppressed rage.

Without warning, his fist jabbed forward and caught my chin. The blow flung me onto my knees as pain exploded through my jaw. I groaned and pressed a palm to my sore cheek.

Scourge leaned down, his fat face mocking. "Not so hot now, huh?"

I said nothing, pushing back to my feet. His open hand slapped the side of my head, forcing me down again. "Did I say you could get up?" he growled. "You gotta stay down 'til I say!"

Scourge was clearly the kind of kid who demanded lunch money from smaller children and pushed their faces in mud puddles when they didn't pay up. I'd become his new target. His target in a world where we would be learning how to kill.

"We gotta teach you some manners, Fiver."

My heart lurched at "we." How many kids could Scourge have recruited in the short time we'd been here? Two girls and three boys began circling us. The others either ignored us entirely or watched with curiosity from the sidelines.

Scourge flung his fist into my face again, and pain spread through my nose as blood spurted over my lips. He paused for a moment at the crimson rush, and I knew this was the first time he'd drawn blood. As his face relaxed into pure triumph, I knew it wouldn't be the last.

Hot anger spewed from me, and I lunged blindly at Scourge's face. He leaped away with a laugh, dodging my wild punch. His next blow sent me stumbling backward, the pain bringing hot tears that I tried to hide.

"Poor little Fiver wants his mommy," Scourge taunted. His leg drew back for a kick. I squinted and braced for the impact.

"Enough!" Bone's voice froze everyone on the spot. "Break it up, Greens!"

Feet shuffled away. Our Ace's furious eyes burned at me. Then they moved to Scourge, who first paled in fear, but then forced his composure and stared back in defiance.

Bone jerked his head. "Get on!" he belted. Scourge balled his fists again, and Bone trained angry eyes on him. "Go!" My tormentor looked at him a moment longer, rubbing his blood-tinged knuckles until he accepted the order and slunk away.

Bone's hard gaze moved to me, to the bruised and bleeding pathetic heap on the floor.

"Get up," he ordered, his voice low.

I blinked at him for a moment, his glare unforgiving. My shaking knees threatened to give out, but I managed to stand.

"Get to the infirmary," Bone commanded, his face firm. "I'll have Ridge go with you." He turned away, then called over his shoulder. "In case you collapse in the hallway."

§

The infirmary smelled of the sharp scents of stinging salves used on cuts. Soap too, harsh and antiseptic. A woman in a gray uniform laid me on the exam table and passed the handheld med-scanner over my face. It examined my injuries with a low hum.

"Nose isn't broken," she announced, watching the scanner's screen. "Just some bruising. We'll give you something for the pain and clean that cut." She smiled, reaching for the laser-suture and bringing it to my split lip. "You'll be right as rain."

From the throbbing, I couldn't believe my nose was still intact. I'd never been in a fight before, never been injured—at least not like this. The closest I'd ever come to fighting was sparring with my father. Self-defense moves he hoped I would never have to use. Moves I was sure I would need in this place.

The woman in gray handed me two pills in a white paper cup and pointed to the drinking fountain in the corner. I climbed down from the table gingerly, my entire body sore. I swallowed the pills as instructed, thankful for the relief the blue tablets would offer, yet leery of them at the same time.

"Oh, one more thing before you leave." She turned back to me, a thin syringe containing a pale, yellow liquid in one hand. I flinched at the long needle.

"I know." She held up her palm, calming me. "It seems scary, but you want to be a big soldier someday, right?"

"What is it?" I croaked. She smiled sweetly again. I hated her for it. Her smile made me trust her less, not more.

"It's for your own good, hon. Everyone gets them at some point."

I closed my eyes as the needle pierced my arm with a sharp pinch. The woman pressed a square of cotton over the drop of emerging blood and taped it there.

She dismissed me, sending me back to Barracks Ten. Not that I knew where that was. "And get some rest, hon," she called after me.

I didn't look back.

SEVEN

THE EAST STREAM'S BURBLING DOESN'T REACH MY senses until I'm almost on it. Daylight has just broken through the trees, weak sunlight filtering through the branches. I have traps to check, food to gather, and wood to store. Inari paces at my side, anxious for her breakfast and my instruction. I fling my hand forward. "Go on," I tell her. "You can catch your own this morning." There's still time enough for her to roam free before the soldiers come. I know their ways too well.

I should go back to Link and his companion. I should drag their bodies to the edge of the Wood, where the cover first begins to thicken. Make it seem they were attacked the moment they infiltrated this forest. But I can't. I've seen what happens to the unattended dead: rigor mortis, the bluish skin, the fleshy heap of a life cut short. I can't face the stiff and silent body of a friend so long loyal to me—fiercely loyal, until the moment when I wasn't loyal to him.

I convince myself that moving Link and the other soldier wouldn't make any difference. Thirty-six hours without contact and Gallander will initiate a search. Wherever the bodies lie—deep in the Wood or on its fringes—his forces will investigate, infiltrating like termites. I'll hide if I can hide, flee if I can't. Or I'll be captured and tortured; Gallander may want me alive, but his soldiers will exact their vengeance on the traitor I now am.

But right now, Inari needs a moment of freedom, and I need her to have a moment of freedom. "Go on," I urge again, answering her questioning eyes. Now confident of my permission, she yips and bounds into the bushes. As easy as it is to let me and my snares feed her, she still loves nothing more than chasing down her own food. Instinct, I suppose.

With her gone, I need to keep my eyes more alert than usual. Fighting the nervous itch I get whenever Inari is away from me, I swing my head from side to side, catching every movement of the forest. My ears might be compromised, but my sight has grown keener without it.

After crossing the East Stream, I continue southward to the bend where my camp lies. It's not long before the trees open up, and the mouth of my cave comes into view. It's partly hidden by boulders and a giant fallen log. The young oak tree atop the cave sends spindly roots snaking down alongside the dark mouth, in search of soft ground and water.

As much as I want to take in the comfort of familiar surroundings, I can't keep my mind from wandering. Lukas plagues my thoughts. He's a Lucian, a Lucian I've let live. Nothing in my past has prepared me for this act of mercy—mercy I thought had long been conditioned out of me. My hands feel empty, yearning for the weight of something solid to ground me. I reach for the old ax I've embedded in a log. One of the many objects salvaged from abandoned outposts, burned-out houses, and forgotten storage facilities. A life built from scavenging.

A cry in the distance. It's muffled by my own ears, but I know Inari's yowl. Her pain resonates through the Wood, carried by the air itself. All thoughts of yesterday's unwelcome guests vanish, and in the next instant, I'm tearing through the trees with a swiftness born of panic. I let her roam free, and now the soldiers have come.

Leading with my good ear yet trying to keep my eyes forward, I scream out, begging her to keep calling. Terror runs through me, my legs pounding as they fly up the foothill, my eyes searching for any sign that she passed this way.

Inari yowls again in painful rage. I burst through the green, sliding to a halt only meters before the cliff. No soldiers here, but a threat just as great: a mountain lion.

A tangled mass of fur and teeth tumbles by me, a furious mix of growls and snarls coming from the spinning heap. Inari wrestles the creature with all her strength, her teeth locked onto the beast's thick skin. Streaks of blood in the dirt: I can't tell if they belong to Inari or to the huge cat attacking her.

"Inari!" I scream, pulling out my knife. Her ears prick at my call, and she sinks her teeth further into the cat's flesh. The creature howls in pain and anger, lashing at Inari with its claws. Inari dodges, saving herself, and in the next second she lunges at the beast again. The two almost become one, too close together to risk a miss with my blade.

"Inari, come!" I yell, but she can't. The whirl of teeth and claws barrels toward the cliff's edge.

I can't wait any longer. I spring forward, aiming my knife at the beast's head. Inari wrenches her attacker to one side, and instead of piercing through the cat's skull, my blade rips into its shoulder, gouging a deep red line in its fur.

The mountain lion swipes its claw-filled paw; a sharp sting burns down my side. Inari lunges again, knocking the cat from me, but the blow throws me off balance, and I stumble even closer to the precipice.

The rocky soil beneath my feet crumbles.

A gasp tears its way out of my mouth, my desperate arms flailing like broken windmill blades. My hands meet nothing but air, and before the moment passes, I'm fully at gravity's mercy.

My frantic fingers scratch against wood, and I latch on with a frenzied grip. My stomach slams against the back of my throat; I'm clinging to the single branch within my reach, to the half-dead tree on the cliff's edge.

I pull, grunting at the strain. Sweat beads on my forehead, a droplet trickling down my temple. The toe of my boot loosens dirt and pebbles from the rock face as I kick forward, trying to brace my feet against the side of the cliff.

The tree cracks above. My body jerks downward a few inches, my arms trembling, my clammy palms struggling for a stronger hold. I'm dangling three feet over the edge, and my weight is slowly pulling the roots of the tree from the rocky earth. A glance over my shoulder sends me reeling. A fifty-foot drop into the craggy ravine awaits me.

A terrified cry squeezes from my throat as the tree falls parallel to the ground above. "Inari!" I choke. She's on high alert, guarding me, lest the beast return. She's giving me all she's got, but that's the only help she can offer.

Pain shoots through my arms, my feet swinging freely beneath me. With sheer adrenaline, I manage to pull my body along the branch, drawing myself inch by inch toward the rock face.

Another crack—the branch itself this time. Any minute now, it will splinter away from the trunk. I can't breathe, panic nearly blinding me.

I can't die here. Not like this.

Just as my feet manage some purchase against the rock face, a frantic arm appears over the edge, frightened eyes behind it.

"Grab my hand!" cries a familiar voice.

Lukas.

EIGHT

Our professor stared down at his young class, a stern frown etched in his ancient face. His name was Thurkan, and he prided himself on his expertise regarding Boquan-Lucian relations.

"To learn to be soldiers?" Link called out.

Thurkan, nodding, pointed at him. "To learn to be soldiers. Why?"

"Because Boqua needs protecting!" a girl shouted.

"And who do we need protection from?"

Over half the class roared the answer. "The Lucians!" Thurkan beamed with pride at the simple statement.

"The Lucians," he agreed, thumping his fist on his desk. He never kept any notes, although he insisted we did; our fingers were poised over our touchpads, ready to record every word the man said. "The Lucians have been a thorn in our side for years. They stole our food and weapons. They didn't care who they hurt to get what they wanted. Yet we tolerated them."

Eyes widened, the class soaking up his words like a dry sponge.

"We let them take what was ours and didn't stop them. Until . . ."

"Until their terrorism campaigns!" another kid shouted.

"Terrible acts," Thurkan said, shaking his head. "Raiding our cities, kidnapping innocent citizens, burning entire towns. Massacring hundreds at a time. They were raising their own army, and if we didn't do something, they'd come for the whole country soon enough."

A chorus of "boos" thundered from us. The fire in my belly swelled, a fury at the Lucians' cowardly, horrible acts against our country—a country that had done nothing to them.

"But we did do something!" Thurkan continued. "We're doing it now." He pointed his finger out at all of us. "You are the future of Boqua, and one day you'll show the Lucians how powerful we are!"

Thurkan was better at pep talks than he was at teaching. By the end of each of his classes, every Green left with renewed vigor and purpose. We trained a little harder and studied a little longer, all in the hopes of becoming true soldiers and protecting and avenging our great nation.

Yet our dream often burst before the day was over, usually in the gym.

"Come on, you've been here a year already! Have you learned nothing?" shouted the Ace.

My hands slipped on the rope, skin burning as I clung to the knots. I gritted my teeth and pulled, my muscles straining until they refused to hang on for another second. Gravity won. My feet slammed into the floor, pain shooting through my legs despite the blue mat beneath them, and I fell backward.

I groaned as the Ace's shadow loomed over me, his grim face staring down at mine. His name was Mole, his moniker taken from the large, round, brown mole on his cheek.

He planted his hands on his hips. "You've got no upper body strength, kid," he growled. "You'll be out on your ass if you can't pull it together!"

"But I'm only nine," I grunted, whimpering in frustration.

"That doesn't matter!" he shouted. "You're not giving Gallander your best! Shape up!"

He scowled at me before stalking off to yell at a Green struggling on another rope. I clenched my teeth and fists, wincing at the pain. My palms glowed red.

Scourge's cackling laugh broke over my shoulder. "Got a boo-boo, Fiver?" His collection of followers hung behind him, watching with hungry eyes as I turned to face him. My insides sank.

Scourge grinned wickedly. "Come on, Fiver," he taunted. "Show me your stuff! Show me your *five*."

Scourge's insults hadn't eased all year, not for a second. When his friends got tired of a particular tactic, he'd devise a new way to torment me, either with pranks or unfounded rumors. I always ignored him, but sooner or later he'd back up his taunts, usually by planting evidence on my face in the form of bruises.

"Did you hear, everybody?" he called. "Fiver cries in bed at night, wanting his big teddy bear."

I ignored the snickers that followed. Scourge led his gang past me, flinging his elbow into the side of my skull. Stars exploded in my vision, and I crumpled onto the mat, gasping at the shock and pain.

Scourge and his gang snickered, continuing toward the climbing wall. I grunted and pushed to my feet, testing my legs gingerly before trusting them to support my weight. Looking up through bleary eyes, I saw Bone in the corner with a younger Green and a practice dummy. He'd paused the lesson for no other reason than to watch Scourge's attacks. Fury ate at my chest. Bone had never once lifted a finger to stop the bully's attacks.

"Dude," Link chuckled as he slunk out from behind the climbing wall. "You look awful."

I grunted in reply and pushed past him, heading for Bone. He'd returned his attention to his pupil, adjusting the boy's arms into a stronger position. "Okay, *now*," he ordered his charge.

"Why do you let him keep hitting me?!" I demanded. The boy sent a fist into the dummy, and Bone nodded in approval before shifting his eyes to me.

"Well, well. You *do* have a voice after all," he said.

"Answer me!" My face tightened, my fists clenching. Shouting at an Ace. I could get demerits for that. Or a beating.

Bone turned, folding his arms once again. "Don't you get it? You scored a five, *Fiver*," he said. "And I've seen your classwork. Nearly perfect across the board. Some people consider that a threat."

"That's not my fault! I thought we're all supposed to be fighting for the same thing!"

"What do you want me to do, huh?" Bone leaned forward, bending until his nose was level with mine. "You're not always gonna have someone to pull you out of a tight spot when you're facing the Lucians. Why should it be any different here?"

I narrowed my eyes, crossing my arms like his. "I should be worried about Lucians coming after me. Not one of our own!"

His eyes mirrored mine, and he lowered his voice to barely above a whisper. "I've seen you, Fiver. You're smart." He blinked, frowning. "Start acting like it."

I glared at him, but he ignored me and returned to the Green, who was now throwing a flurry of blows at the dummy. One punch right after another. I envied him. If only I had someone to hold Scourge's head still, I would show him what it felt like.

With gritted teeth, I stormed out of Training Room One and headed back to Barracks Ten. Free time wasn't over yet, but lights-out was in half an hour. Half an hour until Scourge would collapse in his bed, and I'd be safe while the sleeping giant stored up more jabs and punches for me.

NINE

"COME ON, YOU DUNCE, TAKE IT!" LUKAS'S VOICE breaks through my panic, his hand reaching desperately for mine. I grab at his outstretched fingers, and they clasp onto my wrist. He pulls me an inch or two closer, my other hand sliding along the branch. When another crack rents the air, the branch tears completely away from the rest of the tree. I slam against the rock face, blinding pain searing through my shoulder.

The branch tumbles, hitting the rocks below with a much louder crash than the dull noise I hear. Grasping my other arm, Lukas grunts. His features screw up in pain and effort as he struggles, sweat beading on his dirty forehead. I'm practically dead weight, and I could drag us both to our deaths.

"I could use some help here!" he growls, moaning.

I dig my boots into the side of the cliff. He grunts and leans back, the muscles in his neck straining. I pull upward, bending my elbows, and begin walking myself up the rock face.

Lukas grabs my bicep and rises to his feet, straining to pull me over the top. My shin collides with the edge as I press my knee into the ground. With a final grunt and heave, I lunge onto solid ground and collapse in the dust.

Lukas and I lie there, sucking in air as the adrenaline dissipates in our veins, relief taking its place, our heartbeats slowing. He's shaking, and when I roll over, I'm shocked to see him overtaken by silent laughter. His hand rests on his stomach as he smiles and gazes into the sky.

"We're both crazy, you know that?" he says.

I know. All too well.

Inari's head pops into my vision. Her cold nose touches my cheek as

"

she whines. I push myself up, stroking her blood-tinged fur. Pain flares in my side, and I lift my torn shirt away from the angry gashes the cat has clawed into my skin. Blood, thin streams flowing freely. The wound isn't as deep as I thought, but those claws were razor-sharp. I groan, pressing my hands against the wound to stem the flow.

"What are you doing here?" I ask. Lukas shrugs.

"I heard you leave last night, and I . . . well . . . followed you. Do you really live in that cave?"

My jaw clenches. To my ears, I left in silence last night, but I wasn't careful enough. Now that Lukas knows where my camp is, he can lead someone to it. Boquan soldiers, Lucian brigades. They all can find me.

He sees the concern in my face and holds up his palms. "Hey, don't worry. I'm not gonna tell anybody."

We both stumble to our feet, still on shaky legs. I wince, clutching my side even tighter. Inari whines.

"Endenbough Wood is my home," I tell him, glancing at her.

He frowns. "Endenbough Wood? What's that?"

"You're in it."

His expression doesn't change, but he slowly lifts his head. "Sure."

My knife rests next to his foot, and he bends to pick it up. The back of his shirt rides up, and my relief is replaced with raw fury: a handle of a gun peeks out from his belt.

At my alarm, Inari bares her teeth, and I'm on him before he can move. I grip him by the neck with one hand, the other reaching for the gun. He cries out and tries to break my hold, but I grab the revolver and shove him away from me. He stumbles, catching himself just before he falls.

"What is this?!" I yell, holding the weapon high in the air. His face drains of color.

"What do you think it is?" he mumbles, and I step closer. Inari growls low in her throat. He jerks away as I raise my fist. "Look, I just saved your life, and—"

"—Don't play games with me! You come into my Wood, eat my

food, follow me around, and all the while you're armed! When were you planning on putting a bullet in my back?"

"Why do you always think one of us is trying to kill you?" he shouts. His words sting, and my head pounds. The gun shakes in my blood-covered fist. Enraged, I throw the weapon into the ravine below.

"Hey! Whatchya do that for?!" Lukas cries, anger flashing in his eyes. "I brought it for protection, okay? I wasn't . . . gonna hurt you or anything. I didn't even know you were in this stupid forest!"

I watch his eyes. He's telling the truth. If he'd had any intention of killing me, he'd never have saved me from the cliff. I squint. "What are you *really* doing here? And don't even try lying to me again."

He swallows, his eyes darting from me to the ravine, and then to Inari's stern face. "I . . . " A long, reluctant sigh. "I'm looking for my mother."

"Your mother?"

"She . . . a couple of months ago, she went to Boqua. She has an old friend from before the war in a town there . . . " His voice fades away, and he swallows. "Anyway, her friend got really sick, so she snuck across the border. She was supposed to come home after a few days, but she never did." He raises his gaze, the fear in his eyes replaced with cold defiance. "Everybody says she's dead, but I don't believe it. I followed her trail into Boqua, hoping to find someone willing to help. No one on our side would."

"You went into Boqua?" I can't help but burst out, surprised. Jealous too. "How did you get in? And back out?"

His face darkens. "Look, I found out soldiers raided the town she was in. They rounded up a bunch of people they thought were rebels." His fingers drum against his arm. "They said they took them to some science facility called the Ramius Corporation."

My heart skips a beat. The scientists. "Ramius Corporation?"

"Yeah, it's this big lab the Boquan military took over. They got the scientists working on all kinds of projects there."

I grunt. This doesn't add up, yet Lukas's eyes tell me he isn't lying.

He's telling the truth, at least as he understands it. "What would they want with your mother?" I ask, motioning to Inari to stand down.

Lukas sags down onto a log. "I don't know. What would they want with anybody? All I could find out is the military has put a lot of pressure on the scientists to work on special projects of all kinds. That big shot Commander of yours, probably." He rubs at his temple. "Cures for diseases, new weapons, and some weird plant they're trying to grow."

Something sparks in my mind. The Vitmor. The scientists collecting every plant they could find.

Answers, right in front of me: I fight to keep my interest from showing on my face. "How do you know all this?" I growl.

"I just know, okay?" His fists tremble, he's holding something back.

Every muscle in me tenses. "What else do you know about the projects?"

His eyes muddle with confusion. "What?" he asks.

"Tell me!"

He flinches, his arms flinging up to protect his face. "I don't know! I mean, the guys I talked to didn't tell me a whole lot. Just some stuff about the infections and the—"

"—Tell me about the Vitmor. The plant. What do you know about it?"

"What?" His exasperated voice only tests my patience. "S-something about needing a lot of it. I don't know what for. They're going to claim the Crosswoods, half of it at least. Clear the land, plant whole acres of the stuff."

My stomach shrinks. "Clear it how?"

He shakes his head. "I don't know, burn it, bomb it, whatever! Why's it so special to you?"

Blood drains from my face, a rush of anxiety flooding through me. The Wood. They're coming to the Wood. Everything I have will be destroyed, and Gallander will find me.

Lukas takes a cautious step forward. He stares at me with genuine concern. "Hey . . . what's wrong? Look, if it's about your cave, I'm sure they wouldn't come that deep into the—"

"—Where did you get this info?" I cut him off.

His features contort. "What does it matter? My mother is their prisoner, and you're asking about a stupid plant?"

My glare slices into him and the new information he's let slip. "If you know where your mother is, why are you still in my Wood?"

A twitch in his brow. A tremor in his lips. Inari is on her feet again, ready to pounce.

Lukas looks at the ground to hide his welling tears. "I . . . I can't get to her. I don't know where the facility is."

I glower in thought. Both of us have business with the Ramius Corporation, but only Lukas has the information I need to save my home. Yet there has to be somebody in Boqua he got his intel from—someone with inside info about Gallander's projects, someone sympathetic to the Lucians. The thought nearly makes me dizzy as the terror of soon being discovered sweeps through me. That the Wood will burn.

Trusting Lukas is insane, but it's the only option I have.

Inari senses my thoughts, her body relaxing. Then I remember the object pressed inside my jacket pocket, the one I stowed there. I pull back the flap and stick in my bloodied hand, searching. My hand clasps around the coin, and I pull it free, offering it to Lukas. "I think this is yours."

His eyes bulge. He takes it from my outstretched palm and rubs it between his fingers, staring at the silver surface with longing and hope and a hint of sadness. The skin around his eyes quivers, tears glistening in the blue pools.

"Mom," he whispers, so low I don't hear it—I can only read his lips. He looks at me, a tear sliding down his face. "She used to carry this with her everywhere, but she was too scared to take it into Boqua. I thought she'd want to see it again. When I found her."

I watch his pitiful form shaking like a terrified child, and the words are already out of my mouth before I can consider what they mean or what I'm getting myself into.

"I'll make you a deal."

TEN

HER NAME WAS ATARA.

The first time I saw her, she'd been assigned to Barracks Ten as an incoming Green and had been given one of the bunks across from mine. I looked up from my Boquan history textbook as she came into the room. When she peeked up from her bowed head, her eyes revealed caution and curiosity, but no fear.

Her eyes shone the brightest blue. I'd never seen anyone with eyes that brilliant.

She moved between the rows of beds, searching for the bunk Bone had allocated to her. Her thin hands, which were at the end of even thinner arms, clutched the tan, standard-issue shoulder bag given to recruits at induction. Her head swung from side to side as she counted the beds one by one.

She passed me without a word, not so much as a glance in my direction. I turned, watching her reach a slim hand up toward her head, reflexively attempting to flip now-nonexistent blonde hair. Her fingers quivered in the empty space behind her neck, then finally came to rest on the short, choppy strands left behind by the barber.

"It'll grow back," I offered, folding my textbook closed. She jumped and dropped her bag, whirling around as though I'd poked her with a stick. "Your hair, I mean," I continued, ignoring her stunned face as I stood up. "New Greens always have their hair cut short."

I grabbed a piece of my own hair and pulled it, showing her that the lock reached halfway down my forehead. "I'm a second-year, so they don't shave my head anymore." Bewildered, she said nothing, as if she couldn't believe I was talking to her. I frowned. "Didn't they tell you this at induction? Shaved heads are another way of forgetting our past lives."

Her blue eyes blinked. The caution in them faded away, but something else replaced it. Something I couldn't quite make out. She gazed down, staring at her bag on the floor. Her uniform practically swallowed her small frame, the tan sleeves rolled up so they wouldn't hang over her hands. She picked at a loose thread, pulling on it with her fingernails.

"What if we don't want to forget our past lives?" Her voice startled me. I hadn't expected it to sound the way it did, smooth and soft yet still defiant. Defiance: a trait not envied on the base.

"M-maybe not all the way. Not yet," I spluttered. "But we do, eventually."

She glared at me. "Why?"

I frowned again. She didn't talk like anyone else I knew. Must have been because she was so new. Even I had reservations when I first came here.

"It's what's expected of us," I replied. "The Lucians will destroy us if we don't destroy them first."

Her eyes flashed dark for the briefest second before she turned away and shrugged. "Maybe."

"What's your name?" I asked. "Has Bone given it to you yet? Sometimes it takes a day or two."

Her brows scrunched in disdain. She leaned closer, and I stared into her sparkling blue eyes. "I bet I'm the only one here who remembers their *real* name," she said, her voice low.

I pulled my head back, unnerved. Most of us hadn't been called anything other than our designated names for at least a year. By now, it was only natural that we didn't think about the names our parents had chosen for us. And Atara was right—some of us might have truly forgotten them. Especially those as old as Bone and the other Aces.

But my name floated in my mind, so close I could reach out and touch it. Catch it on the tip of my tongue.

"We don't need those names anymore," I explained firmly. She didn't answer, so I continued. "I'm Fiver. Who are you?"

She was silent for a long moment before she acquiesced, handing me her electro-badge, the word *Queen* written across it.

Her eyes rose to mine, and she leaned in close again. I couldn't back away, her gaze freezing me in place. Her voice became barely a whisper. "My *name* is Atara."

§

Atara was different from the other girls on the base. She was different from most people in general. So different that I had to work to remember her new name. She was silent in classes, even through Thurkan's motivating speeches. She took longer than all the other new Greens to even try punching the practice dummies, and she only threw her first jab after Bone threatened to make her sleep in the training field for a week if she didn't. The other Greens sneered at her and threw wads of paper at her in the hallways. She never flinched. Never lowered her head. Never blinked.

We were two magnets, drawn to each other. I knew she didn't want to be on base, but there was nothing I could do about it except help her endure. Sooner or later, I was sure, she would come around. Once she settled into her new life, she would transform into the soldier that was buried inside each of us. Link accepted her because I did, of course, and the three of us formed an unspoken pact that only grew stronger with every hateful word and spiteful jab Atara was forced to bear. I envied her ability to let the insults bounce off her like rubber.

"Do you think you're here for vacation?!" Bone's steely voice shouted as Scourge and I circled one another in the ring, fists raised. Sweat dripped down my brow, my lungs heaving for air. Scourge's face, red with exertion and adrenaline, broke into a wicked grin.

"Yeah, come on, Fiver," he taunted, waving his balled fists. "Come get me."

I stared at him, watching his movements. Cropped blonde hair flashed in the corner of my vision as I caught sight of Atara on the other side of the gym. She was studying my practice session, concern for me blaring from her eyes.

Sharp pain exploded in my jaw, and the world spun as Scourge flipped me onto my back. I landed hard, the mat offering too-little cushioning. Thick weight pressed the air from my lungs, and I felt my arm wrenched until I saw stars flashing before me. I cried out in pain, slapping his bicep in surrender.

Scourge gave my arm one last yank before letting go and stepping over me. I thought he'd left when he swooped down and kneeled next to my head. "Guess who's getting promoted, lunk?" He bared his teeth. "No more of this Green slop. I'm gonna be a real soldier. Guess that *five* of yours don't mean a whole lot, huh?"

I felt Bone's eyes on me and knew he would do nothing. Watch and wait, as always. If someone was going to end Scourge's bullying, it would have to be me.

Scourge smirked and shifted his attention to Atara, who'd come closer to the boxing ring at the sight of my defeat. Her eyes glistened with worry, but at the sight of Scourge's gaze on her, they widened in dread.

Scourge lit up at her alarm, and he climbed out of the ring. "You next, Queen Lunk?" he jeered. "Come on, show your man how to fight like a girl!"

My face burned, but Atara didn't move. Scourge stepped closer, towering over her like a tidal wave ready to break across her small body. My eyes flicked to Bone, his shoulders now tense. The arms usually folded across his chest were planted firmly on his hips.

He still didn't move, but his watchful glare tracked every movement Scourge made. Scourge, the wolf, circling its new prey. Prey he had scented through me. Dread seeped into my bones, but Atara only stretched her back a little straighter. Held her shoulders a little higher.

"Did Fiver wear you out, Scourge?" she spat at him.

Scourge sneered. "I could break you in half. Just like *that*." He snapped his fingers. Atara didn't blink. I trained my eyes on him as I clambered out of the ring.

"Oh, I see. Gotta find someone small to push around," she challenged. "Can't cut it with the big boys anymore?"

My breath caught in my lungs. Scourge's face darkened into a dangerous shade, his anger bubbling up. Bone leaned forward, but stayed glued to his spot, apprehension leaking from his face. Yet Atara, with her shoulders high and her cropped blonde hair shining under the bright gym lights, looked every bit the queen Bone had named her for.

"Someone *easy*," she continued, challenging Scourge again. "Someone *half* your size."

Scourge froze in shock, then his shoulders went limp in surrender. The queen had backed down the wolf.

Even I hadn't expected such boldness from Atara. Across the room, I thought I saw a hint of a smile play at the corners of Bone's lips.

Scourge turned away, only to find every pair of eyes in the gym focused on him. Watching as he'd hesitated before a girl. Watching as she'd strode away from him without a scratch, her own mark left for all to see.

And the tiny smile melted like ice from Bone's face.

And Scourge launched himself from the ground in attack.

And I lunged.

Scourge roared as I slammed into his back, my arms grappling for a hold around his neck. Bone moved—finally moved—but he was much too far away. This was up to me. If I couldn't save myself from Scourge, at least I could save her.

The sounds around me faded away, Atara's shocked face coming into my field of vision. My grip tightened around Scourge's throat, all my rage coiled inside my arms. He would never touch her. Never hurt her. Never threaten her.

Scourge's knees buckled, but I held firm. I had to. Maybe Atara could back him down now, but he'd wait until no one was around—and only Elorai knew what he would do to her then. I squeezed my arms until they ached, until Scourge stopped struggling.

Strong hands ripped me away.

Scourge twitched on the floor, his chest rising and falling. I hated each of those breaths, and I wished I had been strong enough to snap his neck. But I didn't go for him again. Not after the look Atara shot me from beyond the circle of gawkers.

Bone released me, and the onlookers helped Scourge to his feet. They began leading him to the exit, half-carrying him. Bone shouted at the crowd of whispering Greens, ordering them to mind their own business. His eyes landed on me briefly; a mix of raw emotions gleamed in his gaze before he sprinted toward Scourge. He heaved my tormentor up and helped him into the hallway.

Still whispering in clusters and shooting glances at us, the gawkers began to disperse. Ignoring them all, Atara waited as the crowd thinned, the light in her eyes now dead. I knew it wasn't just the shock of Scourge's attack that had stolen her brightness. I approached her slowly, waiting for her to speak. She only swallowed.

So I spoke. "What's the matter?"

She shook her head. "You . . . you're all becoming mindless killers. I . . . don't want to be like that!"

Treasonous words. Irritation flooded through me without warning. "We're being trained to kill. For Boqua! And you're one of us. It's time you stopped singling yourself out like that."

Her eyes snapped to mine, none of the queen she'd so recently displayed visible within her. She opened her mouth, wrestling with tears she couldn't stem. "I . . . I don't *want* to kill anybody," she whispered.

I felt my jaw slack in shock. "You're going to have to. It's your duty. It's your responsibility to eradicate anyone who threatens our country. We're the chosen. It's an honor."

"An honor?" she hissed, almost in a whisper. "Gallander owns our lives. And he can take them from us whenever he chooses."

"We are Boqua. We are Gallander's army." I was like her once, but how could I ever have questioned Gallander? Who else would protect

Boqua if not for him? If not for us?

When she looked at me again, her eyes were raw and red. Her voice trembled as she fought to keep her composure. "I wonder how many times they told you that before you actually believed it."

ELEVEN

"YOU'RE SURE YOU CAN FIND HIM AGAIN?"

Lukas huffs behind me, tripping over his own feet. I can't hear him well, but I think he says something about slowing down.

"It's a long way to Gesher," I growl. "If we're going to make it by nightfall, we need to hurry."

Inari, ever faithful, trots at my side. I can't take her into town, but every minute she's with me is one more minute I can be sure of her keen ears and calm protection. I won't have those assurances again for some time, and I'm still concerned about the soldiers finding her when they come. Yet with her bloodied and matted fur, she looks more like a stray than a loyal companion , and that will be her camouflage. I hate seeing her hurt, but her wounds are superficial. I force myself to believe she'll be okay without me. At least for now.

"But—" Lukas cuts himself off with a loud cry. When I spin around, he's on his stomach, spitting out dirt. "But I don't know if I can find it in the dark."

"You're gonna have to." Without offering him a hand, I watch him struggle to his feet. "If this man is the only person you have solid intel about, he's our only chance."

"But we don't have to get there *right now*," he protests as I turn my back. "It can wait until morning."

I whirl around, lunging forward and planting myself inches from his nose. "You want to find your mother? Then do as I say! Otherwise the deal is off, and you're on your own."

His face contorts like a child's at the moment before a tantrum. I grunt and turn before Lukas explodes. He says nothing, though, and a quick peek over my shoulder finds him plodding behind me once again.

He hasn't figured out that I need him as much as he needs me, that he could make his own demands. I'll hold tight to the advantage as long as I can, demanding obedience. I had fifty trained soldiers under me two years ago, I can still command.

We continue on until the sun dips below the horizon. When Inari twitches, I realize how close we are to Gesher, the town's lights beginning to filter through the trees. Not long after, I can just make out the muffled sounds of city life—hovercab horns and screeching sirens, the familiar clangs and bangs and crashes I left behind for the Wood.

At the first clear sight line to the city, Lukas gasps and shudders slightly, his face tinging itself green. "Fiver, I sure wish I had that gun, because I don't like this. Did I tell you I don't like this?" He stumbles over a root and nearly crashes into me.

"If you tell me again, I'll bash in your nose," I spit. Half of my brain is screaming, telling me this is a fool's idea. I roll my eyes and ask, "Where's this guy supposed to live?"

Lukas shoots me a sideways glance. "Tēlam Street," he mutters, shuffling his feet.

"What else do you know about him?"

He sticks his tongue between his teeth; it pokes out from his lips. "His name is Yosher Weldtham. He's supposed to have worked at Ramius before the army ditched his project and fired him."

I shoot him a wary look. "*Supposed* to have worked there?"

"That's what the . . . spies told me."

"Wait, you mean you've never met this guy?"

His eyes move nervously, not meeting mine. "Uh . . . no, actually."

"Then how do we know he won't give us up on sight?" How dumb could this kid possibly be?

"They said he was on our side!" he argues. "I just . . . didn't make it to him, that's all."

He won't look at me, won't offer an explanation beyond that, and forcing him to talk right now will only cost us precious time. I blow out a frustrated breath, scanning the buildings in the distance. The smell of smog, fuel cells, and burning rubber makes my nostrils twitch, even from this far away.

This is madness, especially with this terrified Lucian kid in my shadow. My only comfort is knowing that Lukas somehow managed to find his way to Weldtham *and* get out of the city unharmed. Perhaps he can hold onto that shred of bravery just a little longer. Even without his gun.

"Alright." I motion to Inari to stay put before nuzzling her snout affectionately. As much as I hate leaving her, I have no choice. I'm doing this for her. For us. For my Wood.

I swallow, it's time. "Let's go," I command. I step beyond the tree line, fighting the urge to run for the safety of the forest. Lukas moves forward tentatively. We're in this together now, whether I like it or not.

Inari whines behind me, and a sickening dread hollows out my gut. I peer over at Lukas, his face ashen in the dim light. He bites his lip. He'll make a poor substitute for Inari, but he'll have to do.

The deepening twilight conceals us as we slip into the town. I skirt around a brick house, pressing my back against it. Lukas mimics my every movement. I peer around the edge, catching sight of several people on the street. Their long shadows stretch across the sidewalk, their bodies illuminated by the yellowish streetlights. We wait.

There's no way we're going to reach Tēlam Street without being seen to some degree. Lukas might be able to pass for a Boquan as long as he keeps his mouth shut, but in my tattered and mud-stained clothes, I won't make it very far without drawing attention. I need camouflage, and fast.

"Follow me," I hiss finally, moving around the corner of a house. Lukas obeys, his breathing labored. "Why are we sneaking around like this?" he pleads. "I thought you could get us into the city without anyone recognizing me!"

I swallow, peering around the street corner. "I *can* get us there. Without anyone recognizing either one of us."

A brief pause in the flow of traffic. The town is quieting down as night descends. The road is clear, yet it's still a long way to Tēlam Street, and the Boquan patrols guarding the city are out. I don't know the timing of their rounds, and they won't be easy to evade.

We stay in the shadows, ducking into yards and avoiding the sidewalks. We hold our breath as if that will somehow keep residents from looking out their back windows and catching sight of our shadowy movements. Lukas, surprisingly, holds his own, scrambling over the fences between yards with a fair amount of ease.

We pause behind the last house on the street. My mental map of Gesher is blurry; I don't remember as much as I would like, and many things could've changed during my long absence. I haven't been here since I was a kid. Since before they took me.

Lukas tugs on my arm, pointing frantically at something in the grassy alley ahead. A man in dark clothes fumbles with his keys at a side door. I grab Lukas and pull him behind the house before we're spotted. He wisely keeps his mouth shut, although he's as scared as I've ever seen him. Peeking into the alley, I wait until the man turns his key in the lock.

I move. In less than ten steps, I close the gap between us and wrap an arm around the man's neck. He gags and struggles, but my hold is tight; I drag him away from the door, squeezing with all I have until he sags in my grip. I wait a few seconds, making sure he's unconscious, before I let him sink to the ground.

"What are you doing?" Lukas asks in a strangled hiss as he steps from behind the house. I ignore him and reach for the man's long black jacket. Lukas's eyes grow as big as a squirrel's head as he watches me tear the jacket from the man's limp body. A check of his back pocket rewards me with a leather wallet. A quiet groan escapes the man's lips, so low and soft that I feel it more than I hear it.

"What was that?" Lukas pants as we dart across the street. "Did you kill him?"

I shrug into the jacket, shoving my arms into the sleeves. "I probably should've," I grunt. I reach inside my own pocket and pull out the wallet. "But a mugging isn't my style. No one will ever think it was me."

I grab the few bills in the wallet before chucking it into some decorative bushes surrounding another house. The jacket fits nicely, and more importantly, it covers up my worn and filthy clothes. At a glance, I'm an ordinary Boquan once again.

"You're afraid of your own people?" Lukas asks as I step around him, heading for the park behind the next cluster of houses. The trees will provide some decent cover, saving us from traversing the streets.

Trailing five steps behind, Lukas repeats his question. Ducking through the park as though it were my Wood, I don't answer or break my stride. The familiar scents of grass and leaves flood my nose, but they're laced with oil and other city-smells.

Lukas stays quiet until our silence is too much for him. "Hey! Where are you going now?"

I groan. "Tēlam Street. Obviously."

"You know where it is?" He moves beside me, pumping his arms. "I thought you grew up in a military compound?"

"Shut up, Lukas, or I swear I'll—"

"—Okay!" He holds up his palms, ceding.

We cross the rest of the park in silence. When we reach the next street, I shove both my hands in my pockets and lower my head, faking a noticeable limp.

Lukas's mouth gapes open in bewilderment. "You take this whole 'disguise' thing to an extreme, huh?"

"I like to stay alive. I think you do too," I snap. I remember this part of town better. A left at Belmore and straight across both Wader and Hilson. Finally, the street sign reads, "Tēlam."

"Which way to his house?" I demand.

Lukas thinks for a moment, biting his lip before walking to the right. He counts off the house numbers under his breath until his head snaps forward in alarm. I follow his gaze and find a patrol rounding the corner, coming toward us.

He stares with unhidden terror at the soldiers dutifully marching down the street. Any second now, they'll realize Lukas doesn't belong here. What reason would a law-abiding citizen have for gawking at a routine patrol with such fear?

I grab Lukas by the shirt and shove him against a building, my arm across his throat.

"You following me again, lunk?" I shout into his shocked face. His mouth opens but only strangled sounds emerge. "I told you, if I caught you stalking me again, I'd call the patrols on you!"

His eyes bulge. I release him and turn my back to the patrol, now halted in its tracks. I extend a finger in a warning before I ease myself away, walking backward and keeping my face away from the startled, curious expressions of the soldiers.

"Stop following me!" I bark at Lukas.

One of the soldiers says something to me, but his voice is too low to hear and it's too dark to read his lips. I fake a scoff. "Don't worry. Coward lunk won't be bothering me no more."

Continuing my ruse, I keep my back to the soldiers, but I can faintly hear their snickers. His back still against the building, Lukas's face remains paled with fear and he's cowering as though I'd slapped him. He glances at the troupe as they pass him and shoot him snide looks. He flinches but says nothing as they go on their way.

When they march around the corner and disappear, I spin around to Lukas, who's shivering in the shadow of the building.

"What did I do?" he nearly shouts. "I'm sorry, I—"

"You almost got us caught!" I hiss, shoving him. He recoils but doesn't resist as I push him down the street. "You looked like you'd seen a ghost, and they would've called you out for it. I gave you some-thing to be scared of!"

His features contort but relax just as quickly, realizing my ploy. "Oh."

"Which house is it?"

Lukas shakes his head, refocusing, then turns to the doorway we just passed. "This one, here. One-fifteen."

I nod, scanning the drab house. One light shines through an upstairs window. "Right. Let's go."

I reach for the handle and twist, pushing the unlocked door open. Easier than I thought.

"Fiver, what are you doing? You can't burst in without knocking!" Lukas grabs my arm. I shove it away, ducking inside.

"I never knock."

TWELVE

I STOOD IN LINE WITH MY TRAY, WAITING FOR THE cook to dump her masterpiece onto the thick plastic. Today's offering was some kind of meat in dark gravy over rice. I brought it to our table in silence. There was no assigned seating, but most Greens ate with each other at the back tables overlooking the rest of the canteen. Everybody else stuck with their squadron or unit. Nobody wanted to eat with a Green.

I joined Atara and Link, the first two at the Greens' tables. Atara offered to trade her apple for my slice of chocolate cake. I nodded, and her eyes shone.

"Wow, *nobody* ever makes that trade!" She grabbed my cake. "You must really hate chocolate."

"Naw, it's not like that," Link muttered through a mouthful of rice. "It's just that he could eat sawdust and never notice it."

I dug a fork into the meat and said nothing.

"Which is probably a good thing, considering that dinner," Atara said, stuffing the cake into her mouth. "But they sure know how to do chocolate."

Link took a gulp from his carton of milk, then muttered something about the restroom as he shoved his chair back. I waited until he'd slipped through the canteen door before leaning in close to Atara.

"They're watching you."

She licked chocolate from her lips and twisted her face in confusion. "What? Who?"

"The Aces. The Commanders. You're not performing well enough for them."

Her face darkened, but she said nothing, eating another bite of cake.

She took my warning better than I expected, but I had a sick feeling deep inside my chest about her reaction to my next news.

"They're putting me into a squadron."

Her eyes whipped to me, wide with alarm. "What?"

I smiled weakly, a forced thing. "One step closer to becoming a real soldier."

She closed her mouth and looked away.

"I just thought . . . now that I won't be around much longer, you should know you need to shape up. I won't be there to take the attention off you."

She set her jaw. "You think I can't take care of myself?"

"You know what I mean." I met her hard stare. Her gaze softened as she realized I wasn't concerned with her abilities as a soldier; she had remarkable physical prowess that could match mine or Link's, even if she was reluctant to use it. Nor was I afraid she wouldn't pass her qualifying exam; she had brains—and she wasn't so reluctant to use those.

What I feared was someone catching on. Learning that she'd rather be anywhere else than here. That she still cried herself to sleep, even though all the other Greens who'd arrived with her had long overcome their homesickness and embraced their new lives. That she often blinked at her homework in disbelief, sometimes even scribbling out words in her textbooks and replacing them with new, different ones. Words that changed the course of history with nothing but her pen.

That's what I feared, and I almost didn't care if she didn't truly shape up, as long as she got better at faking it. My eyes begged her—I couldn't stand the thought of harm coming to her. I treasured her, treasured our friendship. Atara stayed with me because she wanted to know *me*, not for what she could get out of me. I couldn't lose that. I needed it. Needed her.

She lowered her head. She said nothing.

§

"Welcome to your new home, kid." The older Ace said, his badge reading "Trout." He stared down at me, a grin stretching across his face. He was older than me by two years, and bigger, too. A strange glint came into his eye. "I've heard a lot about you."

I met his stare for only a second before I brushed past him and set my duffel bag on an empty bunk near the back of the room. A strange hollowness had settled into my gut the moment they'd told me I was getting promoted, that I was being assigned to Barracks Six. Others got promotions, too, but not one Green would be coming with me to my new bunk. I was starting over, just like before.

The others, all slouched over their textbooks or sprawled across their mattresses, looked up at me, the new transfer. Most of them were several years older; some of the boys even had the beginnings of facial hair.

A hand clamped down on my shoulder, spinning me around. Trout's red face growled, "I'm talking to you, Green. When your Ace speaks, you listen!"

"I thought that's what I did, sir," I replied, not quite keeping my tone submissive. I was in no mood to deal with his need to lord his power over me to impress his soldiers.

Trout whipped his hand up in a blur of skin and slapped my cheek. I winced at the sting but said nothing. I knew Aces like this. I watched them compete for the best Greens, buttering up their superiors while sabotaging each other. I'd seen them keeping tabs on me in training. This one was luckier than all the rest: either that, or he was the least honorable. I suspected the latter.

My new Ace leaned in close to my face. "You're in a real squadron now, Fiver," he spat. "Nobody's gonna hand-feed you like that babysitter Bone. Here, you work. You work or you *die*. Simple as that."

I had another smart answer, but I held my tongue. I'd infuriated him enough for one day.

"I have four ULs. I'm placing you with Rhino's unit. Which means . . . " He grabbed my duffel bag, shoving it against my torso. "You bunk in the far-right corner."

I glared at him. He smirked. "Don't make me regret choosing you, Green. We have practice every day from two to seven in Training Room Two, except for the two days a week when we practice in the training field behind the building. At the end of every week, we have a mock battle. Don't be late to any of it."

He stalked away, and I was left staring into a group of agog young people. I adjusted my grip on my bag and moved toward the far-right corner, watching for an empty bunk.

"Here, kid, you can have this one," said an older, rough-skinned boy toward the back. He pointed to a rumpled cot against the wall, two bunks away from his. Several pieces of wrinkled clothing were on top of the blanket.

"Someone's already got that one," I replied.

He laughed. "Kid, this is my unit's section. I can put whoever I want wherever I want. Besides, that's all *my* stuff."

"You're Rhino?" The more I looked at him, the more I could see it. The leathery skin, the light hair that seemed grayish in the dim light.

"You got it, sport. What's your name?" He stretched his arms above his head, grunting as he flexed his muscles.

"Fiver."

He paused, pulling his arms down. "Ah, I've heard of you. Impressive little snot, ain'tya?"

"Why does he still call me a Green?"

"Who, Trout?" Rhino shifted on his bed, adjusting the textbook on his lap. "Everybody's called a Green till they prove they ain't one anymore."

"You sure *you* ain't one, Rhino?" said a voice behind me. A rake-thin boy only a year or two older than me slid onto the cot beside Rhino's. Rhino smiled and threw a weak punch across the gap at his shoulder. The boy grinned and blocked, throwing one of his own.

"I got a reputation to prove to the new guy!" Rhino protested as the first boy dodged his outstretched hand.

Another boy with black hair and broad shoulders sank onto the cot on Rhino's other side. "You two at it again?" he said. His voice was deep, and sprouts of hair speckled his dark chin.

Rhino pulled back from roughhousing with the first boy and pointed at me. "Say hello to our new unit member, boys. You've heard of Fiver, right?" He turned to me. "These two useless lumps are Swisher and Moose."

I only had to glance to know which boy was which. Moose lifted two fingers to his dark hairline in a salute, while Swisher held out a skinny hand for me to shake. "It's about time we had some decent blood in this unit," Rhino said. The other boys feigned offense.

"We're the best soldiers in Barracks Six!" Swisher said, narrowing his blue eyes at Rhino. "Ain't nobody got soldiers like Unit Four."

"Handpicked by Gallander himself," Moose said, bowing mockingly.

"Hey, you think he's really as old as they say he is?" Swisher asked. "I heard he's over two hundred!"

"That's ridiculous," said Moose, throwing a pillow at him. "But I heard he can bench press two kids in each hand."

"And that's more believable?"

"Of course it is!"

I half-listened to their banter, absentmindedly clutching my bag to my chest. Gallander's name was barely spoken out loud among the Greens, let alone traded along with ridiculous rumors like these. Among the Greens, nobody ever spoke of him with anything less than respect. Respect tinged with fear, or sometimes straight fear. We all knew what disappointing him meant.

Every head turned as the door flew open. Familiar white teeth flashed. Blond, shaggy hair flopped as Link nodded, scanning us until his gaze finally came to rest on me.

"Fiver!" His face lit up like the sun, and he shot towards our back corner. He dropped his duffle bag and gestured toward himself. "Guess who's transfer got changed last-minute?"

Rhino and the others gawked at me. Link's smile never wavered as he gestured for me to follow him. "I'm gonna grab some dinner. Coming?"

He took off. I remained where I was, glued to the spot. An awkward silence filled our back corner until finally Moose spoke. "So, we get the shadow too?"

I stiffened, instantly filled with the need to defend Link. "He's not useless. He's a good fighter."

Rhino shrugged one shoulder. "We'll see."

THIRTEEN

BY ALL EVIDENCE, YOSHER WELDTHAM IS NOT A VERY stable person. The room I find myself in looks like someone threw it in a dryer for a spin, with blankets and pillows hanging halfway off the sagging furniture. Open books and torn papers litter the wood floor, crude writing scrawled across the pages. Clothing and shoes lay in heaps in corners and across chairs. Used dishes and crumpled napkins cover the coffee table.

I wrinkle my nose and tiptoe through the mess. The stairs are pressed against the left wall; a jacket and a pair of socks hang on the banister. An umbrella stand in the corner has been knocked over, and it peeks out from beneath a coat that fell from the rack on the wall above. The whole place smells like the inside of a shoe.

I move for the stairs, Lukas silent behind me. I climb them gingerly, hoping they don't creak beneath my weight and announce my presence.

Upstairs is slightly better than downstairs. Less clutter. A short hallway holds three doors. One is ajar; light from the room within spills out onto the hallway's floor.

Lukas grips my arm and nods at the door as if I'd missed it. I pull from his grasp and peer inside. A bedroom. A balding, middle-aged man has propped himself up in bed, an open book in one hand and a ceramic mug in the other. Square glasses are perched on his wide nose.

I purse my lips. The man didn't see me, but he is facing us—a sneak attack won't work. I glance at Lukas, who's nearly trembling in fear, and I point down the hall, shoving him in that direction. He lets out a squeak of surprise; his hand thuds against the wall as he steadies himself.

I watch in satisfaction as Yosher Weldtham frowns over his book. He snaps it shut and flings off his blankets, rising to investigate the sound.

Lukas, in the hall corner, is afraid to move, afraid to breathe. As Yosher crosses his bedroom, I tuck myself behind the arc of the door and watch his shadow draw closer.

He steps into the hall, and I grip him by his flannel collar. Yosher freezes and makes no sound that I can hear as I yank him forward, shove the door closed, and pin him against it.

"No, please, I don't know anything!" he cries.

"Shut up." I don't trust this man, he could turn us over in a heartbeat. His eyes blare his fear; that fear is my only insurance against his crossing me. "I've got a few questions for you. The faster you answer them, the faster you'll get back to your book. Understand?"

He trembles, wilting in my hold. He looks up at me, and something flickers in his eyes. They grow wide, as though recognizing something in me.

Recognizing me.

"I didn't mean to do it!" he stammers. "I swear it was an accident!"

Grimacing, I study his square face. Lukas stands himself beside me and watches nervously. Yosher's gaze darts to him, then back to me, his renewed panic making his chest heave.

"You're him, aren't you?"

I straighten my stance. "The traitor? Yes, I am. Now, are you going to answer my questions or not?"

He nods quickly, his mouth hanging open. "Yes, yes, of course!"

"Good." I pull him away from the door and open it, shoving him inside the room. Lukas follows tentatively. Yosher stops in the center of the room, and I shut the door behind us. I nod at Lukas. "Go watch the window."

Lukas becomes even paler. "You're a traitor?"

I grab him and aim him at the window. "Go keep watch."

Yosher, still standing awkwardly in the center of the room, turns. "What do you want?"

"Tell me everything you know about the Ramius Corporation."

His face blanches. "You don't want to hear about that place."

I take a step closer. "You're in no position to tell me what I don't want to hear." He's sizing me up, but he's still afraid. "What are they going to do to the Crosswoods?" I demand. "Why do they want the Vitmor?"

His jaw drops. "How do you know about the Vitmor? It's Gallander's greatest secret."

So it *is* Gallander's project. "Not anymore," I say. "It's gonna stop with me. And nothing's gonna get in my way. You'll tell me everything you know, or . . . " I lift my knife halfway out of its hilt.

"No, wait!" He stares at me for a moment before his eyes gloss over. "He begged me to help, just before they took him." His voice is small and weak, laced with guilt. "He trusted me."

My patience is nearly at its breaking point. I pull him closer, grasping his shirt roughly. "The Crosswoods. Vitmor. Tell me, now!"

He jerks from his stupor, his rheumy eyes refocusing. "Gallander needs it for the serum," he says. "Vitmor only grows in the Crosswoods."

"I have it on good authority they're going to burn the Crosswoods," I snarl. I'm not sure how good the authority actually is, but I need to keep the man focused and talking.

Yosher blinks. "They're close," he whispers, his eyes threatening to float off again. No wonder they fired him.

"What do you mean?" I shake him by his shoulders.

"The Crosswoods is the perfect place. It's large, and it's a de facto neutral-zone. Nobody wants to travel through it, Boquan *or* Lucian. If they're going to clear the land, it means they'll start growing Vitmor in mass quantities, I think. Probably right under the Lucians' noses."

My forehead bunches as I scowl, not understanding. Yosher's face fills with even more fear than when he first saw me. "Don't you understand?" he says, raising his hands to my shoulders. "It means they're about ready to use it. The serum is almost complete!"

"What serum?"

Yosher, nearly in tears, presses his palms over his eyes. "You can't stop it," he wails. "Nobody can stop it. Gallander will kill us all!"

Perhaps fear is not the best way to deal with this man. I relax my angry muscles and pretend I'm on the field encouraging a frightened soldier. "Where is this Ramius Corporation?" I ask, gently pulling his hands from his face. My voice is low and soft. "Tell me. Please."

He looks up at the word *please* and swallows, glancing from me to Lukas. "They'll find you here," he says. "They monitor me."

To keep from slapping him in frustration, I bite the inside of my cheek. "Please tell me where it is," I say, keeping my tone soft. "I need your help."

My pleas seem to have awakened something inside the deranged scientist. His eyes fill with wonder and hope, and his hands stretch out and grasp my arms. "Help? You need my help?"

I nod. He gives a short, oddly gleeful laugh. "He needed my help once, too." The smile falls from his face as quickly as it appeared. "The main facility is in Moleck, but that's not where Gallander is doing the research on the Vitmor. There's a second building, but I don't know where. That's where *he* is."

Before I can ask who "he" is, Lukas leaves his lookout at the window and bounds over to us. "Do you know anything about my mother? Rebekah Garrow. She was taken in a raid a couple months ago."

Yosher stares at Lukas from behind his bushy brows. "You're a Lucian," he finally says, moistening his lips. Lukas tenses, the muscles in his neck contracting. His bulging eyes become his reply.

"Months?" The scientist shakes his head in remorse. "Then I wouldn't hold out much hope. Captives get taken straight to the research labs. They do wicked things to them in those places."

Tears well in Lukas's eyes, but he fights them back. He draws himself to his full height and balls his fists. "I'm going to find her. If I have to tear the country apart, I'll find her!"

Yosher only looks at him with raw pity.

We can't stay here much longer, even if Lukas needs time to absorb this news. If Yosher is under watch, we've already stayed too long. "Lukas," I say. "Let's go."

"But—"

"He doesn't know anything about your mother," I urge. "The quicker we can get to the corporation, the quicker we can find her."

"But what if she's in the second building?" he protests. "We don't know where it is!"

"Nathaniel will know," Yosher says. I turn, training my eyes on him. He squirms beneath my gaze before adding, "Nathaniel's been looking for him, too."

I'm about to ask who Nathaniel is when a heavy pounding from below cuts me off. "They've come, I told you! They see everything!" Yosher wails.

I clench my teeth. Lukas left the window unguarded, and I didn't think to make him go back to it. Sloppy. I haven't been a soldier in a long time, maybe too long.

I cross the hallway to the spare room directly opposite the bedroom. The window here overlooks the street, and a group of soldiers is pounding on Yosher's front door, demanding entry. Half a dozen of them wait below, all clad in black and green, cruel snarls on their faces and weapons in their hands. Likely they've surrounded the place.

Back in the bedroom, Yosher and Lukas quiver in the corner, both begging with their eyes for my leadership when my only defense is a handful of knives.

A handful of knives to save two cowering children. A distraction is the best bet I have.

"Lukas!" I pull him toward the door, pointing. "Go smash out the window in that room! Throw something through it, shatter the glass. Scream. Do whatever you need to do to keep the soldiers' attention on you. Got it?"

He nods in understanding but doesn't move. I blow out an impatient breath and growl, "Go!"

Lukas sprints across the hallway, only marginally less afraid of me than the soldiers. I cock my chin at Yosher. "Go with him." He's frozen, sucking on one corner of his lip. "Now!" I shout, and he bolts from the room.

I kill the overhead light, plunging the room into darkness. Creeping on my knees, I make my way to the window, where I peek my head over the sill just enough to assess the response-unit below. Guns raised, the soldiers inch toward the building, waiting for confirmation that their companions in the front have breached the door.

The pounding below doesn't relent. The orders to come out peacefully have long since ceased, the impatient soldiers now hungry for blood. What's taking those two so long? I wait for several long moments, watching the men.

A scream from across the hall. Breaking glass. More screaming. The soldiers prick their ears in interest. But they have their orders: they can't move until called. They pace restlessly, itching to charge.

I scream in my thoughts to Lukas. "*Come on, more. More! Make them desperate!*"

As if in answer to my silent urging, a powerful explosion rips through the air, nearly knocking me off balance as the building shakes. I scrabble upright, stumbling into the hall, where I can see Lukas waving his fist in front of the shattered window and shouting, "Bring it on, freaks!"

"Get down, you idiot!" I hiss, grabbing Lukas by the shoulder and pulling him away from the window. Yosher, standing a few feet back, peers outside, glowing with pride at whatever homemade bomb the two of them threw out the window's gaping hole. If I stretch, I can see the crater in the ground below, the sidewalk and dirt jumbled together in a round heap. The soldiers have surrounded it, shouting unintelligible words and pulling wounded men from the depression.

"What did you do?!" I demand, releasing Lukas's shoulder.

Yosher smiles at me. "I was in demolitions."

Bullets fly through the window. More shattering glass. A second battery follows, at least one bullet lodging in Yosher's back. His body stiffens in shock. Lukas screams, lunging for him. I grab him, holding him still. Yosher is still on his feet, but life quickly drains from his face, a glaze in his eyes emerging. He looks from Lukas to me, blood seeping from the corner of his mouth. Something catches in my lungs and drives my heart deeper into my chest.

"F-Find . . . him," Yosher croaks, shaking wildly. His gaze becomes glassy. His mouth moves again as he forces one last gurgle, the last fleck of life in his eyes burning into me as the words leave him. "He's . . . waiting for . . . you."

His legs buckle, his body crumpling. Lukas cries and pulls out of my hold. I'm frozen, haunted by the scientist's last words. Words meant for me alone. Words I don't understand.

A new pelting of bullets shocks me from my stupor. Without a word, I tug Lukas across the floor, slinking on my knees toward the door. I pull him out into the hall and then into Yosher's bedroom, moving toward the window. I release Lukas, and he stares at the door. He has tears in his eyes, but I have neither the time nor the patience to console him.

I carefully edge around the window and peer out. Sure enough, the soldiers have left their post, eager for a shot at us from the other side. "Thanks, Yosher," I mutter under my breath before barking my orders at Lukas. "Strip the bed! Tie the sheets together, end-to-end."

He sniffs. "You can't be serious?"

"Do it!"

He wipes his nose and nods as he begins pulling away the bedclothes. We won't have much time. Lukas ties the sheets and Yosher's single blanket together swiftly, but there's not enough material. We'll still need to jump the last two meters at least.

I fasten one end of the makeshift rope around a leg of the bed. Lukas pulls the last knot tightly, and I grab our lifeline, throwing the other end out the window.

"You can't be serious," he repeats, looking down at the freely swinging rope.

"I'm getting out of this thing alive," I reply, scanning the ground below. Still clear. Sticking my legs through the window and holding fast to the sheets, I begin easing myself out of the opening. "It's not hard if you hang on tight."

"I can't!" Lukas whines.

I pause, even though I'm all the way out the window with only one arm clinging to the sill. "You pulled me from the edge of a cliff! This should be nothing!"

He leans forward, looking down again. I lower myself, letting all my weight fall on the sheets. I hope Lukas tied good knots.

Slowly, I inch downward until the sheets are at their end. I take a breath and let go, bending my knees as I land. I peer up at Lukas, who is staring at me from above. "Come on, we don't have all night!" I hiss.

Tentatively, he sticks one foot through the window. Then the other. He wriggles himself out, gripping the sheets for dear life.

"Faster!" I mutter. How did I end up babysitting this soft Lucian kid?

The ground quakes. The soldiers are coming. Tired of shooting at things that don't fire back, they're returning to their post. Lukas, two-thirds down the rope, pauses, craning his head as examines the ground below.

My chest is about to burst. There's no time. They're halfway here already, flowing around both sides of the house like a branching river. The first soldiers spot us. Their hands point, they slap each other on the arms. Guns raise. Ready. Aim.

"Lukas!"

Fire.

Bullets pummel the ground. A spray lands just in front of my boots, and I leap back. Looking over his shoulder, Lukas's face drops in shock. He still has several feet to go on the rope, but before I can shout to him again, he lets go.

He hits the grass hard, and now I can hear the soldiers shouting. They continue to flood around the building's corners, guns raised. On his feet, almost as if in slow motion, Lukas runs for me like a lost child.

"Go!" he screams. But my eyes are no longer fixed on him.

A soldier, now only a meter or so from Lukas, aims his gun. Finger on the trigger, ready to fire. More guns are probably aimed at me, but this one will hit its target without fail.

My knife is in my hand more quickly than I've ever drawn it before, and I launch it with instinctual skill. The soldier's head jerks back, the knife's hilt protruding from his neck. He collapses. The others, confused, freeze in their tracks, unsure of what felled him.

Lukas grabs me, pulling me down the street. "Come on!" he screams. The soldiers are surely regrouping, but we're already gone, fading into the night.

I vow never to return here again.

FOURTEEN

"ʜᴀᴠɪɴ' ꜰᴜɴ ʏᴇᴛ, ꜰɪᴠᴇʀ?"

Rhino smiled down at me as dirt and grass rained onto my head and neck. To gain better traction, he dug his foot into the steep embankment, dislodging more dirt. I grunted in response, waiting until he'd cleared the hill before I continued my own climb.

He reached for me as I struggled, and I heard the shouting of soldiers above. As his hand clasped around my wrist, Rhino screamed at them to cut off the enemy, then yelled, "Come on, Fiver, give me a little help!" I dug my feet into the incline and heaved forward; he gritted his teeth and pulled. I shot up the embankment and collapsed on top of him.

"Unit Four!" Rhino shouted, wriggling out from beneath me. "Regroup, regroup!"

The other three soldiers in our unit appeared over a small rise. Swisher, adjusting his cap, slid next to Rhino. "They're coming, sir!" he panted, laying on his side and pointing at the outcropping of rocks ahead. "At least two units, maybe more."

Rhino cursed. "Trout should've known better than to send us up here without reinforcements."

"What do we do?" Moose rubbed at his fight suit and gripped his gun more tightly. Swisher and Link turned to our commanding officer expectantly, waiting for orders.

Rhino glared at the outcropping and slapped his gun. "We make sure they remember us!" he growled. "Swisher, you and Moose take that rise there." He pointed to the left, where a rocky, earthy mound was partly hidden by a clump of bushes. "Link, go behind those boulders with Fiver." He pointed to the right. "I'll make my way around and come up behind them. Once you engage, I'll bring up the rear, and we'll cut them off."

Link immediately grabbed me by my fight suit and dragged me toward the rocks. "Fiver, let's move!"

We collapsed behind the boulders and peered out, watching for any sign of movement. We could hear the attacking units charging through the underbrush and making their way to the embankment. If they got through, it would all be over.

They emerged from the tree line, moving forward swiftly. Link's hand clenched around his weapon. "Here we go," he muttered. I raised my gun, trying to calm my trembling fingers as I peered through the sights.

Soldier after soldier clambered over the rocks, charging confidently toward the embankment—and the prize.

"Wait for it," Link hissed, squinting into his sights. "Wait . . . hold . . . now!"

He opened fire with a shout, and I heard the others follow suit. The attacking soldiers spun in surprise, caught off guard. I fired with careful aim, the clearing erupting with the sound of gunfire and the acrid smell of its residue. Several soldiers fell at once, the indicator lines of their fight suits changing from black to bright red.

"We got 'em now!" Link whooped in triumph. The attacking soldiers shouted to each other, running for cover from our bullets.

A snap from behind dropped my insides, cutting off any early celebration. I turned and nearly screamed in terror at the soldier rising above us, his gun raised.

"Link!" I cried, pushing him down. A bullet pinged off the boulder a few inches away from us. Link cursed, rolling away from me. "They split up!" I shouted, ducking as the soldier aimed again. I raised my gun and pulled the trigger. His fight suit changed to red. He fell, but another attacker immediately took his place. This siege was more than two units, that was for sure. It seemed like we were up against the entire squadron.

Link lay still, the stripe on his fight suit now bright red. Fear surged through my veins as another soldier bore down on me like a panther. I aimed and fired, but nothing but a click came. Horrified, I fumbled in my pack for another magazine. The soldier up ahead smirked and lowered his gun.

"I'll take care of this one," the soldier called to his unit, letting his weapon fall. Several others came up behind him, watching as he drew a knife and moved closer. My heart became a drum in my chest, dread washing through me. My fingers stiffened in fear and struggled to load the new magazine into my gun. My hands shaking violently, I nearly dropped both.

The soldier lunged forward like a vulture, gripped my suit by the collar, and hauled me to my feet. His dark eyes bore into me, and I slapped uselessly at his arms, forgetting all my training in my panic.

He thrust his blade into my torso; it retracted into its hilt as he stabbed me. I felt the force of the hilt pressing into me, although the knife's tip didn't so much as tear the gray mesh of my fight suit. My suit's line turned bright red, my body tumbling into the dirt as the soldier released me.

I lay there, eyes closed, for several moments before a loud horn sounded. Link, rubbing at his shoulder with one hand, groaned beside me as he rolled over and sat up.

"They warned us about that," he grunted. He stood, shaking the dust from his suit. I pushed to my feet as he continued grumbling. "It don't seem fair. It was just my shoulder, I still could've fought. But no, you get hit *anywhere*, you're out. Like a soldier can't fight with a scratch or two. It's not realistic!"

Link was right, it *wasn't* fair. The Commanders hadn't figured out how to work injury-detection into our suits—that wasn't our fault, we were good soldiers.

"If you can't follow the rules, then get out!" the Ace of Barracks Three barked, pushing toward our redoubt, a pack of ten soldiers behind her. She carried a square flag with a large six on it—the prize and ultimate goal of this war game. Her name was Marble, after the swirled coloring of her eyes.

Trout clomped up close behind her, red-faced and seething. He glared at me; I felt the pinch of his anger in my gut. How could he possibly blame me for his mistake?

The Ace clapped Trout on the shoulder in the tradition of good spirit. "Good fight, my friend. Better luck next time."

She called to her unit, and they broke out in triumphant hoots and shouts, their fists and weapons raised victoriously. Trout glowered at their celebration and eventually stalked away without a word. Link ran after him.

A hand touched my shoulder. I turned to find Rhino giving me a shallow grin. "Your first mock battle. How's it feel?"

I looked away. "He blames me for it."

"Who, Trout?" Rhino snorted. "He blames everybody except himself. You're just the one he hates the most at the moment. Congratulations." He slapped my shoulder and walked away, heading back to the barracks.

Mumbling under my breath, I watched him leave. Next time, I would make sure Trout couldn't blame anybody else for his dumb mistakes.

FIFTEEN

"GO! GO!" I SCREAM, PUSHING LUKAS FORWARD. THE soldiers behind us haven't relented, their pursuit causing us to dodge pedestrians and hovercabs or forcing us down side-streets and alleyways. We make it to the outskirts of Gesher and sprint for the tree line, but the soldiers are catching up fast.

"But—" Lukas protests. I shove him again.

"Move!"

His eyes widen in horror. An enraged cry comes from behind, and I whirl around as the soldier lifts his gun high above his head. Lukas screams in fear, and I push him down, out of harm's way. The soldier, apparently out of ammo, lunges at me like the fool he is as I reach for my blade.

As the metal sinks into his stomach, he drops in mid-cry to the ground. I rush forward and rip the knife from his torso. Another soldier has already taken his place, and I swing the weapon up, slicing her neck. She gurgles as blood gushes from the wound, toppling over.

"Lukas, go!" I order, looking over my shoulder at him.

His face is bone-white, his lips parted in shock. "You . . . you just . . ."

"Get out of here, now!" I scream as another soldier tackles me from behind. His arms are like metal bars around my waist, his weight drives the air from my lungs. He pins me down and wraps an arm around my neck.

"Give up, traitor," he growls. He shoves me harder into the dirt, choking me. I lay helpless, unable to move.

Suddenly, the weight of his body lifts, a sharp cry bursting from him. I gasp for air as he claws at the arms now wrapped around his throat.

Lukas. His head pokes out from behind the soldier's back, his terrified eyes calling to me for help. His first attack on a soldier proves harder than he thought.

"Lukas, let go!" I shout, and for once he listens. The soldier falls, and I land a kick to his gut before he can recover from the stranglehold. As he doubles over, I drive my knee into the bridge of his nose. He grunts and flops backward, the blow leaving him unconsciousness.

Lukas stares at his prone body and swallows. "That was close."

I bore into him with my eyes. "I told you to get out of here. You could've been killed!"

He returns my glare. "And *you* were getting flattened! *I* got him off of you."

I grunt in frustration. "We don't have time for this. The rest of them will be here any minute." In my Wood, my precious Wood. How many soldiers will breach it today?

Lukas jerks his head toward the bushes behind us. I turn and shove him forward. "Go!" I hiss. He obliges, darting into the forest.

I follow him as he pushes through the trees, paying less attention to where we're going than to the too-faint sounds of the soldiers behind. Lukas takes a sharp right, following the tree line. He's assuming our pursuers will delve deeper into the Wood looking for us. It's not a bad strategy, so I trail behind him, pausing only when I spy a dip in the landscape. A cluster of trees conceals a dried-out culvert just wide enough to hide in. Lukas squawks but lets me drag him to the channel, where we take cover.

"What—"

I cut him off with a hand to my lips. "Shh!"

He bites his lip. I press his face flat, my head alongside his. We wait, my ears straining to catch any sound of the soldiers. I yearn for Inari's keen hearing.

After a while, still unsure of my ears, I risk whispering a few words. "You hear anything?"

Lukas shakes his head. "Not anymore."

I wait a second longer before slithering from the culvert and slowly peering out. I scan the trees, looking for movement. Nothing.

When I turn to Lukas, I find him sniffling back tears. "Hey." I slap his arm. "Quit it."

"He's dead!" he blurts out. "Yosher is dead. And it's all my fault."

"Shut up, you had nothing to do with it."

"Yes, I did!" Lukas rubs at one eye like a child. "If I hadn't been so stupid . . ."

Grabbing his elbow, I yank him to his feet. "People die, Lukas." The words catch in my throat. "We can't bring them back."

Lukas scowls. "You don't even care!"

I return his scowl, taking a step closer. "When this is all over, and your mother is safe, then you can cry all you want for Yosher—and anyone else. Until then, we don't have time to sit around feeling sorry about things we can't change."

Lukas balls his fists as if he would actually dare to punch me. Instead, he spins around and takes off, heading in the direction of Gesher.

"Lukas!" I hiss, running after him. "Be careful, they're still out there!"

He ignores me, and I hold in a curse as I begin chasing him. What good does this acting out do anybody, especially his mother?

I could leave him if I wanted, let him run into the city. He's done his part of the deal, and he likely won't contribute anything more without getting himself killed. Yet I still owe him; he's saved my life twice now.

I pursue him through the thinning trees and brush. By the time I realize where he's unknowingly led us, it's too late. Another demon I never wanted to face.

Crumbled bricks. Piles of rubble scattered in haphazard clusters. A house deteriorated. Weeds and grass curl around the remains, growing freely and choking the bricks and burned, rotted floor.

The sight sinks my stomach, an eerie nausea crawling in dizzying circles within me.

"Whoa," comes Lukas's voice. "What happened here?"

"Death happened here," I think.

When I don't answer, Lukas leaps onto the remains of a short stone wall, surveying the devastation. "Looks like this was a house," he says. "A long time ago, anyway." My jaw tightens.

He jumps from the wall and heads into the remains of the house, into a bedroom. Disintegrating rocks litter what used to be the floor. The floor of *their* bedroom.

Lukas moves through the room and into another, kicking through dust and ashes and rotting, charred wood. My fingers curl into fists, my throat tight. Metal bedsprings, blackened doorknobs. A horse figurine that managed to escape the flames; it used to sit on my dresser. In the dim light of my room, I would stare at it from my bed and wait to fall asleep.

I swallow, moving away from the skeleton that was my bed. Lukas leaps over a pile of rubble, landing in the living room. He clambers onto a stack of bricks that used to be the fireplace.

"Look!" he exclaims, dropping to the ground. He picks up a flat object and straightens himself. "It's an award or something."

He scampers over with the plaque I remember well but don't want to see. I steel myself and force my hand to take the scorched, warped thing from Lukas.

The award is my father's. He received it for his work in Branson's science department. It hung on the wall of our living room, displayed with all possible pride.

"Hang on, it's got some writing on it!" Lukas yanks the plaque away and draws it closer to his face. "It says . . . Matthew Endenbough." His pupils widen in realization, and he meets my eyes almost forcefully. "That's . . . " he shakes his head, "the forest. That's what you've been calling it. Endenbough Wood."

I look away, pushing my gaze past him to the tree line.

"He owned the Wood," I lie. "It's only fitting it should be named for him."

Lukas stares at the plaque in his hands, as if only now realizing what must have occurred in this home. "What happened to him?" His voice is small and timid.

I draw in a large breath, taking in the destruction around me. Maybe it would've been better to have forgotten. To not care. All of it, erased for good.

"They died," I reply, my voice as hard as I can make it. "Him and his wife. A fire like this rarely leaves survivors."

"Was it an accident?" His voice harbors an innocent pity for the lost souls. I glare at him, but before I can turn away, Lukas's eyes shoot to the one remaining cluster of bushes in the yard.

"What is it?" I ask, watching him carefully.

"Shh. I heard something," he replies, holding up a palm for silence. With a pang in my gut, I want for Inari again.

But Lukas is not Inari, and he didn't detect the sound fast enough. His face becomes a shocked heap; even he knows it's too late to attempt retreat.

Voices shout, hands clamp onto my shoulders, and a heavy weight crashes into me, bowling me over. I grunt in frustration and twist in the firm grasp, bucking a knee into my attacker's side.

The dark-clad man groans as his grip loosens. He's not a soldier. Not even a Boquan. His simple clothing tells me all I need to know: he's a Lucian.

A fist to his windpipe knocks him backward, and I scramble free, leaping to my feet before the man recovers. But new hands grip my shoulders, two pairs at least. I jab an elbow into one attacker's ribs as I whirl around, slamming my free fist into the other's face. He falls back with a cry, but the first man, now atop a pile of bricks, launches himself at me, screaming in rage as he collides with my body. The force knocks us over, and we roll on the ashy floor, grunting and fighting.

I smash my fist into his nose, splattering the ground with blood. I pin his arms beneath my knees, reaching for my knife. I press the blade to the side of his neck, and, as he realizes my intention, his eyes grow wide with fear.

I press harder, prepared to slice through his skin, when Lukas's choked voice cries, "No!"

Conflicting emotions freeze my hand in place. *"Kill him! Kill him now!"* my mind screams.

"No!" Lukas shouts again. My teeth lock in fury, my fingers trembling around my knife. This Lucian is just one more kill. He deserves it. Why am I hesitating?

The knife clatters out of my grasp as the two other attackers pin me down. My would-be victim spits out a glob of blood and pushes himself upright, reaching for my fallen blade.

"Hold him," he growls, and the other two press their weight into my arms. He hovers over me, the knife in front of my face.

"Let's see how well you kill with *this* sticking out of your neck!" he spits.

"Stop it!" Lukas shrieks, yanking on the man's arm. "Micah, don't!"

"Back off, Lukas," Micah growls, shoving Lukas away. "This has to be done, and you know it."

"You can't kill him in cold blood!" Lukas counters forcefully. "If you do, you're as bad as they are!"

This stays Micah's hand, although his eyes remain cold as he considers what to do with me. I watch him carefully, reading him. His face is older than mine, but not by too many years, and his sweat has turned his brown hair into jagged spikes. His jaw clenches, his companions waiting for his direction. I steady my panting and fight off the panic racing through me.

A huff of furious breath escapes his lips, and he lowers the knife. He grabs my shirt before growling, "Fine." He yanks me to my feet and spins me around, one of his companions jerking my hands behind my back. Metal cuffs click around my wrists, and Micah leans in menacingly. "We'll let Nathaniel decide what to do with him."

Lukas visibly pales at the name. I frown at him, but he won't catch my eye. Micah shoves me from behind. "Get moving, scum!"

SIXTEEN

"Hey!"

The harsh whisper, along with a pressure against my chest, jolted me awake. My arms flew up to find a hand shaking me.

"Shh!" The hiss came from above, and the hand stopped its shaking. I squinted into the dim light at Atara's grinning face. "Calm down, I'm not gonna eat you!"

I sat up, staring open-mouthed at her. "What are you *doing* here?" My eyes flew wildly around the Barracks, searching for any sign that someone else had awoken. A few shifted in their beds, but otherwise no one stirred.

"I never get to see you anymore," she said, sinking into the bed. "Your lunk of an Ace always keeps you over with the rest of your squadron. He won't even let us eat together anymore! And you spend all your free time training with Bone."

I looked around again, sure someone had heard her voice. "Do you know how much trouble you could get in for this?"

"Aw, this whole thing is stupid," she replied, picking at a string on her pajamas. "I don't see what the big deal is. We're just talking."

"How did you get in here?"

She grinned again and fished around in her pocket for a moment before holding up a white key pass. "You'd think Bone would keep better track of his stuff."

"You—"

"—Yeah." She laughed, twirling the card between her fingers. She slipped it back into her pocket. "I told you this whole thing was stupid. Running around like we're big soldiers, getting ready to kill people."

"We're getting ready to save our people," I replied, horrified she still held such thoughts. "Don't talk like that!"

She rolled her eyes. "Oh, come on, Fiver. Don't tell me you buy into all that junk about the Lucians."

"Atara!" I hissed. "You can't talk like that! It's treason!"

"Shh!" she replied, her hand clamping across my mouth. Squirming beneath the weight pressed down on my face, my eyes widened. Someone shifted in their bed, and we froze. She slowly pulled her hand away.

"You called me Atara," she said, her brow furrowing. I stared at her, surprised at myself.

"You should go before someone wakes up." My fingers clenched the sheets. She leaned forward, tugging on my arm.

"Just talk to me!" she pleaded. "Like old times when it was just the three of us against the whole base. Remember?"

She hadn't gone to wake up Link, but I didn't say anything. I only nodded, watching her.

"I miss it sometimes," she whispered. "I miss us. What's it like in a real squadron?"

I swallowed, focusing my gaze on the mattress. "Sort of the same, sort of different. We're split up into units, and we train more outside. We have mock battles in the forest behind the base. The classes are harder . . . more in-depth stuff like outdoor survival and special-ops. We—"

She shook her head and scrunched up her face. "No, what's it *like*?"

I frowned. "What do you mean?"

She looked at me for a moment with her tongue peeking out between her lips before a small smile crossed her face. "Never mind. Can we talk about old times for a bit? Remember when Link dared that kid from Barracks Nine to eat that cricket they found in the bathroom?"

She filled our minds with memories for nearly an hour before Trout stirred from his place at the far end of the room.

"It's nearly wake-up," I said. "You have to go before Trout sees you!"

Atara sighed, but she gave a grin as she pushed up from the bed. She moved toward the door, then pulled the white card from her pocket and waved it near the key sensor. The door clicked open, and she turned. "Thanks, Fiver."

With one last smile she was gone, the light from outside fading into the black of the room as the door closed behind her.

I barely heard the sounds of the Barracks slowly coming awake. Trout's voice shouted at everybody to get their butts out of bed and get dressed, but I ignored all of it. All I could see was her face.

Trout gripped my shoulder and gave it a violent shake. "Get up, lunk!"

I glanced at him. Although there was plenty of risk involved, some part of me couldn't wait for lights out tonight. Hoping she would come back.

And she did. A couple of times a week she would sneak in, and we would talk long into the night, keeping our voices down in the dark. She told me of her life before, what she remembered of it. She lived in a town called Moleck, had a younger brother, and hadn't had many friends there.

"I always knew they were going to come and pick the best of us. They didn't pick us out of a lottery or anything. They watched us. Graded us. Saw if we had what it takes." Her foot struck out and kicked at the bed frame. "My parents told me I would probably be chosen. Because of my marks. My sports. I was good."

I knew very well that Atara didn't want to be in this place. None of us had known what awaited us when we were chosen, but would it have made any difference? Would I have tried to get out of it any way I could?

"Then how did you end up here?" I asked. She chewed on her lips and wiped an itch on her nose.

"I made a mistake."

My stomach churned, reminded once again of her dangerous ideas and what the Commanders, or even Gallander himself, could do to her if they heard her thoughts about the Lucians.

"Why don't you believe what they teach us in history?"

She lifted her eyes. "Because it's not true."

"Who told you?" The sick feeling in my gut rose higher, and I couldn't help but scan the room quickly to see if anyone had heard.

She pressed her lips together. The earlier mirth had disappeared from her eyes, the feelings she usually buried deep within her brought to the surface once again. How heavy her burden had to be. She must have lived terrified someone would find out. I was her only outlet, the only one who wanted her safe, no matter what she said or did.

"I keep praying Elorai will come and rescue us all," she whispered.

I clenched my teeth. No one believed in Elorai anymore. Not really. The Lucians did, and that was all we needed to know about him. But I kept my mouth closed, knowing anything I could say would only cause her to shake her head and sigh.

"I know you don't understand, Fiver," she said. "But maybe someday you will."

SEVENTEEN

 they manage to get this far across the Wood without leaving a sign?

The metal cuffs dig into my wrists, rubbing the skin raw as we walk through the trees. Pain flares from the gashes in my side, but I hold myself upright at the pressure of Micah's handgun pressed into my back.

Lukas traipses along beside me with a lowered head and slumped shoulders like *he* was the one being marched to his death by murderous enemy soldiers. He glares at Micah every now and then, but Micah takes no notice and shoves me forward faster.

"We're almost there," he growls. He grins at Lukas. "Lucky us, right? You know how long we've been trying to find you?"

Lukas turns his eyes on him. "You were looking for me?"

Micah nods. "Orders from the top." He pushes me through a line of trees into a clearing where a black hovercab stands waiting in a grassy ditch. "We're here," he says.

Back when my mother took me with her to the market, I'd see hovercabs rambling down the streets of our town. They're small and boxy, meant for carrying two or three passengers and perhaps a load of groceries. This one is about twice as large, with tinted sureglass windows that can withstand tremendous amounts of force before they shatter. The hull is smooth and rounded, not square like the personal cabs at the market. There are slots on the sides where the wings can extend and retract, depending on the need.

This is a military cab, designed to stealthily transport a small crew through tight spaces, even in the air. If they landed here even a couple of days ago, this far away from my camp, I would have had no way of knowing.

Micah's companions step forward and lift the back hatch. It slides open and over the top, revealing a dark interior with seats lining the sides. Micah shoves me forward. "Get him in there, Tomas. Asher, start the engine."

Tomas grips my shoulders as Micah pushes me from behind. Asher opens the side door of the cab and slides in. A moment later the engine roars to life, and the cab lifts from the ground. Micah gives one last shove and I practically fall into the belly of the cab, with Lukas climbing in silently behind me.

Micah lifts himself inside with a shallow sigh while Tomas pulls me into a seat against the wall. "Shut the hatch and get us home," Micah orders. Asher flips switches and turns dials in the front seat, and the door closes with a click. The cab lurches forward.

"Nathaniel left a message, Micah," Asher says, tapping a screen. I can see nothing but the back of his head, covered in red hair, and I can barely make out his words, my ears straining to hear him. "I told you we should have checked in yesterday."

Micah grunts, shifting his gun. "He'll stop complaining when he sees what we brought home with us."

"Who's Nathaniel?" This is the third time I've heard this name today. First Yosher, and now twice from a group of hostile Lucians.

Lukas's face goes red, and he looks away. Micah grins at me. "Just you wait till this big boy's daddy finds out you kidnapped his son."

"He didn't kidnap me!" Lukas shouts, his fists clenching.

"Then what were you doing out there with him?"

Lukas glares at Micah and looks away again. He crosses his arms and stares at the wall.

"Nathaniel is your father?" I ask him, ignoring the fact that Micah must know that I, as a Boquan, should have killed Lukas on sight. Boquan soldiers don't bother with kidnapping schemes.

Lukas sighs. "He's the commander of the Lucian sabotage units in Dekkan," he answers.

"Lukas!" Micah reaches over and slaps him across the face.

"Hey!" I find myself shouting, but he ignores me. My hands strain against the cuffs, but it only makes the sting in my wrists worse.

"What have you told him?" Micah demands. Lukas's frown deepens, his hands covering the growing welt on his cheek. Micah's eyes flit to it for a moment, a brief flash of regret covering his face before he blinks it away.

"Don't look like much of a soldier to me," Tomas says, sizing me up. He rubs a calloused hand against his jaw. "Fights like one, though." He winces.

"Nathaniel will decide what to do with him," Micah says, leaning back into his seat.

Lukas's father. His family. *Inari.* The thought jolts through my mind and sends a wave of dread down my spine. What will she do? She can take care of herself, but she'll search for me and won't find me. I need her, and now I'm leaving her.

§

Lukas refuses to meet my eyes for the rest of the ride. My palms sweat more the longer I'm confined in this box. I want out. The only other vehicle I'd ridden in for longer was the train to the base all those years ago, and that didn't turn out for the best, either. My bangs fall into my eyes, and I stare through them at the dusky image of Micah, watching me like a wolf guards its kill.

The cuffs have worn deeper into my skin, but I refuse to wince as an unexpected air current shifts the hovercab, jerking us all to the side. Micah's head hits the tinted window with a thud, and he yelps.

"Watch it, Asher!" he growls. Asher doesn't reply, likely tired of Micah's overpowering sense of control. Tomas lets out a weary sigh but says nothing.

Lukas crouches on the edge of his seat, his body facing away from me. If it weren't for him, I'd send my foot into Micah's throat right now. But he asked me to stay my hand, and for some reason, I listened. Why, I'm not sure. Even Lukas doesn't like these people. What could he possibly gain from letting them live when they're taking him away from finding his mother?

"You're awful quiet over there," Micah says to him. Lukas ignores the comment, pulling his arms tighter across his chest. "This Boquan got you scared?"

"Shut up," comes the stiff reply. Micah opens his mouth, but whatever he'd planned to dump out is cut off by Asher's voice.

"We're coming in over the town. Nathaniel wants to see us as soon as we land."

"You tell him about our friend here?" Micah asks.

Asher shakes his head. "No. Only that we found Lukas."

Micah smiles. "Perfect. Put her down right in front of the courthouse."

Tomas locks his jaw but says nothing as Asher twists the controls to comply with Micah's order.

"Yeah, make sure everyone can see us, Micah," says Asher, his voice dripping with sarcasm. "Don't want anyone to miss out."

I twist my neck and peer out the window at the brick building. Two stories tall, with broken and cracked gray columns barely supporting an overhang that hides the front door. Dying grass and the remains of wilted flowers frame the foundation. Crumbling stone steps lead to the veranda.

Not exactly what I think of when I hear the word *courthouse*.

Reverse thrusters on the hovercab kick in, and the wheels deploy to catch the body before it hits the ground. Dead leaves swirl around the machine as it slowly sinks onto its wheels and hisses to a stop. Asher reaches for a button, and the back hatch pops open and slides up over the roof, letting bright sunlight stream into the hovercab.

With my hands cuffed behind my back, I'm unable to shield my eyes, and I blink at the sunshine. Lukas turns and leaps out without a word, Tomas close behind. Micah grabs my arm and pulls me down beside him. "You give me any trouble and you'll make nice fertilizer for our gardens," he hisses in my ear.

I say nothing and let him drag me toward the decaying building. My eyes take in the similar state of the rest of the area. Grass grows from large cracks in the sidewalks, and only a few rusted hovercabs are parked on the sides of the street. The buildings stand quiet with chipped brick and cracked wood. The streetlamps are adorned with "City of Dekkan" banners.

But what chills me are the stares. Dozens of people peeking out from behind curtains and around corners, observing me with suspicion. Some of them are brave enough to stand completely exposed in the streets, staring at me with blank looks as if they're not sure what to think. Even the children, who clutch at their parents' clothes with small fists, watch me like they've never seen a stranger before and have no idea what to do with the sight of me.

Micah shoves me up the steps and through the creaking wooden courthouse door, with Asher, Tomas, and Lukas dragging behind us. Inside, bright lights illuminate the lobby, and wooden floors groan beneath our feet. The room is nearly bare; only a few chairs are scattered about, and an abandoned wooden desk is in the back. Micah pulls me across the room and through a door in the far wall. We move silently down a carpeted hallway lined with photographs of men and women in gray suits.

There's a creak, and a door opens to our right. A tall man in dark gray pants and a black button-down shirt steps through. His hands freeze around a packet of papers as he spots Lukas.

"Lukas…" His lips part, and Micah's grip tightens around my arm. The man's gaze darts to me; he studies my face with startled curiosity. His eyes move to Lukas again, who's hunched at the back, picking a clod of dried mud from his tattered shirt. The man's mouth hardens, and he tilts his head. "My office. Now."

He crosses the hallway and turns the knob of a door, disappearing inside. Micah pushes me through right behind him into the office. Two windows let sunlight pour in from the left wall, and a desk, cluttered with papers and large envelopes, sits against the far wall. Three framed pictures are displayed alongside a flag stand bearing a miniature of the Lucian colors. As if the huge cloth flag covering nearly the entire back wall wasn't enough patriotism. The man stands behind the desk, rubbing his forehead with a pale hand.

I eye his tense body with caution, watching every intake of breath, every flutter of his dark hair. He's probably in his early to mid-forties, his black hair barely touched with gray. But the thin nose, the shape of the lips, the blue eyes, all of it is familiar, and I know this must be Nathaniel, Lukas's father.

The door shuts behind us with a dull click, and Nathaniel pulls his hand from his face.

"Lukas, what have you done?" Frustration is pressed into his voice. Lukas grumbles and pretends to focus his attention out the window.

"He was out in the Crosswoods, practically on Boqua's front doorstep," Micah offers, "with this scumbag." He slaps the back of my head. I suck my lip between my teeth and keep still.

Nathaniel doesn't seem nearly as interested in me as he does with his disobedient son. "Lukas, you've been gone without a word for three weeks. Answer me!" he growls. Heat radiates from Micah's face.

"I went looking for her." Lukas whirls around to confront him, resentment burning in his very movement. "Somebody had to. You're too busy organizing raids and babysitting Micah."

The words sting. Nathaniel's eyes strain even further than they already were. "Lukas." He sighs. Micah stiffens even more behind me.

"Whether you help me or not, I'm going to find Mom," Lukas spits at him, and Asher takes hold of one of his arms. Even then, the son's eyes have jumped the distance and slapped his father across the face. Nathaniel swallows, sympathy showing in his weary expression.

"Your mother is dead, Lukas."

"She is *not* dead!" Lukas throws off Asher's grip and takes a step forward. We all watch in awkward silence, and even Micah says nothing.

Nathaniel's lips tighten into a thin line, and he mirrors his son's glare.

"Do you have any idea what you've done?" His voice nearly trembles. "I've received word from Seth. Peter and Philip are dead!"

Lukas's face drains. His glare softens into grief and guilt, his gaze sliding to his feet.

Nathaniel slams his palms on the desk with a loud thump. Even Micah jumps. His entire unit is frozen in shock at this news, their jaws falling open. "You snuck into my files and found their names, and then ran off to Boqua like some big hero! You compromised them, Lukas. You understand? Two of our operatives are dead because of you!"

Every face in the room has gone pale. No one dares to speak, and even Micah's fist around my arm loosens its grip as he stares at Nathaniel in utter shock. Lukas's features contort in dread, his mouth twisting, his eyebrows fusing together.

"But . . . I . . . it wasn't supposed to . . . "

"—The Boquans found them right after you left their houses," Nathaniel interrupts. "Their cover was blown the minute you stepped across their doorways. And who knows what the Boquans learned before they killed them." He marches around to the front of the desk, facing his son. "What was in your head, boy?"

Lukas's hand shakes uncontrollably, and I know now why he was hesitant to return to Gesher. Why guilt had flashed in his eyes when Yosher's body crumpled into a heap. Why he was hiding in my Wood like a frightened child. Without another word, he breaks from the group and bolts for the door, slamming it shut behind him.

Nathaniel watches him leave, staring at the door for a long moment before giving a deep sigh and pinching the bridge of his nose. His clean-shaven face is a mixture of relief and utter fury. Worry is still there, hiding in the lines around his eyes. He knows Lukas won't give up. That he'll try again.

He lowers his hand from his face and suddenly seems to remember his prisoner. He turns back to me, his teeth clenched, the muscles in his jaw tightening.

"Put him in the pit," Nathaniel orders, and Micah sneers in grim satisfaction before grabbing my arm and yanking me from the room.

The pit turns out to be a decaying gray building with gray walls and gray doors hidden behind the courthouse. Micah and Tomas pull me down a long hall, up a flight of stairs, and down another hall before they stop in front of a narrow door with a square sureglass window. Micah swipes a card at the lock sensor, and the door beeps open.

It's a prison cell. With a grunt, he shoves me inside onto the cold, tiled floor, leaving my hands cuffed behind my back. "I hope he lets you rot in here!" He snarls at me and draws the door shut with a loud clang. His seething face appears for a moment in the sureglass before he draws away.

I grunt, shifting on the floor to view the small room. The cell is probably ten feet square, with a porcelain sink and toilet against one wall and a steel-framed cot against the other. The gray, concrete walls are bare and cold, and a single light bulb inside a wire cage stubbornly shines its weak light from the center of the ceiling. The stench of mold permeates the space like a cold fog.

The cuffs have no give in them, and every movement causes another burst of sharp pain screaming from my wrists. But still I struggle to my feet and press my nose to the sureglass. There'll be no breaking this window. The door has no handle from this side, and all I can see outside are gray walls and the closed doors of other cells.

I spend ten minutes trying to wiggle my legs through my linked arms to bring my hands in front of me, but all I get for my trouble is an even worse stinging in my raw wrists and a flare of pain from the wound in my side. I wince, sinking onto the stiff cot as spots flash in front of my eyes. I blink them away and fight the growing nausea settling into my gut.

They are going to kill me. I've slaughtered enough of them to deserve it a thousand times over. Maybe more. Maybe someone here has lost a son or daughter to my hands. Once they get past the shock of my arrival, that will likely be the next thought to cross their minds, and what will they demand Nathaniel do to me as punishment? I try not to think about it, but in the silence of the tiny cell, my thoughts wander easily. They take me through the deep caverns inside of me where I push all the things I don't want to remember.

My darkest thoughts are bubbling to the surface, fighting their way to break through, and there's not enough of my mind to keep a hold of them all. I can't shove them back where they belong before they rise up and choke me. My pulse pounds at my temples, blood simmering beneath my skin. My muscles constrict and my shoulders hunch, and suddenly I can't breathe, can't breathe, and she's not here to calm my stubborn brain. She's not here to press her fur against my skin and look at me with those eyes that tell me it's over, it's over, it's okay, it's okay, and without her I know it's not over, and it's not okay.

My stomach seems to shrink into itself, panic rising like bile in my throat. I suck in straggled breath after straggled breath, trying to picture her my memory. Remember what it feels like to have her paws resting on my legs. Breathe. In. Out.

It's not working. My heart pounds, sweat beads on my forehead. Her face. Her face. Calm brown eyes. She would look at me like that before she rested her chin on her paws and let out a sigh. And I would copy her and blow out all the bad dreams and memories, and she wouldn't move until I didn't shake anymore.

Slowly, my muscles unwind. I study her face in my mind, remembering every detail I can about her. The pointed tips of her ears. The silky black fur only parted by a streak of white down her chest and across one paw. The way she would perk up when I finally smiled at her to show her it was over, that I could breathe properly again.

Finally, after what seems like hours, the trembling subsides. The bubbling ocean beneath my skin sinks back down to where it belongs, and the flashes stop. I watch the light bulb still flickering overhead, refusing to die.

I can't wipe the cold sweat from my brow, but I focus on my breathing until I remember that soon they will come for me, and then it will all be over.

And some part of me is relieved. Because I deserve it.

EIGHTEEN

"COME ON, FIVER, FOCUS!" BONE REACHED OUT AND slapped my cheek, the sting bringing my attention back to him. Mirroring his steady stance, I raised my fists to protect my face. The sun beat across my shoulders, sweat pouring down my temples. Bone kicked at the sandy earth beneath our feet. "Pay attention," he said. "Every feed has a different response. So if I do this . . . "

He threw his fist in a wide arc. I blocked the punch and drew myself to him, flinging him over my shoulder. He crashed to the ground.

He grunted, but he smiled up at me. "Better," he said, hopping to his feet. "Much better." He grabbed for his towel and drew it across his forehead. "Trout'll be impressed." He looked up from the cloth. "Oh, by the way, you're about to get a new member in your squadron."

I paused in mid-stretch. Such information was rare for a squadron member to be given. "Who is it?"

Bone grinned. "Queen." He watched my face closely, and I tried to keep any betraying expression from crossing it. "So she won't have to keep sneaking out to get into your Barracks anymore."

He laughed as I felt the blood drain from my face. "Don't wet your pants, kid. I've known for a long time. Why do you think she kept getting so lucky swiping my key pass?"

I swallowed. "You let her take it?"

Bone dropped the towel, stepping closer to me. His voice fell an octave, his eyes became hard and unwavering. "Know this, Fiver. Not everyone agrees with everything that goes on in this place. But everyone knows what happens to those who don't keep it to themselves. You be careful with what you hear and say. Understand?"

I nodded, watching his stern eyes. If he knew what was inside

Atara's mind, who else did? How long could she keep herself under the Commanders' radar? Just how much influence did Bone have over who went to which squadron, and what did it mean for him to place her with me? Did he think I could keep her safe?

Bone broke through my thoughts. "When you're done here, they want you in the infirmary."

I blinked. "Why?"

He shrugged. "Dunno. I just don't argue with them, know what I mean?"

I nodded again, but he made sure I noticed the warning in his eyes.

§

"Go! Go! Go!"

I clapped Swisher on the back as he darted forward, my teeth bared and head low. Whip followed close behind, slipping in the mud and falling to his knees for a moment before charging forward again. Both collapsed behind the boulder up ahead as bullets rained down around them. Atara kneeled behind me, gripping her rifle in both hands, her knuckles white. Her blonde hair was nearly brown with dust.

"We're taking an awful lot of heat!" Whip shouted over his shoulder at me.

"Link!" I whirled around, searching for the last member of my unit. How was I supposed to lead this unit without Rhino? To make things worse, he'd also taken Moose with him when he became the Ace of Barracks Eight, leaving me with Atara, Link, and Swisher. Whip came up from the Greens, completing this ensemble of sorry soldiers who worked about as well together as ice cream and whiskey. My first command. I still wasn't sure if Link resented me for it, or if he simply figured he just had to wait. He thought of himself as next in line, as far as I could tell.

Link's head popped over the ridge and ducked back down again as another spray of gunfire threw dust and dirt into his face. I growled.

"Link, get your ass over here!"

His head appeared again. "I'm sorry if I don't want to get half a mag embedded in my face! You know how bad those things hurt when they hit bare skin?"

He waited until the wave subsided, then flung himself over the ridge and scurried like a mouse to the clump of bushes we were crouched behind.

"Where are they all coming from?" he grunted, wiping sweat from his forehead.

"Same place they always do," I replied, scanning the trees behind us. "You should take it as a compliment."

"Why the hell would I—" he ducked as a bullet zinged above him, "—do that?"

I peered around the bushes and tried to spot the attacking soldiers. "They're singling us out. They want to get us out of the way first." I let a half smile slip. "Means we're the best in Barracks Six."

Link watched my face. "Or it means we're the weakest and they're just picking us off."

I shook my head. "Not with Howler leading this army."

"How do you know?"

"Because I've known Howler for three years now. He's just as dumb as Trout. Predictable." I spotted movement in the trees ahead. A figure, slinking through the underbrush, aimed his weapon at us. I threw up my gun and squeezed off a single shot. His fight suit turned red, and he dropped to the ground. I faced Link. "And he hates me like Trout does, too."

"You seem to have a talent for getting on people's bad sides," Link muttered as he took out another soldier.

My fingers clenched around my gun, and I pressed it tight into my shoulder.

"Queen, we could use that gun of yours!" Link grunted. I glanced down at her and found she hadn't moved since we'd taken cover behind the bushes. I reached for her and nudged her.

"Come on, get your weapon up!" I hissed. She opened her eyes, her lips trembling.

"I . . . I can't—"

I heard a cry and a shout, and I knew either Swisher or Whip had been eliminated. Likely, both of them. Only Link, Atara, and I remained.

Wonderful.

"We're *so* dead," Link muttered. "Some Unit Leader you turned out to be."

I gripped the arm of Atara's uniform in one hand. "Listen to me! We need you on this! Pull it together, it's only a mock battle. You're not gonna kill anybody."

She looked at me with those eyes, blue shining out from beneath the dirt on her face. "But that's where it starts, Fiver."

"Straight ahead!" Link shouted.

I leaped to my feet, mowing down the line of soldiers moving in on us before they could fire a single shot. Link took my place as I reloaded my weapon. "What's your problem, Queen?" he grunted.

I sighed. She'd have to do a better job. We'd talked about this. I couldn't protect her forever; she was in a real squadron now and couldn't be viewed as a simple-minded child any longer.

I stood beside Link and aimed out at the rustling bushes, watching red lights from fight suits flash with nearly every shot.

"What do we do, Fiver?" Link cried. I looked ahead as they crashed through the trees, so close that I could see the gleeful expressions on their faces. A full unit, tearing toward us, guns raised. I aimed and pulled the trigger; all I heard was a click in response. I swore, tossing the weapon aside.

"I'm out," I grumbled.

Link's face fell. "I've got two rounds left."

"Make them count."

Link took careful aim and picked off two attacking soldiers, but still they kept coming. His gaze shifted downward, and he grabbed the only useful weapon we had left.

"Someone's got to make use of this thing," he growled, but I frowned.

"They're not firing," I said, noticing the lack of bullets. "They must be out, too."

Before Link could reply, the attacking unit let out a terrible cry and swarmed ahead at full speed. The leader flung himself at me and tackled me, knife raised. But before he could bring it down, he jerked backward, the line on his fight suit turning red. A pair of hands flung his limp body away, and Swisher's face filled my vision.

"Now what would we do without our brilliant Unit Leader?" he asked, grinning at me.

"I thought you were a goner," I said, rolling to my feet as another attacking soldier tried to plow me down. I pulled my knife and slammed the collapsible blade into him.

"Nah, Whip got it. Not me."

Two more soldiers tried their luck, but between the two of us plus Link's semi-decent shooting, we left their bodies on the dusty ground. When the horn finally sounded, Link shot to his feet and practically threw himself at Atara.

"What's wrong with you, Queen?" he screamed, and she shrank beneath his anger. He waved the gun he'd taken from her in her face. "You didn't fire a single shot!"

"Link!" I shouted. He whirled around to me.

"I'm tired of this!" he shouted back, stepping closer. "She keeps clamming up like she doesn't even want to win!"

I glanced at her, my brow furrowed. The others stared, waiting. She refused to meet my eyes, but she could probably guess what was going through my mind. Now the soldiers were noticing. How long before it reached Gallander?

I stepped toward Link. "Hey, let it go, man. We won."

His features twisted in anger. "She almost lost it for us." He glared at me with disdain. "*You* deal with it, Fiver."

He stormed away, and it wasn't long before the others followed him out of the trees and back to the base. I looked down at Atara, who was fighting tears where she kneeled.

"You see?" I told her. "If you don't fight, bad things happen to the people you care about."

She sniffed and raised her eyes to mine. "That's not why we're fighting, and you know it."

I leaned closer to her, hoping she could see the frustration in my gaze. "Then what are we fighting for?"

She turned away and said nothing, as I knew she would. I bent over to pick up my discarded rifle and walked away without another word. I didn't want her to see the other emotions swirling inside my mind. Things even I didn't understand.

Things that terrified me.

NINETEEN

THE DOOR CLICKS. I BRACE MYSELF FOR MICAH'S SCOWL,
and he does not disappoint. He snarls and marches through the door, then grabs my arm and hauls me roughly to my feet. Asher stands behind him, his face fixed and firm.

But the face behind his is what surprises me.

Nathaniel steps across the entryway, his hands behind his back and conflicting expressions on his face. Intrigue. Anger. I don't care for it at all. My insides flip; moisture drips down my temples.

"What's your name?" he finally asks.

Micah prods me from behind. "Don't say much, this one," he grumbles. "About three words since we found him."

I watch him in the corner of my vision, calculating how high I'd have to fling my foot to catch him on the chin. I could do it, even with my hands tied behind me. I poke my tongue out and taste the blood caked in the corner of my lips.

Nathaniel cocks his head at me, his quiet eyes considering. "Well?" he asks after a moment.

What difference does my name make? Just so they can have something to carve onto my gravestone? Even if Lukas told Nathaniel everything, it wouldn't be enough to absolve me from everything else I've done.

Completely ignoring Micah's impatient huff, I swallow, then reply, "It's Fiver."

Nathaniel squints for a moment, analyzing me. Searching my face, scrutinizing it. I try not to squirm beneath his gaze. No stories about Boquans caught by Lucians were ever told *by* Boquans caught by Lucians.

"What's your real name, son?" he asks.

I press my lips together, silent. Why is he asking me this? Why does he care about the name my parents gave me? My fingers jerk, tapping each other between the handcuffs behind my back.

Nathaniel looks at the gray floor and takes a step closer. "Lukas seems to think you're some kind of hero."

A wave of dread nauseates me, with my stomach threatening to crawl into my throat. Nathaniel's voice grows louder, and he shoots it over his shoulder. "Isn't that right, son?"

He makes a half-turn and trains his eyes on the door. He's waiting for something. The door opens slowly, and Lukas's sheepish face peers through. Nathaniel chastises, "I told you to go home."

Flashing me a grim smile, Lukas grips the doorframe with one hand. "I just wanted to make sure Micah doesn't beat him up again."

Nathaniel sizes up my split lip and the bruises around my nose, and he shoots a frown at Micah. "Get in here or get out," he says to Lukas. "Make up your mind."

Lukas keeps his eyes to the floor and steps through the doorway, then slinks along the wall across from me. He gives me a glance before he crosses his arms and looks straight ahead, like he's a self-appointed bodyguard.

"Get out of here, kid," Micah growls at him, gripping my arm tighter. "This has nothing to do with you."

"Thank you, Micah, you can take your unit and go," Nathaniel says, folding his arms. Micah stares wide-eyed at him, as if the idea of being dismissed was a completely new concept.

"Sir—"

"—But before you do, take those cuffs off." Nathaniel levels a glare at him before Micah can voice his protest. Red creeps over the skin of his neck, filling his face with anger. But he complies, albeit not gently. I wince as he yanks on the metal rings, grumbling while he fiddles with the key that unlocks them. The cuffs fall away, relief floods through me, and Micah storms out of the cell, slamming the door behind him.

Picking at a scab on his thumb, Nathaniel watches him go before he turns to me. "Lukas tells me you two have struck up some kind of deal?" He squints at me. "That's a bit strange. A Lucian boy and a Boquan soldier."

I squint back at him, baffled by his odd behavior. Dismissing Micah wasn't a show of power, nor is he afraid that I'll lash out and attack. Whatever he wants to discuss is something he doesn't want the younger soldier to hear. My fingers rub over the sore rings around my wrists, and I scan Nathaniel's face for any hint of his plans.

Nathaniel knows I'm not a soldier anymore. Not a real one. Anyone with a cool head could see that. My clothes are so worn that I've patched up patches, my face is rough with a few days' growth, and I can't remember when I last cut my hair. Nathaniel also knows I didn't kidnap his son, but there's something about me he can't quite work out just from looking at me. He's no fool, that's for sure, and he would see right through any lie I could come up with.

I try not to squirm beneath his eyes, eyes that are searching, scanning, digging beneath my skin as though answers will ooze from my pores like my sweat does now.

I finally give him an answer. "I told him I would help him find his mother if he gave me all the information he could about the Ramius Corporation."

"I told you," Lukas says from his corner. He scuffs his shoe against the concrete floor. "He's different. He doesn't want to hurt us, he just wants to save the Crosswoods."

Nathaniel looks at me. "Endenbough Wood, I think you call it?"

My spine stiffens. I turn to Lukas, who only nods in encouragement. I swallow but say nothing, wary of Nathaniel's motives. He clears his throat.

"Interesting name, Endenbough," he says. "I knew a man with that name, a long time ago. He had a wife. A son."

Heat rises in my face. My heart pounds so hard I'm sure he can see it beating beneath my shirt. His gaze is intense enough to bore a hole through my skull.

"His name was Matthew," he says, and my heart nearly breaks all over again. I can barely keep eye contact with him, and I struggle to control the trembling in my hands. He knew my father. My mother. Maybe even me.

"I heard about what happened," Nathaniel continues, and I clench my fists. White flashes behind my eyes and mixes with my memories of ashes and crumbling brick—the only traces left of the old house. "Terrible thing. The son was already in the army, but the wife died in the fire. And Matthew? Well, Matthew . . . "

He swallows, and I wish he would just say it. Get it out, get it over with, stop this strange mental torture and get straight to his point. Why is he doing this? Who is this man?

"Matthew was taken prisoner before they even got to the house."

"*What?*" screams my brain. My head flies up in shock and my throat goes as dry as a riverbed in the heat of summer. My father was dead. I knew that, accepted it. Both my parents were dead.

I almost can't process what he's telling me. The blood rushes from my face, leaving my head as light as a blue-jay feather, with my legs becoming nothing but limp rags. Under my shirt, my pendant seems to burn against my skin.

Nathaniel never takes his eyes off of me, watching every inch of me, every twitch of muscle. "Would you care to know where they're holding him?"

TWENTY

A STAMPEDE OF FOOTSTEPS POUNDED AGAINST THE floor. Squeaks from skidding shoes, sharp intakes of breath, jumbled shouts of excitement.

"Fiver!" Link's blond head poked out from behind his thin arms. His hair nearly touched his eyebrows now, and he brushed it across his forehead as he beamed at me. His face suddenly contorted in confusion. "What are you doing in the library? Come on!"

"What is it?" I asked, shutting the dusty book on past battle strategies. The final exam on Boquan military history had been breathing down my neck for two weeks, and every second spent studying the material could mean the difference between success and failure.

Link's face leaned forward, his eyes blazing in delight. "A Rabbit Hunt!"

His head disappeared. The sound of dozens of kids spilling from doors and hallways echoed in my ears. I listened as they made their way to the assembly room, chattering in mindless anticipation, a random high-pitched squawk here and there. We had waited years to witness a hunt, and it would likely be years until we saw another. Of course we were excited; blood pounded in my temples.

Yet my gut shrank and dropped like a stone. I stepped from the library, where Atara hovered by the door. Her face blanched as she looked to me for any sense of comfort. I turned away and marched with the others to the assembly room, which was already filled with restless kids and their near-endless babbling.

I sank into a chair toward the back, then I felt her hand grip mine. The wide media screen spread across one entire wall of the assembly room, and I glued my eyes to it even though it was still blank.

Link's head bobbed a few rows ahead of us. He turned around, searching for me, and waved with a grin big enough to crack his face. Atara sucked in a hitched breath.

The door flew open as though caught in the winds of a hurricane. All heads spun forward as a huge figure filled the doorframe. Gasps sounded from every throat before silence fell and everyone jumped to their feet.

I felt my stomach shrink to the size of a walnut and the thunder-crash of fear racing through every inch of me. I remembered. Walker's face. Wide open, dead eyes. The hands that ended his life.

Commander Gallander strode into the room, his huge arms pulled behind his back as he towered over us. He swept dark eyes across us, and my insides squirmed when they lingered on me for several seconds before moving on. He walked to the front of the room with heavy steps, every gaze planted on him, with some kids seeing the great Commander for the first time. He was as big as the rumors that preceded him, with broad shoulders and thick limbs.

After a long moment, Gallander's eyes softened into a warm glow. "Many of you have never seen a Rabbit Hunt," he said, his voice booming like a thunderclap. His gray head nodded. We watched him in awe, hungry for every word from his mouth. "Yes, they are a lot of fun, but don't forget what you can learn from them. Someday, you might have the honor of joining one."

Looking patiently up at the screen, he slipped us a broken smile and strolled toward the side of the room, hands behind his back. His position sent an eerie buzz through the room: Gallander was going to stay? Was he assessing us for leadership? Even something as simple as a Unit Leader promotion packed a lot of weight.

The lights clicked off and plunged the room into darkness, silencing most of the ruckus. The vid screen flared to life, bathing the room in dim blue light while kids still fidgeted in their seats. Eyes glued to the screen, they leaned forward, knees bouncing like pistons, fingers tapping out symphonies on armrests.

Stories of past Rabbit Hunts haunted these halls. Even those of us who had never seen one knew exactly how it worked. It is both a blessing and a curse, an incredible thrill and the source of deepest fear. It all depends on whether or not you are a rabbit.

Rabbits are chosen from a pool of names that have all found their way there by means of weakness. Their Commanders have deemed them, for one reason or another, unworthy of the Boquan army, and as such, they have all earned the right to the chance of being a rabbit.

The opposing side is chosen from a pool of the exact opposite. They are the hound dogs. Their Commanders choose them for their strength.

And every few years, thirteen names are selected from the rabbit pool, with six chosen from the hound dogs. Commanders compose the list of participants with great care: not one participant has ever seen another. Not a familiar face will be found.

When the list is complete, the Rabbit Hunt begins. And nobody knows exactly where the Hunt takes place, not even the winners. Certainly not the rabbits.

The screen flickered, and an aerial view of a secluded wooded area appeared on it. All participants were given an area to stand in too far away from any others to even see each other. The only thing each of them knew was whether they were the hunter or the prey.

The faces of those in the Hunt flashed across the screen one by one. Something hard pressed against my chest as I recognized the third face.

Scourge. I could tell he was a rabbit by the wild look in his eyes, the desperation gouging deep wrinkles in his features.

The anticipation built in the room, especially as more of us recognized Scourge.

"Hey, it's him!"

"They never said *that* was where he was going!"

"Is he a rabbit or a dog?"

All heads from my Barracks turned, looking for me. I was famous for my fight in the gym with Scourge, which was the last time anyone had seen him before his transfer to a new base. I remained hunched in the back, hiding the hand that gripped mine tightly beneath my jacket. I ignored them all, watching the screen as the view switched to aerial again.

A long horn sounded, and rabbits and hounds alike scattered like bugs beneath a light. They had to run. Because they tell everyone to run. Especially if you're a rabbit. Because the dogs are coming.

The object of the game is for each of the dogs to kill as many rabbits as they can. The dog who kills the most rabbits is the winner, and they are lauded with the highest praise. Laden with gifts and honors, they return to their Barracks a hero, and they are likely to receive a command of their own.

As the participants spread out over the vast wood, Atara's grip tightened on my hand. Her eyes widened in shock as she watched the screen. Any attempt by the rabbits to form an alliance was thwarted as soon as enough of them were foolish enough to form a group. Dogs weren't dumb, after all. It wouldn't take much for one to convince a terrified rabbit he was one of their own, use that rabbit to find more, and slaughter them all in a matter of seconds.

The rabbits apparently were too stupid to realize they could do the same thing to the dogs. But even if they did, their fear would eventually find them out; their very eyes were glazed with it. This is why the rabbits would never win, even though—according to the rules—they could wipe out the dogs and regain their honor within the army. But no one ever had.

Nearly the entire base had jumped to their feet, shaking their fists at the screen. They cried out with shouts of praise for a clean kill, with degradation for rabbits cowering in fear. They cheered their favorites on as each dog's body count rose, and they watched the lower corners of the screen as points were added to each dog's tally.

Atara sniffed beside me. I tore my gaze from the bloody screen, and she wiped her nose on her sleeve, tears leaking down her cheeks. Gallander shifted from the wall, and one glance told me he had noticed. I bumped her arm and told her to hush, but she let the tears roll, her eyes bloodshot and bleary.

I looked up at the screen as Scourge's neck snapped beneath the strain of the thick arms strangling him. Atara dug her nails into my skin, and I tried to pull away. I only succeeded in knocking my jacket off balance enough to send it sliding to the floor.

My heart pounded in my ribcage: our hands were clasped together without my jacket to cover them. Atara choking on tears.

I took my other hand and pried her fingers from mine and sat straight forward, praying to Elorai that Gallander hadn't noticed my compassion for her.

The room erupted in victorious shouts as the last rabbit fell, the winner's face projected across the screen along with his tally. The screen faded to black, and I heard a faint rustle beside me. A slim shaft of light shot across the room, a lone figure slipping out through the cracked door.

The lights came on, and the seat beside me was empty. Caught up in the rush of the Hunt, no one in the room noticed her absence. Still bursting with excitement, none of the kids bothered to leave the assembly room. I stood up and took a step toward the door when a hand fell onto my shoulder.

"Didn't you enjoy the presentation, Fiver?"

I caught myself right before nearly jumping out of my skin. Gallander's voice haunts even deeper when it is directed only at you. Turning to him, I stared up at his impossibly tall frame, his hard, dark eyes searching my face. A hint of curiosity as well. I wasn't completely screwed yet.

"I didn't like the ending," I replied, holding a steady gaze. Gallander's bushy eyebrows lifted.

"Oh? Rooting for someone else, were you?"

"Yes," I replied, my heart pounding again. "Myself." The surprise in his eyes was enough to set me at ease. I could have walked out then, but if I did, he would never leave me alone after that.

"If it were me, I could have halved the time it took that brute to hunt them all down," I said. Gallander crossed his arms and leaned backward, looking at me as though I were an impetuous child bragging about his simple accomplishments.

"And how would you have done that?"

I crossed my arms and mirrored his look. "Kill everyone I see," I replied. His eyes opened wider, and his mouth sagged. "Whether they're a rabbit or a dog. Either way, you've upped your count or taken out the competition."

Gallander stuck his tongue between his lips and bit down. His eyelids drooped, and he exhaled. "You have an interesting mind, Fiver," he said. "Very interesting indeed."

He turned away from me and walked toward the door, where a sea of young soldiers was finally funneling out of the room.

A sense of dread gnawed away at my insides. It wasn't me Gallander had been asking about, and I knew it. He was onto the scent; he wouldn't stop until he found his rabbit. And destroyed it.

TWENTY-ONE

MY HEART HAS STOPPED COMPLETELY. MAYBE I DIDN'T hear him right. Maybe I didn't read his lips right.

My father is alive?

The tension slips from Nathaniel's face. My reaction to this news seems to have sated his curiosity for the moment, though I know there is more.

Lukas only looks from one of us to the other in utter bewilderment. "What?" he says, his arms unfolding.

Nathaniel continues to stare at me, and I still can't suck in enough air to calm my heaving lungs. He knew my father. My father is alive. My throat is swollen with shock, and only one word manages to slip through, cracked and broken.

"Where?"

The Lucian commander's eyes narrow with a tiny twitch. Lukas is still demanding to know what's going on, his voice rising in pitch with every repeat of his words.

"You knew him too, didn't you?" Nathaniel voices what he sees in my face. My muscles tighten, and I lift my gaze to meet his. "You're his boy."

Lukas shouts again. "What? What are the two of you talking about?"

"Where is he?" I practically plead, and I hate myself for it. The Wood no longer matters—he's alive.

"What happened, son?" Nathaniel says. "Why aren't you with your army?" I barely hear him. It doesn't make a difference, anyway.

I shrug one shoulder. "I left."

Nathaniel seems consider if he should ask me again. Maybe I'd eventually tell him if he kept it up. He must decide against it since he moves toward the door and raps on it loudly.

"Micah!" he shouts. "Get in here!"

Not five seconds later, the rattle of the lock fills the room, and the door swings open. Micah is still furious at being dismissed, but there's a flicker of hope in his eyes. Hope, I assume, that Nathaniel will let him do what he wants to me.

My stomach plunges into my shoes again.

Nathaniel motions to me. "I'm letting him go. No soldier, including you, is to touch him, you understand?"

The shock takes a moment to register on Micah's face. After a second, his jaw falls open as though someone had slapped him. I can't help my own mouth dropping in surprise. Let me go? Who was my father to this man?

Micah finally seems to gain control of his voice. "Are . . . are you serious?" he chokes out. "Do you know who this guy is? What did he tell you? That he was just following orders, or that he's changed his loyalties?"

"Don't question me, Micah," Nathaniel begins.

Micah's glare could melt steel. "He'll run straight back to them. Tell them everything he knows about us." His voice hisses out between clenched teeth, his shoulders shaking with rage.

Tomas and Asher appear in the shadows behind him. Their faces mirror his. Tension weighs in the air, enough to press my lungs flat. Nathaniel could easily change his mind, and if I were him I would do just that.

"Sir, are you sure you want to do this?" Tomas says, his long fingers wrapping around the weapon at his hip. "It might be best to—"

"—We should kill him now, before he sees anything else," Micah interrupts, reaching for his weapon.

"Stop it!" Lukas shrieks. "He's not gonna tell them anything!"

My insides burn. Every muscle tenses, and I'm aching to fly at them. The pounding in my head grows even more intense as faint clouds spot my vision.

Micah turns his steely gaze on Lukas, his crooked teeth tight together. "And how do you know that? You can't believe a word that comes out of their mouths!"

Lukas's voice nearly reaches its breaking point, his cheeks flushed red. "I know because he's half deaf, alright?!"

The room goes quiet as a graveyard, with every eye trained on Lukas and, eventually, me. Micah stares down at me with confusion, and my face is filled with heat, fingers trembling. My gut sinks, and even if I wanted to speak, my voice is gone. The overwhelming desire to run, to fight, to kill, grips my heart. All the fear and anxiety compressed inside of me squeeze through the cracks in my defenses, and soon it will all erupt. The only thing that keeps me still is knowing that to stop me, they'll have to kill me.

Nathaniel's voice breaks the heavy silence. "Deaf?" He looks at me in awe.

My breath comes in weighted gasps, panic threatening to spill from my chest. I watch as the sympathy on Lukas's face grows. He turns away.

Even with his head turned away, I know his next words are for me. "I'm not that stupid, okay? I just noticed things." He rubs at his eye and addresses Micah again. "I mean, he cocks his head all the time when people talk to him, and he hardly ever lets his dog out of his sight. She's like a personal alarm system. He reads her like a book."

Nathaniel watches his son for a long time before he turns to me. His eyes are hard. Sorrowful. "What happened?"

I slide my eyes to his. He seems more curious than anything, his face devoid of all hostility. But he knows I didn't answer the last question he asked, and I won't answer this one, either.

They will kill me now. Lukas has killed me. They know my weakness. They will exploit it. Lucians always do.

I challenge them with a smoldering stare. I will not go down without taking out many of them with me.

Nathaniel reads my eyes, and his soften. "Steady, young man."

I search, but I find no malice in his gaze. Only something that troubles me even more. A hard emotion to pinpoint, it's a sense of pride along with sorrow, joy mixed with pity. It makes my gut churn again.

Nathaniel leans forward and blinks slowly, looking me over as he lets out a sigh. "I said let him go."

Micah's face is a picture of unsuppressed rage. "You've lost your mind," he says, stepping inside the cell. "He's a Boquan soldier! They kill on sight. Who knows how many of us he's murdered?!"

Nathaniel looks at me. "I heard he gave up the chance to shove a knife into your neck earlier today."

Micah's scowl deepens. "It doesn't make up for anything," he growls.

"No, it doesn't." Nathaniel seems unshaken by Micah's hostility. "But neither would killing him."

Micah grumbles but says nothing. Nathaniel points at me. "Take him to my house and see that he gets anything he needs."

His house? Micah glances between his men as if making sure he heard Nathaniel right. I'm dangerous even here in this prison cell; sooner or later I'll escape or break someone's neck, and it's likely I'll do both. Why would a Lucian want me in their home?

Nathaniel's not finished with me yet. There are still things he wants to know about me. About who I am. And he knows I won't leave, not now. He's dangled the perfect bait right in front of my nose, and I can't ignore it. Not if it can free my father.

Is he trying to win me over with a gesture of kindness? My throat still feels like a bed of sand, and my temples throb. Micah steps ahead and grabs my arm, jerking me forward. I wasn't expecting such a sudden movement, and my head snaps up in surprise.

I let him drag me out of the cell with one last look to Lukas before his nervous smile disappears. As soon as we're out of Nathaniel's view, Micah takes out his pistol and trains it on me. He starts leading me out of the building. Through the leaf-littered street and into a two-story brick house on the corner. Not a soul meets us on the way. The town has fallen into an eerie fog, and not even one set of curious eyes peeks out from the windows.

Micah says nothing. He pushes me up the stairs, down the hall, and into a small room. He slams the door, but I doubt he's left me alone here. I could have killed him. Easily. Even with his pistol shoved roughly against my back, I could have snapped his neck and bolted.

A chilly wind slips through the cracked window, sending a shiver up my arms. The room isn't much bigger than my cell back at the pit, but I would take it over that dreary place any day. A simple bed with clean sheets is shoved beneath the window and against a pale wall. A wooden desk and chair, along with a carved dresser, line the other walls. All of it is illuminated by a single lamp opposite the bed. A mirror is mounted above the dresser, and I catch my reflection in its smooth surface. I haven't seen myself in a mirror for more than two years, and I'm shocked at how much my face has changed. The chin flatter, the jaw sharper. Eyes, somehow darker. Bloodshot. I close them and turn away.

I move to the other side of the room and sink to the carpet, trying to calm my rapid heartbeat as shaky breaths wrack my body. My father is alive. Somewhere in Boqua, my father is alive.

I clutch my silver pendant, staring down into its intricate circles and curved lines. My fist clenches around it tight enough to whiten my knuckles, imprinting the design on my palm.

What do they want with him? How long have they had him?

He is alive. And I will find him.

A shadow moves, interrupting my thoughts. The door opens slightly, and someone spews out angry words that I can't make out. But I recognize the voice as Lukas's. The door opens all the way, and he sticks his head through, looking at me apologetically before sliding all the way into the room.

"Sorry," Lukas mumbles, his hands deep in his pockets. He winces. "You alright? You look awful."

I rub the back of my hand over my forehead, feel the sweat dripping from my skin. My fingers tremble.

"Where am I?" I ask.

He shrugs one shoulder. "This is my dad's house."

"But not yours." I frown.

He shrugs again. I push up from the thin carpet. The room spins for a moment, and I blink, waiting for it to still. Something's wrong. "What did you come here for?"

"Told you," he says, turning away. "Sorry."

I sigh and look toward the window. At this angle, all I can see is the cloudy blue sky and the treetops, the leaves quaking in the wind. I shake along with them, sweat sticking my bangs to my skin.

The room spins again, spots flashing before me. Lukas's hand grips my arm, then touches my brow. The coolness of his skin is a shock.

"Fiver, you're burning up!" he says. I blink again, trying to clear my vision, but as I take a step forward, my legs quiver beneath my weight, and I stumble. Lukas's grip goes back to my arm, hauling me upright.

"Get off," I mumble, pushing weakly at him.

"Shut up. You need help," he replies, ignoring my hand. He calls out for his father as my legs give out completely and the ground rushes forward. Lukas's arms keep me from smashing into the floor with my face, but my eyes are already closing, bringing a suddenly welcome sleep.

TWENTY-TWO

I found her in the training field, crouched in the sand near the dummy targets. I pretended I didn't see her, making as though I were merely preparing to practice with the dummies until I realized she was in my way.

No one thought it the least bit suspicious. I listened to them all, grunting and sweating and straining as they tumbled in the sand, hauled their strong bodies up ropes or over logs, or fired at prepared targets and cheered when the dummies glowed bright red for a kill shot.

"You're not like them," she said. I turned, watching her red cheeks darken. "Neither am I."

I took a few steps forward. "They're looking for you. Gallander says you might need a mental evaluation."

Atara snorted. "We all do, Fiver."

"Get serious!" I closed the gap between us and reached for her arm, hauling her to her feet. She yanked it away.

"*You* get serious!" she shouted back. Her eyes glared for a long moment before they softened, and she pulled them away from mine. Her voice came as a whisper. "What are we doing here, Fiver?"

"We're saving our people," I replied, as I always did. She shook her head.

"When we were younger, I thought it was all a silly game." She sniffed, brushing sand from her shirt. "But people are dying. Real people, dying, and they're not coming back."

I stared at the ground, then moved beside her. "That's what happens in war," I said, searching for her eyes.

She finally raised her blue eyes to mine, fire blazing in them. "This war is wrong!"

The familiar sick feeling washed over me again. She looked at me, pleading. "You feel it, I know you do. They're liars, Fiver. We're just killing machines to them, nothing more."

I gripped her shoulders and turned her to me. "You can't talk like this, understand?" I said, watching in fear as her tears welled up.

"Fiver, you know what they said was going to happen to Scourge? That they were going to transfer him to another training camp? But yesterday one of our own soldiers killed him in that Rabbit Hunt!"

"That's what this is about?" I replied, eyeing the group of people nearing the target stations. They gave us angry scowls, but they moved on and found another station to practice at. "Scourge could have failed at his new training camp. He could have broken any kind of rule to get him into the Hunt. It doesn't have to have been a lie!"

"I checked into his file," she said. "Right after they kicked him out of here."

My eyes bulged. "What? How?" I glanced around to make sure no one had heard her.

"Doesn't matter," she replied. "I did it. You know what it said?"

I bit my lip, heart pounding. "You can't—"

"—It said, 'Immediate termination of career. Transfer to holding facility for complete termination.' You know what that means, Fiver?"

I twisted my head, refusing to look at her.

She reached up and took my chin in her hands, holding my face in front of her. "It means they lied."

I let her hold me like that, her hands warm against my suddenly cold skin. "Please . . ." I whispered. "Please, let's just . . . go back to the way it was before."

She softly shook her head. "It was never any different before."

"Yes, it was! I can't keep their attention off you like I used to." My heart pleaded with her, the strain audible in my voice. "I . . . I don't want anything to happen to you."

A grim smile lifted her lips and she let go of me. "I thought that's what happened in war."

"Don't do that!" I protested. "That's not what I meant."

Her smile broadened. A strange expression came over her features. She took one of my hands in both of hers and turned her head toward our intertwined fingers. "Alright, Fiver," she said, squeezing my palm. "Let's go down to the lake and see if we can catch that old cranky turtle."

I scrunched up my face. "That's what all the Greens do. They've been trying to catch that thing for years now."

She leaned close. "Let's show them how to do it, then, huh?" She smiled, the spark back in her eyes. My heart swelled, and I knew, for her, I'd do anything asked of me. "Race ya!" she cried, and with a laugh, she flew to her feet and took off across the field. Bolting after her, I spluttered, spitting out the sand she'd kicked up into my face and thinking maybe this time she'd be okay. That I could sleep soundly at night, knowing she would be there the next morning.

TWENTY-THREE

I HEAR VOICES IN THE DARK. SOMEONE WIPES A COOL cloth across my brow, the relief from the heat as brief as a drop of water in the desert. My skin feels blistered, my clothes are damp with sweat. A voice whispers soothing things I can't understand. A familiar voice, like a ghost from the past. It dances with the other voices inside my skull, pulling my mind this way and that.

I try to open my eyes, but all I manage to do is peek out from behind my eyelashes at the blurry figure. The voice comes again. In the fog, I can make out the face. His soft eyes. It can't be.

"Dad?" My voice cracks.

He shushes me, wiping my brow again. "Just sleep, son," he says.

And her face is there. Pulled from the walls like a summoned spirit, she floats above the bed. Seeing her drives a nail into me, into lungs that are already struggling to keep drawing in air. Atara's blonde hair, long and full like I used to imagine it, swirls around her head as though she were underwater.

But her eyes have welled up with bloody tears, and they spill down her cheeks in red streaks. "No," I moan as she studies me with a pained sorrow. As she weeps out her own blood, I watch the red drops drip from her chin. They fall onto my shirt, where they sizzle and burn into my chest.

"Fiver," she says, but it's my father's voice. Her face fades away and I see nothing but the walls of the room. They sway to and fro like they were made of cloth.

And I let the darkness take me again.

It takes me to the base, where the blackness is draped over every-thing like a fuzzy blanket, distorting all I thought familiar. Atara. I had followed her out that day, past the training field and almost to the tree line, waiting for her to tell me what she wanted to show me. Though I knew we were treading on dangerous ground, I thought if I humored her just this once, the light would come back to her eyes.

She took my hand in hers and pointed toward the sky. "See them all up there? Sometimes it's hard because of the clouds, but tonight they really shine."

I followed her finger, staring into the black. Faint dots of light shone through. "It's just the stars."

"They say Elorai lives up there."

I pulled my hand away. "Nobody believes in those fairy tales anymore."

"I bet there are some that do," she replied. The starlight reflected in her eyes, her lips slightly parted as she drank in the glow.

"None that I've ever met," I replied. "We shouldn't be out here so late. Curfew is in ten minutes."

She took a deep breath as the breeze ruffled through her hair, now grown long enough for her to pull into a mini ponytail. Beautiful blonde strands whipped out from behind her, and part of me wanted to reach out and run my fingers through them.

I shook my head. A ludicrous thought.

"I think he's out there," she whispered. "I think he's right here, too."

I frowned. "What's that supposed to mean?"

She turned back to me and reached for my hand again. In the next instant, she drew herself close to me and leaned her head forward. I felt her lips touch mine, a gentle pressure that was gone almost as soon as it came.

She pulled away, and my body refused to move, jolts of electricity freezing it in place. My mind whirled, thoughts jumping at me from all directions. Torn two ways, I could only stand there and watch her with dumbfounded eyes.

I saw her smile, but the sorrow embedded behind it gave her away, and I knew that though she was closer than she'd ever been, she couldn't be further away. But still I cherished the moment, as if some part of me knew someday, somewhere, somehow, I would need it.

"Fiver."

At the sound of this new voice, the sky dissolves in a cloud of dust, taking the memory with it. Bright lights sting my pupils. I search desperately for her, but I can't catch a glimpse of her through the glow.

"Fiver."

I'm trying to reach her, but something holds me back.

"He's burning up."

I sling my head to the side, a wet cloth on my face. Where is she? *No, please don't go.*

The brightness fades away, and blackness takes its place. I look one last time before I let myself slide under. She's gone.

TWENTY-FOUR

THE BARRACKS WERE NEVER COMPLETELY DARK AT night. Shallow light from the hall always filtered in beneath the door, enough to see the outlines of the bunks and the sleeping soldiers buried beneath their sheets.

Something woke me in the night. A nagging in my ear. A bug in my brain. Listening, I stared at the ceiling's smooth paint, my thoughts blurred and hazy. The sound came again, like something vaguely remembered right before falling asleep.

I rolled to one side, and the sound stopped. Then it began again. I squeezed my eyes shut, then cracked them open. A shadow danced across the wall. A thought from the recesses of my mind grew clearer.

A shadow?

I pushed up from the bed and squinted at the moving shape a few bunks down. "Is that you?" I whispered.

Atara whirled around at my voice, and her knapsack fell from her hands, a jumble of clothes spilling from its mouth, the soft noise painfully loud in the silent room. "What are you doing?" I whispered, throwing my legs over the side of the bed.

Her face, twisted with terror, dropped open like a kid caught snooping in Gallander's office. "Please, go back to sleep, Fiver," she begged.

I ignored her and crossed the room in three bounds. "What is this?" I hissed, eyeing her bag. She bent to pick up the straps, shoving the contents back inside.

"What does it look like?" she replied, hoisting the bag onto her shoulder and making for the door.

"You can't!" I winced at my voice; a boy shifted in his bed across the room. Atara ignored me, swiping her key pass at the door sensor. It beeped, and the door cracked open. She pushed it forward just enough to slip through. I followed her, grabbing at her shirt.

"You're deserting!" I hissed.

Biting her lip and looking at the ground, she turned as the door shut. Tears blurred her blue eyes. "I can't take it anymore, Fiver," she whispered. "I can't."

"What, being a soldier?"

"Being a murderer!" She threw her head up. "All this training, all these lessons, all to do exactly what they did on that screen today!"

"I don't understand!" My voice rang against the walls, and I cringed. "Why is it so hard for you here? Don't you want to defend your country?"

Defiance flared in her eyes. "Fiver, what we're doing is wrong! And I've been pretending long enough."

"They will kill you!" I said, watching her face fall in dismay. "You understand? Deserting is worse than being a rabbit. They'll hunt you down faster than any hound ever could."

"I don't care," she replied. "I've had enough. I'm going home."

She jogged down the hall. I went after her, my footsteps silent behind hers. I reached out to take her arm. "Please!" How could she go home? What home was there to go back to? Home was here, with the other soldiers. With me.

She pulled away, blinking back tears. "I'm sorry, Fiver." She wiped her cheek. "You could come with me."

My stomach flipped, nausea spreading through my insides. Her eyes pleaded with me, but I could only shake my head.

"I can't. You know I can't." The dread filling me intensified as she sniffed. She rubbed her nose as her blonde hair fell across her forehead.

"Could you at least . . . help me?"

No. There's no way. We'll both be dead, with Gallander's staring down at our bloody bodies. He would . . .

Her eyes. I swallowed and closed mine. "Alright. But we have to hurry."

She nodded, a small smile creasing her face. "Thank you."

"This is the stupidest thing you've ever done," I grunted. My chest tightened. Atara gone? The thought was hardly recognizable. And what was I doing helping her? She'd likely be dead by morning, but then, she could very well be killed if she stayed, too. I sighed. "Door three is right next to the teacher's quarters. I'll take you—there are hardly any guards that way. Once you're outside, head straight for the training woods, and don't stop until you can't run another step, understand?"

She nodded again, and I brushed past her down the hall. Door three was at the back of the building, luckily on the same floor. The corridors were dangerous enough to navigate without stairs to add to it.

My gut clenched more tightly with each step. I couldn't believe I was doing this. If we were caught, I'd be as much of a traitor as Atara, and yet I continued through the hall, ears alert for any sound of a night patrol.

"I'm sorry, Fiver," she whispered behind me. "I—"

"—Shh!" I hissed. Footsteps ahead froze my limbs. A patrol. I yanked her away from the center of the hallway, and we pressed our backs against the wall. The footsteps grew closer, and I held back a curse. Atara looked at me with wild eyes, and I fought to keep the panic at bay. Backing down the wall, my hand brushed against something hard. Turning, I saw the handle, the hinges.

The janitor's closet. Without another thought, I yanked on the handle, flinging the door open and shoving Atara inside among the mops and cleaning supplies. I slipped in behind her and eased the door shut, just as the footsteps rounded the corner. Pressing my ear to the door, my lungs filling with ammonia-tinged air, I listened as they drew closer, paused, then continued onward until they faded away.

I let out a quaking gasp. "We're never going to make it," I groaned.

Atara pushed the door open and wiggled out of the closet. We slipped through the hall in silence, peeking around corners and watching out for more patrols.

"Look, there's the door!" Atara whispered. I nodded grimly. Door three was in sight, but nothing more.

And never destined to be. As she took a step closer to the black sliding door, the lights above flared bright and blinding. I squinted, turning around to find three Commanders staring at me. Staring at Atara.

The dread in my heart sank my stomach to my shoes. Atara sucked in a quivering breath. One of the Commanders lifted a hand and touched his earpiece. "Sir, we have an interesting situation by door three," he reported.

Whatever the reply, the man simply lowered his arm and raised his weapon. "Very interesting indeed."

They held us there for only a moment before a shadow flickered behind them.

Gallander.

He smiled. "What have we here, then?"

I swallowed. Our lifeless bodies. Bloody and broken. Dead.

Atara stepped forward, hands raised. "Please, don't let him hurt me!"

At first, I thought she was talking to me, but her eyes were aimed at Gallander.

The towering Commander flicked his eyes to her. "And why would he do that?"

She looked to her feet, her body quivering. "Because I was trying to leave," she replied, her voice tiny.

Gallander's eyebrows rose. I doubted it was out of surprise. He scrutinized me for a long moment. "And what were *you* doing, young Fiver?"

"He caught me," Atara interjected before I could reply. "H–he heard me leaving and followed me. He gave me a chance, but I–I didn't listen to him. He said he'd have to do something about it."

Her eyes met mine, the fear in them directed at me. My heart thudded like a drum, my mind screaming for her to stop. But her acting was too good, her face positioned just right for Gallander's viewing. Keeping me off his radar. Just as I had done for her.

It worked. Gallander smiled at me with pride. "Well done, Fiver. Although I can't say I would have been so generous. Still."

I nodded just slightly and gulped, trying not to let the terror coursing through my veins show.

Gallander slowly squared his shoulders and turned to Atara, his eyes as cold as granite yet ablaze with anger and disgust. "Everyone knows what happens to traitors," he snarled. Walker's lifeless face floated in my mind once again.

"Please, no," Atara cried, but I could already hear the resignation in her voice. I tried to catch her eyes with mine, but she wouldn't peel her gaze from Gallander's pitiless glare.

He reached to his side and unsheathed his knife, the blade gleaming in the light. My stomach shrank yet again.

"Here's your chance to prove your worth, Fiver." Gallander stepped forward and flipped the knife, catching it by the blade and extending the hilt to me. "You caught her. You punish her. As you would any traitor."

My throat seized. Blood drained from my head, leaving me woozy. My legs threatening to give out beneath me. I bit the inside of my cheek to keep my face composed. Inside, my gut twisted, a knot constricting my lungs. No, no, he didn't mean . . .

Kill.

I stared at the knife, the sharply filed edge, the narrow point. Flashing steel soon to be stained with blood. Atara's brilliant eyes leaking large, hot tears that even her bravery couldn't quite hold back.

Gallander stared down at me, his *C*-shaped scar white against his tan, rough skin. He would not wait much longer. I watched my hand move, fingers wrapping around the hilt. Pulling it from his hands. I turned to her as her face drained of all color.

"I know it's difficult at first," Gallander's voice came from behind me. "The first kill is always the most frightening. The most painful. Especially when it's someone you know . . . perhaps even cared for. But I have faith in you, Fiver."

The knife trembled in my grasp. Atara met my eyes, her lips parted, lungs heaving, looking every bit the twelve-year-old child that she was.

Her gaze burned with fear, but behind it shone a glimmer of defiance. A shred of forgiveness. She clenched her fists and dipped her head in a tiny nod. *It's okay. Okay.*

I shook my head. She stood there, alive, her heart pumping blood through her veins. Two Commanders breezed past me and took her arms, holding her. She cried out at their unforgiving grip, but she didn't fight them. I felt Gallander's breath on my neck. Something wet stung my eyes, but something worse pierced my heart. Atara nodded once again, biting her lip as her body trembled.

Behind me, Gallander cleared his throat. The man didn't even need to speak for me to understand his meaning: either I punished the traitor, or I became a traitor. I took several shaky steps forward until I was inches from her. She lowered her head, resigned to her death. All because I had failed. And she was going to take the blame.

I willed her to look at me, to lift her eyes, look into mine, and see in them the words screaming, *I'm sorry. I'm so sorry.* My fingers shook like leaves in a violent storm, but when she raised her head and locked her eyes on me with the greatest look of defiance and courage I had ever seen in her, my heart cracked worse than it had the day they'd tossed me onto the train and taken me so far from my home in Gesher.

Gallander's voice boomed from behind me. "Fiver!"

And I thrust my hand forward.

The knife sunk in down to the hilt, meeting little resistance. Her mouth fell open with a quiet grunt, an involuntary gurgle escaping from her. Tears again appeared, this time flowing freely. Something warm and sticky ran down my fingers; it dripped to the floor in quiet taps. The Commanders released her arms, and her knees, no longer capable of holding her weight, buckled. The knife slipped from her body and remained in my suddenly steady hands. I let it drop, my fingers streaked with red.

Gallander's hand clamped down on my shoulder, but I refused to turn to him. My gaze remained on Atara, with her gasping and writhing on the floor. Dying. I stifled a horrified scream.

Her eyes met mine, her hand slowly curling. She was motioning to me, urging me to come closer. I squinted, my insides shattering like glass. But I sank to my knees and inched closer, the ache spreading through every inch of me. The Commanders stepped away, leaving me alone with her.

She swallowed painfully, blood pooling in the corners of her mouth. She coughed, splattering red down her chin and across the floor. "Please," she whispered, her voice strained. I cringed, guilt soaking through my lungs. "Please, Fiver. What's your name?"

The question surprised me. I expected anger, revulsion. But she looked at me without accusation. "Please, Fiver."

Anything she wanted. I leaned over, pressing my lips to her ear, and in a small voice, I whispered the name I'd never forgotten. "Joshua. My name is Joshua."

The wound in her torso allowed for one more small spark to flicker in her eyes; one last burst of life shone through me before the smile on her trembling lips slipped away like water in a stream. And she was gone. The light in her eyes dead.

My face burned, a tearing in my chest as I squeezed her body to mine and begged her to forgive me. Holding her tight, I rocked her as my eyes stung with tears I wasn't supposed to let flow. I pressed her face against me, stroking her hair, her beautiful blonde hair, watching my tears fall into it. I held her as tight as I could, held her until my arms grew numb. Until I felt hands encase my shoulders.

They pulled me back, yanking on my fingers until my grip loosened, and I felt her slipping away. I screamed. Kicking and twisting in the grasp of the strong hands that dragged me further and further from her, I cried for her lifeless body. Someone else took her wrists, dragging her across the corridor and out the door. The last I saw was the bottom of her shoes, the initials she'd carved into the sole: A.D.

Her secret rebellion. Never forget who you are.

My eyes caught on the other sole. No initials had been engraved there. Nothing but a number, immortalized on the bottom of her left shoe.

The number five.

§

Two days later, the same strong hands came and took me from my bunk, led me down the hall, and placed me before the door to Barracks Five. The Ace gave me a brisk salute and stepped aside, revealing all the staring faces, boring eyes, and intense stares. They told me this was my squadron. That I was the new Ace.

Whispers of surprise and disbelief spread through the boys and girls in the room. No one got made Ace before their sixth year, and I had barely been here for five. I ignored them all and their accusing faces.

"You can choose up to five soldiers to take with you," one of the Commanders said. "They can come from any Barracks, but their names must be on this list." She handed me a piece of paper. I didn't look at it.

"Link," I said. They glanced at each other. I raised my voice just slightly. "I want Link."

Everything in my world was changing, and I would cling to whatever stability I could find. Even if it meant Link's constant presence hiding in my shadow. The Commanders eventually nodded their consent, and I nodded in return.

"You have until next week to decide on any more," the lead Commander said. "And your take must be replaced by someone from Barracks Five. You take five, you give five."

I locked my jaw. The number five was starting to leave a bitter taste on my tongue. I brushed past them and stepped fully into the room. The faces never left mine. The eyes followed me, challenging me, testing me.

The door slammed shut behind me.

"Alright, you lunks of Greens!" I shouted, more anger than I'd ever felt pouring into my words. Their faces changed at my tone. Eyes wide. Alert. "We're gonna rip some Lucian hide!"

TWENTY-FIVE

I open my eyes and am surprised to find the room the same as I remember it. The pounding in my head is gone, and the light above emits a comfortable, low glow. I look toward the front of the room at Lukas, who's leaning against the doorframe, his back to me.

Nathaniel's voice drifts through the open door, but I can't make out his words.

I shift in the bed, and Lukas turns to face me. His face lights up, and he rushes to my side. "You're awake!"

I grunt. "Barely," I choke out. My mouth feels dryer than tinder.

Nathaniel steps through the doorway, joining his son at the foot of the bed. "Gave us a scare there," he says

"How long was I out?" I stretch a stiff arm.

"Just a day," Lukas replies. "Who's Atara?"

I freeze. My eyes dart to Nathaniel's, though I'm not sure why. He only lifts a questioning eyebrow and remains silent.

"You were calling out for her in your sleep," Lukas continues.

I swallow the growing lump in my throat. My fists clench to keep from trembling, my jaw tightening. Nathaniel sees my tense body and touches Lukas on the shoulder. "I'll go get him something to eat. You should let him rest and get his strength back."

Lukas seems as if he's about to argue, but instead he turns away without a word. Nathaniel gives me a nod and walks out of the room. Lukas mumbles an apology and starts to follow him, but I suddenly don't want to be left alone. I prop a pillow against the headboard and push myself up.

"Lukas?"

He pauses, looking over his shoulder. I force a weak smile. "Would you stay for a bit?"

He returns the grin and moves back to where a chair sits beside the bed. He drops himself into it and sighs, staring at the hardwood floor for a long moment. His quiet presence calms my tense muscles, and I relax into the pillows. They're almost too soft after years of my sleeping on rock.

"Dad said your name was Joshua."

His voice fills the silence, and I cringe. "Nobody calls me that anymore."

"Why not?"

"It's just a name. It's stupid," I think. *"It's something I can never be again."*

"They gave us new names in the Barracks," I reply, my voice stiff.

Lukas's voice fills with quiet horror. "What else did they do to you there?"

I turn my head to the wall. Beneath the blankets, my hands quiver. I lean forward, and there's the sharp pain in my side again. I press my hand against it and find a thick padding covering my wound. I pull aside the blankets and lift the tattered cloth of my shirt to find a white bandage.

I lift my eyes to Lukas, who nods at the dressing and says, "It got infected. Really bad. Dad patched you up."

I pull my shirt down. "You shouldn't take your father for granted."

He snorts in disdain. "My father," he scoffs. "The only reason I came to this town is because they made me. After Mom disappeared, I got sent off to him." Red creeps into his face. "He makes it his job to find people. He sends them into all kinds of covert operations, getting information, pulling people out, yet he won't lift a finger to find her!"

I say nothing. I doubt Nathaniel would have refused to help his son out of spite for Lukas's mother, even if the two were separated. Her picture still stood on his desk. He had to care for her still, no matter what their situation had been.

Lukas rubs at the back of his hands, then runs his fingers through his hair. A wet sheen coats his eyes. "I can't lose her, too."

I twitch. I remember that first night, his shaking shoulders. Muffled cries. It wasn't his mother he was weeping for, not then.

"Who was it?" I ask softly.

He gazes into his palms, a tear slipping down his face. "My sister. Eden." He wipes the moisture from his cheek. "She was eleven. Almost twelve. There was . . . an accident, and . . . " He shakes his head. "There wasn't nothing anybody could do."

Lukas looks up at me. "My older brother Jakob went off to enlist in the army as soon as he turned twenty. He won't help me. He keeps saying Mom is dead."

I swallow, remembering the silver coin I found near the North Stream. I think of my father, alive. Lukas's face is streaked with red blotches: a boy still grieving and convinced he's alone in his fight to keep his own hope alive. Torn by guilt yet still longing to find his father's approval, even if he despises the man.

I lean my head against the pillow, silently rolling this new information over in my mind.

It's several moments later when Lukas's voice comes again, small and timid."Fiver?"

I tilt my head. "Yeah?"

"Is our deal still on?"

Something tugs at the strings inside of me, and it pulls up one corner of my mouth. A grin. It feels like the skin cracks around my lips and eyes, breaking a mold that had long encased my face.

Weakly, I slap a hand against his shoulder. A calm settles over me. "Sure," I say, "but one more thing." Lukas raises his eyebrows at me. "We're getting my father out, too."

TWENTY-SIX

"STUPID SLEEVE."

Link's arm swung sideways, barely missing my head. He turned in awkward circles, struggling to shove his hand into the sleeve of his dress uniform. I looked up from hooking my jacket buttons and gave him a smirk as he turned again. All the other soldiers had finished dressing and had gone to join the commotion down the hall, leaving me to fiddle with my buttons and watch Link bop around like a ball on a string. I suppressed a smile and reached for his jacket.

"Hold still. Stop your dancing, will ya?" I chided, shoving his arm into the narrow sleeve.

"Ow!" he grunted. He mumbled a curse. "I don't see why we have to get all fancied up for this silly thing, anyway." His eyes darted to mine. "No offense."

I lifted one corner of my mouth in reply. "Come on, they're waiting for us out there."

"Right," Link grunted, shifting his jacket over his shoulders. "Waiting to cheer and get drunk. I guess that's not so bad, huh, Fiver?" He grinned and nudged me with his shoulder.

Listening to the cacophony coming from the other side, I took a deep breath before the door. I reached for the handle, and we stepped out from the dressing room, moving toward the auditorium where the audience waited.

"Oh, get over it, Fiver," Link grumbled, shoving the auditorium's door open with a grunt. I flinched at the crowds inside, watching the soldiers milling about the enormous room now decorated with the nation's colors. The purples and golds covering the tables, chairs, and walls nearly stung my eyes. Soldiers stood with drinks in hand, nibbling finger sandwiches and congregating in small groups to gossip. The lights shone too bright overhead, and suddenly I felt heat travel across my neck.

Link strode inside with his arms in the air. "Ladies and gentlemen!" he shouted. My stomach dropped, sweat beading on my forehead. "May I present . . . the new senior-grade Commander from Barracks Nine!"

He whirled around with a flair and pointed both his index fingers at me. Every head in the room turned to stare as I entered, sweat rolling down my back. Link let out a yell and began clapping. Those nearest to us followed suit, and soon the whole room filled with applause. Link grinned wider, grabbed me by the arm, and pulled me further inside the room. If he had any hard feelings about my surpassing him for the command, he certainly didn't let them show.

"Come on, Fiver, live it up!" he crooned. "It's not every day you get promoted!"

"I'm not promoted *yet*!" I hissed at him. "They haven't even given me a command."

Link jerked his chin toward my shoulder. "You got the stars, you got the job, man. That makes it official."

I rolled my eyes and shoved him away. "Go find someone else to embarrass, will you?"

He laughed and backed into the crowd, joining up with a couple of junior-grade soldiers we once shared a Barracks with. I stood alone on the outskirts of the celebration, watching them all take pleasure in my achievement. I was the youngest junior-grade trainee ever to be promoted to a senior-grade command. I would be in charge of a squadron of real Boquan soldiers, and I would finally be able to make a real difference in the war.

I was ready to kill. I wanted to kill. I ground my teeth at the thought of the battles I would fight. The chance each one would give me to wipe her blood from my hands—or at least cover them with someone else's.

I caught sight of a man lurking outside the chattering groups. Seeming slightly uncomfortable in his dress uniform, he wiggled his shoulders inside his stiff jacket. He turned my way but didn't notice me as he stuffed a sandwich into his mouth and washed it down with a long gulp from his glass.

I recognized that face. The dark hair and strong arms. Older, and somehow smaller than I remembered, but still him.

"Bone?"

He looked up, and a smile spread across his face as he swallowed. I stepped closer, and he shook his head in astonishment as I stood toe to toe with him. My eyes were the same level as his.

"Fiver!" He clapped his hand on my shoulder, admiring the five stars pinned across them.

"What are you doing here?" I asked.

He slapped my back. "One of my former Greens makes command in senior grade? Of course I'm gonna show up!"

I allowed a small grin. "You finally got promoted out of the Greens, huh?"

"Yeah, well," he sniffed and stretched his arm. "They found somebody younger to take the job. I'm gonna miss it, actually." He paused, a faraway glint in his eyes. "I did what I could for my kids. To prepare them. Teach them. I even knew their real names."

I blinked. "You knew our names?"

He looked at me as though it were obvious, his eyes slightly hazy as he lifted his glass and took a sip. "Of course, I had all your files. I knew your names, your parents' names." He lowered his head and his voice. "I know a lot of things about you, Fiver. Things even you probably don't know."

My lips trembled. Something spread inside my stomach like a fog, making me sick as I pushed away Atara's voice from my mind. "What things?" I asked.

He sipped from his glass again and hiccupped. "You wanna know why they called me Bone?"

I frowned. "What has that got to do with—"

"—Most people think it's because I broke a lot of people's bones while I was in training. Beat 'em up pretty good. But that's not it . . . " He let a wistful smile touch his lips. He set down his glass and pulled at his jacket sleeve, yanking it up his forearm. He turned his arm to reveal a scar running in a jagged line to his elbow. I remembered seeing it before, but I had never asked him about it.

"I took a fall on the rope on my second day here," he said. "Landed in a pretty bad way. Broke my ulna clear across, and two inches of it were sticking right out of my arm."

He rolled his sleeve down and adjusted his jacket. "By the time I was fit to begin training properly, it was too late to prepare for my exam."

"But . . . if you couldn't do it, then why didn't they . . . " I struggled to meet his eye. *"Why are you still here?"* I thought.

"Because I made it, Fiver," he replied. "Barely, but I made it. And it's why they made me the Greens' Ace. They don't like to throw away good stock."

I narrowed my eyes at him, and my jaw clenched. "What do you know about me, Bone?"

His dark eyes met mine for a long, silent moment. He blinked. He reached into his jacket pocket and pulled out a small silver disc on a leather string. "They took this off you when you first came to base." He pulled my hand open and pressed the pendant into my palm, closing my fingers around it. "I'd be careful with that, if I were you."

"How did you—"

"—They kept it in your file. Funny how we've got all that technology, and yet we still keep paper copies." He shrugged. "I guess the big shots are more worried about the Lucians hacking in than breaking in."

I pulled my stare from my balled fist. "What else was there?"

He shook his head. "Fiver—"

"—What else was there, Bone?"

He took a step back. "Don't do this. I've already done enough to get you put six feet under!"

"You said they don't throw away good stock!" I protested, leaning closer.

Bone hissed. "They don't *like* doing it, but they will, Fiver, believe me. You may be the best soldier they've ever seen, but even you are expendable if they don't like what you know."

I glared at him. "And what do I know, Bone?"

His eyes filled with a warning and a challenge, stirring fire in my gut. He clapped a hand on my shoulder again, then turned to leave. "Congratulations, Fiver," he said. "I wish you all the best."

He paused, his head angled so I could only see a fraction of his face. His voice was low as he spoke again. "And I'm sorry about her, Fiver." My chest tightened as his gaze rose to mine. "Really, I am."

I blinked and looked at the floor, forcing down the bulge growing in my throat. Her face flashed behind my eyes over and over, the noise of the party around me fading into cries of pain and anger.

Tears threatened to burst down my cheeks, as I lowered my head and made for the door, not caring that I was skipping out on my own celebration. Bone's words echoed in my skull as I walked away.

TWENTY-SEVEN

I LET THEM NURSE ME FOR THREE DAYS BEFORE I finally decide my body is well enough to take care of itself. Nathaniel finds me out of bed one afternoon as he brings me lunch, just as I'm stretching my muscles and shaking out my hunting jacket.

"Feeling better?" he says, setting a tray on the dresser. I look at the sandwich and vegetables, and my stomach lets out a loud, hungry growl. Nathaniel chuckles. "I guess that's as good an answer as any."

I slip my arms through my jacket. "Thank you for what you've done for me." He sizes me up with those eyes again. "It's not what I would have done in your place."

A tiny smile pulls at one corner of his mouth. "Oh, I don't know. You did more for my son."

I swallow the lump in my throat. After all the time I've spent here, I still don't know what to make of this man. He's a military commander in charge of sabotage and infiltration, and he must know the best way to get what he wants out of someone.

"I imagine you know what I'm going to ask you," I say, straightening the jacket on my shoulders. He gives a nod. "What do you want?"

The sturdy expression wavers for a moment. My words were not what he was expecting. My eyebrows pinch together, as do Nathaniel's. "What do I want?"

"In exchange for the information about my father." I cock my head, watching his puzzled face. Why else would he have withheld it from me? Why else would he have told me anything about my father in the first place?

His tongue moves into the space between his teeth and his upper lip. "You like to make deals, don't you?"

I glare at him in response. He nods again. "Alright then," he begins, "here's my deal. We'll talk about anything you want, but first . . . " He takes a step closer, then winces. "When was the last time you had a shower?"

§

Nathaniel's bathroom looks too much like the ones in the Barracks. Clean white walls. Bright lights. He's been trained to keep his living quarters spotless.

The showerhead sprays out jets of warm water, filling the stall with light clouds of steam. Standing inches from the spray, I strip, tossing my clothes into the corner. I stick out one arm and let my fingers break the showerhead's stream.

The water pounds onto my skin like a heavy rain, droplets sliding down my arm. The water gets colder and colder. Too cold. I reach for the knob, turning it a bit. Old habits snap back into my brain as though I'd left the Barracks only yesterday. I like the water just barely warm. Never cold.

I run my hand through my hair, now snipped short and off my ears once again. My head feels lighter, the familiar swish of my bangs gone. I scrub soap suds through my hair and across my skin, digging out years of embedded dirt and grime that water alone refused to cleanse. I repeat several times, letting the pounding water soothe my stiff, aching muscles.

Without warning, the pressure in my ribcage is too much to bear, and my knees crumple. I bend at the waist and lean against the shower's wall, gripping my sides as uncontrollable sobs wrack me. Link's dead body is out there in the Wood somewhere. My mother is probably buried beneath ash and rubble. Atara. Who knows what's happened to Lukas's mom? They all died, even now they're dying. My father, dying. The water pours over my head, dripping from my hair and into my eyes. It mixes with my tears, and I stand for long minutes watching it all wash down the drain.

When I finally step out from the shower, I can smell my old clothes from across the room. My nose crinkles in disgust, the greasy pile nearly turning my stomach. How could I have not noticed such a stink?

I reach for the clothes Lukas offered me. A thin, gray T-shirt and a dark button-down shirt. Gray shorts, a pair of sturdy jeans, well-bleached socks, and a leather jacket. The clothes fit surprisingly well, and even the boots slide on with little effort, the insoles springy and comfortable on my feet.

Whoever these clothes belong to, they're not Lukas's. They smell as though they've been tucked away in a closet for some time, and I briefly wonder if I'm wearing the old clothes of a dead man.

I push the thought away, reaching for the jacket. The leather is smooth and supple; it's used, but still in good shape. I lift it and push my arms through the sleeves. The fit is even better than my hunting jacket. It drapes over my shoulders as if tailored for me.

I take one last look in the mirror, staring at my clean-shaven face and neatly cropped hair. That one lock in the front that always used to stick up stubbornly is standing proudly once again, no longer drowned by the weight of my thick mane.

I frown at the image staring back at me, watch as the creases form around my eyes and lips. The familiar contours of my face, now changed in subtle ways. I am a soldier again, but different. I don't belong to them.

I clench my teeth. Nathaniel is waiting. I head downstairs.

As I step off the stairs and into the living room, Lukas's first reaction is a mixture of amusement and surprise, his mouth dropping open and spreading into a wide grin.

"Wow," he says, rising from his seat on the couch. "So that's what you look like clean."

"Thanks," I grunt at him, moving toward the bay window overlooking the gloomy front yard. People have gone back to their routines, as far as I can tell. Back to their normal lives.

"Where's Nathaniel?" I ask Lukas. He pulls his glass, which is filled with a dark-purple liquid, from his face and smacks his lips.

"He's in the war room." He takes another sip. "Said he wanted to talk to you as soon as you were ready."

"The war room?"

He nods. "It's like the hub of operations around here. Information comes in from all over Lucia and Boqua, and they plan their hits based on what our spies can give them."

"Sabotage?" I step from the window, catching sight of the fireplace mantle. It's lined with framed photos of Nathaniel's family. Children, teens. Babies. A beautiful woman. A proud man. A happy family. I turn away. My father kept pictures on the mantle, too.

Lukas gulps his drink. "Yeah, it's super-secret spy stuff," he grunts. "Come on, I'll show you."

"You know where it is?" I raise my eyebrows.

Lukas scoffs. "Of course I do. Where do you think I got the information on those spies in Boqua?" He flinches at the memory and moves for the door. I follow, determined this time to get the answers I want.

TWENTY-EIGHT

EVERY TIME I LOOKED AT THEM, I SAW HER FACE. IN their terrified eyes, in their fear mixed with beneath-the-surface rage. Whenever I went to cut a Lucian down, I saw her, then I watched as their blood seeped into the ground, coating the stones and grass. The satisfaction lasted only an instant. In moments, it was always replaced once again by the insatiable desire to kill. To avenge.

"Fiver! On your six!" Link cried, but I'd already noticed the Lucian soldier creeping up behind me. Why he hadn't fired his weapon could have a dozen answers, but I didn't bother with any of them as I whirled around and caught the arm wielding a large combat knife in its hand.

The Lucian growled and tried to sling his other fist into my chin, but I ducked and slammed his arm against my leg. He howled and dropped his knife, then flew backward as I pounded my knee into his face. Blood ran from his nose and cracked lip, but I wasn't finished yet.

"You're not keeping this post," I warned him as I stepped beside his writhing body, the crumbling cement crunching beneath my boots. "It belongs to Boqua." The walls of the bunker were nearly destroyed, but somehow they still held up the roof overhead as my squadron searched for any survivors of our assault. The Lucians hadn't put forth nearly as much of a fight as we'd expected.

Link laughed at my side, eyeing the soldier on the floor. From the holes in the walls and ceiling, beams of hazy, dusty light streamed into the small room. His hair coated in the pale white dust, Link held his wrist to his mouth, radioing the rest of the squadron and telling them we were nearly finished here. Everyone was to return to our meeting place.

The broken soldier glared up at me. "This isn't a post, you idiot," he grunted, wiping at the blood pouring from his nose. "It's a refugee camp. There are innocent people buried underneath all this rubble!"

I narrowed my eyes, lifting a boot and laying it across his throat. "You tried to overtake our forces stationed here," I said, my patience wearing as thin as paper. "Did you think we wouldn't crush you? Just like this." I pressed my weight onto my foot. He choked and gripped my ankle.

"That's . . . what they told you?" he gagged. "Look around! We were . . . barely surviving here! Barely a weapon . . . for half the adults."

"You're lying." Holding my foot still, I frowned. He pulled and coughed, but he couldn't move me from his throat.

"Why would I lie?!" he spluttered. "You can see for yourself! My daughter . . . " Tears sprang to his eyes, one hand motioning at a darkened hallway where part of the ceiling had collapsed. "She's . . . " He coughed again, looking straight at me. "Oh, Elorai help us. What have they been filling your heads with?"

"*Lies. They lie.*" Atara's voice in my mind surprised me. I felt my eyebrows nearly touch as I screwed up my face. The soldier saw the flicker of doubt in me and pounced on it.

"They've been lying to you! We haven't—"

"—Shut up!" Link shouted. He lifted his weapon and fired a single shot into the soldier's torso. I jerked back at the sound, realizing my heart was racing.

"What was that for?"

Link waved his gun. "He said nothing worth listening to," he muttered. "You should have killed him on the spot!"

He pushed past me toward the exit, and I stared down at the soldier's body. I knew he had to die. All Lucians would die, sooner or later.

But I'd never spoken to one like this before. Some part of me wanted to hear what he would have said if Link hadn't put a bullet into him. I bit the inside of my cheek and shook my head to clear it. It had to be the heat talking. Nothing more. I didn't need to look closer. I didn't need to lift the slab of fallen roof the soldier had pointed at to see if there was a girl's body underneath.

I would have believed myself if Atara's voice hadn't floated into my mind once again.

"*They lie.*"

§

She couldn't have been right. I didn't want her to be right. I fought her voice all the way back to the base, barely hearing the excited, triumphant chatter of my squadron, proud of their newest achievement for the Boquan cause. I said nothing, and fortunately, they expected the silence.

At the base, I went straight to my quarters and locked the door behind me. On the top of my bookshelf sat a collection of thick volumes recounting famous Boquan battles and victories, but I reached behind those and pulled out the smaller book I'd hidden there.

I wiped the dust from its cover and sank into my desk chair, thumbing the book's edges before slowly letting it fall open in my hands.

Atara had snuck several books out of the base's library; she tore out pages to make paper animals with. With this book, however, she'd taken a knife and sliced out a large square in half of the pages, leaving a gaping hole inside the book. Her secret hiding place for her paper animals.

I lifted them out one by one, gazing at all the shapes and colors and shadows she'd drawn. I knew I should throw them away. I should throw everything away. But without them I feared I would lose her memory forever, and so they'd stayed hidden on the bookshelf all these years.

I let the cover of the makeshift box close, running my finger along it. I swallowed, pushing against the turmoil raging inside my chest. She had to go. She couldn't interfere. Not anymore. I lifted the book by one cover and flung it into the trashcan.

Something hard hit the floor at my feet.

I looked down, frowning at the plain white card between my shoes. It must have fallen from the other pages left untouched in the book. I bent over to scoop up the card. This was a passkey, the kind made especially for visiting Commanders. I flipped it over to reveal the impossible name inscribed on its casing.

Abraham Gallander.

I had no idea how she'd gotten Gallander's passkey, but it had to be how she'd broken into the records and discovered Scourge's true fate. I could almost hear her voice in my head, prodding me: *"You can see for yourself. Prove me wrong, if you can."*

I ran my sweaty palm through my hair. I gripped the white card in my trembling hand and tried to push away the Lucian's last words.

Atara's words reflected right back at me.

"They lie."

TWENTY-NINE

THE FIRST FACE I SEE WHEN LUKAS PUSHES OPEN THE heavy metal door is not one I find much pleasure in seeing. His glare alone is enough to make an angry heat wash over me like a wave, though the underground room is much cooler than outside. I clench my fists.

"What's he doing here?" Micah growls. He looks up from the 3D projection of a series of buildings and empty streets created by the broad holo-table in the center of the room. Tomas and Asher stand behind him. Besides the three of them, only a handful of people surround the table, including Nathaniel. A few more people mill about the room, some typing at keyboards or swiping fingers across other holo projections on touchpads; some talk in low voices into microphones attached to their earpieces.

Several heads turn at Micah's voice. Eyes widen as a hush falls on the room, then they shoot to Nathaniel at the holo-table. He catches sight of us at the door; he immediately straightens and excuses himself.

"Well, you clean up nice, don't you?" he says, grinning. I slowly scan the nervous soldiers who are trying not to look at me.

"Why have you brought me here?" The war room is barely two blocks from Nathaniel's house, but I can't believe he's allowed me into the heart of his operations. I fight to keep the confusion from my face as the soldiers return to their duties, and the room resumes its work. Lukas picks up a small touchpad and scrolls through the news on the screen searching, I assume, for reports about a Boquan soldier running free in the middle of Dekkan.

Nathaniel squints at me. "I did get the name right, didn't I? Joshua?"

I bite my tongue until the pain flares. He nods, accepting my silence, and gestures to his men. "This is the real reason Dekkan exists," he says.

"I am the head of the Sabotage and Infiltration sector of the Lucian military, and this city is our base of operations."

Micah growls and marches up behind Nathaniel. "So, you've just decided to welcome him with open arms, have you?" he spits. "Show him everything?"

Nathaniel ignores him. "This used to be a farming community. When we transformed the town, we decided to keep as much of that as we could to keep suspicion off us. It's worked pretty well so far. Some of the original families even still live here, working on their farms like they always have."

I grimace inwardly. "So you're all pretending to be simple, innocent farmers while sending spies and saboteurs into Boqua?"

He nods. "This room is the information center, if you want to call it that. It's where all our contacts in Boqua send us what they know, and we send them instructions in return. We also organize raids and operations for the units to take on."

I lick my lips. "Why are you telling me all this?"

"Because," Nathaniel replies, eyeing Micah. "I want you to know where my information comes from. That it is reliable."

Clearly consternated, Micah shakes his head.

Nathaniel cocks his chin at me. "I know Matthew Endenbough is your father."

Of course he knows. How else could he have guessed my name? Still, I can't help the tightening of my ribcage. I'm consumed by the overpowering desire to know how he knows my parentage. Why is he so interested in me?

I swallow. "And you know where he is."

"I do," he replies, taking a mini touchpad from his pocket. He taps the screen several times. "We know he's in Boquan custody. Commander Gallander took him eleven years ago to get him working on some kind of project at a lab called the Ramius Corporation."

Blood falls from my face faster than I can suck air into my greedy lungs. Gallander has had my father for eleven years? Every time he looked at me, was he thinking of him? Did the Commander ever wonder what I would do if I found out?

"Ramius?" Lukas says, frowning. "That's where they took my mother."

I know what he's thinking. If Gallander has kept my father alive for eleven years, who's to say he isn't doing the same with Rebekah Garrow? Nathaniel shakes his head, squashing the idea before it can get out of his son's mouth.

I manage to squeeze out the words. "What kind of project?"

Nathaniel taps on his screen again. "All we know is that it's an experimental serum. Lucian scientists tried to produce it over two hundred years ago, but the results were so catastrophic they had to close down the project. The details were locked away, and all access is forbidden, which means that whatever it does, it can't be good."

Like a cold hand, dread presses against my chest. "You don't know what the serum does?"

He shakes his head again. "Even my access to the info is limited. Most researchers don't know that the project existed in the first place."

"Oh, beautiful," Micah grunts. "So now let's tell that to every Boquan soldier who comes to our door."

"Micah, please," Nathaniel begins, but I cut him off before he can say anything else.

"No, he's right. How do you know you can trust me?"

Nathaniel's eyes flicker for a moment, as if he's unsure he should let the others hear what he's about to say. He slides his touchpad back into his pocket and gives a small cough.

"I knew Matthew well," he says finally. "Even though his son was a stolen child and raised to believe every ounce of propaganda those Commanders threw at him, I want him to at least have the chance to know the truth."

The lump in my throat has grown sharp edges. They pierce me with every word he speaks.

"What truth?"

THIRTY

"YOU OKAY, FIVER?" LINK CLAPPED A HAND ON MY
shoulder, and, pulled from my memories, I nearly jumped out of my
skin. He lifted his eyebrows as if no further question was needed.

I sniffed and wiped my forehead. We were the only two people in
the library, and my table was buried beneath a tower of books. Just
about every book I'd ever read on Boquan military history was before
me. My eyes blurred and ached, and my mind struggled to digest all
the information I had been feeding it. Filling it with little things, like
dates and places. Things that made my head spin.

"You've spent days in here," Link said. "What in the world are you
doing?"

I grunted, slamming a huge textbook closed. "What are *you* doing?
I haven't seen you inside a library in years."

He let a sly grin cross his lips. "Someone had to come pull you out."

I tossed the book onto the table and pushed my chair back. I looked
into his face and tried to remember what his eyes had been like years
before, like when I'd first seen him on the train. He'd changed so much;
we all had. There was a glint reflecting in his gaze that hadn't been there
before, not even when we were training. Not until he'd shed Lucian
blood.

He leaned down and sized me up. "You sure you're okay?"

I nodded, pushing him away as I stood. "I'm fine."

He shrugged. "Well, either way, they sent me to tell you they want
you in the infirmary as soon as you can." He paused for an uncomfortable moment. "You sure there's nothing wrong with you that I should
know about?"

I stretched stiff muscles. "They probably want another blood sample," I grunted.

Link frowned. "Blood? What for?"

"I don't know. What do they tell you when you have yours done?"

Link shook his head. "They've only taken blood at the yearly physical. That's not due for another couple of months."

I froze. They were taking blood almost once a month now, the frequency increasing over the past few years. Link shrugged as if it were nothing to be concerned about and walked out of the library, leaving me alone with ragged thoughts racing through my brain.

§

"Fiver."

I blinked. A female voice. A tug at my sleeve. "Fiver?"

My eyes moved down. She smiled back at me with a gap-toothed grin. A sickly pale face framed in blonde curls. She pulled at my sleeve, rolling it up my arm. "I'm about to take the sample now, alright?"

She held up the phlebotomy needle, and I leaped from the cold infirmary bench with clenched fists. She let out a surprised gasp and took a step back before composing herself. "Now really, Fiver, you've had plenty of blood samples drawn before—you should be used to this by now."

"What do you need them for?" I asked. She offered her smile again, and I felt I might rip it off her face.

"It's for your own good, Fiver," she replied, the smile evaporating at my dissatisfaction with her answer. "To make sure everything's as it should be."

"Then why am I the only one getting my blood taken?" I wasn't entirely sure about that, but I knew Link didn't get his blood drawn all the time.

Her face faltered for a moment. She fiddled with the needle, keeping her eyes from me. "Everyone gives the samples, Fiver. Everyone."

A lie.

I looked away. She gripped my sleeve and tugged it higher, then came the cool swipe and the sting, the collection tube filling with my blood. When it was full, she taped a square of cotton over the injection site, then ushered me from the infirmary without another word. The door shut with a dull clank, and I stared back at it, a mixture of anger and distrust slowly boiling beneath my skin.

"*They lie.*"

Atara's words floated inside my mind, a whisper in my ears. She'd seen through it all, whereas I had never suspected a thing. I looked down the hallway and toward the Barracks under my command. All my boys and girls. Good soldiers. Trained fighters.

I turned and walked the other way, down the deserted corridor toward the back elevators. I pressed the button and stepped inside, eyeing the blue screen where the floor numbers glowed. My finger hovered over number thirteen, the deepest level in the base. The level that housed the records room.

Bone said there was something in my file. Something he knew, something I never could. Something that could get me killed. I jerked my finger forward and touched the circular disc for level thirteen.

The circle around the floor number changed from green to red, then flashed. A grinding beep, then a mechanical female voice:

"Access restricted. Clearance passkey required."

I reached for my passkey, swiping it across the screen's sensor. The beep came again, and the entire screen glowed red. The voice:

"Access denied. Improper clearance."

The screen resumed its default setting, the blue screen glowing in the background behind the green, numbered circles. I frowned. I was a Commander. My card gave me clearance to every level, every door. Why not this one?

My teeth grit as I knew the answer. More secrets. More lies. But I also knew that if basic Commanders didn't have clearance to venture into level thirteen, there was only one man here who did.

Gallander.

I slipped my hand back inside my pocket and fiddled with the small piece of plastic hidden there.

How much trouble could I get myself into? What could they do to me if they found out? I bit my lip. Atara's seed of doubt flourished, and I found my hand pulling Gallander's passkey from my pocket, the card held tightly between my fingers.

How would they ever know? Atara had never been caught. She'd managed to get the passkey in the first place, and who knew how lucky she had to have been for that to happen. But if I were caught, there would be no explaining my way out of this one. No one to take the blame for me.

I held my breath and swiped the card in front of the sensor.

The screen flashed green. "Access granted." The elevator jolted, nauseating me as it sank downward. I watched the numbers on the screen until thirteen appeared, and the elevator slid to a smooth halt. The doors swished open.

Slowly, I stepped from the elevator and into the dimly lit hallway. One single hallway, lined with several doors. One large door at the back. The records room.

My head cocked, I paused outside of the elevator, listening for any sign of human presence.

Silence. I tucked in my chin and trotted for the door at the back. A request for the passkey came again at the terminal, and I swiped Gallander's card at the sensor. The door beeped. I pushed it open and found myself in an enormous room full of metal towers lining the walls and covering the floor like the bookshelves in a library. I held in a small gasp. This had to be the biggest room on the base. Bigger, even, than the Commanders' training rooms.

Each tower stood a few inches below my head and had several small drawers labeled with a name. I ventured further into the room, glancing at the names in straight type across each of the drawers. *Admas, Blaine* to *Avers, Marcen.* A few towers over came *Beckers, Gervinda,* to *Bunrava, Clash.* Ordered alphabetically by last names, it seemed. All soldiers of the Boquan Army, kids I knew as Boomer and Splicer and Falcon and Tank.

I thought briefly of Link's file, curious as to which tower it would be in. I had never known his given name, nor would I ever ask it. Atara hadn't told me her last name—although I knew it started with *D*—and finding her file would be more of a challenge than I had time for. There was only one name I needed to find here.

Several towers down, I found the *E* section and opened a drawer: *Easmas, Halban; Edran, Ruby; Eklemos, Auriel; Eldrich, Predwin.*

Endenbough, Joshua.

My heart leaped into my throat. My hand shook as I reached forward and gripped the handle. One breath, two breaths. Atara's voice echoing in my ears: "*They're liars, Fiver. We're just killing machines to them, nothing more.*" Bone's sympathetic gaze: "*I know a lot of things about you, Fiver. Things even you probably don't know.*"

I yanked at the drawer. It creaked on its warped treads, but it opened fully enough for me to pull out my thick file. Inside were white folders, all labeled with years and dates, all cataloging my progress as a Boquan soldier. The names of the soldiers under me, the records of our defeats and victories. All things I already knew.

One folder in particular, labeled "Entry/Induction," caught my attention.

I released the others and grasped the white folder, pulling it from the collection and flipping it open before my trembling hands could drop it back inside, before my feet could make for the door.

A picture of a small boy, brown hair hanging to his eyebrows. A smooth, innocent face filled with fear blazing out from chocolate eyes. My eyes. I didn't remember them taking a picture of me at induction.

Below the photograph were my name, age, birthday. Next to that were my height, weight, and all kinds of strange measurements of my body. My entire physical overview from the doctor at the induction center. My aptitude test score, the blaring five. My birthplace.

Gesher, Western Province, Boqua.

Further down were my parents' names. Matthew and Anna Endenbough. Ages, weights, basic physical descriptions. Birthplaces.

My insides plummeted as I read the next lines. Sweat clung to my forehead, my clammy palms gripping the file tighter. It had to be a mistake. They couldn't be . . . I couldn't be . . .

Mother: *Northern Commonwealth, Lucia. Defected to Boqua in year 1007 of the BR.*

Father: *Western Commonwealth, Lucia. Defected to Boqua in year 1007 of the BR.*

Lucians.

Black spots flashed before my eyes, my knees knocking beneath me. I gripped the side of the metal tower for support, the file falling from my sweaty hands and back into the drawer. Deep breaths ravaged my lungs as waves of anger and despair rushed from my chest.

It wasn't possible. I was . . . I couldn't be . . . But it was true.

I was a Lucian.

THIRTY-ONE

"You're Lucian?" His stunned eyes flit to me. My stomach is churning as though trying to digest itself. Nathaniel knew? How could he possibly have known this?

Nathaniel swallows at the question in my face. "Matthew is my half-brother on my mother's side."

My head drains of blood, and I focus on Lukas, who stands staring at his father as if seeing a complete stranger. My chest feels hollow. My father was an only child, as far as I knew. What is happening?

Lukas's eyes have bulged out like a frog's, while his mouth hangs agape. "What?!" The touchpad he holds drops to the concrete floor, and its screen shatters. "Nobody told me you had a brother!"

Nathaniel gives a sigh that seems to express his eternal frustration with his son. Thankfully, Micah seems to have lost his voice, but the shock in his eyes bleeds through the mask he's trying to display.

Only one word will form on my tongue. "How?"

Nathaniel looks at me. "Your father worked in Boqua as a botanist, back in the days before those sick Commanders started blaming Lucia for everything they could think of," he says. "Your mother was one of my contacts stationed in Gesher. They met, and when her mission was complete, she and your father decided to stay in Boqua. You weren't too far behind."

I shake my head, still shocked at the fact that this man, *this man,* is related to me. That Lukas is my cousin. "But why?" I manage. "Why would they want to stay there? The war was just around the corner then. There had to be tension between Lucia and Boqua by that time."

A strange look haunts Nathaniel's eyes. "I can't answer that one.

All I know is they never came home. Matthew was a good scientist and earned a reputation for himself here in Lucia. Gallander noticed and offered him a job. He worked for him for several years before something went wrong."

"What?"

"We don't know. But one night Matthew returned to work after-hours and never came back. Then they went to his house some-time after midnight and burned it to the ground, with your mother still inside. We don't know why, or what happened after that, only that Matthew went into the Ramius Corporation and never came back out again."

My heart shrinks inside me, struggling desperately to hold together the giant crack splitting it down the middle. Heat flushes through my face, my fingers shaking uncontrollably.

"Why haven't you gotten him out? Eleven years. He's been there for eleven years."

Micah scoffs but says nothing.

"We've tried," Nathaniel answered. "Ever since we knew for sure that they had him. But it's impossible. Even with all my resources, *and* even with my men inside the corporation, we couldn't find out a single thing about him. Not one shred of information."

Lukas meets my eyes, and a spark flares. Silent communication across the space between us conveys only two words: Yosher Weldtham.

Lukas inhales deeply. "He's in another building."

Nathaniel fixes his gazes on his son. "What?"

Lukas's mouth gapes, and I feel as though I might drop to my knees at any second. Yosher knew my father—the "he" the old man kept mumbling about. *He begged me to help,* Yosher had said, *just before they took him.*

"He's not there, he's in another building!" Lukas's eyes dance. "Just like Yosher said!"

"What in Elorai's name are you talking about?" Micah shoots.

Nathaniel ignores him. "Wait, wait a minute. Yosher?" He holds up a hand, trying to calm Lukas's excited squawking. "You've met Yosher Weldtham?"

"You knew him?" asks Lukas. Yosher claimed to know Nathaniel, so it only makes sense.

Nathaniel nods. "By name, yes. He was a friend of Matthew's while they worked at the Ramius Corporation. He's the one who was with him when they took him away."

"But how did he escape?" I can't imagine Yosher ever being able to slip through anyone's guard, much less a crowd of trained Boquan soldiers.

Nathaniel shrugs. "We have no idea. He's the only reason we know Matthew was taken into custody. What else did he tell you?"

I frown, remembering the mostly one-sided conversation. "He said something about the Crosswoods," I answer, my mind reeling. "The Vitmor there. That they needed it for the serum. That they were close to finishing it."

Nathaniel's face mirrors my own shock. We both know what it means: if my father has finished the serum, then there's no need to keep him alive any longer. Any hope my information brings also comes with an unknown time limit, and whatever Gallander's plans are for his serum will soon be underway.

"We've gotta get him out now!" I take a step forward. "We don't have much time left!"

Despair washes over Nathaniel's face. "If he's not in the main building, he could be anywhere. Gallander could use any place to set up his research."

"There's got to be someone who knows," I say, hating the desperation that creeps into my voice.

Nathaniel stares at the floor, his eyes moving as his mind frantically searches for an answer. "The rebels might," he says, his voice low but clear.

"Rebels?" My interest spikes to the ceiling. "What rebels? Where are they?"

He rubs his hand through his hair. "They're mostly Boquan parents who've lost their children to the violence. They know the reasons Boqua gives for starting the war are lies, but they can't prove it. Their numbers are pretty small, and they're not all that effective. Gallander keeps them pinned down pretty tight. He hunts them like rabbits every chance he gets."

Rabbits. A shudder passes through me, although I try not to let it show. "What do they know?"

"We can't say for sure. They won't have anything to do with us. Every operative I've sent to find them has come back with the same message: they won't deal with us, and next time we make contact, they might not let our operatives live."

"A bunch of lightweights, if you ask me," Micah grunts. "Too stubborn to take any kind of help."

I don't answer him. Perhaps they're stubborn. Perhaps they're jealous that the Lucians only take volunteers for their armies. Perhaps they just don't trust outsiders.

"Where can I find them?" I ask Nathaniel.

Micah scoffs. "Oh, yeah, that'll fly," he says with a sarcastic smirk. "A Boquan soldier trained by the most ruthless man in the entire Boquan army? Whose father is working on a secret project for that same man? Who, by the way, is responsible for the child draft in the first place?" He scoffs again, louder this time. "They'll bury you faster than they can shoot you."

"Maybe they'll talk to me *because* I was one of those soldiers," I shoot back at him.

"They won't talk to us, the only people who can help them. Why would they talk to you?" Micah snorts.

"There's more information now. If we show them we can stop Gallander's project, they may be willing to help get my father out."

Nathaniel rubs his jaw. "It's possible," he says. "But it's going to be hard to find them after we've tried so many times to ally with them. I can give you a general location, but no specifics."

I bite the inside of my cheek. Even if I can find them, it'll be even harder to do it without giving myself away. Gallander hasn't stopped searching for me, and the more I expose myself in Boqua, the easier it'll be for him to catch me and do what he wants with me.

But suddenly, her face comes to me, beaming back at me from somewhere deep inside my mind. Almost shaking her head in mockery at my stupidity.

Atara.

Her ideas had to come from somewhere, most likely her parents. All the warnings about the soldiers and the Commanders and the way things really were out there. Desperate parents attempting to keep their kid from conforming to the lies. It's possible they were part of the rebels all along. If that's the case, even if they're not still alive, there have to be people who knew them. People who knew the resistance.

It's a long shot, but the only one I have. "It's possible—"

Micah cuts me off with a grunt. "This is ridiculous!" He flings out his hand as if dismissing the whole affair and jerks his thumb toward the door. Tomas and Asher take his signal and follow him, offering sympathetic glances at Nathaniel before they disappear outside.

I bite the inside of my mouth again. "What did the Boquans do to him to make him so hostile?" I ask.

A flash of pity flares in Nathaniel's eyes. Hesitant at first, eventually his lips part. "Micah had a twin brother, Marcus. The two were inseparable from birth; they did everything together, even joining the army. They both were stationed under my command from their twentieth year." He pauses and sighs. "They were good infiltrators. The best. But not perfect."

Lukas is riveted to his father; he's apparently hearing this story for the first time. "What happened?" he asks. He's discovering a lot of secrets today, as am I.

"They volunteered for a mission I never did feel good about, but one that had to be done," Nathaniel begins. "They snuck into a Boquan bunker, extracted what we needed, and snuck back out again. They thought they'd made it out clear when the alarms sounded."

I flinch at the familiar tightening in my throat. Nathaniel looks away. "They were discovered, and Marcus was killed in the fight. Micah and the rest of the team made it out alive, but he never was the same after that. Tomas and Asher are his brothers now."

"So Micah lost his twin." I shake my head. "I can't imagine two of them."

Nathaniel gives a grim smile. "Actually, there were three. Micah and Marcus were part of a set of triplets. The youngest baby died with his mother at birth."

My eyes widen. Three?

Nathaniel rubs the back of his neck. "I've never seen siblings so close, even for twins," he says. "Marcus lost his life at Boquan hands, and in Micah's mind, all of them are guilty for it."

I gaze at the door through which Micah disappeared. "He needs his brains kicked in."

Nathaniel sighs as if a weight is pressing down on him. "What he needs is something we can't give him. Only Elorai can, if Micah would let Him."

I cock my head, but he turns to his son. "Lukas, take that broken touchpad over to Helen. If there was any data on there not backed up to Central, she needs to get it for us. I'll meet you at the house shortly."

Lukas looks to me as though waiting for confirmation. I peer at him, and he glances back at his father before grabbing the broken device and disappearing through the door.

As soon as he's gone, I face Nathaniel, who sighs heavily and steps closer to me. "I want you to leave him here," he says.

My eyebrows arch upwards. "What for? He has as much right to find his mother as I do to find my father."

His hands slide into his pockets, his blue eyes piercing. "I've already lost his mother and his sister. I will not lose him as well."

"And what about your other son?" I ask, stepping around him.

At my mention of another son, Nathaniel seems momentarily

surprised. "Jakob is out of my reach. I could never call him away from his duties like that."

"And how is Lukas any different?" I snap.

"Lukas is still under my authority. He's only eighteen, two whole years from coming of age. He's reckless and naive, and not trained for any sort of combat. I'll protect him as long as I can, whether he likes it or not."

I snort. "You've done a great job of that so far. He stole your information, took off, and nearly got himself killed in Boqua."

"Exactly!" Nathaniel steps forward again. "If he goes with you, he'll die."

I fold my arms, anger bubbling beneath the surface of my skin. "You have no idea what happened after I found him." He tilts his head, and I grit my teeth. "Lukas isn't helpless. And he's not alone."

He swallows, pain reflecting in his eyes. "You can't protect him forever."

"Neither can you." I push past him toward the door. I turn back to him with my hand on the knob. "I'm leaving as soon as I can, and I won't stop Lukas if he decides to come with me."

I pull open the door, but I pause when Nathaniel calls out. "You're right." I look back. His face is broken, heavy lines pressed deep into his skin. Tears hide in his eyes, the sheen brightening the blue. "I couldn't protect him. I let him and the rest of my family slip away right under my nose."

My hand slides from the doorknob. I open my mouth, prepared to ask him what happened, when a startled cry erupts from one of the computer techs at his station. He jumps to his feet, watching the holo-screen in front of him with frozen horror.

"Sir!" he shouts, his eyes still on the screen. Nathaniel rushes to his side, peering over the man's shoulder.

"What is it?"

"Incoming, sir," the tech breathes, pointing at a series of quickly moving dots converging on a single point I have to assume is Dekkan.

"How many? How soon?" Nathaniel demands, swiping his finger across the holo-screen.

The tech's fingers fly across his keyboard. Sweat breaks out on his forehead, and my heartbeat quickens. They don't have to tell me who is coming.

The tech stops his typing and slowly shakes his head, his jaw falling open as his face crinkles with confusion. "I . . . I don't understand." The confusion is soon replaced with sheer terror. "How did we not pick it up?"

His fingers fly again, a drop of sweat sliding down his temple. Nathaniel's face has gone ghost-white as he leans back from the screen.

"Sir, they're nearly on us!" the tech cries.

Panic begins its icy race through my body, even before their eyes all train on me. Every single one of them is glaring at me with an unhidden accusation.

Nathaniel pushes back from the table and marches straight for me, his features stern and tight. "Paul, start the emergency alarms, and keep your eyes on that screen! Everybody else, get to the main streets and start getting our people to the safe houses."

Confident nods around the room. They all look to him for leadership, and they trust him to give them the orders they need to survive. Paul turns to the keyboard and taps at it. An earsplitting wail erupts from the speakers mounted on the walls, loud enough to make me jump. People leap from their chairs, the sound jolting them into action. They rush past me like river water flowing around a boulder and disappear through the door.

Nathaniel grabs my arm with one hand and pulls me toward the door. He leans in so close that I can feel his breath on my skin. "Find Lukas," he says, his voice grave. "Take him and get out of here."

I pull from his grasp. "You want me to take him?"

He nods impatiently. "The Boquans have identified this town. How they did it isn't important right now, but he's better off with you than he is here." He grips both of my arms in a strong grasp. "You have to find

Matthew. You've got to stop Gallander from completing that serum."

A loud explosion cuts through the air, and the building groans and shakes with the force. Nathaniel and I glance at each other and run for the stairs, bursting out the front door and onto the street.

Into utter chaos.

People running and screaming, children crying. Arms flailing, legs pumping. And down the street, the familiar flapping of dark fabric. Soldiers marching in coordinated lines. Pounding black boots, weapons lifted, eyes menacing. It's too late.

Nathaniel is frozen in shock. "How . . . "

But at the front of the line, one face stands out from all the others. A sinister grin, teeth gleaming in the sun. His glare sweeps across the street like blades of grass in the wind, and I duck with Nathaniel into an alley before they can land on me.

Gallander.

"He's here," I hiss, panic and rage mixing together in one ball of emotion inside my head. He's here, he's found me.

Nathaniel grabs my shoulder. "The house. Lukas is at the house!" he says. "Go get him, now!"

He gives me one last hard look before he rushes into the fray, shouting orders I can't make out and pointing in different directions. Even if I manage to get Lukas and get out of here, I have no idea where I'm going. He never told me where to find the rebels.

I set my jaw and peek out from behind a building, breathing heavily. I won't have to worry about finding anybody if I don't get out of here. The soldiers haven't opened fire yet, but they could at any moment. My eyebrows pinch together. What are they waiting for?

I swallow a hard lump in my throat and sprint for the alley, skirting around side streets until I make it to Nathaniel's house. In through the back door. Past the kitchen, into the living room. I find Lukas poised at the front door, a fireplace poker in one hand, raised and ready to swing.

I lurch forward and grab his shirt before he can run out the door. I yank him backward into the house. The poker drops from his hand

and clatters to the floor.

"W-wait!" he shrieks, craning his neck and looking over my shoulder as he pulls against my hold. "My dad!"

I slam the door shut. "There's no time," I tell him, still shoving him further into the house. He thrashes in my grasp, harmlessly slapping against my torso.

"Dad!" he screams as fists pound at the door. I hiss at him to shut up and force him toward the back door before they surround the house. I grip his arm and throw him forward, weaving through the rooms. I don't hesitate as I fling the door open, sending Lukas tumbling down the steps to the grass below.

I yank him to his feet. "Come on! If they find us here, we're dead!"

"My dad! They'll kill my dad!" he protests, lunging for the door. I hold him back with a strong grip.

"He'll have to fend for himself!" I growl. What will Gallander do to the leader of this place? A shudder rips through me that I ignore. "Right now, we've gotta move!"

I whirl Lukas around and push him forward again. He cooperates as we dart away from the house, picking up speed and aiming for the tree line beyond. Screams of terrified people reach my ears in muffled cries, pulling me into countless memories. Someone has ignited a shed in a neighbor's backyard, the timbers creaking under the strain. People file out of their homes at gunpoint, hands-on-heads while soldiers bark orders. One takes his weapon and strikes a woman across the back with it. She cries out and nearly falls, catching herself before she loses her balance.

There's no time for them. Right after the thought crosses my mind, one of the soldiers lifts his head and spots us from across the yard.

"Move, move now!" I scream at Lukas as the soldier lifts his weapon. The tree line is too far away; we'll never make it. Lukas pales, and I shove him toward the fence that separates Nathaniel's yard from his neighbor's. The soldier screams at us to halt, but we've reached the fence, and I grab the top and vault over it.

My feet have barely hit the ground when something black and heavy plows into my face, stars flashing behind my eyes as I careen toward the dirt.

THIRTY-TWO

They must have thought it funny. I could imag-ine them looking into my file, realizing who I was, and letting out amused chuckles. A Lucian trained to kill other Lucians without a second thought.

But now what was I?

"Get moving!" I prodded the man forward with the barrel of my gun. My words were forced and hollow, and the man turned to me with hopeless eyes. Accusation tearing through me like a bullet, I looked away, prodding him again to keep up with the others.

"How many is that altogether?" I called ahead, joining with the rest of my squadron as they herded the refugees into the clearing. We were on a remote mission to the border, and we'd traced a whole pack of them to an area called Crosswoods. We'd come upon them crouching in the brush like terrified pigeons ready for flight.

Fox trained his gun on the cowering group in front of him. His pointed chin and narrow eyes matched perfectly with the fire-red of his hair that gave him his name. "Thirteen," he shouted, answering me. "Pathetic little bunch, if you ask me."

I sized up their looks and found I couldn't hold their anguished gazes for long. Most were young men, probably only a few years older than I. A few were women, and one was a child, maybe seven or eight years old. She kept her eyes on the ground, clinging to a man's filthy T-shirt as he kneeled beside her.

The rest of my squadron joined us in the clearing, hoisting their guns. I could tell they were itching for blood. I swallowed. A week ago, I would have been itching right along with them. But today . . .

All I could see was my file. The words inscribed there. My parents,

Lucians. Did they perhaps know any of these people? Could I even be related to one of them?

The girl sniffed and rubbed her dirt-streaked face. We had destroyed her village. We had blamed it on others. We had taken her family's livelihood from her. All she had left was the young man holding a protective arm around her, looking up in defiance at us.

Poison ran in my veins.

Link stepped forward. "Orders said no witnesses, Fiver."

My hands quivered. I tightened my grip on my gun to steady them, hoping no one would notice. Fox shrugged. "Well, if you won't take the first bite . . . " He leaned forward and gripped one of the men by his collar, hauling him to his feet. The others cried in protest, but he swung his gun at them in warning.

"Shut up, all of you!" he yelled. The man tugged weakly in his grasp, but Fox only grinned and pulled him closer. He adjusted his grip and wrapped his fingers around the man's neck before he squeezed. I grimaced, my eyes meeting Link's questioning stare. I shook my head and turned away.

Fox let his rifle swing at his side and reached for his handgun. "Before we get started, is there anything you'd like to tell us?" The man in his grip gagged, trying to pull in air through his strangled throat. Fox grit his teeth and shoved the barrel against his temple. "Like which one of you Lucian dogs was in charge of the raids that killed half the people in a dozen of our towns?"

The man's face morphed into shock. "That . . . " he spluttered, "that wasn't us."

"The hell it wasn't!" Fox screamed, shaking him. I flinched at the wrath he held. Of all the soldiers under my command, he was the most brutal. The most ruthless. "Thousands of our people died, and what did we ever do to you to deserve it?" The man gasped for air. Fox pulled him higher, his grip tightening. "Why did your people attack us?"

The man's eyes rolled back in his head. "Lucians . . . never . . . attacked anybody."

Fox grit his teeth. With a furious cry, he threw the man down, pulling up his rifle once more. "Then we have nothing more to talk about."

He aimed, finger on the trigger, waiting. Waiting for my signal. For my authorization. I stood frozen, examining all their faces, seeing the Lucians for the first time as actual people, not animals. I looked at Fox, at his hate-filled eyes and clenched teeth. We were the animals. We even named each other after them.

He glanced at me, his impatience turning into suspicion. I stepped forward and opened my mouth. He took it as the beginning of my command and opened fire. The others did as well. Before I could utter a word, I watched in horror as vain cries erupted from the Lucians, bodies slumped over, and red coated the earth.

The little girl was screaming. Fox showed no remorse as he planted a bullet in the back of the young man who was protecting her, his body trying to shield her tiny one. He fell with a cry and landed on top of her, trying to protect her even in his death.

All too soon, the Lucians stopped moving altogether, and Fox finally pulled up his gun. The others followed suit. He grinned at me. "Too fast for ya, huh, Fiver?" He stepped over to the fallen young man and gripped his body in one hand, flinging it off to the side. The little girl cried out, but he pulled her from the ground with little effort, her tears drenching her face as she held out her arms for her protector.

Fox hauled her to her feet and shoved her to her knees, his gun trained on her head. She didn't move, quaking in anguish and fear.

"She's all yours, sir," Fox said. "Get your dose of revenge." His eyes met mine. "For Queen."

The name screamed at me, piercing me like a hot dagger. I looked at the girl's tiny face, tears leaving streaks through the dirt on her cheeks. All I had to do was lift, point, and pull. Something I'd done countless times. Something I couldn't do just this once.

Fox frowned, confused at my hesitation. "What are you waiting for? Waste her already!"

Sweat rolled down my neck, my chest pounding wildly, the word repeating over and over in my mind: *Lucian, Lucian, Lucian.* I could see them all, every life I had knowingly taken, countless numbers of my own people brought down under my command. And today's victims, they hadn't known about the raids; they surely didn't have anything to do with them. The truth was plain in that man's eyes.

My fingers shook, the tremor spreading into my limbs, my head. Fox glowered at me. "Fine. I'll do it myself," he snapped.

"No!" I screamed, but my protest was too late. He pressed the gun to the girl's head and pulled the trigger. The blast echoed for what seemed like hours, her body stiffening like a board before it collapsed.

My heart froze in shock. Fox never wavered as he scrutinized me with anger and distrust. "What the hell is wrong with you, *sir*?"

Hot, boiling rage rose within me. My eyebrows knit together, my teeth grinding against the pounding in my temples. "She was a child, soldier."

Fox's face grew red, matching his hair. "She was a Lucian!" he screamed, pointing at her dead body with his gun. "They all should be wiped off the face of this planet!"

And I couldn't hold back. Anger and fear and pain churned too fast beneath the surface, pressing through the cracks, boiling over, hissing like a thousand snakes. I lifted my gun and pressed the barrel against his chest. For a fraction of a second, I watched Fox's eyes widen in disbelief before I pulled the trigger.

The sound of the blast echoed away, and silence took its place. His body hung motionless for an instant before it tumbled to the earth, breaking the quiet for a split second. His blood streamed into the ground, mixing with the Lucians' and soaking the grass. My chest heaved, shock sending my pulse racing. Slowly, I lifted my head, the gun hanging limply at my side.

Five pairs of eyes stared at me. Faces I once knew, all alienated in a single moment as the realization sank in. For all of us.

Link was the first to move, the first to break out of the stunned stupor. His face twisted into pure hatred, blazing with disgust. "You . . ."

His voice choked in fury. "What have you *done*?!"

He stepped forward, his hand on his holster. The others did the same, the chain of command now shifted. I was a traitor. I saw it in their eyes, and soon heard it from their lips, the word pounding inside my own mind.

"*Traitor. Traitor. Traitor.*"

THIRTY-THREE

Colors flash in my eyes—greens and browns and the blue of the sky—for just a moment before a snarling face fills my vision. It's followed by the black metal of a gun.

My head screams in pain, spots still floating before me from the blow. I groan, reaching my hand to the wet, bleeding spot at my hairline.

"Well, well, well," the soldier growls down at me, a hint of a grin playing at his lips. My fingers flex as the spots finally fade. "Look who it is."

I glare at him. "What's next then, huh? Gonna gloat a little, rough me up, then put a bullet in my brain?"

He takes a step forward. "Believe me, there's nothing I'd like better. But the Commander wants you alive and in one piece." He waves the gun. "So turn over. Stomach on the ground, now."

Lukas's head appears over the fence, eyes wide as two fists. My surprise comes out as a grunt. What happened to the soldier chasing us? How did he get away from him?

"What's Gallander want with me?" I ask, keeping focused on the soldier in front of me.

"You'll find out soon enough," the soldier says through clenched teeth. He grips his gun tighter. "Now, turn over."

Lukas nods quickly at me, and I slowly slide my legs underneath me and roll onto my stomach. The cold metal of the soldier's gun presses into my shoulder. "One wrong move and you'll regret it."

A hand grabs my arm and pulls it behind my back—then there's a grunt and my arm is released as a heavy weight slumps on top of me. I groan and roll out from underneath the fallen soldier. Lukas stands a meter or two away, glaring at him with a Boquan rifle in his hand.

I lurch to my feet. "Where'd you get that?"

He jerks his head at the fence. "From that soldier chasing us. I ducked behind the house, and he chased me instead of you. When he came by, I jumped out and tackled him."

I raise my eyebrows. "You knocked him out?"

He gives a small, lopsided grin. "Well, actually, he hit his head on a rock when he fell."

I roll my eyes. "Nice. Come on, we've got to get out of here."

We skirt through the backyard to the tree line and disappear inside the forest. Lukas pants heavily, leaning against a tree, cringing at the sky. His hands grip the gun tighter. I think of his pistol, still at the bottom of the ravine in the Wood. He's the last person who should handle a rifle, but I decide to let him keep it. He's earned it.

Tears build in his eyes. "Are they going to kill them all?" he whispers.

I say nothing, drawing breath into my anxious lungs. He looks at me with desperation. "Those soldiers never fired a shot," I say. "They marched those people out instead of opening fire on them inside their homes. Boquan soldiers would have never bothered with that on a simple raid. They were searching for something."

Lukas shoots me a confused look and swallows hard. "What will they do when they find it?" he asks.

I peer downward. "Depends on how mad they get searching for it."

"What if they don't find it?"

I level my gaze at him. He meets my stare, but I push past him further into the trees, flinging aside branches like a tornado ripping through a forest. If Lukas is keeping up, I can't tell, and I almost don't care. My gut has twisted into knots, my stomach squeezed tight.

Link wasn't lying. The rage has spread to soldiers who've never even seen me, and they all are ordered to bring me to Gallander alive. Whatever he's got in mind for me sends a stab of fear through my chest.

I push it away and continue through the trees. It will take nearly a full day to reach the cave, and we need to get as far away from Dekkan as possible. I glance behind me to find Lukas jogging in step, dodging branches and fumbling over logs. I slow down enough to make him feel as though he's keeping up on his own.

Suddenly, I'm very tired of running.

§

The sun is just starting to set when we reach my camp. I dive into the cave, Lukas hot on my heels. "What are you doing?" he asks.

I ignore him, crossing the stone floor to the storage shelves. On my knees, I reach back onto a lower shelf, tugging tools and trinkets out of the way. My arm disappears up to my bicep, fingers searching until they find it lurking in the dust at the back. My hand clamps onto the material and pulls it out, revealing the thick burlap sack I haven't touched in years.

"What's that?" Lukas asks, peering over my shoulder. Gingerly, I unfold the flap and reach into the sack, fingers wrapping around the cool, familiar metal.

Lukas's eyes pop from his head and his mouth drops as I pull the object free. "You've got a *gun*?" he exclaims. "You've had one all this time?"

I ignore him for the moment. I check the magazine and grab the black ammo boxes out of the sack. I remember what it's like to be a soldier, weapon in hand. Death in hand.

Inari hasn't come back, and it worries me. She would have waited for a while where I left her, but eventually she would have made her way here to wait. This is where I always come back, and she knows it. I try to calm myself with the possibility that she's simply out hunting, but the churning of my insides doesn't subside that easily.

Curiously taking in my habitation, Lukas follows me out of the cave. A strange look of awe and nervousness crosses his face with every new thing he sees.

"What do we do now?" he says. "Yosher didn't even know where the second building was. How do we know the rebels will? And how do we know they won't kill us on the spot? We don't even know where they are!"

I ignore his questions and reply with one of my own. "Do you actually know how to shoot a gun?"

He pales. "Yes." His eyes move everywhere but to me, and I sigh. Our asset list does not fill me with overwhelming confidence, but it can't get much worse from here.

"We'll get them out, I promise," I say.

Lukas throws up his hands. "How? We have nothing! A couple of guns and a wanted traitor! How are we supposed to do this?"

I lower my head, lips drawing into a thin line. We'll do it the only way I know how.

"We'll just have to raise an army."

THIRTY-FOUR

MY FOOT CAUGHT ON A TREE ROOT, THE MERCILESS ground coming up to strike me in the face as my balance left me. I groaned, rolling onto my back while gulping in air.

I could hear them in the distance, tromping through the woods, screaming at each other. Screaming at me. Link's voice rose above them all. "You can't hide from us forever, Fiver! We'll find you! We'll kill you! Filthy traitor!"

Panic drove me to my feet, and I kicked up soil and dead leaves as I rose. I shoved branches out of my way, pushing through the trees in a desperate frenzy. A shot flew above me, landing in a tree with a thunk and a spray of wood chips. Hands over my head, I ducked and blinked at the dust raining into my eyes.

Thorns tore at my clothes, whip-thin branches slicing at my face. The soldiers—my own men—were closer, following my trail easily through the dense forest. They let out whoops of triumph; one bullet grazed me as my pursuers tried to shoot and run at the same time.

They were close enough to see me through the trees. Sooner or later one of them would get in a lucky shot, and it would be my blood oozing into the dirt.

For a second, I considered letting them kill me. It probably was no less than I deserved. But the fight instilled in me since I was eight years old didn't leave that easily, and so I plowed on, taking the cuts and the scrapes.

But never in my life had I felt so close to death. I could practically feel their breath ruffling the hairs on the back of my neck. I dared not turn around, fearing I would trip again. A fall now would surely mean my demise.

"He's too fast!" someone shouted.

"He's blazing the trail for us. It'll slow him down."

"Someone put a bullet in his back already!"

I ran. One of them shouted, saying he could see me clearly through the brush, and a rain of bullets came once more, a drenching downpour sending dust and tree branches pelting onto me. I covered my head and ran blindly, dread pressing its weight into my limbs, forcing me to flee even faster. My heart beat loud enough that I was sure they could hear it over their sprays of bullets.

I waited for the lucky bullet to hit its mark. Waited for the pain as it tore through my flesh, seeking out my thumping chest and planting itself there. Waited for my own death to descend upon me.

But it never came. Instead, an explosion rocked the Earth.

The blast tore every thought from my mind. The hail of bullets that had been tearing through the trees now seemed like a light drizzle compared to the flood of debris that filled the air. The force of the grenade's impact flung me high into the air as though I were made of grass. Dirt and leaves and twigs all swirled around me in a furious whirlwind.

I didn't feel myself land. I opened my eyes to a haze of smoke and dust, my body lying like a dropped rag in a pile of dead leaves. My hand slipped from my side and landed in something wet. I looked down, blinking.

Blood. So much blood. Slick on my cheek, matting into my hair. And the ringing. So much ringing in my left ear. I lifted my palm to it as the pain stabbed through the left side of my head.

Blood coated my fingers, sticky and wet. My vision blurred. My ear rang. Why the ringing? I could take the pain pounding through my skull, but why the ringing?

And then it was gone. And there was nothing.

THIRTY-FIVE

MY EYES SWIPE BACK AND FORTH THROUGH THE TREES, on the alert for any flicker of movement. Never has Inari's absence left me so uneasy. Out of habit, I glance down every now and then, but without her warning signals to guide me, I'm left relying on my own limited senses.

One more thing to add to my growing anxiety. I miss her steady pace at my side, the feel of her fur at my fingertips, her calm and reassuring gaze.

I shake my head.

Lukas grabs my arm. His hand flails out in front of us, and I move, taking hold of his collar and yanking him behind a tree beside me. His white face peers up at me in horror. Someone is coming through the trees. Fast.

He looks between me and the trees beyond. They are nearing our position. I lift my gun in two hands, lowering my head and widening my eyes at him. "*Tell me when.*"

He sits for a moment, listening, then gives a quick nod.

I jump out from behind the tree, gun aimed and ready to fire before the person has a chance to even register my presence. I peer down the sights at the startled figure lifting his arms and giving a terrified, angry shout. I freeze.

Micah. Three more figures materialize behind him, their weapons raised, but I've already lowered my gun. I recognize Tomas and Asher, but the woman with them is a face I don't know. She grips a handgun, watching me with sharp blue eyes that tell me she wouldn't hesitate to put a bullet in me.

"What are you doing?" Micah shouts, trying in vain to compose himself into some picture of control.

His question is lost in Lukas's voice. "What's going on? What happened back in town? Is everybody okay?"

Micah glares at him. "You don't know?" Lukas frowns hard. "Once the Boquans finished dragging everybody out of their homes, they started tearing the town apart. Half of it has been reduced to ashes, the other half isn't worth repairing."

Lukas's face fills with horror. "My dad?"

Micah shrugs his shoulders, and my insides clench in dread. "Don't know. The last I saw of him, he ordered me to take Jael and my team and get out." His eyes dart to me. "To find you two."

My eyebrows pinch. "Find us?"

He grits his teeth. "Yeah, and considering our base of operation was being overrun and torn to shreds, I would really like to know why he would tell me to do that."

My lips press together in a hard line. I'd thought I'd escaped Micah's accusing stares, but Nathaniel apparently had other ideas.

Micah shakes his head in disdain. "Who knows what the place looks like now? But there's one person we found for you, Lukas." He twists his head over his shoulder. "Yo! Garrow! Hurry up back there!"

A few seconds later, a tall, blond young man steps through the trees, a hardened expression on his increasingly familiar face.

Lukas's eyes bulge as he leaps forward. "Jakob!"

The young man's features soften at the sight of his brother, accepting the embrace without a hint of embarrassment. "Hey, kid," he murmurs, ruffling Lukas's hair as if he were a child.

"What are you doing here?" the younger asks. "You're supposed to be stationed three towns away!"

"Me and my unit got a week's leave," he replies. "We were on our way back to Dekkan when the raid started." A flare lights in his eyes. "We met up with Micah and his unit just outside of the city, and I decided to come with him. The others in my unit went into Dekkan to see what they could do, but who knows what's happened to them."

He chose his brother over his father. Jakob's gaze links with mine for a moment, his expression unreadable. It hits me that whatever he knows of me has been filtered through Micah, and yet he doesn't seem to hold any hostility toward me. Perhaps Nathaniel isn't the only one who's learned to ignore Micah's stark temper.

The others have lowered their weapons, but they still regard me warily. Did Micah tell them of my Lucian blood?

Asher pushes to the front, his hands still gripped on his gun. "Someone want to tell us what we trekked all the way out here for?" he grunts. "Cause we could have done a lot more in Dekkan, fighting off those soldiers."

"They would've smeared you across the pavement," I say. His eyes, narrow blue flints embedded in his freckled face, meet mine. "Nathaniel sent you out here for something much more important."

The woman named Jael speaks up from behind Micah. "Which is?"

"Oh, don't even bother," Micah tells her. "It's all a load of lunk."

I take a deep breath, then tell them everything I know. Their eyebrows raise when I tell them of my Lucian parents, and I know Micah hadn't told them anything about that part. When I mention Gallander, their eyes narrow as one.

"That freak?" Tomas blurts out. His chocolate eyes burn. "He's the one responsible for this?"

Freak?

"He's a traitor," Micah grunts. "That's all that matters."

"What are you talking about?" My stomach fills with a sick dread that winds up my spine.

Micah sighs. "Remember that experiment Nathaniel told you about? The one they locked away and forgot about?" He pauses, taking a deep breath. "Abraham Gallander was the only test subject who survived it."

Blood falls from my face fast enough to make my head spin. "He can't be," I choke out.

Micah snorts. "Yeah, and neither could you," he says. "He was a Lucian, born and raised. Turned traitor decades ago. Started stealing

Boquan children from their parents and raising his own little army." He spits on the ground.

My mind is reeling. The rumors. If he truly was a part of the Lucian experiment, it *would* make him over two hundred years old. How could that be possible?

"But . . . his age."

Micah nods. "We figure it has something to do with the experiment. We can't get any more details, though."

My shock isn't wearing off. "But wouldn't the Boquans question this? Want to know how he was living so long?"

Micah shrugs. "The man has more power than the Boquan government does. You should know that. And besides, he was giving them the results they wanted, so they probably didn't question it."

"But he's trying the experiment again," I say. "He's got my father prisoner, forcing him to work on it."

Micah rolls his eyes, and the others open theirs wide. We've hit on another detail he apparently left out.

Tomas breaks the silence. "You can't be serious."

"I'm going to stop him," I reply, trying to shove as much confidence onto my face as I can. "But I'll need your help."

"And how do we know we can trust you?" Jael shoots at me. A lock of dark hair sweeps across her eyes, and she stares at me through it. "Maybe you've forgotten what the Boquans have done, but we sure haven't. How do we know you won't slaughter us in our sleep?"

A small voice inside tells me I don't have to do this. I only want my father alive. I only want to see him again, to hear his voice. To show him I'm still his son.

But even if I managed to get him out on my own, the running would never stop. We would do it for the rest of our lives, hunted by Gallander and his soldiers. I don't even know if my father wants anything to do with me, I realize with a jolt. What if he hates me? What if he looks at me and only sees a monster, a Lucian-killing machine?

I search at their faces, and I can't let it continue. Gallander has spent years convincing us to hate each other, but it can stop.

It will stop.

I pull myself straighter. "I've been told nothing but lies my entire life," I tell them. I let my voice fall back into the cadence I used as a Commander to invigorate my soldiers. But now every word is used not as a tool to manipulate, but as honest speech reflecting everything deep inside, everything I had locked away and all but forgotten. "I believed them. All of them. I killed for them. And I was proud of it."

They scrutinize me. A flicker of pain. A prick of worry that they won't accept my words, or worse; that they'll retaliate. But like it or not, I need this group of ragtag soldiers, even if they do hate me.

"You can believe me or not, but know this: Gallander stole my childhood, my freedom, and my family, and he's done it to countless others for who knows how long. It has to stop. But I need help. Soldiers. Trained to fight."

Their eyes pierce deep. I see the doubt in Asher's, the mistrust in Tomas's. Jael's burn with pain, Lukas's with determination. Micah looks at the ground. But it's Jakob who finally steps forward.

"Well then," he says, his voice breaking the long silence. "Guess we've got a job to do."

THIRTY-SIX

I HEARD NOTHING BUT THE POUNDING OF BLOOD IN MY ears. I still felt the echo of their words in my mind. They would hunt me down, no matter how long it took.

I stumbled through the trees, crashing into bushes and low-hanging branches, barely keeping myself upright. Pain ached in my left ear, the agony and loss of hearing setting me off balance. Propelled by sheer panic, I didn't stop running until my foot caught on an upturned root, and I hurled forward, slamming into the forest floor with a painful thud.

Groaning, I let my forehead rest in the dirt, my bloodied hand pressed against my ear. My exhausted body shook, and my thoughts whirled with fears, flashes of dead bodies, and spurts of red. I felt tears prick at the corners of my eyes, and I blinked them away. *"Deep breaths,"* I told myself. I sucked at the air like a fish out of water and listened to the muffled sound of my ragged lungs taking it in.

What was I supposed to do now? I needed a doctor, I needed water. Needed help.

When I looked up again, something about the tree line in the distance seemed oddly familiar. I blinked and clambered to my feet, examining the forest in front of me more closely.

The trees were younger here, the undergrowth not nearly as thick. Smoke rose from chimneys a few miles in the distance. But those trees . . .

I stumbled forward, pushing aside sapling branches and cracking through overgrown grass and weeds until the Wood opened up to the crumbled remains of a house in a clearing. A broken road, cracked and abandoned, was barely visible underneath all the growth that choked it. Leading back into Boquan territory and the nearby town of Gesher, it wound its way toward the scent of the chimney smoke.

But my gaze rested on the house. Burned to the ground, nothing left but charred and rotting wood and broken stacks of brick and stone, but I recognized the shape. I took in what was left of the garden, grown wild and clustered with green. The back yard, where the swing set sat rusted and dented, the poles sagging into the earth, the chains of the swings broken. The trodden path where he used to take me into the Wood was overgrown and barely visible.

What was left of the old house. My old house.

My legs quivered and eventually gave out, sending me to my knees. My parents, my father, my mother. Despite all else, I'd always longed to see them again, and some part of me always believed I would—once Boqua won the war we could all go home. Go back to the places we never talked about and always pretended didn't exist.

My chest ached. It cracked and tore and screamed, and I didn't stop the tears that rained down my cheeks. I trembled with exhaustion and pain, my ear still ringing like a swarm of mosquitoes trapped in my own head. Choking on sobs, I dragged myself underneath the low branches of a nearby pine tree and curled into a ball on the carpet of moss.

That night dragged on, no relief from the memories. They haunted me in nightmares, leaving me quaking in the darkness, begging for the light of the rising sun that never seemed to come. I hovered around sleep, pain keeping me awake while exhaustion pulled me under. By the time the morning came, I had wrapped both arms over my eyes and pulled my body into itself as far as I could.

They flew open at the feel of warm breath on my skin.

Jerking up, I slid backward. My bleary vision cleared, and I finally made out the fur and pointed ears of a dog. It looked at me with dark brown eyes that never left mine, a floppy tongue hanging from its mouth.

I stared as the dog sniffed at my feet, then turned away and trotted a meter or two ahead, sniffing the ground. Five small pups trailed after her. A collar hung around the dog's neck, a metal tag swinging from the silver ring attached to it. A household pet wandering away from her home with her pups in tow.

I realized with a jolt how close I was to Gesher. My family had enjoyed living beyond the outskirts in the fresh air and the trees, but the house was still close enough to the town for someone to find me here.

Brushing pine needles from my clothes, I pushed myself to my feet. The dog circled the old house, nose inspecting the destroyed structure. Her pups followed her with energetic leaps, nipping at each other's ears and tails.

A sharp whine cut through the air, muffled in my left ear. My hand instantly reached up to tug at it, while my gaze moved to the side where, out of the trees, another pup struggled and limped into the clearing. Blood dripping down one of its front legs stained its black fur. The pup let out another painful yip and collapsed, the tiny body heaving for breath.

I frowned, watching as its mother went about her business as if her injured pup didn't exist. Inching forward, I approached the exhausted dog, its bleary eyes barely noticing me.

I sank to my knees, looking at the swollen paw and long angry gash across its front leg. I reached out and touched the top of its head. It barely moved in response, its pain-filled eyes looking up at me. Blood dripped into the dirt.

I turned to the five pups, the mother moving further into the trees with her litter trotting along behind her. The pup at my feet let out an agonized wail and tried to follow, but its legs refused to take another step, and it collapsed again. Fallen, it let out a defeated huff.

It wasn't my problem. It was only a runt, barely worth the walk over to it. It couldn't possibly begin to make up for anything.

Its body trembled, its head sagging to one side, its leg continued to bleed. I clenched my jaw and reached inside my pocket for a handkerchief.

No more blood would be spilled today. I cleaned the wound as best

I could, wrapping it in the handkerchief to stop the bleeding. With one last glance at the mother as she disappeared into the trees, I bent and scooped the tiny pup into my arms, cradling it gently in my hands as I carried it deep into the Wood.

THIRTY-SEVEN

"SEVEN PEOPLE DOESN'T MAKE MUCH OF AN ARMY." Lukas turns and faces me. "If we even get that many of them to agree to come."

The others have huddled around each other, arguing over whether to trust me. From what I can read from their lips and body language, Jakob and Jael have deemed me trustworthy enough, with Micah, Tomas, and Asher giving most of the arguments against. Nothing I didn't expect.

I shrug. "It's five more than we had before."

"You don't even know him!" Micah shouts over my voice. "None of us do! How can you say you trust him?"

"He's a Lucian, isn't he?" Jakob says.

"That's not enough!" Micah replies, tightening his grip on his rifle. "He was raised as a Boquan."

"But you heard him!" Jakob throws a hand in my direction. "Imagine if it were you, finding out you'd been killing your own people all those years."

Micah growls.

"They must think you're totally deaf or something," Lukas says with a smirk. I find myself returning his lopsided grin. Seeing my response, he leans forward. "So how bad is it, really? Your hearing, I mean."

I instinctively raise my hand to my left ear. "Almost completely gone on this side. Some loss in the right one."

"What happened?"

I hesitate before answering him. I lower my hand. "A grenade went off too close."

His eyes widen. "Wow. Guess you're lucky to be alive."

Fiddling with the strap of my holster, I reply, "Yeah, I guess you could say that."

He takes a big breath. "So what's the plan?" he asks, shifting closer to me.

"The plan is: you do as I say," Micah's voice booms. Lukas jumps, then scowls at him as he marches closer, his company in tow.

"I'm going with Fiver," Lukas says, glaring at him. "You can't tell me what to do."

"Fine." Micah doesn't even glance at him. "You two can walk around in circles together in this forest forever for all I care, but if you want to get your people out and stop Gallander, you're gonna have to take orders from me."

I cock my head, trying to figure out what he means, and he meets my eye, one hand propped on the rifle he's slung over his stiff shoulder. Realization hits me, and I know exactly what Micah's going to say before he says it: "I know how to find the rebels," he announces.

I press my lips together. Micah's glare bores into me, and I try not to look at the grim stares of those behind him. His voice takes on a sharp and angry warning.

"So. This is what's gonna go down: we're gonna find out what we can from the rebels, stop Gallander, and get Lukas's mom and your dad out if we can. And we're gonna *allow* you to come with us." I square my jaw, but he's not finished. "You'll be under my command, and you'll do what I say. If you can't live with that, then I'll shoot you like the dog you are."

Micah looks away without waiting for the response burning at the back of my throat. "Alright, we're moving out!" He leads his people into the trees without another word.

Lukas turns to me with a gaze that seems to ask what my plan is now that Micah has taken complete control. I shake my head, and he gives a shrug. He jogs away to catch up with the others.

I swallow my anger and trudge along behind, forcing away thoughts of Micah's face with my fist in it. I opt instead to think of my father, alive. Free.

§

We travel in silence for a long while, and eventually, Jakob lags back to where his steps match up with mine. I wait for him to spill out whatever is on the tip of his tongue, but he says nothing for a long time, watching his feet.

"Lukas idolizes you." His voice surprises me. He's placed himself at my right side and leans closer to my good ear. I lift an eyebrow in his direction. He nods at the ground. "I think he felt like he had his older brother back."

A twinge inside me turns my head away. I nearly killed the kid. Twice. Jakob has no idea of the danger his brother was in with me.

"I don't think I would have made a good older brother," I reply, a sour tinge in my voice.

"Better than me, probably," Jakob says. "I took off for the army the first chance I got. And I abandoned Lukas and ran right back to my battalion when Eden died, and it nearly tore him apart."

"Eden. Your sister, right?"

He nods and kicks at a bush, sending leaves floating to the forest floor. "It was just after our mom left for Boqua. Lukas forgot to pick Eden up from school, so she took a public transport. A hovercab slammed into the side of it minutes after she got on."

My throat constricts. The guilt living in Lukas's eyes was much heavier than I'd realized. The mask he'd worn since I'd first met him was slowly falling away from the sheer weight it pressed onto him.

"It wasn't really his fault, it was mine," Jakob says, still watching his feet. "Mom asked me to take a few days' leave to watch Lukas and Eden. And on the second morning, before we really knew Mom was missing, I . . . I put Lukas in charge of picking Eden up." He pauses, now somehow watching his feet even more attentively. "I should have made sure he remembered."

He looks up at the leaves fluttering in the dwindling sunlight. He bites his lip, grief plain in his eyes. It's in the fine lines around his mouth and across his brow, too. "That was some three months ago," he says, his voice choked. "She hadn't turned twelve yet. Lukas had planned a surprise party for her and everything. He was even going to let Nathaniel be part of it."

"You call him Nathaniel?"

Jakob gives a grim smile. "Dad was never much of what you'd call a 'family man.'" He whacks a tangle of leaves and vines, pushing through the obstruction.

"So I heard."

He glances at me and nods. "Lukas told you?"

I focus my attention on the swish of my feet as I tread through the Wood. Jakob lets the silence linger for a few more strides.

"He hates our father," Jacob says too softly; I barely hear him above the muffle in my ears. "I did too, for a while."

Lukas had screamed for his father when the Boquans attacked. I duck a low branch. "What made you stop?"

"I grew up," he replies. "No matter what Dad did, he was still my family. So I left home, found out what was so important to him out in the rest of the world. Why he did what he did."

Watching his face, my throat clenches. Would my father feel the same about me? Would he overlook the things in my past? I resist the urge to grip my pendant between my fingers.

"Why was that?"

Jakob shrugs, gazing straight ahead. "He was searching for his brother."

The knot tightens in my throat, winding downward until it squeezes the air from my lungs. I study the ground, taking in the blur of greens and browns. Jakob shifts his rifle to his other shoulder.

"I've never had a cousin before," he says, a smile tugging on his lips. "What are you supposed to do with one? Play brackel ball and wrestle in the mud?"

I don't want to admit that I don't know what brackel ball is, but the corners of my lips pull themselves up, despite the turmoil inside. "I dunno," I reply. "Maybe it's kind of like having a brother." Jacob turns his head and looks me full in the face, but I can't read the expression there.

Micah's voice suddenly breaks our stare. Though I can't make out his words, and I'm too far away to read his lips, I can tell by the way the others swivel their heads toward me that he's made some comment in my direction.

"Don't listen to him," Jakob grumbles. "He's just in a permanent bad mood." He pauses, then continues, "Whether Micah admits it or not, he still needs you for this. You're a good soldier; it's the only reason he let you come. Plus, you know the tactics, how the Boquans think."

Renewed anger bubbles inside. "Of course I know how they think. I'm one of them."

"But you're not with them anymore," Jakob replies, his voice smooth despite the bite in mine. "You're with us."

"Doesn't mean I'm one of you."

He nods. "True. But you could be. If you decided you didn't want to straddle the fence anymore, you could be one of us."

The thought is insane, and I nearly stumble over an exposed root. "What makes you think that's even possible?"

He looks at me with a sort of puzzled expression, as though my words didn't make any sense to him at all. He frowns, lines appearing at his lips.

"We're family."

THIRTY-EIGHT

WE CAMP NEAR THE LUX RIVER. TOO CLOSE TO WHERE the scientists ripped the ground apart for my liking.

"Will you calm down?" Asher brushes past me, throwing his worn pack beside the campfire. He sizes me up and squats in the dirt so he can rifle through his bag. There's just enough sunlight left to see by.

Jakob, flipping twigs into the flames, looks up from feeding the fire. "You do seem a bit nervous."

I narrow my eyes, but I recognize that the tense muscles in my hands and my pointless pacing have given away my state of mind. "We're too close to Boqua," I say, watching the trees sway in the wind.

Micah snorts. "Gee. I thought we were heading somewhere else." I resist the urge to slap his sarcasm right out of him.

Jael walks behind him and playfully smacks the back of his head. "Leave him alone, will you?" Micah lets out a yowl of protest, but the softness in his eyes betrays him. She looks at me, her face blooming into pink shades as she turns away.

I don't want to stay here any longer than I have to, but we all need sleep. We will be in Boqua tomorrow, and we need all the rest we can get before then. From what I can see, Lukas's eyelids seem as though they weigh a hundred pounds, and he struggles to keep them open, his head dipping in exhaustion.

Tomas reaches into his pack and pulls out a small, worn notebook and a pen. Leaning against a tree, he opens to a page and begins scribbling, and he's soon lost in concentration. The others ignore him, apparently having seen him do this on more than one occasion, but I watch, fascinated, as his hand moves across the page. Sharp, hatched lines and smooth, long strokes come together in the perfect way to make the shape of the face, the hair, the nose, the lips.

I find myself moving closer, wanting a better view, until I'm right over Tomas's shoulder, observing him as he puts the finishing touches on her face. A beautiful face. A hint of sorrow in her eyes mixed with the slight downward curve of her full lips. This is a face from memory, not conjured by Tomas's mind, and I can't help but ask.

"Who is she?"

Tomas jerks, his pen making a jagged line in the woman's hair. He slams the notebook shut. "Mind your own business," he grumbles, shoving it back inside his pack as he glares at me.

"Nobody ever drew anything like that in the Barracks," I find myself telling him, even though he hates me like the rest of them. "It's very good."

He scowls at me, but even beneath his brown skin his cheeks flush. "It's nothing," he mutters. "Asher used to tease me about it all the time until—" He cuts himself off and clears his throat. "It's nothing."

Asher and Jakob pull ration packs out of their bags. They toss one to each of us.

"I don't want chicken!" Lukas complains, holding his ration pack out with two fingers.

"Alright, how about boiled turngrap legs?" Asher replies, a gleam in his eye.

Jael grins and shakes her pouch at him. "I'll trade you for some raw mouse meat." Lukas scrunches up his face, and Asher gives him a playful punch in the side. Even Micah joins in the ribbing as he drapes his arm casually over Jael's shoulders. She lets it sit there, even as she spoons her food into her mouth and jokes with the others.

I see their camaraderie; they're as knit together as my squadron and I had been. Normal people, keeping their fear and loss at bay with laughter and the comfort of each other. All they want is to protect their own, just as we had done.

Micah reaches for his rifle. "I'm taking first watch. Tomas and Jael, second. Jakob and Asher take third. And you—" he points at me,

"You're with me."

He turns away, and Lukas calls after him. "What about me?"

Micah barely breaks stride. "Get your rest, kid. Can't have you falling asleep on us in Boqua."

Lukas's face burns red, but he says nothing. The others pull out blankets from their packs and settle down around the fire to sleep. I duck and obediently follow Micah to the edge of the camp, swallowing the sick feeling swimming around in my gut as we move out of sight of the others.

Is Micah keeping an eye on me, or does he have something else in mind? Am I safe alone with him, or is this a setup? He could say I attacked him; he could lift his gun and blow me away, and no one would question him.

But he doesn't even look at me as I come up alongside him, his eyes squinting into the dark of the evening. I watch as his rifle shifts in his arms, but there's no bunching of muscles or twitching in his neck that indicate he's about to swing it around at me. The firelight flickers off his face, and his Adam's apple bobs as he swallows. Perhaps Jakob was right. Perhaps he does think he needs me.

I know I need him.

"Nathaniel told me about your brother." My voice breaks the silence; it's as unnatural to me as breathing underwater.

Micah swipes his hand under his nose and shifts his feet. "And here I thought I'd picked a watch partner who wouldn't talk the whole time."

I ignore his comment. "I wanted to say I'm sorry. Maybe things would have been different if he'd lived."

His jaw muscles tighten. His eyes shrink, his irises even darker in the low light. He presses his lips together and tightens his fingers around his weapon. "You Boquans murdered him."

"I'm not talking about Marcus," I tell him. "I'm talking about the baby."

Surprise glints on his face for a brief moment. How different might things have been if the child hadn't died at birth? If Micah had had someone to turn to after Marcus was killed. Would he have come back from whatever dark place he's hidden himself in?

Micah refuses to speak to me for the rest of the watch, and I'm useless without Inari's warning signals. Being forced to rely on Micah's senses doesn't fill me with any sense of comfort, and I can tell he's noticed my studying him. His eyes slide toward me often, his scowl deepening with each glance.

Two hours later, Tomas and Jael relieve us, wiping sleep from their tired eyes. Micah stomps off to his makeshift bed, and Jael pauses long enough to give me a sympathetic look before Tomas pulls her away.

Lukas sits up as I sit beside him, his blanket sliding down his skinny body. "Fiver?" he mumbles, his hair matted and twisted on his head.

"Go back to sleep," I say, folding my arms over my torso and letting my head rest on the rocky ground.

"Fiver?" he repeats, and I shift.

"What?"

"Here." He tugs off his blanket and holds it out in front of me, a lopsided smile pasted on his face. He waves it a bit when I hesitate, and eventually, I reach up to take the offering.

"Thanks."

His smile grows, and he lies down again and closes his eyes. I watch his chest rise and fall with sleep as I wad the blanket into a ball and tuck it beneath my head. On my back, I stare at the dark sky and the stars that shine through the canopy of trees above. For a moment, I can imagine I'm at my old house, lying on the front lawn with my father beside me. We used to point out constellations or come up with our own and give them silly names like, "Horse With Fat Feet" and "Bunny Has No Tail." On warm summer nights and long into the fall, we would stay out until my mother called us in.

Micah coughs in his bed, and the memory vanishes like breath on a cold morning.

THIRTY-NINE

THE CITY MICAH LEADS US TO IS CALLED MESER, AND it's three or four times the size of Gesher. Here there are more people who could spot us, but there are more hiding places as well. We skirt around some abandoned buildings that have been left to rot on the outskirts, slowly making our way through. We stay with the forest at our side, ready to sprint into it if someone sees us.

Crouching behind a shed in someone's backyard, Micah says, "We have to get deeper in. The rebels don't come out this far."

Taking in every sight they can, my eyes move like bouncing rubber balls. Out here, the earthy smells still permeate the air, but there's the underlying scent of burning oil from further into the city. The buildings here are still a good way apart from each other, but if we were seen, soldiers would be upon us in less than five minutes. In a town like this, a squadron is never too far away, especially as the barbwire-covered building further up the hill must be a prison.

"How do we get close without being spotted?" Jael asks, shifting her weight from one boot to the other. She jerks her thumb at me. "They all know him." Micah glances at her, then slowly brings his asking eyes to me.

"You have to blend in," I answer. All heads swivel to me, surprised to hear my voice. "You should be able to without much trouble." I instantly think of Lukas's near panic at the sight of the patrol in Gesher. I hope the others do better under pressure. "But if any of you are seen with me, the whole thing is over. They'll take you in as accomplices before they even guess you're Lucians."

"Oh, no you don't." Micah shakes his head. "I'm not letting you out of my sight, not even if—"

The rest of his response is consumed by the whirring of a hovercab engine, the dark shape descending from the sky like a thick black cloud. Micah shouts and dives for cover; the others follow suit.

I watch from behind a huge flowerpot as the hovercab slowly begins landing outside of the barbed wire of the prison, its hull gleaming in the sun. It's a transport hovercab, similar to the one that Micah took me to Dekkan in; it's large and meant for carrying supplies, or in some cases, prisoners. The landing pads descend, and the hovercab settles down on them like a cat tucking its paws beneath itself.

The driver steps out from the vehicle and waves at someone up ahead. I follow his signals and see a handful of soldiers marching in a double line from the prison toward the hovercab. A cowed, shackled man is in between each pair.

Micah exchanges a questioning look with me, and I can only shrug my shoulders. These people could be common criminals for all I know. The others try not to let their fear show at the sight of Boquan soldiers, but I can feel it radiating from their wide eyes.

The driver moves to the rear of the hovercab, where he opens the hatch and lets it slide over the body of the vehicle. He shoulders a rifle and moves to meet the other soldiers with their six prisoners. Hands behind their backs, each one keeps their head low as the soldiers haul them toward the open hatch and lift them inside one by one.

The last man in the line shakes his shoulders away from the soldiers' hands, and they shove him from behind. He stumbles to the concrete with a cry, nothing to break his fall but his face. His shoulders slump inside his tattered black shirt, but he lifts his head defiantly at them.

At the sight of his dirty, bloodied face, my insides drop, my breath catching in my lungs. Shock drowns out any thought of how he wound up here in the first place.

It's Bone.

The surprise hits me like a punch in the gut. I can only imagine what he did to deserve such treatment. One of the soldiers barks something at him and swings his fist into Bone's face. The blow knocks him backward, a spray of blood from his nose coating the ground. His features twist with pain, his arms straining at the cuffs.

And suddenly blood is rushing in my ears, my heart pounding out a flood so hard it bursts beneath my skin, veins protruding like twisted tree roots. My fingernails cut into my palms, my body wracked with furious tremors.

A hand lands on my arm. "You okay?" Jakob's voice whispers in my ear. "Do you know him?"

It's only after hearing his voice that I realize I've leaped from my hiding place. My feet move, nimble and quiet as ever, and I'm dashing across the street, dodging parked hovercabs until I'm right behind the soldier who punched Bone.

Micah shouts an alarm, but not before I've wrapped my arms around the soldier's neck, prepared to jerk his head to the side until I hear the telltale crack, until he falls lifeless at my feet.

But my hands don't move. The soldier freezes in my grasp, and I can feel the blood pulsing through his veins, pushing faster with every second his dread rises. But the other soldiers don't move either, their faces filled with fear, and I frown. My hesitation should have meant my death. They know how to deal with situations like this. But they do nothing.

So I change my mind: I pull his head down as I fling my knee up. The force crunches into the bridge of his nose hard enough to knock him unconscious. I release my hold on him and let him tumble to the concrete with a groan.

Now the others move. Two of them, all shouting and pulling up weapons, but I grip the barrel of the closest rifle, ripping it from the soldier's hands and swinging it like a bat at his head.

He crumples into a heap, but the second soldier steals my idea and slams the butt of his rifle into my back. Pain explodes through me, and the force of his blow sends me to my knees. He stands over me, his face a mixture of rage and excitement, his gun raised, barrel aimed at my face.

A body slams into his torso just as he starts to step closer, a startled huff escaping him as his attacker takes him down. An angry cry, a series of thumps, and the soldier goes limp beneath Micah's tall frame.

He turns to me, his chest heaving, his knuckles scraped raw from the punches to the soldier's head. I suck air into my starving lungs, the pounding in my temples slowly subsiding. The first soldier lays flat on the ground, not moving; Jakob and Jael train their guns on him.

Micah pushes off the second soldier. He looks at me with contempt and shakes his head. "What are you trying to do? Get yourself killed?"

I have no answer, instead peering over to where Bone crouches. He's staring at me as though seeing a ghost.

Micah shakes his head again. "Idiot."

"Guys, we've got company," Jael warns, looking toward the prison. I follow her gaze, and a stream of soldiers flows from the jail's doors. My insides shrink at the loud cracks of gunfire, and my mind screams out my stupidity. Of course the other soldiers would see us. Of course they would try to stop us.

"Move, move, move!" Micah shouts as he grabs Jael's arm and pulls her away from the hovercab.

"Wait!" I shout, flinging my hands up to stop him.

"So help me, if you don't get out of my way—"

"—The hovercab!" I shout over his threat. "We'll never outrun them on foot if they chase us from the air."

He pauses. A split-second decision. "Asher! Take the controls! Jakob! Get those people out of the back, now!"

The others jump into action, helping to drag the prisoners out of the hovercab as bullets start slamming into its side. We duck, but Micah is still shouting as he grabs a prisoner by the collar and throws him into the street. Red explodes from the man's chest, and he groans and tumbles to his side, spasming on the hard pavement. The other prisoners let out cries of fear, or they simply shove one another out of their way with their shoulders as they run from the hovercab.

"Come on," I hiss at Bone, helping him to his feet. I push him toward the open hatch as the vehicle begins to hover. The others are already aboard, Asher at the helm.

"What are you doing?" Micah shouts at me, glaring at Bone. I ignore him and shove Bone forward into the belly of the hovercab. Asher shouts we have no more time, and the door starts to slide shut.

Bone collapses inside. Sparks fly at the ping of bullets hitting the side of the hovercab. I flinch, my feet still on the concrete. The hovercab lifts into the air, the floor as high as my elbows. I grapple for a hold on the inside of the vehicle, but my fingers can't find a grip. Lukas screams my name. A jolting fear races through me: they might leave me here. Leave me to the soldiers, their bullets, and Gallander and his sick experiments.

Jakob lurches forward, and his hands take hold of my wrists firmly just as my feet leave the ground. My shoulders burn from the weight of my dangling body, but Jakob doesn't let go. Jael takes hold of one of my arms, and together the two tug me into the belly of the hovercab just as the door slides shut.

The three of us collapse inside, heaving for breath.

Micah stares at us with a grim face. "Well, that was dramatic," he grumbles.

"It's about to get a lot worse," Asher replies from the driver's seat. He punches several keys and flips the autopilot switch. He slides down the seat, fiddling with a hatch built into the side of the vehicle.

"What are you doing?" Micah asks him. Asher grunts, pulling off the square of metal. Underneath is a series of colored wires and small black boxes crisscrossing like a spider web inside a dark cavern.

"As long as our navigation system is active, they can track us in the sky or on the ground," he says, pulling at a wire. "I can disable it and make us invisible to them. But . . . " He yanks on one wire entangled with three others until it snaps. "We won't be able to see where they are, either. Or where we're going."

Micah purses his lips. "So we'll be flying blind."

Asher nods.

"Great." Micah runs his hand through his hair. He looks up and seems to remember his extra passenger. "What's he doing here?"

I ignore him and move closer to Bone. "Are you alright?" His face, streaked with dirt and blood, is full of shock and something else I can't pinpoint. Almost embarrassment.

"Fiver?" he asks. Bone swallows and lets his mouth drop open, looking from one strange face to another. "What are you doing here?"

I ignore him and nod at Micah. "Do you have anything to get these cuffs off?"

He scoffs. "You're joking. Who is this guy?"

"Who are you?" Bone growls. Micah shoots a glare at him, crossing his arms.

"His name is Bone," I say. "I knew him. Back in the Barracks."

Micah snorts. "Just what we need, another Boquan. You have any idea why he was in that prison? He could be a serial killer for all we know."

"He's got information we need," I say. "You may know where the rebels generally hang out, but he can give us names, addresses, spot-accurate locations."

That gets Micah's attention. Bone trains his bewildered face on me, and I stare at him until he pulls his eyes away.

Micah clamps his hand on Bone's shoulder and shakes him a little."This guy knows more about the rebels than Nathaniel does?"

"Yes. He was one of my Aces back at the base. He knew everything there was to know about every kid who came in. Including their families."

"What has that got to do with it?" Micah's hand moves up to Bone's neck, gripping his collar.

"Not all of those kids believed the lies," I reply, staring hard at him. "Some of them didn't agree with anything we were taught, and they even died because of it. Where do you think they got all those ideas?"

Micah scowls at Bone, who scowls back. Slowly, he releases his stiff hold on Bone's collar, shoving him backward until he hits the wall. "Fine. What do you know?"

Bone sizes him up, his tongue rubbing against his teeth. "Can't think too well with these cuffs on."

Micah snarls. But Bone's eyes narrow in contempt, and Micah whirls around, grabbing his pack and shoving his hand inside one of the outer pockets. He pulls out a device made of several pieces of long, thin metal folded into a small handle. He unfolds one of the pieces and moves in behind Bone, shoving him forward while he fiddles with the lock on the cuffs.

Bone's hands come to the front of his body, and he rubs his bruised and raw wrists. Micah grunts and tosses the cuffs to the floor. He folds his device back together and shoves it into his pack.

"Well?" demands Micah. "Start talking."

Bone refuses to look at him and straightens the collar of his tattered shirt before saying anything. "How do I know you won't take what I say and kill me?"

Micah reddens with anger. "I could kill you now."

The corners of Bone's lips curve up slightly. He eyes Micah, evaluating him. Calculating, even now, after having more or less exchanged one captor for another. "I don't think you will," he counters. "You want this information as bad as Fiver does. You wouldn't throw it away."

Micah sizes Bone up for himself. Eventually, he leans back and sighs. "Fine. What do you want?"

Bone's features relax into a satisfied smirk. "Now we're talking."

"Spit it out!" Micah demands.

Bone's face hardens once again. "First of all, you don't touch me. Ever. Change your mind about that later, and you'll never breathe again." Micah's eye twitches as he listens. "Second, you do as I say. When I tell you to duck, you'll bury your head in the ground so far that you'll taste nothing but dirt for a week. When I tell you to stay put, you'll be a human statue. When I tell you to run . . . you'll fly."

Micah glances at me, but I keep quiet. He finally shakes his head and turns away. "Whatever. Deal."

In the space of thirty seconds, Bone has taken over the leadership of our group. "Now, what in the name of Elorai are you doing?" he asks me.

I look him full in the face. "I need to find Gallander."

"Gallander?" Bone goes pale. "What for?"

"You know he hates the Lucians more than anyone ever could," I say. "He's got a plan to wipe them out, and it's not through the old-fashioned ways he's been trying for decades. We've got to stop him."

Doubt flickers in Bone's eyes, and I beg him with mine not to press me. But the expression he replies with tells me I have to give him more.

"He's got my father," I tell him. "He's making him work on his serum project."

Bone's face twists in a strange sort of way. The corners of his lips retreat toward his chin, and his eyebrows touch in the center of his forehead. "You don't want to find Gallander," he says under his breath. "If you do, you'll wish you never laid eyes on him."

I lean forward. "Please, Bone. Tell me what you know."

He presses his lips together and eventually nods. "What do you want?"

"You saw into everybody's records on base. You knew their names, their parents' names, their birthplaces, everything."

"So?"

"I need you to remember. I need all the information you have on someone that used to be at the base."

He looks at me with a miserable glare. "Who?"

I swallow.

"Queen."

FORTY

BONE STARES AT ME FOR HALF A MINUTE BEFORE HE speaks."Fiver, you—" He gulps. "What do you need that for?"

I ignore his sympathetic look and the tearing open of a wound in my chest. This wasn't supposed to be easy, but he isn't helping anything.

"I knew her, Bone. Better than anyone on the base. If anyone had a family that was against the government, she did. And they couldn't have been the only ones."

Bone glues his eyes to the floor. "You better know what you're doing," he says, his voice so soft I can barely hear him. "Because what you're talking about doing is not going to end without blood."

I frown at him. "If someone you cared about was in danger, is there anything you wouldn't do to save them?"

His face darkens, a hint of agony reflecting in his eyes. His lips press together into a thin line. "Nothing." His back straightens, despite the obvious pain in his muscles.

I wait for a second before I nod. "Then tell me what you know."

He sucks in a breath, holds it, and releases it in one long exhale. "It's not a pretty picture," he says. "They've been cracking down on the rebels hard, and the rebels have gotten more and more cautious."

"So they'll be hard to find," Micah snorts. "We expected that already."

Bone flicks his eyes to him. "They've buried themselves so deep they're barely any threat to Gallander anymore. But they're trigger-happy. Even if Gallander doesn't find you and kill you, the rebels might, out of fear of being discovered."

"They still have to have some information. Contacts, spies, something," I say.

Bone shrugs. "Last I heard, someone was trying to stir them up, get them to pull their heads out of their shells and strike. But I've been out of the loop for a while." He holds up his bruised wrists as he speaks.

Micah squints at me. "Before we get too far in this whole 'trusting Boquans' adventure, does someone want to ask this guy what he was doing in prison? In a *Boquan* prison?"

"Does it matter?" I grumble.

"As a matter of fact, it does," Micah says, his teeth glaring. "We're about to put our lives in this guy's hands, and even if you two were best buds back in your Barracks, that doesn't mean he won't turn on us the first opportunity he gets."

I press my teeth together and look at the others, but they all avoid eye contact in silent agreement with Micah. I slide my jaw to the right and face Bone. "Fine. Tell us why you were locked up."

Bone's features twist into a terrible mix of sorrow and hate. He rubs at his wrists and licks his lips, the answer clearly accompanied by painful memories. What did they do to him in that place?

"I betrayed them," he says finally. His bleary eyes lock onto me. "Just like you did. But they caught me."

I blink. "Then why are you alive? There's no prison for traitors."

He lifts his shoulders. "I dunno, man. For some reason, they wanted me alive. Gallander wanted me alive."

There is more in his eyes. He's not telling me everything, but I'm distracted by the fact that Gallander wants me alive as well.

His answer isn't enough for Micah. "What did you do?" He glares at Bone as if waiting for him to say something he doesn't like so he can have cause to throw him out of the hovercab.

"I killed a man." He offers no more information as he turns to me. "I remember Queen's parents' address," he says, ignoring the looks the others give him. "But who knows what you'll find there? It could be bullets in your face, or it could be a whole lot of nothing."

"Still, it's the only lead we've got," I say. Micah harrumphs from his seat but doesn't say anything.

"Yeah," Bone says, shaking his head. "And what if Gallander orders one of his raids while we're there? Last time he raided a rebel hideout, he carted off people who weren't even rebels. It doesn't matter to him, they all go to the Ramius Corporation. I've seen it over and over again."

Jakob slides forward in his seat. He reaches a hand inside his jacket and pulls out a folded square of leather. From inside it, he takes a small picture and holds it in front of Bone's face. It's a woman—the same woman who smiled back at me from Nathaniel's desk.

"Did you ever see this lady get taken?" he asks, and I can hear the strain in his voice. "Would have been a couple of months ago, so I don't know if you were . . . " His voice trails away, and he swallows awkwardly.

"In prison?" Bone scoffs, but he squints at the picture. Jakob and Lukas stiffen in hope, leaning forward with pricked ears. Bone shakes his head. "Sorry, kid, never seen her. But if she was taken, I wouldn't hold out too much hope. Awful stuff happens to folks in that place."

I swallow the lump in my throat. Lukas's face falls in disappointment for just a moment before he squares his shoulders.

"If anybody could survive it, she could."

I clutch my father's pendant to my chest. I don't hear Micah approach until he leans over my shoulder and frowns. "What's that?" he asks.

I jump and back away from his stare. "Nothing."

He cocks his chin toward my hand, and I reluctantly open my fingers to reveal the pendant resting in my palm. His frown deepens. "That's the symbol for Elorai."

I nod. "Yes. I know. My father gave it to me."

Something shifts in his eyes. "You've had that this entire time?"

I shake my head. "The Commanders took it from me when they put me in training. Bone got it out of my file for me."

Micah glances at Bone, then brings his gaze to me. There's still a hardness to him, but there are now cracks in Micah's stubborn resolve. "From what I've heard, he was a good man, your father."

I blink, not expecting kind words like that. Micah slides his eyes downward and coughs, scratching his nose. "Now let's go get him out."

FORTY-ONE

BONE DOESN'T HESITATE TO EXERCISE HIS LEADERSHIP, much to Micah's disdain. He takes us down side-streets and alleys, skirting through the city with cautious steps that miraculously keep us from being spotted. He's split us into two groups to remain inconspicuous, and Lukas, occasionally looking back at his brother, crouches by my side behind Bone.

"The Deagan house is just up the street," Bone says in a loud whisper from behind a tall brick building at the edge of an alley. He peers into the street while we crouch behind a couple of trash cans further back. "That's where Queen's parents lived."

"Lived?" Jakob says, shifting his pack straps across his shoulders. Bone made us ditch our weapons in a hollow tree just outside the town, and nobody feels comfortable unarmed, Micah least of all. He'd thrown a fit nearly half an hour long over the matter, but Bone had argued that nothing screamed "Lucian" like a group of rugged people with rifles walking down the street.

"Besides," he'd said, "the less of a threat we appear to be, the less likely the rebels are to kill us out of fear."

"The military pretty much owns Boquan streets!" Micah had shouted back. "There's always a patrol right around the corner, especially in cities this close to the border. What if one of them makes us?"

I didn't like the idea of putting so much faith in something that could fall to pieces in so many different ways any more than Micah did. But my choices had been limited at that point, and Bone had refused to lead us one step closer to the house until we'd ditched every knife and bullet.

Bone looks over his shoulder at us. "I told you, my information is from fourteen or fifteen years ago. Anything could have happened in that time."

"So what's so special about this girl, Queen?" Jakob says. The name falls off his tongue like he can't figure out how it should feel in his mouth.

"Atara Deagan," Bone says, turning to the alley. "But who knows what her parents were, or if they're even alive."

"Atara?" Lukas's eyes twitch in recognition at me. "That's . . ."

I grimace at him, my throat swelling and cutting off my air. Bone peeks back at me, his face guarded. I shake my head. *No, they don't know what I did to her. They won't know.*

"She was the only one I knew for sure who didn't worship the ground Gallander walked on," I say. And I leave it at that.

"So what's the plan?" Jakob asks, scanning the area for any kind of danger that could pop out at us. "Micah and the others should be here by now."

"Don't hate me," Bone says, peering around the wall again.

I level my gaze at him. "What?"

Bone gives a grimace. "I brought you three and sent the others on a wild goose chase."

Jakob and Lukas nearly jump to their feet in shock. "What?"

Bone's grin turns grim. "I know Micah still has a piece on him somewhere, and he won't hesitate to use it if he gets too nervous. I'm not leading him or any other trigger-happy soldiers anywhere near the rebels."

Jakob's eyebrows raise, but he's come to the same conclusion I have and has to agree with the reasoning behind Bone's decision. I give him a reassuring nod.

"The fewer people we have, the better, anyway," I say, thinking how nice it is to have a break from Micah's big mouth. "Although he'll kill you when he finds out."

Bone's lips stretch over his teeth. "I ain't scared of that bully."

Jakob glares at him. "Anything else about your plans you'd like to share with us?"

Bone shrugs. "I think that's about it."

"So what do we do now?" Lukas asks. He swallows nervously.

"Now, nothing," Bone says. "With any luck, the rebels already know we're here, and we won't have to wait too much longer."

"Wait, 'with any luck?'" Jakob asks, holding out a hand. "You *want* them to jump us?"

"Assuming Fiver is correct and Queens's parents are alive and still part of the rebellion, it's better to let them find us than the other way around," Bone replies, sticking his head out of the alley again. "I've been givin' them plenty of views of my face. Where are they?"

I'm beginning to wonder if my entire idea was wrong. I start thinking we're just standing here waiting for a patrol to find us when there's a muffled voice behind me. I turn around to find the barrel of a gun pointed right between my eyes. My blood freezes in my veins at the sight of the man's snarling face, his finger tight around the trigger. Jakob and Lukas already have their hands in the air as two more guns appear from the alley and train on us.

A second look reveals no uniforms on any of them, only civilian clothes. Whoever these people are, they're not Boquan soldiers.

"Don't move," the man behind the first gun warns. His dark eyes flash, but not in recognition of my face, and not in hatred at the sight of me.

In the corner of my peripheral vision, Bone gives a big grin and takes a step to my side, holding his hands together in front of him. "Well, it's about time y'all showed up."

The lead man frowns, not lowering his weapon. "Who are you? What are you doing here?"

"Look, we don't want any trouble, we just want to talk to the rebels," Jakob says, trying not to move and glancing at his brother with a silent command to do the same. Lukas's face has gone bone-white. "We need their help."

The man looks at Jakob's uniform, at the patches on his shoulders. "Lucians," he grunts. His grip tightens around his gun. "We told you people we don't want nothin' to do with your war."

He moves to swing his rifle at Jakob, and I lunge forward. "We only want some information, and we'll be gone!"

"Don't lie to me," the man growls. His lips sag down his scruffy chin, deep wrinkles lining his dark, leathery skin. "You'll only get us killed. You've probably already given us away."

He may kill us right here and now out of anger. Even if someone heard the shots and cared, he could always say he'd captured us but killed us when we tried to escape.

Whatever I say next will decide the man's actions. "Listen," I begin, holding out my hands in a gesture of peace. "I know you've lost your children to Gallander's draft. Even if they survive the war, they may as well be dead. You'll never see them again."

His eyes cut into me, the barrel of the gun only inches away from me. The danger in striking this particular nerve is clear, but it is also the best bet for keeping his attention.

"My name is Joshua Endenbough, and I was one of Gallander's soldiers," I say. I watch the man's face drop, his grip on his gun wavering. "Maybe you didn't trust anything Nathaniel's men said because you didn't think it would help. And maybe it was true then, but I think we have a real chance at this. All I'm asking is for you to hear me out."

He knows who I am. His eyes are agog, his lips trembling. All of a sudden, I'm hit with a wave of worry he might shoot me out of fear. But slowly, the gun moves toward the ground, and he lets out a huff of breath. The two men behind him cautiously follow suit, looking to him for guidance.

"E-Endenbough?" he stammers, still staring at me as though seeing me for the first time. The rifle falls limp at his side. I nod. He tilts his head toward the other two men. "Bags!" he orders.

My heart skips a beat. The men step forward and reach into their pockets for pieces of black cloth that they stretch between their hands. Lukas shouts and puts up a fight as one of them goes to fling the black bag over his head, but Jakob hushes him.

"Don't worry, everything's gonna be okay," Jakob assures him. Lukas gives him one last despairing look before the bag envelopes his head. Jakob turns to me, his eyes pleading, *I'm right, aren't I?*

I can only hold his worried stare until the man fits the bag over his head, and his face disappears in a swath of black cloth. I say nothing as another bag is pulled over my head and tugged tightly around my neck, my world dissolving into darkness.

Someone takes my arm and moves me forward, and my arms instantly fly out in front of me, panic jolting through my nerves. My eyes are my life; without them, I'm completely lost. Someone says something to me, but the voice is garbled, and I can't see his face to read his lips. So I let him lead me away, still taking cautious steps, although his hand never leaves my arm.

With two senses gone, I try to let my mind relax and focus on the others I still have left. We move over hard concrete, crunching gravel, and even grass, but I don't know this city, and for all I know we could be marching toward the training camps. I can still smell the scent of burning oil and rubber, but there is a waft of fresh grass now and then.

The others grumble, especially Bone, his familiar voice grating out his complaints to an uncaring audience. The men keep marching us forward as the minutes tick by in darkness and semi-silence. But then we pause, and there's a muffled grating sound, and the air changes. Musky, stale air. Smooth, hard ground beneath our feet. We've gone inside a building. Then we go down some stairs—clumsily, I hang onto the man's arm for support. More walking down a long stretch. The air grows even more stale, and it's damp too. Underground? A tunnel?

Time passes even more slowly with blind eyes, and this tunnel, or whatever it is, is impossibly long. Eventually, we stop again, and again there's a flight of stairs—up this time—and then the air is clearer.

They march us around some more before finally stopping and mumbling some garbled words. Something to the effect of "sit," and when I strain forward trying to determine if I've heard right, a firm hand pushes down on my shoulder. My knees buckle from the pressure, and

I collapse onto a chair.

Hands tug at the strings of the bag, and when it's ripped off, my eyes sting from the light. I squint, letting my pupils adjust, scanning the room for Lukas and the others. There they are, blinking at the brightness, their hair ruffled and matted, but they're here.

I look forward and find myself face-to-face with a dark-skinned woman. Her brown eyes rake over us, taking us in, glaring out a warning. Yet beneath that is the shadow of fear. Her black hair is pulled into a bun at the nape of her neck, and she wears a simple button-down shirt and jeans.

"Jolan, what were you thinking, bringing them here?" She whirls around from us to the leader of the merry band who's brought us to what appears to be someone's living room. Only a few pictures grace the eggshell-white walls, and a small media screen sits in one corner. We're all in chairs on one side of a wooden coffee table, which is bare except for a small vase of flowers in the center. A simple home, but well cared for.

Jolan holds out his palms. "You don't understand, he says he's—"

"—I don't care what he said," the woman spews back. "We can't risk getting tangled up with Lucians!"

Jolan shakes his head, his hand waving. "Marria, listen—"

"—And bringing them here? How crazy do you have to be? If it were up to me, I'd—"

"Marria! He said his name is Endenbough!" Jolan shouts over her ranting. The words she'd prepared to say evaporate from her tongue, and she freezes in astonishment. "Joshua Endenbough."

Marria's throat makes a strange noise, her eyes flicking to us and eventually landing on me. I try to keep any emotion from my face. Why does that name mean so much to them? The others glance at me, but no one says a word, and their hands remain at their sides, unmoving.

Her gaze never leaves mine. "Are you sure?" She whispers her words, but I can read her lips clearly.

Jolan scoffs. "Look at him and decide for yourself."

She pores over my face, taking in every contour, every detail. She steps closer, and I try not to flinch.

"The eyes," she murmurs. "He's got her eyes." Her hand shoots out and grabs my wrist in a tight lock. I jerk, but strong hands on my shoulders keep me planted in the chair, even as Jakob and Lukas howl in protest.

Marria keeps her hold on my wrist and pulls my sleeve up to the elbow. She runs a finger over the horseshoe-shaped scar in the crook of my arm. "Anna said her boy had this kind of scar here," she says, her voice lowered to nearly a whisper. Her eyes jump to mine. "How did you get it?"

I swallow. "Playing with one of my father's knives. I was seven."

Her eyes watch me for a long moment before they glisten with tears. She releases my arm. "It's him," she says, taking a long breath to calm the emotion in her voice. "It's Anna's son."

FORTY-TWO

"THAT'S NOT RIGHT, MY MOTHER DIED IN A HOUSE fire," I tell them. Marria wipes her tears away with the back of her hand.

Jolan grins from his place behind her. "Oh, son, you have no idea what your mother did," he says. "We lost a lot of ground when she passed." His face loosens into a look of sorrow, and I can't help the bite in my stomach at the sight. A stranger, mourning my mother.

"What are you talking about?"

"Anna Endenbough." The grin returns. "Never thought I'd sing a Lucian's praises before I met that spitfire."

"She took over the leadership here, after you . . . " Marria clears her throat, "were taken. Her house burned, yes, but she was gone long before it happened. She spent the rest of her life helping us try to free our children." A flash of pain crosses her face for a brief moment before she tucks it away.

My mother, a rebel? The thought is impossible, and yet these people knew her. Knew about me. Suddenly, more questions than I can keep straight are whirling through my mind. What was she like with them? Did she talk about me? How did she find them?

"Did she say anything about my father?" I ask, letting a little bit of hope rise into my words.

Marria and Jolan frown. "He died in the fire, didn't he?" she says.

In that moment, all my dreams deflate like a punctured tire with air rushing from it. They know nothing. How can they know nothing?

Lukas shakes his head. "He's not dead. Gallander has him."

The two rebels' eyes grow wide. "He's still alive?" Even Jolan's two men, now stationed at the door as guards, turn to us. Who was my father to these people?

"It's why we're here," I tell them. "We were hoping you might have an idea about where he's being held."

I tell them what I know and watch their faces go white. "The Lucian serum?" Jolan says, his hands falling at his sides. He exchanges glances with Marria. "We knew he'd been tryin' to start the project up again, but we had no idea . . ."

Bone shifts uncomfortably in his chair. He's putting up a good front, but I can tell he's as nervous as the rest of us.

"Then you know what it is?" Lukas pipes up. "What it does?"

Marria nods slowly. "It's a kind of super drug. It was meant to cure neurological disorders, but the project failed, and nearly all the subjects died."

"Except Gallander," Jolan says. "The man survived it. He tried to get the Lucians to start the project again, but they'd sealed it up, and they threw away the key. That's what made him turn to Boqua—he figured we could give him what he wanted."

The blood in my veins nearly seizes. "What else does it do?"

Jolan shrugs. "Most of the details got locked away. Even Gallander had a hard time gettin' at the few bits of information he collected. No wonder it took him this long to get things goin' again."

I ball my fists. "But what does it *do*?" I ask stubbornly. "Why does he want to finish the serum project? So he can make soldiers who live for two hundred years? There has to be a more immediate benefit."

Jolan shakes his head. "I'm sorry, Joshua, we don't know any more."

I flinch at the name. The word is foreign: a strange name on a strange man's tongue. Some part of me wishes I'd never remembered it.

"You knew he was working on this?" Jakob asks, his face growing red with anger.

"We knew he was tryin' to get it started again, but we didn't know he'd already begun," Jolan says.

Jakob's eyes darken. "He's not just started, he's nearly finished!" he says. "And what happens when he's done?" Anger flashes on his face again. Jolan and Marria both clench their fists, returning his hard look.

"We just need to know where Gallander is working on his underground projects," I say, keeping my voice calm and hoping it will cool off the tension. "He's keeping it quiet—even the Boquan leaders don't know anything about it. You're the only ones who could possibly know where he's working from."

Marria blinks, moving her gaze to me. "There is one place Gallander kept hidden from the officials. We thought maybe that was where he was plotting his projects, but nobody could ever get close enough to find out for sure. He chose his help very carefully."

"Where is it?" I ask, unable to keep the anticipation from swelling in my voice.

"Havena."

The name sparks something in my memory. "The Felled City," I whisper. "The one the Lucian rebellion destroyed over a decade ago."

Marria's eyes flash with anger. "It wasn't a Lucian rebellion," she nearly spits. "Nothing like that ever happened. It was all a ruse."

A gnawing in my stomach makes me feel sick. "Gallander destroyed it?"

"Gallander did a lotta things," Jolan says. "Kept the government from rebuildin' Havena. Spoutin' nonsense about 'preserving what was taken from us' to remind our kids what Lucians'll do to them." His features contort into a mix of disgust and anger. "He sure knows how to rile an army up."

I believe it. I've seen it.

"How do we find the lab?" Bone asks from his chair, his curiosity piqued.

"There are only a few buildings left standing in Havena. He has to be working out of one of those," Marria says.

"You got a school, an office building, and two apartment buildings," Jolan offers. He sniffs, rubbing a finger against the side of his broad nose. "You want my opinion? He's in the school."

"You don't know that," Marria protests, latching a cold look onto him.

"It's the building that makes the most sense," he says, ignoring her icy glare. "Plenty of space, even some of the equipment he'd need. Not too big, not too tall, but big enough to run an operation like his out of. I'd bet a month's pay," he shakes a finger in our direction, "he's in the school."

Bone nods in agreement. "The school it is, then."

Jolan cracks his knuckles. "Wonderful. Next stop: home base. Nova's gonna be awful surprised to see you folks."

Marria snorts derisively. "Surprised? She'll eat dirt before she'll agree to this."

Jolan shoots her a warning glare. "Marria, please." She rolls her eyes in response, but she says nothing.

"Um, who's Nova?" I ask. The tension on Marria's face relaxes just a bit when she notices me looking at her.

"Nova's our chief," Jolan answers. "Trust me, you want her help on this." He turns to Marria. "Just try not to shout at her this time, okay?"

Marria grunts a reluctant reply. "I'll do what's best for our children."

FORTY-THREE

NOBODY SEEMS TOO PLEASED WITH THE DETOUR INTO the countryside to fetch Micah and the others. When we find them, Bone only smiles and looks at the sky while heated words from all sides fly at his impenetrable shell.

"You risked the entire mission with this crazy stunt!" Micah shouts, pacing in front of Bone like a caged animal. The others stand with arms crossed, glaring, but the slightest smile plays at Jael's lips.

"Why didn't you tell us there were more of you?" Jolan asks, sizing up Micah and the rest of the Lucians.

"Does it matter?" Bone sighs. "We've got more important things to worry about."

Micah's eyes flit from Marria to Jolan, and the two of them return his stare until he finally wipes his hand across his nose and turns back to his soldiers. "Alright," he grunts. "Pack up, we're going with them."

"What about the hovercab?" Asher asks.

Marria shakes her head. "We'll be less conspicuous on foot."

"We need to stop and get our weapons first," I say. Bone nods in agreement, as do Jael and Tomas.

Jolan slaps his palms together. "Alright, after that, we'll split up. Two groups. I'll lead one, Marria'll lead the other." He grins before Micah can protest. "Someone's got to show the way."

§

Marria leads our group through alleys and side streets, all of us angling our faces away from any passersby and carrying our weapons with loose, lazy grips. I keep my eyes on her, slowly catching up to her until my feet are in step with hers.

"What happened?" I ask her eventually. "I saw the old house; it was burned almost beyond recognition. I thought . . ." Emotion overtakes me, I can't finish the sentence.

Marria doesn't look at me, but her eyes flash with pain. "Anna didn't talk about Matthew for a long time. We didn't press her. When she finally did, it was in fragments we had to piece together."

She swallows hard. "Apparently, Matthew found out that Gallander was using his research to conduct experiments on humans. Some of the subjects were Lucians. Some he knew. A man named Yosher Weldtham showed him what was going on in those labs."

My heart flares at the name. "I met him," I say softly. "He was the one who helped us escape from Gesher." My hand brushes the lobe of my left ear.

Marria backs us into another alley, ducking behind garbage cans as a patrol passes. "The night of the fire, Matthew never came home. Anna finally left the house to go find him, and that's when they attacked."

My throat tightens. "All this time, I thought . . ."

A small smile touches Marria's face. "She thought the same. You were all she had left to hope for, so it was only a matter of time before she showed up on our doorstep." She chuckles. "Anna learned from the best, that's for sure. With her knowledge and skills, we'd just started to organize ourselves into something that could make a difference for our kids."

My jaw clenches. Looking for me. My mother was looking for me. Risking her life for me—and not just me, but the other children as well.

I almost can't bear to ask, my throat dry as sandpaper. "What happened?" The words come out in a small voice. One I barely hear over the muffle in my ears and the sound of my own heartbeat. The others have lowered their heads, keeping their eyes away.

Marria doesn't answer for a long moment, the memory harsher than I thought it would be. A part of me hates her for it. "Anna was good, but not impenetrable," she finally says. I take a breath but say nothing, waiting for her to continue without my prompting.

"There were rumors floating around that another rebel group had set up in the city, and that they had information we needed. Anna decided to find them." Marria pauses, taking a deep breath. "The whole thing was a hoax. Boquan soldiers waited until she and the others showed up and opened fire."

I flinch, my insides becoming rot. Marria shoots a sympathetic glance my way. "She would have been so proud to see you now."

Her praise only makes the hollow in my gut grow deeper. I turn away and press my lips together to keep them from trembling.

I stay quiet for a moment, collecting myself, and I decide to change the subject, even if only for my own comfort. "So, you think Nova won't go for our idea?"

Marria's face tenses. "Nova's nothing like Anna was. Some of us think we should take more risks, like your mother did. Nova has big ideas, but ever since she took over, it seems all we do is *talk* about saving our kids."

The hardness in her eyes expresses more than her words, and I wonder what kind of trouble we're about to get ourselves into with this Nova woman.

I force myself to refocus. We're in a rough part of the town: buildings crumbling, streets cracked and deserted. Eventually, Marria looks up and down the street before ducking into another alley and pausing beside an old, rusted metal door.

"What is this?" Tomas breaks the silence, watching as she pulls open the door and ushers us inside the dark cavern. Dank air meets my nostrils; the entire space reeks of oil and mold.

A weak light sparks to life in the ceiling. Marria turns away from the switch and moves further into the narrow hallway, motioning for us to follow.

"It's an access door leading to the old transport systems below," she says. "Back in the days when people traveled underneath the city instead of above it."

"This is where your base is?" Lukas asks, looking at the sweating walls.

Marria smiles. "We've made our own additions. Nobody comes down here anymore, so it's mostly useless to anyone else."

Following the light switches along the wall, Marria leads us through the hallway, and then down a few flights of narrow, metal stairs. "We're the first ones here. Jolan's group will seal the way again once they come through."

She leads us to an old door at the back of a long hallway before she pulls a white card from her pocket and slips it inside the crack beside the knob. Tomas's eyes widen at something he hears, and the door pops open.

"Card reader," she says, pointing at the thin, black slot on the door-frame. "No visible locks, keypads, or scanners. Nothing to make anyone interested in what's behind this door."

Inside is a large, circular room with doorways leading into several hallways. She picks the nearest one on the right and leads us into a damp-smelling space with a bright light at the end. Hearing something I can't, the others fixate their attention on the light.

After a moment, I can make out the faint sounds of people, and the hall eventually opens up into another room. This one is filled with a dozen rebels seated around a long table, plates of food in front of them, laughing and smiling with each other. The smell of cooked meat and vegetables makes my stomach rumble with a hunger I'd forgotten I had.

They look up at our arrival, pausing in mid-chew. Their eyes all flick to me, and I know they recognize my face. Silverware drops onto plates as their gazes shift from me to Marria. They're quiet for a long moment, stunned. It's not until a young woman leaps from her chair and shouts, "You found him!" that they snap out of their surprised stupor.

The young woman turns to me, her gray eyes eager. "What happened?"

Solemnly, I return her gaze. "We need to talk to Nova."

FORTY-FOUR

THE LOOK ON NOVA'S FACE DOESN'T CHANGE MUCH AS
the young woman opens the metal door to her quarters. The leader
glares at us from her chair, an old wooden thing behind an old wooden
desk. She's a moderately sized woman with the first signs of gray in
her brown hair. Green eyes size us up from within deep sockets, her
jaw naturally square. An unmade bed sits pushed against the far wall,
buried in the dim light of the corner, and dirty plates are strewn across
a small table. The room practically reeks with the familiar isolation of
someone in charge.

The space is small, and only Marria, Jakob, and myself are allowed
in the room. Before we entered, Marria had whispered something to
Jolan—if I read her lips correctly, she'd ordered him to radio someone.
Micah had protested at being left in the hall, but Nova's men shut the
door in his raving face without flinching.

Inside, Nova listens in silence as Marria explains, then leans forward
in her chair. "You want to do what?"

Marria sighs. "Think about it, Nova. It's our best chance to get to
Gallander. Anna helped us this far. Now we have her son to help us
the rest of the way."

I bite the inside of my cheek. From the look on Nova's face, I can bet
that mentioning my mother was not the wisest thing for Marria to do.

Nova's eyes slide to me, scrutinizing my face. "So, another one of
your clever little plans, Marria? Bringing him here? Making more people doubt my authority?"

"That has nothing to do with this. You know I—"

"—How does this plan help free our children?" Nova interrupts.

Marria presses her lips together. "It's only a first step, but it's the best option we have." Her eyes become slits. "Anna would have leaped at the chance."

The stab digs deep. Nova's stony expression wavers enough to wear lines in her face, and it seems as if her skin turns a shade darker.

Marria smirks. "Just how are *you* helping to free our children?"

Nova shoots to her feet fast enough to send her chair toppling. The others jump at the noise, and she plants her fists on her desk. Jakob surges forward, palms outstretched as a call for peace.

"You tell me," Nova says, her voice surprisingly calm, "how helping the Lucians will save our children."

"Because it's not just about Lucia," Jakob says, his hands still parted.

The rebel leader frowns at him. "If Gallander can wipe out the Lucians with his serum, there'll be no need for child soldiers."

Jakob's face transforms from serious to grave. "You really believe that?" Nova snorts at him as he continues. "I don't know what's going on between you and Marria here, but use your head. If Gallander finishes that serum, who do you think he's going to use it *on*?"

The two exchange one last fierce glare while my head spins. Bile rises in the back of my throat. The thought had never even crossed my mind: the children. He's going to use it on the children.

Nova either doesn't get it or doesn't believe it, because she steps out from behind her desk and looks directly at Marria. "My answer is no," she says. Her eyes dart to the rebel soldiers standing at the door. "Beams, get rid of them." She returns her attention to Marria. "And the next time a Lucian comes to us begging for help, they'll get a bullet in their brain. Understand?"

"Nova!" Marria's alarmed cry doesn't shake the woman.

Beams drops his hand from his earpiece. "Yes, ma'am." He shoots a glance to the second soldier, telling him to engage.

A hand grips my arm, and despite our protests, Jakob and I are dragged into the hallway. Without Nova's help, infiltrating Havena will be impossible, and my hopes all but vanish as I struggle in Beams's grip.

§

"Get going," Beams says, the muzzle of his rifle jabbing into my back. I stumble, trying to keep my balance. As we're marched down the hall, Jolan, his face grim, hands something to Beams, but I can't see what it is.

"What now?" Micah huffs beside me. He throws his icy glare over his shoulder at Beams. "You're just gonna plant a bullet in us and call it a day?"

Beams doesn't reply. The other rebel soldier with him is silent as well. As they march us away, I catch sight of Lukas's terrified face. His skin pale, he walks stiffly and with his fists balled. Jakob murmurs something to him, but the younger Garrow's eyes show no sign of being any less frightened.

We finally come to the end of the hallway. To the left is another hall ending in a set of stairs. Beams motions for us to turn, and once we're around the corner, he lowers his gun.

"Go up the stairs and through the last door on your right," he says. "Jolan has pulled the guards from there, so it should be a straight shot for you."

My jaw goes slack. We all exchange shocked glances before Beams turns to the rebel soldier behind him. "The key," he orders, snapping his fingers. The soldier obediently hands him a silver key, and Beams places it in my palm.

"The first door on your right is where we stored your packs and weapons," he says. He reaches into his pocket and pulls out a folded square of paper that he gives to Micah. "This is a map of Havena. You'll need it."

"Why are you doing this?" Micah doesn't hide his wariness.

Beams turns to him. "If what you say is true, we're gonna need all the help we can get. Nova's much too cautious—it'll get our kids killed." He clenches his teeth. "I got a daughter in that army, she was taken fourteen years ago. I got no idea whether she's alive or dead. Or what kind of monster they've turned her into." His cheeks flush, his eyes tinged with pink. "Now go before Nova gets suspicious."

"What will you tell her?" I ask.

He gives a grim smile. "The truth. Hopefully, if she sees that enough of us agree, we can convince her to change her mind. Until then . . ." he shrugs one shoulder, "we do what we have to. There are plenty of us who are willing to take matters into our own hands."

Jakob lowers his head. "Thank you."

Beams watches us until we've funneled through the door, but it's only after Micah slams it shut that I realize something was bothering me the whole time I was looking at the man's face.

Beams is a rebel, clearly filled with fanatical ideas. Beams's daughter is one of Gallander's stolen children, and she was taken fourteen years ago, one year after me.

Beams is blond.

FORTY-FIVE

THE ODDS ARE AGAINST IT. IT'S JUST A COINCIDENCE. What if it isn't?

My heart pounds behind my ribcage, and not just from the mad dash that Micah leads us on. He throws out his directions, and I'm forced to focus on finding cover in this broken part of the city until we reach the hovercab.

Asher bounds into the pilot's seat and starts the engine. Bone ushers us all inside, and we collapse on the floor, panting in exhaustion. We're airborne in less than a minute, Asher confident at the controls.

Clutching our sides and still trying to catch our breath, we slowly pull ourselves into our seats. Micah grunts and drops his rifle. "Talk about a complete waste of time," he grumbles.

I only see Atara's face. Beams's face is right next to it. Is there any resemblance at all?

Beside me, Tomas tugs at his pack, tossing the flap back and digging around inside. He pulls out his ratty notebook, apparently still in one piece, and he gives a relieved sigh. Slowly, his fingers pull at the pages, opening the notebook to the same girl I'd seen him sketch just a few days ago.

His hand lingers on the drawing, his fingertip passing over the carefully placed lines of her sharp cheeks, her full lips. It brushes against her curly hair as delicately as if the locks were really there on the page.

When he sees me watching him, he doesn't slam the book shut like I expect. His eyes twitch at me as if trying to figure out whether to be embarrassed or angry, but then his expression softens as he looks back at the girl's face.

"Her name is Naomi," he says. "She didn't like her picture being taken, so . . . " He offers a weak smile. He lifts the front of the book and flips through the pages with his thumb, Naomi's face flashing a dozen times over. Always the same girl, different angles, different hairstyles—some images are of her laughing, some crying, some with her hands covering half her face in embarrassment. Tomas has created his own photo album, one nearly as realistic as a book of snapshots.

"I'm afraid I'll forget what she looked like," he says. "This is all I have."

I meet his gaze, and it nearly tears me apart. The pain in his eyes—in all of their eyes. Can he see it in mine as well?

He studies me closely before a gruff smile curves one side of his mouth. Surprisingly, he reaches out and touches my shoulder. "Micah was wrong about you, Fiver."

Micah's face burns, though he keeps it buried in the map of the Felled City. My chest aches at the thought of my mother, but my father is waiting.

Concentrating, Micah spreads the map out on the floor between our feet and hunches over it. "The tree line here would give us good cover, but beyond that, we'd need to find a route to the school without being seen."

Asher cranes his neck toward me. "They never told you anything about what Gallander was doing in there?"

I press my lips together, but I push out an answer. "We didn't even know he had a lab there."

He grunts. "Not to be a downer, but how are we supposed to get into this place? We don't even know how heavily he's guarding it. What kind of firepower they have."

Jael sets her jaw. "We'll have to draw them out somehow. Pull them away from their posts."

"We need a bomb," Jakob says. "Plant it in one of the buildings, get clear, and blow it. Wait for whoever to show up." He mimes pulling a trigger. "Double boom."

"But we'd have to get there without anyone seeing us, killing us, or figuring out what we're doing and causing the whole plan to backfire," Asher argues. "Literally."

"We don't have to go too far in," Bone says, scooting forward in his seat. His eyes blaze with excitement at the idea. "They'd hear it anywhere in the city. The smoke alone would draw their attention. By the time they get there, we'll already be inside the school, finding Endenbough and Gallander."

My heart seizes."It won't work."

"Which part?" asks Bone. "The bomb or the infiltration afterward?"

"Any of it!" I reply. "They won't fall for it. Gallander has to know I'm coming for him by now. They'll be waiting."

Bone suppresses a grin. "You ought to know better than anybody," he begins, "Boquans are very attracted to things that explode."

I'm wary of his plan, but it doesn't matter. Bone has got the idea in his head, and he likes it.

"Where should we plant it?" Asher says, twisting around again. I wish he'd keep his eyes on the sky.

Bone jabs a finger on the map. "Here," he says. "This is the largest building we can get to safely."

Micah nods thoughtfully, rubbing his cheek. "Okay. How much explosive will we need? And where are we going to get it?"

Bone reaches under his seat and withdraws a tan pack. "Our good friend Beams came through."

Micah's eyes bulge. "*That's* what's in the extra pack?"

Bone smiles. "Never know when you'll need to blow something up."

Micah is too bewildered to be angry. "What's our ETA?" he calls to Asher. Our pilot glances at his instruments and half-turns around.

"Four hours," he says. "But we'll need to touch down far enough away that no one in town will see the hovercab."

Micah huffs, folds his map into a square, and slides it in the inside pocket of his jacket. "Get your weapons ready. Make sure they're cleaned and loaded."

Everyone moves, and I check the single pistol strapped to my belt.

How long can it last me? All the ammo I'd scavenged from my years in the Wood is tucked away in my various pockets, but altogether it doesn't amount to much. I'd stopped collecting it after the nightmares refused to leave me. That, and because gunshots tend to draw a lot of attention.

But it could be worse: Bone doesn't even have a weapon. His face is slightly pale as he nervously twists his battered shirt in his hands, wrinkling it.

A hand touches my arm, and I turn as Lukas gives me that same limp smile I've come to recognize as his front for his fear. "You don't think it will work, Fiver?"

I can't lie to him. "Without the rebels' help, I'm not sure."

"You think we're gonna die, don't you?"

Bone's head jerks up, but he doesn't say anything. I bite my tongue and place a palm on Lukas's shoulder as if I could squeeze reassurance into him just by my touch. "We can do this, Lukas," I tell him. "We have to do this."

He's not convinced, but he flashes that smile again and nods. I look at the pistol I'm holding and sigh: bravery comes so much more easily with a weapon in hand. I take the gun by the barrel and hold it out to him. "Here."

Lukas reaches forward hesitantly. "But . . . you won't have a weapon," he says, the pistol now weighing down his hand. He stares at the barrel, and I dig into my pockets for the bullets, filling up a small bag. I pass it to him and take the gun from his weak fingers.

"Here, this is how you load it," I say, pushing the button that slides the magazine out. "Like this, see? One bullet at a time." I jam the magazine back into place, then pull back the slide and release it. "This loads the first round. Push this button here to take the safety off. Aim down the sights."

Lukas blinks at the gun like it's some alien creature. I clap my hand on his shoulder again. "And don't worry about me. I've got my knives." He doesn't believe me for a second, but he offers a weak smile anyway.

Jakob watches us, unhidden worry etched in his face. But he regards me with gratitude, and I nod in reply. We've just made an unspoken agreement: Lukas lives through this. No matter what, Lukas lives.

FORTY-SIX

THE FELLED CITY IS JUST AS DESTROYED AS I IMAGINED it to be. There's a permanent layer of dust and grime on every surface, with vines crawling their way over abandoned hovercabs and up devastated buildings. Huge chunks of pavement and warped lumps of steel line the streets as we slowly creep into the town.

"Alright," Micah says. "You know what to do."

Bone grins, trotting off with his pack slung on one shoulder. Micah frowns but follows him, leading us to the building Bone has chosen.

"They may already know we're here," Tomas says, ducking his head. "They may have cameras all over this place."

"I doubt it," Asher assures him. "Nobody has a reason to come here."

The building is tall and covered with dust. Shattered windows loom down like jagged teeth, daring us to come closer.

"Come on," Bone says, jumping up the small incline leading to the building. He turns and shoves a block of explosives into each of our hands. "Find the support beams." His eyes sparkle with excitement. "Spread it out."

We nod and comply, and in no time, we're running from the building and back toward the outskirts of the city. We slide around a corner, dodging craters in the street and kicking up dust. We enter one of the few remaining buildings, and once inside, we climb its rickety stairs to watch from above.

Bone holds up the detonator. "Everybody ready?"

"You sure we're far enough away?" Jael asks, pulling her hair away from her eyes. It's fallen out of its ponytail and hangs limp down to her shoulders.

"Don't worry, we're safe," Bone replies.

He thumbs the switch, and we all cringe, waiting. There's a deafening crack, and we watch the debris and smoke from the charges fly out and up. The building quivers and shakes and groans, then it caves in like a house of cards collapsing, sending out thick clouds of dust and smoke and glass.

"You can bet they heard that!" Bone shouts over the noise.

It isn't long before we can make out figures scurrying toward the wreckage, and Micah nods. "Alright, there they are. Let's go!"

We pile out of the building, Bone leading us. "Come on!" he says. "The school is this way."

We follow him blindly, racing through the littered streets. Broken pieces of concrete and glass and piles of dirt and brick flash by as we run.

"Almost there," Bone says just as a bullet slams into the ground a foot or two ahead. Shouts of surprise come from us all, and Bone's face goes white as another bullet misses its mark, this one only inches from his toes.

"Get back!" I scream, reaching for Lukas's collar. I yank him toward what's left of a department store's brick wall and shove him down. The others follow, eyes wide with surprise and terror. A sniper. Dread rises within me, my whole body quaking. No. Not here. Not now.

"Where's it coming from?" Jael calls. Her next breath is a cry of pain, her legs giving out beneath her. Micah screams her name and lunges for her. She holds up her head and shifts position, cradling her arm as blood seeps out from between her fingers.

"I'm okay," she says, gasping at the pain. "It's just a scratch." Her face is bone white as Asher kneels beside her and presses his flattened palm across the wound.

"You've led us into a trap!" Micah screams, whirling his gun around and pointing it at Bone.

"I didn't!" Bone shouts, ducking as a bullet slams into the wall above him; dust and crumbling brick rain down on us. The others keep their heads low, their rifles raised with nothing to shoot at.

"How did they know our location?" Micah yells. I grit my teeth at his single-mindedness, pressing my back against the cracked wall. My heart thumps out a terrified rhythm, and I make myself take deep breaths. I can't panic here, not when all our lives are at stake, and suddenly I wish Inari were at my side.

My eyes scan the remnants of the destruction, watching for any betraying movement. And there, on the roof of a destroyed office building, I see the flash of a uniform. The glint of a weapon pointed in our direction. Pointed at Micah, the tallest of us all, and the biggest target.

I push off from the wall and grab Micah's jacket in both hands. His eyes boggle with surprise and fury, but I've already caught him off balance and yanked him down before he can open his mouth again. Or get his head blown off.

Micah thrashes beneath me, but I press my weight into his torso and keep a firm grip on his arms. "Stay put, you idiot!" I hiss. "Sniper, on the roof over there!"

He stops squirming, and I grab his fallen rifle. The weapon feels light in my hands, unlike the hefty guns we carted around in the army. I steady the barrel against the wall and take aim, the sniper's head coming into stark clarity through the scope's lens.

Another bullet slams into the brick, and broken chips spew across the ground. I peer down the barrel of my weapon, biting the inside of my lip. My finger tightens around the trigger, ready to fire.

But wait. I squint and lift the crosshair slightly. The sniper is further away than I first thought. Deep breath in. Let it stream out. Pull the trigger.

The kickback is barely noticeable, and I pull the rifle down to find the soldier no longer on the roof. Micah stumbles to his feet, his eyes round with surprise. He quickly composes himself when he sees me watching him.

"Nice shot," he mumbles. He casts an awkward glance at his boots.

I look at the rifle clutched in my hands. "This is a good gun," I tell him, holding the weapon out.

He's barely reached forward to take it when a barrage of bullets slams into the rubble. I dive for cover, the brick wall crumbling with countless bullet strikes. Where are they shooting from?

The salvo is unrelenting, leaving us all scrambling. Jakob screams for Tomas to duck, just as Tomas's body jerks, and red spews from his chest. He crumples into a heap while Micah yells orders at his team.

Asher lunges for Tomas, but his friend's lifeless eyes stare at the sky. Jael lets out an anguished cry, one hand pressing on her wounded arm while the other reaches for her fallen friend. "Tomas!"

Lukas flings his arms up to cover his head as more bullets crash into the wall. Grief surges in Micah's eyes, but he reaches for Lukas's arm, hauling him beside him and against the brick. My pistol trembles in Lukas's useless hands, and Micah rips it from his grasp, looking at me once before tossing it my way.

As much good as it will do for me. We're sitting ducks here. We have to move. Micah's arm waves, Bone and Asher and Jael fire off shots in random directions, and more dust flies into the air. In a swirling panic, we're left clambering for cover.

I fling my arms away from my head and scream, "Everybody to the woods!" I don't know if they heard me or not, but I reach for the nearest arm and haul the stumbling body to its feet. I blink back dust and find Jael staring at me, her mouth agape in terror.

"Come on!" I urge, pushing her in front of me. She lumbers through the sea of debris, her arms out to steady herself as she picks her way through. Her head swings around constantly, searching behind us for her companions.

Someone grips my bicep. I whirl around, and Bone's face fills my vision. "Up there!" he shouts, pointing. "Get to the trees!"

I nod and follow him toward the forest, expecting the others to come too, but when I turn, the spot where Jael stood is nothing but dust and rock. I can't see Lukas or Jakob anywhere. My eyes search frantically, my useless ears hearing nothing above the muffle and the gunfire.

An explosion from the projectile throws me backward, my body slamming into the detritus below me with a painful crash. I look up as the fireball grows, consuming everything in its path with a great, angry flash of heat. Chunks of rubble tumble to the Earth like stones tossed by a giant; huge clouds of dirt fly into the air and rain down in hot cinders all around me. I block the painful downpour with one hand, my stinging eyes struggling to see through the haze of dust.

"Lukas!" The thought has barely crossed my mind when it's out of my mouth, a loud, horrified scream tearing across the destroyed city.

They're all dead. Every single one of them. They're now nothing more than scattered bits of flesh and bone, all blown to dust by soldiers I once would have called friends. The hollow in the pit of my stomach grows into a pain-filled gnawing that threatens to consume me from the inside out.

The motion of the world slows, the muffle in my ears fading to nothing. All of them gone, and it's all my fault. Gallander knew we were coming. I told them the plan wouldn't work, but I let them go through with it anyway.

Someone grabs my arm. I hear his cries, but I can't understand his words. It's not until he wrenches my elbow just enough to make me turn that I see his lips and know Bone is asking me if I'm alright.

I'm not alright. "I did this," I mumble. "I brought them here."

His face shows his pain, but he shakes his head. "We don't have time to argue blame. They're coming. We have to move." Bone leans down and grabs Micah's rifle, dropped in the chaos.

"They're dead!" I shout, pulling my arm away. Sorrow clenches my gut as tight as a knot. Guilt joins it in the pit of my stomach, squeezing until I might be sick.

Bone grips me firmly by the shoulders, hauling me to my feet with familiar strength. Without a word, he pushes me through the rest of the rubble and into the stretch of trees. He shoves me downward and positions himself beside me, his rifle raised, scanning the area for any soldiers who might have seen us go.

"I can't see anyone," he says after a moment, and the pain consuming me only grows. Any hope that they might have survived disappears with his words.

"We may as well let them shoot us," I mutter.

Bone turns to me, his mouth twisted. "What?"

"This mission was doomed before it ever began," I say. "Gallander knew we were coming, probably even before we left Dekkan."

"What are you talking about?" Bone says, shifting on the ground. He gestures toward the massacre beyond us. "This mission is the reason they came here. The reason they kept risking their lives over and over again! All of it, because they knew it needed to be done. It's what a soldier does, Fiver."

My head lolls forward, and when I try to lift it, I can't summon the strength. Staring at my boots, I realize how exhausted I am. I feel it deep in my bones, a weariness that has finally begun eroding me from within. I'm tired of running. Tired of fighting. Tired of living like a cowering rabbit in a hole.

"I'm not a soldier anymore," I say, my voice too soft for me to hear.

Bone grips my arm, squeezing it in reassurance. "Yes, you are," he says, his eyes boring into mine. "As long as there's a battle to fight, we'll always be soldiers."

I close my eyes. Atara. Her blood staining my hands. The blood of countless others dripping from my fingers. The faces I trained myself to ignore, swimming into my vision again. The overpowering scent of death in the air. How many lives have ended at my hands? How many more will I have to take? And Nathaniel. How can I face him again, knowing I led his sons to their deaths?

I don't want to go back. I don't want to go forward. It would be so easy to let them take me. Burn me, dismember me, parade me through the streets like a great war trophy. It wouldn't matter; it would all be over.

But little faces also come to mind. Young faces of countless children and teens, all in Gallander's hands right at this very moment. They're being trained to slaughter innocent people, just as I once did. More cities will burn, and more anger will spread, along with the blood, until there's nothing left but death. And he'll keep taking them, keep destroying their lives to better his own, and nobody will be able to stop him.

Unless someone stands up.

The rebels are too fractured to pose any serious threat. Micah and his soldiers are torn to pieces in the wreckage of the city, and if Nathaniel and his people aren't dead already, they're still too far away to offer any help. The only thing that remains is us. Bone and me. Up against Gallander's entire force.

I always did like a challenge.

I strengthen the grip around the pistol I'd given to Lukas. Facing Bone, I push myself to my feet, ignoring the pain in my muscles and bruises on my skin, drawing strength from the new resolve rising inside.

"You're right," I say. "And Gallander's going to regret giving me that five."

FORTY-SEVEN

The building itself is, on the outside, nothing more than a pile of bricks slapped together to form a slightly crooked square stretching two stories high. On the inside, my father, a prisoner, has spent years of his life concocting Gallander's sick experiments. I scan the building. Whether the Boquan Commander is in there or not, I can't tell, but the sight of the school drives my thirst for blood.

"What do you see?" I ask Bone, the two of us crouching behind a rusted hovercab abandoned along with other scraps of metal strewn about the streets. He's propped himself up on one knee, peering over the hood of the vehicle with an eye scope.

"Not much," he grunts, twisting as he slides back onto the pavement. He frowns at the scope. "Where'd you get this heap of lunk?"

I shrug. "Did you see any soldiers?"

"Not one," he replies. "They could all be out there, searching the bomb site, or—"

"—They could be hiding around the next building, waiting for an attack," I finish for him.

He nods. "Either way, we can't sit here forever."

"Then what's the plan?" I ask.

Bone bites his lip, turning his head over his shoulder and around the hovercab. "I'm going in. You follow, but stay far enough behind that if they see me, they won't see you as well."

"Bone—" I start to protest, but he cuts me off with a wave of his hand.

"—Don't. Someone has to do it, and I'm keeping you alive as long as I possibly can." His lips flutter, a hint of a smile. "Don't worry, I'll keep my head down."

He slaps my arm and rises to a crouch, Micah's rifle lifted and ready to fire. A sickening dread fills me as Bone darts from slabs of stone to rusted metal heaps in the street while watching for any flicker of movement ahead.

Not a single shot is fired. Slowly, I move out from behind the hovercab. Bone is several meters ahead, peering around a small building that's barely standing. Surprise morphs onto his face, and in the next instant, the gun is at his shoulder, and he's firing shots faster than my feet can pound against the pavement. The soldier comes into view, but I barely catch a glimpse of his flailing hands before he drops to the ground.

My heart throbs with a terror that's become too familiar. Bone ducks behind another rust-covered hovercab, firing over the hood. I race for him, my arms extended with my fists clenched around my gun.

Two more soldiers turn the corner; they're mowed down by our shots. I heave for breath as I slide myself next to Bone, his own shoulders rising and falling rapidly.

"How many more?" I call out to him, and in response, he fires again. His gun clicks, and he ducks to reload.

"Can't tell," he grunts, grappling with the weapon. "I don't think too many, though."

I take his place, watching over the hood of the hovercab, and for several seconds all is quiet. There's no immediate danger that I can see.

Bone finishes reloading and slips up beside me. "You think that's the last of 'em?" he heaves, still shaken by the surprise attack.

"Maybe of this wave." My eyes flit from one pile of debris to another, searching for any more movements. "But there'll be more, sooner or later. They'll have heard the gunfire for sure."

"Then now might be our best chance," Bone says, smearing dirt across his skin as he wipes his forehead. "They'll all flock here."

I scan the city one last time. "Alright. We have to get out of here, anyway. Our ammo won't last nearly as long as theirs will."

Bone nods. "Come on. I think I know the best way to get there."

§

We have to gun down four more soldiers before we stumble into the school. The first floor opens into a small lobby with office doors leading off to the right. Behind them, a long hallway extends with doors lining each side. The offices are empty, as is the lobby, and Bone leads me to the stairs.

"Come on," he says. "The science labs are on the second floor."

"How do you know?" I hiss at his back.

He turns, shrugging his shoulders. "Aren't they always?" he replies. With that, he jogs for the stairs. I follow him—my father is in one of these rooms, and we will find him sooner or later, whether we start with the first floor or the second.

At the top of the stairs, we find a hallway identical to the one below with dim lights overhead. Still, not a soul in sight.

A chill runs through me. "You think they all went after us back there?"

Bone shrugs. "Could be they didn't have that many soldiers to begin with. After all the excitement we caused, the ones who were in here probably joined the others outside."

"But they'd still have to have some here to guard my father. Where are they?" I survey the hallway, even turning behind me to glance at the rest of it. It stretches even farther in the opposite direction.

"They might be in the rooms themselves," Bone says, but his voice wavers. He shifts his gun and trains his eyes straight ahead. "We'll have to check them all. You take this half," he motions behind us, "and I'll take this one."

I check the ammunition in my pistol. Empty. All the extra bullets were with Lukas. All I have left are my knives. Not the greatest position to be in, but I've had to make do with less. My pulse increases at the thought of how close I am to finding my father. What will he look like after all this time? Will he even recognize me? Or want to?

I shake my head, pocketing the pistol and reaching for a knife. I'm ready.

I've only checked a couple of rooms—dark classrooms filled with dust-covered desks and blank, cracked learning screens—when Bone waves at me from down the hall, pointing at a section of doors at the end of the hallway. My heart jolts, and I start jogging toward him.

"This way!" he calls, motioning for me to come closer. "These are the science labs!" I pick up my pace, and he leads me further down the hall, scanning the windows of the doors as he goes. He passes one, skids to a stop, and grabs for the handle. He peers inside and waves to me.

"Come on, in here!"

"Can you see him?" I ask, jogging faster.

Peering through the glass of the door, he nods. "Yes, yes, hurry!"

I come up beside him as he fiddles with the doorknob. He's blocking my view of the room. Sweat beads on his face, a drop trickling its way down his temple. His hand shakes, his eyes flitting back and forth from me to the door. "Almost there," he stammers. He gives the door a push, and it opens a crack, stale air filling the hallway.

He smiles quickly, then motions for me to go inside. I stare at his trembling fingers. He won't meet my eyes, and his forehead is slick with sweat.

Something's wrong.

I turn around and lean closer to him. A tiny hint of dread crosses his face, and he steps back, giving a nervous laugh. "What's the matter?" he asks.

My brow creases. "You tell me." My hand reaches for the knob, and I fling the door open hard enough for it to slam against the wall. He flinches, his fingers laced together, his eyes darting from one side to the other.

"Look, I—"

"—You first," I interrupt, reaching forward and grabbing his shirt. He gasps as I spin around with him in tow, shoving him in front of me and into the room. He stumbles, trying to catch his balance. I stand in the doorframe, watching. Waiting. The only light in the room comes in from the hallway, and the only thing inside that I can see is a wheeled table, much like a medical bed in an infirmary. Only shadows loom behind it, the walls lined with shelves and cabinets.

Bone meets my gaze, holding it for a second. His palms open, fingers splayed. "See?" he says. "Nothing's wrong."

"Where's my father?" I demand. "You said he was here!"

A low moan, just loud enough that I can hear it, comes from behind him, and he stiffens. The blood drains from my face, my muscles growing lax. It comes again, and my mind reels. Without another thought, my feet sprint forward, pushing past Bone and into the room. "Where is he?!" I shout. All I can see in front of me is darkness as I squint into the gray of the room.

Something sharp pricks my arm. I grab at the fabric of my sleeve, whirling around. Bone stands there with a guilt-ridden face, a spent syringe in one hand.

"I'm sorry, Fiver," he squeezes out. My head spins, confusion mixing with shock. White-hot anger flares within me, my jaw clenching as I take an unsteady step forward. He backs away, and a dizzying wave crashes over me. The anger slips away into fear, and my knees buckle, my hands grasping for the table to keep myself upright.

"What . . . what did you do?" I mumble. Bone looks away, his eyes swollen. My vision blots in and out, my eyelids struggling to stay open against the weight that's pulling them closed. My hands scrabble for a hold on the table as my legs give way completely. I crumple to the floor in a dazed heap, feeling as though my body will sink through the tiles as if they were made of gel. I groan, clenching my fingers, straining to sit up.

"You don't understand!" Bone's voice verges on hysterical. "I had to do it! You don't know what they would have done to me if—" His voice strangles.

Shadows flicker overhead. My head lolls on my neck, my throat letting out a weak moan. My limbs refuse to move, and strange hands clamp down on them. Faces swirl before me, blending with the dim light as they lift me up.

"No . . . " I grunt, a flash of alarm pressed back into the grayness. "No, don't."

They ignore me. Lights turn on as I'm forced onto the table. Three faces, blank stares on each one. I try to tear my arms away, but they barely budge against the grip holding me.

The hands pull my wrists to my sides. Fabric brushes against my skin, and I force my eyes downward. Straps on my wrists and ankles. The soldiers pull them tight and hook them around the metal support beams of the table. I tug weakly at the straps, but they don't give.

The three faces back away, leaving me bound and as helpless as a newborn kitten.

"Well, well, well."

I hear the voice, but the man stays hidden. It's a voice I had hoped I would never hear again. It echoes in my mind like cymbals in an orchestra, firing a wave of panic that is swiftly dulled by whatever drug they've shot into my bloodstream. Ice fills my veins.

He comes into my sight, not a hair on his head changed. A sick smile pasted on his lips.

Gallander.

"Still the fighter, aren't you, Fiver?" he says, his voice thick with delight. "Even after all this time."

I can barely move my head to face him. The drug coursing through me keeps me pinned to the table, my limbs useless.

"Good work," Gallander says to Bone. "You'll find your transport waiting outside, as promised."

Bone looks from the Commander to me, his face green. He seems on the verge of throwing up, and he quickly turns and leaves the room. Gallander snorts and rakes his eyes over me. "He'll never know what he's done for us."

Who was he talking to? Dizziness overtakes me, my vision blotting out. I remember I need to do something, something important, but it floats just out of reach. Wait. Someone I need to find. My head flops to one side, and I blink.

Gallander gives my shoulder a pat and walks from one end of the table to the other, stopping just at my feet. "Take him to the lab."

The table wobbles as they release the brake, the squeaking wheels protesting against the weight. My body jostles on its surface as they push me through the door and down the hall. I watch the lights on the ceiling pass by, and soon they begin to fade. I shouldn't sleep, I have to find . . . But the pull is too strong, and eventually, it all fades into nothing.

FORTY-EIGHT

MY TEMPLES THROB. BRIGHT LIGHTS SWIM BEHIND MY eyes, blinding me even with my lids tightly shut. My mind moves closer to the light as if bobbing at the surface. I stifle a groan. I don't want to wake up. The heaviness in my head compels me to sleep, but some sense of urgency pushes me forward into the light.

My eyes open.

Gray ceiling. A round light embedded in the tiles. Fuzzy blotches clouding my vision.

My memory comes back with a snap, and with it returns the fear. Bone. Bone betrayed us. Betrayed me. My arms jerk, but they're pulled to a painful halt by the straps still wrapped tightly around my wrists. A quick check finds my ankles still bound as well.

"*Why?*" Why had he done it? The guilt was plain on his face, but still he'd led me straight to them, let them drag me away. I kick myself at my stupidity. My father had been all that mattered, and I had willfully ignored any hint that Gallander would use him against me.

My vision clears, and soon I can make out the room I'm imprisoned in. I'm still flat on my back and on the same metal table, but now I've been pushed against the far wall. The only other furniture in the room is an unoccupied stool in the corner. Strange machines beep around me, dull lights flashing blue and green hues.

"Boy, are you a sight for sore eyes."

The voice whips my head around. Gallander. He's now perched on the metal stool in the corner. My heart leaps—how did he get in here without my noticing him? I glance at the door. Shut, as I assumed it had been moments before.

Gallander gives a low chuckle. "Didn't hear me come in, did you?

But you didn't see it, either." He lifts his gaze to mine, eyes boring into my skull. "Now, doesn't that get you to wondering?"

He stretches his long legs and crosses the room in slow strides. His finger points inches from my nose, and with a practiced discipline, I don't shy away from him. I glare into his snake eyes, pulling at the straps holding me until my muscles bulge from the strain.

He smiles, ignoring my anger. "You are a very interesting case, Fiver. Or do you go by Joshua these days?"

I swallowed hard. "What do you want with me?"

His eyebrows twitch, and he licks his lips. "Your father was pretty good at making deals. I imagine you will be too."

A hot flash of angry, piercing fear races through my chest. "What did you do to him?"

Gallander twists his face into a cruel grimace.

I tug at the straps. "Tell me!"

He laughs. "Relax, boy. Your father is perfectly safe. Has been for . . . what, ten, eleven years?"

My face blisters with heat. "Working on your serum experiment!"

He doesn't seem surprised I know of the serum. He scrutinizes me, studying me as if determining whether I'm worth the breath it would take to talk to me.

After a long moment, Gallander gives a tiny but sharp nod, and I can tell that he's come to some sort of conclusion in his own fiendish mind. Something in his demeanor shifts, and the tone of his voice changes with it. "Imagine having your life stop just before it began," he begins slowly. "A freak accident leaving you paralyzed from the waist down." I watch him pace the room, every now and then glancing at me. "All your dreams gone up in smoke. Endless weeks of pain and depression. Then they tell you that you'll never walk again." His eyes flash at the memory.

"Two centuries ago, Lucian scientists came to me. I was eighteen. They told me they thought they had a cure for people with damage to their nervous systems like me. They were looking for test subjects. Of course I agreed—I thought I had nothing left to lose. I went to their facility, and they injected me and dozens of others with their serum, and we all waited. Years we waited."

I silently thumb the straps securing my wrists. Lost in his memories, Gallander's eyes are focused on a distant point somewhere off in space. I let him talk, hoping he'll distract himself long enough for me to get free.

"At first, they thought it was a total failure. Then things began to change. Slowly, I found I could nearly support myself on my own legs. Then I was standing. Not long after, I could walk all the way across a room by myself. And not just me. People unable to talk, or swallow, or write, or even breathe on their own could do those things again. It was a miracle drug, that serum."

"That's not how I heard it," I scoff. "All the subjects died except for one."

A smile plays at the corner of his mouth. "Not for a while, they didn't. It wasn't long after we were back to normal that we noticed . . . other abilities strengthened tens of times. Senses heightened to pick up on the smallest sounds, the tiniest movements." His eyes sparkle at the thought. "We could smell other people's emotions, taste blood in the air. Reflexes enhanced beyond any normal human capacity. We could sprint so fast that we could cross full rooms without a soul noticing us. We even stopped aging normally."

"Then why are they all dead?"

"Everything was fine for years, and then . . . something went wrong. The serum's effects began to degrade. After a few years, the subjects were back to normal, but a few years after that, well . . . " Gallander shakes his head. "They kept going backward, like rewinding a film. The Lucians couldn't do anything to stop it. Eventually, almost all the subjects were bedbound, their nervous systems nearly destroyed. One by one, they started dying."

"But you didn't." I manage to spit, launching a glob to the floor.

The smile returns to his tanned face. "There were four of us altogether who kept our abilities." He shrugs. "To this day, I'm not sure why. Maybe something in our DNA, maybe something the technicians missed when they injected us. Who knows? But we waited, and still nothing happened to us. We were perfectly fine. And a little idea popped itself right here." He taps the side of his head. "Imagine what you could do with this kind of power? Imagine if you had a whole army of super soldiers under your command? Who could stop you from doing anything?"

My insides churn, a sick, nauseated feeling creeping up from my gut. "So that's it, then," I say. "You've turned two countries against each other just to seize power?"

"To become the greatest Commander this world has ever seen!" Gallander nearly shouts back, his nostrils flaring. "No one could stop me, not with the army I would build. Nobody would have that kind of power!" He inhales deeply, and then his face calms as he shrugs one shoulder. "Of course, it hasn't always been an easy road. The Lucians shut down the project and buried all the research. They'd offered me everything . . . only to take it all away. So I went to my fellow survivors for help."

He grits his teeth, one hand curling into a fist. "The cowards refused. Said there had been too many lives lost to try the project again, and it wasn't worth anymore deaths. I had something wonderful to offer them, yet they threw it away. And so . . . well, I'm the only one left."

His grizzly implication sends another wave of nausea through me. "You killed them all?"

He grins. "It wasn't difficult. They were afraid of what their bodies could do, so they did nothing with them. Not one embraced their new potential, choosing instead to let it go to waste." He shakes his head, almost in shame. "I slaughtered them like fattened calves bellowing for their mothers. Too easy. Made me wonder what kind of a man I was."

"I'd have thought it pretty obvious," I grunt.

He laughs, a harsh, grating sound. "Oh, Fiver, those Lucians sure have changed you." He moves to the foot of the table and begins fiddling with an ankle strap. "I remember when you'd rip a man apart just because there was a rumor he might be a Lucian. Now look at you." He flings his hand in my direction.

"That was a long time ago," I say.

He trains his gaze on me. "Was it?"

I glare back at him. "Maybe you're right. I'm looking at a Lucian right now, and I'd like nothing better than to put a bullet in his brain." He may have defected, risen in ranks in the Boquan army, and gathered enough power that even the government didn't know what he was doing, but he's still a Lucian. A Lucian turned into a monster. Just like me.

Gallander laughs again. "So what now?" I say. "You inject your entire army and unleash your super-mutated soldiers on the Lucians to wipe them out?"

The smile drips from his face. "Well, I have to admit, I was a bit hasty there. I mean, even if you start out with an eight-year-old kid, the serum still takes years to start working. And then you have to wait to see if it kills the kid or not. But imagine, once it takes hold and stays, look at what you'd have? A perfectly trained army, ready to march across the world."

My jaw tightens as I remember what Jakob said to Nova in the rebel base about the children and the serum. "Those kids . . . you've already ripped them from their families, and now you're going to use that poison on them?" I growl.

He looks offended. "Of course. Where else would I get the perfect mix of people all living in the same place for years at a time? Controlled environments. All the chosen subjects close by, easy to keep tabs on, integrated and trained along with the controls. It was perfect. If they started degrading, all I had to do was hold a Rabbit Hunt, and they would all disappear with no questions asked."

I focus on the ceiling, fighting the urge to vomit. The kids. He's already begun injecting the kids. How many of them had been his test subjects? And the Rabbit Hunts, nothing more than a cover for his sick experiments. Scourge: the name races across my mind. Had he been injected with the serum? I think back to the last time I saw him, his increased rage, his eyes ringed red. Were those signs?

Gallander points a finger at me. "Your father is a brilliant man, Fiver. I knew he could figure out how to keep the serum from killing the subjects sooner or later. Especially if his own son would one day be claimed by it."

The nausea in my gut is joined by a deep, black fear shooting through my stomach like a wildfire. Gallander gives a grin at the shock on my face. "Oh, don't be so nervous, Fiver. The serum's been crawling around inside you for years; much longer than anyone else has had it. Well, besides me, of course. Why do you think I've tried so hard to find you?"

"But I . . . " My tongue is dry, the words coming out raspy and hoarse. "I don't have any special abilities."

Aiming both pointer fingers at me, Gallander claps his hands together, his face giddy with excitement. "That's the interesting part, Fiver. The serum did absolutely nothing to you at all. It didn't give you any added abilities, and it certainly didn't kill you. I tried it on you twice, and still, nothing." He pushes away from the table and paces at the foot of it. "I've never seen anything like it before. You're the only one the serum didn't work on."

I squirm against my restraints, a chill freezing my blood. Gallander stops his pacing. "And I want to find out why. So," he bends over the table, arms crossed, "we're gonna have ourselves a little experiment."

Blood drains from my head. "You can't . . . This is what you wanted me for? For your serum?"

"You know, it was disappointing how good of a soldier you became," Gallander says, ignoring me. "And all on your own talent, too. I thought it was too bad you probably wouldn't survive the serum, and then you did, yet I couldn't touch you without drawing too much attention to myself."

His grin widens, teeth flashing. "But then you rebelled, ran away, and became fair game. I hunted you for two years, and you *still* kept away from me. And I can't use any of that talent. You're a waste, Fiver. But there's one last thing you can do for me."

I swallow a lump the size of an apple in my throat. My skin crawls with fear and disgust, the straps biting into my wrists.

He smiles down at me again. "Don't look so glum, Fiver. The best part is just ahead. Everything you've been searching for." He turns toward the door. "Bring him in!"

The doorknob twists. The hinges creak, and the door slowly swings open, revealing a thin man in a white lab coat clutching a touchpad to his chest. The world crumbles beneath me, and if I hadn't already been strapped to the table, I'd have collapsed from the weight of the face before me. Familiar eyes, dark and more sunken in than I remembered. Wrinkles marring his now-bearded face, graying and disheveled hair, and cracked lips don't stop me from recognizing him.

My father.

FORTY-NINE

FOR WHAT SEEMS LIKE HOURS, I CAN'T BREATHE. CAN'T move. My heart freezes its once-relentless pounding, my blood threatening to burst from inside. I can barely believe my eyes; surely, Gallander has somehow tricked me into thinking my father is really here. Alive.

He lifts his weary gaze, and it lands on me, taking in every inch of my face. My father's mouth opens in stunned silence. "Joshua?"

His voice is haggard and dry, nothing like the strong sound I remember. I tell myself it's just my damaged ears, but it's clear that the years haven't been kind to him. His lips quiver, and blood drains from his face, his fingers gripping his touchpad so tightly his knuckles turn white.

"What . . . what have you done?!"

It takes a second for me to realize the question was directed at Gallander, not at me, and the panic rising inside me decreases a little.

The Commander gives a steely grin. "You've done such a wonderful job with that serum, Matthew, but ultimately, we still saw the same results with the gershawn rats as before. They may have lasted longer, but they still wound up dead." My insides lurch as he gestures at me. "But don't worry. I've brought you the perfect test subject."

My father swallows, his head shaking back and forth. "You said . . . you said he was on the battlefield. That he wouldn't survive the next couple months because of the degradation."

"Well, obviously, he's surpassed even your expectations," Gallander says. "Now I want you to find out why he's unaffected."

My father looks at me, sets his jaw, and drops the touchpad onto the counter. "No."

A muscle in Gallander's face twitches. "You're not in any position to defy me, Endenbough."

"You need us," my father throws back, his gaze steady. "You won't kill me . . . or him."

Gallander says nothing; he only moves around to the side of the table. His face is passive, the color only slightly risen in his cheeks. "You're right, Endenbough," he says. His calm voice sends nervous shivers down my spine. He stares into my father's eyes. "I wouldn't ever kill him."

Before I can blink, there's the glint of metal, and my arm is locked in Gallander's iron grip. A sharp sting flares as the knife presses into my skin and erupts into burning fire. I brace myself against the pain, muscles clenching as the blade digs deeper, dragging further down my arm. White stars flash behind my eyes, and I can no longer hold back the scream tearing from my throat. The knife moves beneath my skin, slicing it from my arm like you would the flesh of a bagged rabbit. My chest heaves, and my heart pounds out a terrified beat, pumping blood out through the wound. Sticky and warm, my blood becomes a rivulet dripping down the side of the table. I try to buck away, but between the straps and Gallander's powerful arm, I'm helpless.

My father is screaming. "Stop it! Just stop!"

I barely hear him over the thudding in my ears and the constant shriek of pain in my arm. Gallander's hand only tightens as he drags the blade even further. "That's up to you, Endenbough," he says. Tears blur my vision, and a choked cry presses out of me as my father screams again and again.

"Alright!" he shouts. His face is blood red as he draws in hurried breaths. "I'll do it! Just stop! Please!"

The knife retreats. Gallander releases his hold. I gasp, drawing air into my desperate lungs, looking at my torn, bloody skin. Sweat trickles down my temples.

"Very good, Endenbough," he says. He holds up the knife, blood dripping from the blade. "That was only a couple of inches of skin. Imagine how it'll be with his whole arm."

"You can't." My father's face is ashen. My arm screams in pain, but I hold back a moan, blinking away tears.

"Of course, more than likely it would get infected, and that might kill him. So we'd have to cut the limb off altogether—"

"—Alright!" My father's nostrils flare in fury as he seethes. Gallander smiles in amusement.

"I thought you would come around eventually. Now, nurse your boy and have a long chat about old times, and then I want you to get those answers for me." He gestures toward the door. "As usual, your dear friends and mine will be waiting outside should you try anything foolish."

My father glares at him, his eyes scintillating in raw instinct. Instinct to protect one's offspring at all costs.

Gallander gives his head the tiniest of shakes. "I'll start on his other arm next." He steps forward, then gives us one last warning scowl before heading for the door, slamming it shut behind him.

My father practically leaps to my side. His fingers brush over the straps, but he leaves them on and moves to the gash still welling with blood on my left arm. He lets out a sympathetic groan and moves across the room, where he starts rummaging in the cabinets that are pushed up against the wall. He returns with several bottles and sprays the contents of one across the wound.

I jerk at the suddenness of the scorching sting, tugging at the straps around my wrists and ankles.

"Sorry," my father breathes, dabbing at my arm with a cloth. "I should have warned you about that."

I'm not sure if he's talking about the burn of the antiseptic or Gallander's torture. Trying not to flinch as he cleans and dresses the wound, I watch the ceiling or stare into the black behind my eyelids.

Finally, I speak. "Can you . . . can you please take these off me?" I pull at the straps, and my father's face nearly melts in guilt and regret.

"I'm sorry, son." He shakes his head. *Son.* It sounds foreign on his lips. "I didn't expect any of this to happen." He reaches toward me and unbuckles the strap around my wrist. He moves to the foot of the table and unbinds my ankles as I pull off the other wrist strap.

"How did Gallander find you?" he asks.

I swallow. "Long story," I tell him.

His eyes soften, finally moving away from the wound on my arm and looking at my face. "I thought . . . I thought I'd never see you again." He leans forward, pulling me into his arms. "Thank Elorai you're alive."

He's so close. I had dreamed of the moment when I would find myself back in his embrace. I'd wondered if being reunited were even possible or if he would reject me as a traitor and curse the day I was born. But now I'm here with him. It's been fifteen years, and now he's finally here, but I'm still partly empty because we have a mission to accomplish.

I pull away from his arms, and he looks me in the eyes, a renewed fire burning deep inside.

I take ahold of him by the shoulders. "We have work to do."

§

I can't imagine Gallander left us alone without some kind of observation, but I can't find any cameras or microphones hidden in the corners or crevices of the room, and no one has come in to stop anything we're doing.

"Gallander doesn't need them," my father explains wearily. "He knows I would do anything to keep you safe, and there's no way I'm getting past his men and away from here."

I should have known the place was too barren the moment I stepped inside. I bite the wall of my mouth and fight the anger flooding my system.

"Where is your research?" I ask.

"In the other lab. Why?"

I take in a gulp of air before answering him. "We need to find out why I'm immune to the serum."

His mouth mashes into a line. "You know what Gallander will do with that serum once it's finished." He scrutinizes me, silently prodding my brain to see just what the army has turned me into. What kind of monster his son is.

My jaw clenches. "What about the kids who've already received it?" I ask. "They're dying right now, and Gallander is just going to keep giving it to more and more children until he gets what he wants."

My father's eyes dart to the bandage on my arm. Muscles twitch in his face. "And when he succeeds, he'll march his soldiers across Lucia and wipe everyone out." He looks back at me. "We can't let that happen."

I step closer. "We won't. They don't *have* to be his soldiers. They can make their own choices. We only have to take out one man."

He sighs, weary. "One man and his advanced abilities, plus a squadron or more of loyal soldiers underneath him."

"We have to try," I urge. "If we do nothing, he'll still find a way. He won't stop, not until he's dead or killed every other human being on the planet. You know he won't."

My father shakes his head. "It won't work."

He's tired. He's lived in fear of Gallander for more than a decade, his wife dead, his son taken, countless children dying from a serum he'd helped create. Lives resting on his conscience. It's not something so foreign that I can't understand.

He moves his gaze to me again, and I'm surprised at the glimmer of amusement on his face. "Look at you," he says. "Risking your life for me. For the kids. I thought for sure they'd wipe that part of you away."

The words burn into me like hot cinders to the skin. Does he know the countless lives I've taken, all in Gallander's name? How can he look at me with pride? How can he look at me at all?

He touches my shoulder. "Let me show you something." He moves across the room to the second door, leaving it open as he slips inside. I hesitate, but I follow him through. Inside is another part of the lab, only this part is covered in plants. Plants growing in pots hanging from the ceiling, in glass containers, and in planters lined up against one entire wall.

Not plants. Plant. They're all the same: streaks of yellow cross their leaves, a small, yellow-and-red flower sprouting from the center of the bigger ones.

"I know this," I murmur, running my fingers across the leaves of one nearby. My father ignores the plants, heading straight for a metal cabinet against the far wall. He opens a drawer and fishes around inside.

"It's Vitmor," he replies, pulling out one fat folder after another. "It's the key ingredient for the serum." He selects one folder from the stack and drops the rest back inside the drawer.

"Where did you get so much? I've only ever seen it growing in the . . . " My voice trails away as the realization hits me. The scientists in the Wood. Taking their samples in carefully marked containers.

"Gallander was going to destroy the Wood," I say. I fight the pang of nausea that hits me.

My father looks up from his folder. "Vitmor can only grow in the soil of the Crosswoods. Gallander needs large amounts of land to mass produce it for the serum. The plan was to clear the land with fire. Or bomb select areas best for the plant's growth so they could get the most out of smaller pieces of land. He could explain it to the Lucians as a forest fire out of hand, or an accident, or anything. He'd hoped to start as soon as the serum's formula was complete, then harvest before the Lucians ever suspected anything."

I hold up a Vitmor leaf. "But he hasn't even finished the serum yet. Why does he need so much right now?"

My father shrugs, giving a weak sigh. "Gallander is too ambitious. He thought for sure by now I'd have finished the formula for him. Which only means he's getting more desperate every day."

He tosses the folder onto a table in front of me. "This is the summary of my research." He swallows, grimacing as if in pain. "The things we had to do . . . I'm not proud of them."

"I know the feeling." I take the folder and open it. My father swallows but makes no comment, and for that I'm grateful.

Inside I find a stack of papers with graphs and symbols and numbers on them, all of it meaning absolutely nothing to me. I flip through the pages, searching for paragraphs of text and familiar words.

"How does it work?"

"The serum coats the axons of the neurons like a second myelin sheath," he says. "It not only speeds up the conduction of the electrical impulses across the axon, but it can repair damage to the neurons like nothing we've ever seen."

I blink, positive he'd slipped into another language. "What?"

He bites his lip as if concentrating on a better way to explain it. "Your nervous system depends on a substance called myelin that coats neurons' axons." He opens the folder to a page and points to a picture of something that looks like a curved, uprooted tree. "This is a neuron," he says. "The axon is here." He points to the trunk of the tree. "The bulges along it are myelin. Without it, the neuron can't send signals across your body that let it function as it needs to. The serum coats over the myelin, in some cases replacing it where there was very little before. It can even repair damage to neurons when nothing else could help."

"So, it basically supercharges the neurons, whether they were damaged or not," I reply. I pause and wait for my father to confirm my understanding with a quick nod. "But why did it extend Gallander's life so much?"

My father gives a small shrug. "That part is a mystery. His neurons are permanently protected by the serum, but that doesn't explain why he hasn't aged like he should. I think it has something to do with the Vitmor, but Gallander hasn't let me try to find out. He's too concerned with fixing the serum's . . . hitch."

"The fact that it kills people," I say.

He nods. "The serum is unstable. It only sticks to the axons for so long before it begins to degrade, and when it does, it takes the natural myelin with it. The nervous system breaks down, and eventually the person dies."

"But you've fixed it?"

"The gershawn rats we use have a very short lifespan. They were bred to live only for a few weeks, which speeds up the serum's processes. The most-recent batch we injected lasted much longer than any other test, but in the end they still died. Gallander thinks I'm on the brink of discovering a way to stop the degeneration, and he's convinced you are the key."

My eyebrows lower. "But if the serum didn't kill him, why does he need me to experiment on? Why can't he use himself to figure it out?"

"He's already tried it." My father shakes his head. "Everything short of exploratory brain surgery, which might possibly give us some answers if we thought he would live through it. He thinks he and the other survivors were a fluke—likely a mistake someone made in the lab. Fluke or not, it only makes him more determined to find out why, especially since he knows it's possible but can't figure it out."

I imagine Gallander regrets killing the others who survived. With them, he'd have three more chances to find his answers, three more bodies to rip apart, three more living souls to torture.

I swallow, feeling as if something were squirming in my stomach. I start imagining all kinds of sharp metal things piercing my skin, ripping it from my body, burning me alive from the inside out. It's so real, the ache in my arm springs to life once more.

But I nod. "What do you need?

FIFTY

THE NEEDLE MY FATHER IS HOLDING SOMEHOW SEEMS more intimidating than half a Boquan squadron breathing down my neck. I sit with my legs dangling over the side of the metal table, the straps looming in my vision as my father reaches for my right arm. I let him move my hand palm-up and aim the needle at a vein on the inside of my elbow.

It stings, but my father is the one who flinches. The thought of experimenting on his own son has tinted his face green. I watch the red flow from my arm into a tube, and I place a tentative hand on my father's shoulder.

"Hey. It's okay," I tell him, recalling the soothing words he once used on me when I wanted to crawl beneath the blankets and hide from the monsters peering out at me from the closet.

He glances at me but says nothing as he fills the tube with my blood. He pulls the needle out and presses a cotton square onto the puncture site. He caps the tube and turns toward the other lab.

I slide off the table and follow him, tossing away the cotton. "What are you going to do with it?"

"Evidence of the serum is in the blood," he replies, crossing the lab toward a strange-looking machine in the corner. "When it's injected, several different proteins get into the bloodstream and stay there. As I've been told, you've been injected twice, so the first thing we're going to do is see if those proteins are in your blood."

He approaches a machine—a squat, tubular container with various buttons and dials on the top—and lifts a metal bar on one side. There's a popping sound, like a suction cup being torn from a window, and the lid opens, revealing a dark interior with a small, hollow, open-ended tube suspended in the center. My father slips the blood-filled tube inside, flips the lid back, and lowers the bar back into position.

He moves to a two-foot-square touchpad mounted on the wall next to the machine and slides his finger across the screen. He types in commands I don't recognize, and the machine whirrs to life.

My father reads the touchpad screen with one hand on his chin. The whirring slows, a beep sounds, and my father gives a strange grunt. "They're not there," he says.

I watch the screen, but all I see is a swirling list of strange configurations—spheres and lines labeled with paired letters and numbers that mean nothing to me. He skims the touchpad with his finger, and the screen shifts, showing the spheres from different views.

"Nothing," he says, pinching and flicking at the screen. "Not a single one."

I lean in closer. "Which means?"

"Which means something happened to them. If the serum was in you at all, we would see the proteins. Even if something was counteracting it."

The statement troubles him. "Gallander will assume the serum degraded without any of the negative side effects. He'll take it as more proof that the serum can be fixed." He shakes his head slowly in confusion. "Although it still doesn't explain why you never had the advancements. The serum got out of your body, somehow."

"How?" I ask, thinking of all the times I'd had my blood taken in the Barracks.

My father shakes his head again, his hand rubbing at his jawline as he stares at the touchpad. "No idea. Something must have destroyed the serum before it could take hold of your neurons."

I'm not sure I'm fully inferring his meaning. "Otherwise, I'd be dead or dying right now, right?"

My father responds with a grim nod.

"So now what?" I ask, looking away from the touchpad's screen to keep the swirling from making me dizzy.

The door flies open and crashes against the wall. My father jumps, and both of us turn as six soldiers pour into the room. His hand quickly swipes across the touchpad's screen, and it goes black.

"Alright, enough father-son sappy time," Gallander's voice roars from the other room. Slowly, he follows his soldiers inside as they surround my father and me. "Perhaps a few minutes isn't quite enough time to catch up after all these years, but I'm through waiting."

Hands reach out for my arms. I lash out, grabbing one soldier by the wrist and jerking him toward me; my elbow greets his chin. He's knocked backward, but three more soldiers take his place, one wrapping an arm around my neck while the other two hold my arms.

"Stop!"

We freeze at my father's booming voice, and for a second, I see the man I remember from my childhood. Strong, unwavering. He flits his gaze from one face to another, my own included.

"Just stop!"

Gallander gives a grin. "Thank you, Endenbough," He turns to the soldiers still holding me in their grasp. "Somebody give daddy's boy a punch. Anywhere you'd like."

The hands tighten on my arms, and just as I move to counter, I see the expression on my father's face. Balling my fists, I restrain myself, and I examine him as he examines me.

My father can see it in my eyes. The desire to kill, still not quite extinguished. At the look on his face, the desire mixes with a sick shroud of guilt, and there's a burst of pain as someone throws a fist into my jaw.

I taste blood. My father gives a furious grunt and shoots daggers at Gallander, who only smiles. "Again," he orders.

It's a blow to my stomach this time, doubling me over as the shock and pain flare through me. The hands drag me upright again as I gasp and cough at the ache. Then the fist comes once more, right across my cheekbone. Spots dance in front of me from the impact.

"Now I want you to start analyzing him, Endenbough," Gallander says as the soldiers hold me up again. "I let you have your little reunion, and no doubt you've told him all you know. Surely your son is now trying to devise some desperate scheme to get the both of you out of here. But you better start running those tests and find me those answers, or you'll get to see this lovely scene every day."

Gallander gestures to me, nods at his men, and one of them grins wickedly and pulls back his arm. My father barely keeps his mouth closed as the punch lands across my face again, blood dripping from the gash on my cheek. I grit my teeth and try to push past the pain, but my chest heaves for air, my body weak in their arms.

They tighten their grip on me, with one of them squeezing the patch of torn skin on my arm. I gasp in pain as the wound blazes to life again. The soldier chuckles and presses harder, forcing a groan from my throat while the others laugh alongside him.

My father speaks through teeth locked together. "I told you I would do it, Gallander."

"Good." He nods again to his soldiers.

One of them leans down beside my face. "That's just the beginning, Fiver boy," he sneers into my ear. "Your own daddy is gonna rip your body to shreds, and guess who gets to watch every second of it?"

Anger flares ten times higher than the pain in my arm. It burns behind my eyes until all I see is red, and I lose all restraint. "Certainly not you," I growl. I kick his shin, almost grinning in pleasure as he grimaces in pain and relinquishes his hold on my arm. My other arm is still firmly gripped by another soldier, but all I care about is plowing my fist into this one's face. Tactics and planning have gone out the window.

The soldier gives a shout of alarm, but it's too late to save his nose from busting beneath my knuckles. My hand explodes in pain at the force of the blow, but a satisfying spurt of blood gushes from his nose, and he crumples to the floor.

The other soldier wrenches my elbow behind my back with enough force that I cry out. An arm around my neck squeezes tightly, bending me forward while another soldier rushes to the aid of his fallen comrade. He touches the soldier's mangled face, his fingers becoming slick with blood. He turns his head to me, his features clouded with anger. "You could've killed him!" he spits, seething.

I grunt between clenched teeth but say nothing at the irony of it all. The soldier looks to Gallander for direction, but the man only locks his eyes onto me.

"Get him out of here," he points to the fallen soldier. The others glower at me, but they obey the order, retrieve their injured and groggy companion, and carefully help him out of the room.

Gallander doesn't move from where he stands, his hands pressed into his pockets. My father only shoots a furious stare at him before he crosses the distance between us and touches the bloody cuts on my face. I wince in pain, and he sets his jaw.

Gallander snarls. "I've changed my mind," he says, and my father blanches like a ghost. The Commander takes a step forward, and in the time it takes to blink, his arm is around my neck, clutching me tightly.

I blink in surprise, my hands flying to his forearm. I tug, but it's like pulling on a lump of stone. His grip doesn't waver, and neither does his stance, and no amount of struggling lessens his hold. My father watches with terror etched in the wrinkles of his face. His eyes widen as Gallander's other hand holds something in the air.

"No!" shouts my father, his voice nearly pleading.

Gallander mutters something back at him, but I can't make it out. I yank on that rock of an arm, but it still doesn't budge, and the reality of his abilities sinks in better than the punches to my face. He's stronger than I ever thought he was, even when I was a child. His reflexes are faster than a cobra's strike. My prayers to Elorai waft up to the ceiling, but I can't tell if they make it any higher.

"Don't!" my father shouts, but I feel the prick of the needle in the side of my neck. Gallander tosses me aside like a used rag. I hit the floor, and whatever was in the syringe is now swimming inside my veins. Fear washes over me, especially at the horror in my father's features.

The Commander throws the spent syringe onto an empty tray. "Figure it out, Endenbough," he says. "And don't be so dramatic. He's survived it twice before. What could be so different about this time?"

And without another word, he turns and marches for the door, slamming it behind him. I catch a glimpse of a soldier posted outside, sneering at me, before the heavy door abruptly cuts off the view.

"*He's survived it twice before,*" I think, the words echoing in my own mind.

That, combined with the sickened look on my father's face, confirms what I already fear.

Gallander has injected me with his serum.

Again.

FIFTY-ONE

I CLAMP MY HAND OVER THE SPOT WHERE THE NEEDLE pricked my neck. My eyes meet my father's, and they must be filled with fear because he shakes his head. He holds his hand out and helps me up from the floor.

"Come on, we need to get a sample," he says. I peer at another needle in his hand. Another tube, empty and waiting for my blood.

"Why?"

"It takes a few years for the pieces to come together and start working," he says. "But you can see the proteins almost instantly after the serum is injected."

His fingers tremble around the tube. "I don't like admitting it, but this is the best way to find out what happens to the serum when it . . ." His face becomes a picture of anguish. Sweat beads on his brow. Guilt-ridden eyes, a down-turned mouth. "We . . . we can see what happens to . . . to make it . . ."

"*To make it not kill me*," I think, not daring to say the words aloud.

I feel a painful swell in my chest. He doesn't know for sure that this time I will be so lucky. Neither do I. Any number of things could have prevented the serum from killing me. I may not have even been injected with it at all—someone could have made a mistake. There are too many uncertain variables to guarantee that I'll live.

My father knows this. He's terrified for me.

There's no room for more fear here. My hand clamps on his shoulder. "Dad." His head jerks at the word, something he hasn't heard in years. Something he isn't sure he is anymore. It's in his eyes. In his face, so much like my own.

"Come on, we'll get through it," I say. "I didn't come all this way to find you, only to watch you give up." I grip his wrist right above the hand that holds the needle. "So let's get on with it, alright?"

His hand no longer shakes, but the heartache still fills his face. He takes a deep breath, refusing to look at me, and I know he's caught between his conscience and his love for me. "I thought . . . I thought for sure you would hate me. For everything."

I frown. "What?"

He rubs his forehead with his free hand. When he speaks, his voice is barely audible. "We could have fought for you. We could have tried to get you away before they took you."

The muscles at the corners of my eyes twitch. "You couldn't have known. They send you that letter, then they show up the next morning and take your kid."

"We wanted to," he says, meeting my gaze. "When the Peacekeeper handed us that letter, a thousand ideas flew through my mind. A thousand questions: why didn't we leave Boqua before you'd been born? Why didn't we do more to hide you from them?" He bows his head, almost ashamed. "We wanted to fight them, but we were terrified of what they might do to you if we refused. We'd heard stories . . . " He sniffs. "And we let them take you. We knew what they were going to do with you, yet we let them take you." My insides burn.

My father sighs. "And all those people in the labs. All the kids who have died from my formulas. I thought that even if I ever managed to see you again, you'd be disgusted with me. So, I thought the best thing I could do was to keep fighting. Keep trying to find a way out of this mess, but nothing's worked. And you're no safer than when it all started."

The pang of Bone's betrayal rings again within me. He'd led me every step of the way, and I'd fallen for the whole thing, but there was one truth to everything he'd said: I did find my father.

A swell of determination rises inside me—the same invigoration that used to fill me at the critical moment of battle. "That doesn't mean we give up now. It just means it might be a little harder."

"You sound like my brother," he says.

I give a casual shrug. "I suppose I do."

His eyes widen. "You've met Nathaniel?"

I nod, a pang of sorrow in my chest at the thought of Dekkan torn to shreds by Gallander's soldiers. Is Nathaniel even alive?

I gesture at the needle in my father's hand. "Come on. Let's take a look at those proteins."

§

Another tube of scarlet blood sinks into the analyzing machine, and my father stares at the touchpad mounted to the wall.

"What is all this?" I ask, pointing at the swirling shapes on the touchpad.

"Everything that's in your blood," he replies. "The machine can identify every molecule in any substance it analyzes. It also can tell us the quantity in real time."

I peer at the screen. "So, what are we watching out for?"

My father's hand swipes across the screen, scrolling through the list of molecules. "There." He stops at one, tapping the three-dimensional image to enlarge it. The image fills the whole screen, and I see a great mass of spheres and lines, beneath which is a list of properties, including the size and number in the blood sample."This is berculan, one of the proteins from the serum."

I squint at the spinning picture. My father resizes it and slides it into one corner, where it remains as he scrolls through the list again. Two more molecules are added to this separate list in the corner.

"So this is what the stuff inside your blood looks like," I comment.

"Well, actually, this is just the chemical structure," he says. "A representation of what makes up the molecule, the atoms, and the bonds holding them together."

I stare at him. "You realize chemistry wasn't at the top of Gallander's education plan, right?"

My father smiles, still scrolling through the list. "You're a smart young man."

I frown. "But what's their purpose? What do they do?"

His finger swipes across the screen, flipping back to the list of selected molecules. "These proteins mostly catalyze the chemical reactions that let the serum attach to the neurons. Some of them work to carry out messages from your cells and tissues to keep your body making what the serum needs to work right. It can get complicated, but without them, the serum wouldn't work at all."

I chew the inside of my lip. "And they're inside me now."

He squints at the pictures on his list, and a number beneath one of them changes. His finger jabs at the screen. "Look!" he says, his arm extended. "See that?"

"What?" I peer closer at the screen, but all I see are the swirls.

"The number on this one changed," my father says. "The amount in the blood sample went down." There's a giddy glimmer in his eye.

"How is that possible?"

"Something destroyed it." He turns to me, his face beaming with relief. Another number changes on the screen. "Something in your blood is destroying the serum's proteins. It's too early to say, but it's possible that the serum won't function in you at all."

I look back at the screen. "What's doing it?"

He shakes his head. "No idea." He slides through the main list once more, scanning the screen. "But I don't think it'll help us figure out how to keep the serum from degrading. These proteins have nothing to do with that. It's a completely different problem."

"But people are dying from this," I tell him. "If we could destroy those proteins, it might save them."

He shakes his head again. "Even if we could figure out what's destroying them and stop the serum's effects, it doesn't mean it won't degrade in them anyway. The serum hasn't attached to your neurons yet, but it's been on theirs for years."

I clench my teeth. "And they have even less time left." The serum is killing them as we speak. Gallander is itching for answers he won't find in me, and my clogged brain still can't think of away to stop him from slaughtering us and countless others.

"You don't understand." My father taps at the touchpad. "Once the serum attaches to the neurons, it can't be removed. Not without stripping the axons clean."

"No, there has to be a way," I reply, scanning the screen desperately. "The answer has to be here, somewhere. We can't just give up and let them die."

My father sighs. "Joshua, the last round of subjects died two days ago."

Blood drains from my face. "What?"

"I'm sorry, Joshua. There was nothing to be done for them. Even if they could've been saved, they would have lived their lives as vegetables. The best I've been able to do is slow the rate of degradation, but nothing will stop it completely."

His features reflect sympathy and remorse, and even as the anger floods my veins, I know he did everything in his power and knowledge to stop the deaths. Gallander's face fills my mind, and I let him feed my fury. The others may not have had a chance, but we have the opportunity to make sure they were the last ones to die.

"Can you figure out what's breaking down the proteins?"

My father rubs the top of his head, examining the screen. "Yes. Possibly. But there are countless molecules in this sample, and I have no idea where to even start. It would take weeks to isolate a handful and test each one of them against each protein to see if it had any effect, and . . . "

I rub my eyes, a headache creeping across my temples.

" . . . even then, it wouldn't fool Gallander if we put our discovery into the serum. The gershawn rats would prove we'd tampered with it before we gave it to humans."

"But there may be a way to figure out how to make it into a cure. Maybe you could sort of hide it in the serum. We know the serum doesn't start working for years—couldn't you make the cure take a long time to start too?" I look at the screen where, with its list of countless spinning structures, the answer lies.

My father's brow furrows. "But how would we even get it to the—" He stops abruptly and turns his head toward the door to the other room as if some sound has alerted him.

"What—" I begin, but he holds up a hand and cuts me off. He watches the door intently, and my fingers flex in anticipation. Whatever he heard was not a reassuring sound, if such a thing could be found in this place. His muscles tense as he slides closer to the other room and slips inside. I follow him warily, senses peeled. We wait, breaths held.

I hear it. On the other side of the door to the hallway. A thump and a clatter. My father pulls on his beard as he listens, and I nearly leap for the door at the rattle of keys in the lock. The door flies open, revealing a soldier on the other side, his face gray and nervous. I squint in confusion, but a familiar face pops up over his shoulder, the deep voice hissing into his ear.

My gut squirms in a mixture of disgust and anger and shock. I thought I'd never see him again, especially with the determined gleam in his eye in such stark contrast to the look I'd last seen there.

"Move it, lunk!" Bone growls. The soldier jerks, his body arching as though something sharp had poked him in the back. "One squeak out of you, and it'll be the last sound you make."

The soldier scowls in anger and poorly suppressed terror, but he complies, moving slowly into the room, his arms raised. Bone shuts the door behind both of them. His eyes sweep the room and land on the metal table with its straps.

"Get over there," he orders, pressing whatever he has pointed against the soldier's back further into him. The soldier gives a grunt of irritation and a hard frown. But he obeys, marching toward the table and sliding up onto it. Bone pivots around behind him.

"Fiver, get over here and help me," he grunts.

I'm too stunned to move. Bone raises his eyebrows at me, as though his betrayal only hours ago never happened—like I've woken up from a bad dream and everything can return to the way it was before he stabbed me in the back and left me in Gallander's grip.

"Joshua, who is this man?" my father asks, his confusion evident.

I ignore him. "Bone? What are you doing here?" I force out.

"Get those straps, will you?" Bone says, an edge in his voice. I stare at him until his face clouds over with desperation and the soldier seems as though he's going to make a run for it, threat or no threat.

It's the same soldier who punched me earlier. I cross the room and grab him by the shoulders, shoving him onto his back while Bone fiddles with the restraints. When he's finished, my old Ace looks up at me, but I turn my head away and find my father's eyes waiting for me.

"Here." Bone holds out a roll of tape. "Keep him quiet."

The soldier glares at me as I slap a strip across his mouth, but he doesn't budge. Bone watches me solemnly, still holding the hunting knife. My knife. One of my larger ones, with the chip in the handle. Rage bubbles up inside like a swollen river threatening to burst over its banks. I hold out one hand.

"Give it to me."

He seems confused at my request, but then his face sparks with recognition. "Oh, yeah, I guess you'll want these back."

He pulls open a long leather jacket he didn't have on earlier and reveals my belt around his waist, each knife strapped into place. He undoes the buckle and slips it off. He passes the belt and the large hunting knife to me. I snatch them from his grasp, aiming the point of the knife at his neck.

"Give me one good reason why I shouldn't slit your throat," I growl.

He doesn't even flinch. "Fiver, I'm sorry, okay? I'm *sorry*. But—"

"—Don't you *dare* say that again!" I take a step forward, and Bone holds out his palms, his eyes glancing at the knife as if wondering if I would do it. And I would. I really, really would.

Except my father puts a gentle hand on my forearm. "Joshua," he says, his voice soft and pleading. I pause, debating fighting with him because all I feel is rage coursing through me. But the look in his eyes is enough, he doesn't need to say anything more, and I let him pull my arms down far enough for him to take the knife.

Bone lets out a breath, and I summon all my rage into my glare. "It wasn't just for me, Fiver," he finally says. "Gallander told me he'd get me a hovercab. Said I could put anyone I could fit in it and fly out of the country, no questions asked. Even someone in their prisons."

"What are you saying?" I growl at him.

His next words come out in nearly a whisper, and I have to read his lips to get what he's saying. "I wasn't the only one they kept in those cells, Fiver. They took my entire family. Made us watch while they tortured us one at a time. My brother almost died in there."

Pain flares in his face, the memories obviously clear and pristine in his mind. It never occurred to me that Bone had a family. Certainly not one he remembered or cared about. But, judging by the fervor in his eyes, this time, there is no lie.

"I would have done anything to get them out of there, Fiver," he says, his teeth pressed together with raw determination. "Just like you would for your father."

It doesn't stop the anger or the sick feeling of betrayal I feel radiating off him. "Then why are you here?" I spit. "Why aren't you with them?"

"They're safe," he assures me. There's a spark of relief in his eyes. "I made sure they got out. They're in Lucia, and they're being taken care of." His hand rubs at his forehead, smoothing the wrinkles etched in his skin. "But I had to . . . I had to come back. I got what I wanted, and you paid for it. Whatever happens to me now . . ." he shrugs, " . . . you could say I'll get what's coming to me."

"You want to help us?" my dad asks, clearly confused. He can't know that Bone betrayed me, but he must know something terrible has passed between us.

I twist my head as I stare at Bone with suspicion.

"I want to set it straight," he says.

I scoff. "What have you got to offer us? You're one man. They've got guns and bombs and numbers to back them up."

He shakes his head. "What happened to the guy who's always breaking out of impossible situations?"

I tense, my hands clenching. "Don't start that with me."

His mouth twists upward in a broad grin.

"Just wait, Fiver," he says. "The cavalry's coming."

FIFTY-TWO

"You think you can just waltz in here, and I'll trust you again?"

Bone ignores my question, moving away from the furious soldier on the table and toward the other room.

My father steps beside me, tilting his head. "Maybe the real question should be: how did he waltz in here in the first place?"

Bone offers a cocky grin, familiar except for the flash of guilt behind it. I scowl and turn away.

"Come on, Fiver," Bone says. "You can hate me all you want later, but right now we have more important things to worry about."

"Spare me," I growl, pushing past him into the other room. But before I take two steps inside, a heavy, large weight crashes into me from behind. I gasp in shock as the force drives me downward. Bone deftly flips me on my back and pins me there, one arm barred across my neck while his other hand clasps my wrist.

I could reverse his hold in two moves, but I stop struggling at the glint in his eye. "Listen to me, you thick-headed lunk!" Bone hisses. "I hid three Boquan bodies in closets, and I nearly got captured trying to make my way back here. I've got no more second chances—if they catch me, they'll execute me on the spot. You're pissed and have every right to be, but I'm not dying for you because you're holding a grudge when all our lives are at risk!" He sucks in a breath. "You wanna kill me? Fine. Just wait until you know for sure that you and your father are safe first."

He waits a moment, seething down at me, before he loosens his grip and steps away. I push off from the floor and growl at him, but he ignores me.

"I need to know what assets you have here," he says to my father, as if I automatically accepted his whole speech. "What you have access to, what you can control."

My father grimaces. "Not much. Gallander has many scientists on his team, but I'm isolated from all of them."

Bone paces the room, scanning the equipment. "What are all these machines?"

"Mostly analyzing equipment. The cabinets in the back hold chemicals and lab supplies."

Bone thinks for a moment. "Is there anything you can think of, or create, that would help us get out of the building?"

My father bites his lip. "I've been trying to do that for over a decade," he answers, a hard look in his eye. "It's impossible. There are too many guards and too little opportunity."

Bone steps closer. "Yes, but what if you had backup?"

I screw up my face. "What do you mean?"

Bone refocuses on the plants. "What is this stuff?" he asks, fiddling with a leaf. He plucks it and holds it to his nostrils. "Smells a bit like strawberries."

My father takes the leaf from his hands. "It certainly doesn't taste like strawberries, and it's the cause of this whole mess, so—" His face pales, his mouth falling open as he stares at the leaf. He brings it to his nose and inhales. My heart flutters, and I must have flinched visibly because he asks, "Joshua, what is it?"

"Smells like strawberries . . . "

My father stares at me, my face twisted with confusion. Bone mirrors my look, his arms crossed.

My father glances at Bone, then back at me. "You remember the plant?" I nod as he continues, "You remember where we used to live?"

I nod again, a jerk in my gut at the thought of the old house. "Right next to Endenbough Wood," I choke out.

An amused expression crosses my father's face. "Endenbough Wood? Is that what you call the Crosswoods?"

I lift my shoulder, anxious to hear what's going through his mind. "I used to think you owned the Wood." My voice is thick. "So I thought it should be named after you. When I went back and found the house destroyed . . . I went into the trees. It was the closest thing I had to home." A mix of gratitude and sorrow gleams in his eyes.

Bone clears his throat. "This is all very touching, but what does it have to do with this silly plant?"

My father swallows, still focused on me. "You remember how we used to take walks through the forest? We'd even camp there overnight sometimes."

I nod again. How could I forget? I'd dreamed of those days, when everything was simple, and each day was sure to bring nothing but security and love.

"On our walks, I used to catch you eating random things all the time. You thought it was fun, living off the land like a pioneer, finding your own food."

His words cut uncomfortably close. Does he know how I've spent the last two and a half years of my life?

My father holds up the leaf. "One of them was this plant. You said it smelled like strawberries, and I caught you eating it more than once." He smiles at the memory, stroking his palm with the leaf. Then he crumples it into a ball and lets it drop, bruised and crinkled, from his hand.

"Again," Bone says gruffly. "What does this have to do with anything?"

My father looks at him. "I have an idea."

§

The white rat wiggles its nose in my direction, but it scurries to the other side of the glass tank as my father lowers his gloved arm in its direction once again. He clamps his hand on the rat and holds it steady as his other hand moves down with the second syringe. The rat squirms and tries to bite, but all too soon the needle sticks, and my father releases the animal, letting it scurry off.

"And what is this experiment of yours supposed to prove?" Bone asks, glancing at the clock on the wall. "We only have so much time before someone finds those guards. I wanted to use the few minutes we have here to figure out an escape plan, not poke at rats."

"Shh!" my father says, tossing the syringe away and reaching for another needle. "It's been over ten minutes now. I need to get this blood sample as soon as possible."

He grabs the rat again, and blood fills the tube. My father releases the animal and takes the tube back to his analyzing machine. He taps the touchpad once again, pulling up a command list. He taps "Full Analysis," and a blue cube fills the screen and begins flipping over and over as the machine does its work.

"What are we looking for?" I ask.

My father holds his chin in one hand. "The rat has never been exposed to the serum before. That's what the second injection was. The first was a solution of Vitmor in its natural state."

"So what?" Bone asks, his arms crossed again. He squints as he watches the screen.

"The particles that the serum needs to work come from the plant. But what if . . . "

The machine beeps, its command fulfilled, and my father quickly runs through the populated results, picking out specific proteins and placing them in a separate list. When he's finished, we stare at the screen, and I suspect I know what will happen next.

Sure enough, after a moment, the quantity of one of the proteins drops. Then another. And another. My father smiles.

"What?" Bone nearly shouts.

"How did that happen?" I ask.

My father nods, looking at the screen. "I'd need to do more extensive tests to be sure, but I would guess when the raw form of Vitmor is introduced, the body sees it as foreign and makes antibodies for it."

"Anti-what?" snaps Bone. His patience with scientific experimentation is thinning.

"Antibodies are the immune system's way of destroying things that can make you sick when they come into your body," my father explains. "If your system sees something that doesn't belong, it can start making special particles that will target it. Then, the next time your immune system comes in contact with the threat, it can destroy it."

"And you think that's what's happening now?" I ask, watching the screen as more numbers drop.

"You ate the plant. Your immune system saw the particles and produced antibodies. When Gallander injected you with the serum, those antibodies destroyed it before it could attach to your neurons. It's the only explanation that makes sense."

I shake my head. "But the serum contains the proteins," I say. "Why doesn't the body produce these antibodies after it's injected?"

He turns from the screen. "By the time they could be produced, the serum would have already attached itself to the neurons and changed their shape. The new antibodies wouldn't recognize it after that."

"But wouldn't the antibodies form almost instantly, like they did with the rat?" I ask.

"No. It would take a week or two for them to form completely in humans. The process is sped up in gershawn rats because that's how we've bred them. A few minutes to us is like a week to them."

"So, wait a minute." Bone holds out a hand. "You're saying, if you eat this plant before you get injected with Gallander's wonder drug, you become immune to it?"

My father's head wobbles before it dips in a nod. "I think so, yes."

"Well, that's well and good for Fiver here, but how is that going to help everyone else? There's no way we could get that plant to everyone on the planet before Gallander figured out what we were doing. If we even managed to get out of here in the first place."

My father grips his chin again, moving away from the screen. "There is . . . one other thing we could do." His gaze settles on me, causing an uneasy quiver in my stomach.

"Destroy all the Vitmor," he says, his voice deep and grave. "A few years ago, I started working on a way to do it, but I had to stop before Gallander found me out."

"How could you do that?" Bone asks.

He sighs. "Vitmor only grows in the Crosswoods because the soil there is incredibly unique. I figured out the exact compounds that the Vitmor feeds on. And I figured out how to kill it."

"Well, that sounds promising," Bone replies. My father looks at me, then reaches deep into a cabinet below the countertop and fishes around for a moment before pulling out a cylindrical canister. "I kept this information from Gallander as best I could. I hoped I'd be able to use it later. The virus I created is in here. The compounds in the soil will be destroyed on contact, and the effect can spread across the Crosswoods." He pauses and shakes his head. "But we need a way to deliver the virus. I thought perhaps, if I got lucky, I could use Yosher and his explosives to do it, but now . . . "

"You want to destroy the Wood," I say, the weight of the statement pressing heavily on my chest.

"If we can destroy every plant, and the compounds in the soil that allow it to grow, no one will ever be able to harvest Vitmor again."

The Wood. My home. My throat swells, a pang piercing in my heart. But even as I try to convince myself that there has to be something else we can do, the reality of it solidifies in my head: we're not going to find the answer in my blood, and the only way forward is to destroy the serum's essential component.

Destroy Endenbough Wood.

"But how would we even do that?" Bone asks. "We're going to have enough trouble getting out of this building alive, much less blowing up a forest."

Just as my father seems to figure it out, I know the answer. "Gallander was going to bomb parts of the Wood to clear it," I say. "If we can take over that system, there's our means." I turn to Bone. "Now what were you saying about backup?"

His lips widen into a grin. "I did mention the cavalry, didn't I?"

My eyebrows pinch together. "What—"

My question is cut off as the building quakes with such force that we're nearly thrown from our feet. The room blurs as the machines rattle, papers blow off tables, and glass shatters from falling beakers and instruments. My knee strikes the floor with a sharp burst of pain, and my arms fly out for something to hold onto as another violent spasm rips through the building.

Bone's face radiates with shock as he clings to a table to keep himself from toppling over. My arm catches something soft—my father's jacket—and I cling to it and pull him close, his face wan with fear.

"They're storming the gates!" Bone shouts above the noise.

It takes a moment, but slowly, the room stills. We're left surrounded by scattered papers and shards of glass.

"Who is it?" I demand, pulling my father next to me. Bone turns, giving me his classic grin, the one that tells me he's about to reveal something I should already know.

"Who do you think?"

FIFTY-THREE

 in the room into a large, mechanical canister that makes loud, grinding noises and opens up empty whenever he lifts the lid to add more Vitmor. Every piece. He even tosses the folder filled with his research inside. He'll either make it out of here alive or not; either way, he won't be needing it any longer.

"Of course, we don't have much to show them now, thanks to this little jaunt into the scientific jungle," Bone grumbles, watching my father move. "But at least we'll have more bodies to back us up."

"Are you telling me they're alive?" I step in front of him, eyeing him with caution. He nods.

"Alive and well. All of them. Well, except for Tomas, of course. Shame, that. I didn't mind him all that much."

I feel the pang of Tomas's loss. The notebook of pictures he carried. "How did they get in here?" I ask.

The room buckles again, more glass clattering to the floor and breaking into shards. Bone shields his head from more flying debris and shakes it. "They're not in yet. Boquans put up a good fight, you know. Especially ones trained to protect Gallander's secrets."

Lukas. Alive. I can't stop the surge of joy inside my chest. Jakob, Asher, Jael. Even Micah. I lunge forward, toward the door. "We have to help them!"

"Easy there." Bone stiffens his arms in front of me. "They can handle it. It's you they're coming to save, not the other way around."

As if on cue, the door bursts open and two Boquan soldiers fall to the floor inside. A familiar figure steps over them without glancing down and hefts his rifle in the air. His smirk still remains, but the tone of it has changed. More sincere, somehow.

"Well, will you look at that?" Micah says, moving further into the room. "The traitor actually told the truth."

The others follow close behind, weapons drawn. The last one in is Lukas, who's gripping a rifle he instantly drops at the sight of me.

"You're alive!" he shouts, his face beaming. He dashes away from the others and slams into me, wrapping his arms around my torso. I'm taken aback. How can they all be here? I saw that bomb explode with my own eyes.

But Lukas's grip is real, and when he steps back, his eyes are alight with relief. I crack a small grin.

"You're alive, too." My forehead furrows. "But how? The bomb . . ."

"The bomb never touched us," Jael assures me. "We got lucky. It landed in front of us, and we got knocked backward, but it was nowhere close to a direct hit. But when we couldn't find the two of you in the debris, we thought the blast vaporized *you*."

"Until this lowlife found us outside the facility," Micah says, gesturing at Bone with his gun.

Bone smirks. "And you'd still be wandering around like a bunch of lost puppies if I hadn't told you Fiver was alive."

Micah glares at him, and the others match his furious expression. He steps closer, hefting his gun in both hands. "Actually, I thought about bashing this lunk's head in for what he did, but then I would have to admit I've got a soft spot for you."

Micah turns to me, and I feel that odd feeling again—some kind of acceptance. The strange air of his tone, the look on his face. Almost . . . respect? No. Can't be. But the others stare at me with the same look— even Asher, whose best friend was lost while executing my plans.

"Nova was a surprise, though," Micah says. "Didn't expect her to personally come on this raid."

My features fall into a heap. "Nova? She's here?"

Micah's smile stretches across one side of his face. "Marria's one determined lady," he says. "Almost every squad Nova has is downstairs, pulling the guards off of us up here. Don't know how she convinced Nova to do it, but we never would've gotten this far without them."

"Between Marria, Jolan, and Beams, they must have talked some sense into her," Asher adds.

Micah's smile disappears. "Now, we won't be alone in this room for much longer, so what do you know?"

My gaze flicks to my father. His eyes are hollow, but he blinks and shakes himself out of his stupor. He sets his jaw and tells everyone our plans.

Micah rotates his shoulders. "Well, Gallander's never going to sit still for that."

My back straightens. This plan has to work. It's the only one we have left. My father, as if agreeing with my thoughts, passes the canister holding the virus to me.

"We'll have to attach the virus to the missile's systems and set it off," Bone says. "Gallander's got a whole store of explosives in the basement. It's always good to keep an arsenal around to protect your secret research facility."

Jakob frowns. "You want us to launch one of Gallander's own missiles?"

Bone nods. "Do any of you know anything about explosives?"

All eyes train on Asher, who steps forward with determination.

Bone holds up a hand. "No, I'll do it. We're gonna need our best tech guy up here to set it off."

"What do you mean?" Micah says. He's got an expression that tells me he doesn't like the plan he's heard.

"The missiles can only be launched from the command center, which is somewhere in this building. We'll have to go down to the basement, pick a missile, and put the virus inside it. We need someone up here who can set it off as soon as we get it in position."

"But *you*?" Jael says, her eyes skeptical.

Bone grins at her. "I'm full of surprises, sweetheart."

She glares at him as Micah scowls. "Call me sweetheart again, lunk, and I'll bust your nose," she snaps.

Bone ignores her. "We have to find the command center," he says.

"Second floor, back hallway. Third door on the left." We turn and look at my father. He doesn't wither underneath our surprised stares, but instead he lifts his head in determination. "I've been here for a long time," he says. "At least I should know something about the layout."

I slowly nod. "That's where we need to go, then."

"It'll be crawling with soldiers," Jakob says. "Nova's forces wouldn't have pulled them out of there. We'll have to fight our way in."

Micah jams a fresh round of ammunition into his gun. "We're ready for them," he says in a grim voice. "They'll pay for Tomas. Pay for everyone. Let's go."

As soon as we step into the hallway, it's a barrage of shouts and bullets. Micah screams for cover fire, and Jakob sprays the end of the hallway with bullets while the rest of us tumble away in the other direction. I reach for my father's jacket and haul him in front of me, Lukas next in my grasp. Jakob glances behind to make sure we're moving before laying down a few more shots and sprinting after us.

We careen toward the corner, sliding around it on our knees. Micah slams himself up against a wall, peering around the corner as the onslaught of soldiers barrels toward us.

"Jael!" he shouts, squeezing off rounds. "Cover our six! The rest of you get to that door!"

We move, but soldiers from the other end of the hallway have rounded the corner. They shout, and Jael fires, putting several of them down before they can even lift their guns in defense. "Come on, go!" she shouts. "Third door on the left!"

My father nods, his face white. Micah fires again, then grunts as his ammo runs out. Asher takes his place smoothly while Micah bends to reload, bullets taking off chunks of the concrete wall above.

Armed with just my knives, I'm not much help beyond hurrying my father along and making sure Lukas doesn't blow his own head off with the rifle he's carrying. I watch him squeeze off a few rounds, and the sight takes me back to the Barracks. To me at his age. Killing. Not thinking twice. Bile rises in my throat, but I swallow the bitter taste as we arrive at the door.

We're exposed here in the hallway, but I still hesitate to open the door. No sounds that I can hear come from the room within. No movement, either. Have all the guards left, joining the search? Or are they inside, waiting for us?

Micah shouts again. The shots ring out somewhere down the hall, and he throws his rifle up to his shoulder, ducking behind the doorframe. The others brace themselves as well, most focused toward the sound of the shots, but Jakob has pivoted himself to keep one eye on the other direction as well.

Micah fumbles in his vest pocket and produces a small, black walkie-talkie that he tosses to Bone. "We'll let you know when we're ready. Let us know which missile to launch," he hisses. "And don't get lost on the way!"

I glare at him, soldiers pounding down the hallway for us. We're not even inside the command center, and he's sending us away now?

Micah snarls. "Go!" he hisses. "We'll hold them off!"

I want to ask him what his plan is after I get the virus in place, or what he's going to do if I don't make it at all, but he doesn't give me much time to say anything as he lets off a round from his gun.

"Come on!" Bone grabs my arm and propels me forward toward the stairwell. I fight the overwhelming urge to back away—the last time he encouraged me to follow him, I'd ended up strapped to a table and looking up at Gallander's sneering face. Bone's excited expression falls away at my scowl, but I don't give him a chance to respond as I push past him toward the stairs.

We've descended into the depths of the school, where boiler rooms and storage closets once had much different purposes than they do now, when Bone jerks to the side and whirls around at the same time, his hand on his pistol.

I reach for my knives, but the shadowy figure holds up both hands and steps closer.

"Easy, it's me!" Lukas says. I exchange a relieved glance with Bone, who lets out a tired sigh.

"What are you doing?" I say. "Get out of here!"

"You think it's safer up there with all those bullets flying around?" he responds, crossing his arms.

He has me there, and I bite my lip. "Fine. But stay close and stay quiet!"

Lukas smirks. "You wouldn't hear me, anyway."

I roll my eyes at him. While he has yet another point, this is no time for fooling around.

"It should be close," Bone says, holstering his gun. "There's not much space left big enough to hold the arsenal."

The next door we try is locked. Bone levels a kick at it, and it flies open. Shocked, a curse flies from his lips at what's inside. Not missiles. Cells. A row on each side of the room and a cowering, fearful prisoner inside of each one. Some of them call out, while others can only manage a moan or a grunt.

My breath hitches in my throat. Bone said they'd been using humans in dozens of experiments—Gallander had to hide them somewhere. My stomach rebels at their pain-filled eyes, all watching me in fear.

Bone grimaces, and he backs out of the room. "Come on. We have to move."

"Wait, you're just going to leave them there?" Lukas protests.

"There's no time," Bone replies. "With all the shooting, they'll be safer in there than out here."

Lukas's head flies around, searching out the source of some sound. Bone lifts his gaze as well, and I turn as one figure struggles to pull herself to her feet. Mangy blonde hair covers her forehead, and although her lips move in a whisper I can't hear, I can still make out the single word she speaks.

"Lukas?"

His eyes grow wider than I've ever seen. With a gasp, Lukas sprints across the room. He crashes into the cell door, reaching for her hands.

"Mom! Mom, it's me!" he cries. Rebekah Garrow blinks as though she's not sure she's seeing what's right in front of her. Red welts cover her face and arms, and long gashes mar her skin. Her clothes are blood-stained and tattered, and she pushes her thin arms out between the bars to touch her son's face.

"Is it really you?" she whispers. Lukas nods his head like a bouncing rubber ball.

"I'm here, it's me," he says. "Don't worry, I'll get you out."

Rebekah gives a weak smile and runs her fingers down his cheek. She lets out a relieved sigh before a racking cough grips her. Lukas cries out as she stumbles away from the bars, gripping her sides as she struggles to breathe.

"Mom!" he screams, grabbing hold of the bars. Rebekah moans, wincing in pain, as her legs give out and she collapses, her body twitching in violent spasms.

Lukas screams louder. "Mom!" He glances back at us, practically begging. "Get this door open! Hurry!"

Bone's face is etched with sympathy, but he makes no move forward. Lukas turns desperately to me, but Rebekah has stopped moving, her eyes closed, her lungs no longer pulling in air.

"Lukas . . ."

"Get it open!" he yells, tugging at the bars. I move closer and pull his hands away. He yanks himself from my grasp, and his palm flies up and slaps me hard. The shock of it stings far more than the pain.

"You promised!" he cries, his tears welling up. My chest aches with his pain, my throat tight.

"I'm sorry, Lukas," I croak. "There was nothing we could—"

Rebekah's body gives a rasping cough.

All eyes fly to her, her head lolling to one side. My heart surges, and Lukas's features reflect a renewed panic. I whirl back to Bone, and above his head, on a nail in the wall, is a sight that nearly drives the air from my lungs.

A set of keys.

"Bone! On the wall behind you!" He turns, grabs the keys, and tosses them to me. I fumble with them, jamming various keys into the lock on Rebekah's cell. As soon as I find the right one and the door opens, Lukas is on his knees beside his mother.

"Mom, wake up!" he pleads, brushing the hair away from her face.

"Get out of the way!" Bone orders, pushing his way into the cell. Lukas leaps back as Rebekah gasps for air.

Bone reaches into his jacket pocket and pulls out a small metal box. From inside it, he takes out a thin tube with a cap on one end. He pulls the cap off, revealing a tiny needle.

Lukas winces as he jabs it into her thigh. Within seconds, Rebekah's breathing has returned to normal, and she lets out a long sigh as her head falls to one side.

"Teluriam fever," Bone grunts, tossing aside the tube. "I had a bad case of it last year. Gotta carry meds in case my throat seizes." He rakes over Rebekah. "Looks like they've been exposing her to it for a long time."

"Will she be alright?" Lukas inches closer, his face ashen.

Bone nods. "Meds'll help. She'll sleep for a while, but if she gets a regular dose every day, she should come out of it."

Lukas looks up at him, relief swimming across his features. "Thank you."

Bone grunts. "We've wasted enough time here. There's no telling what's going on upstairs. You coming or not?"

Lukas's eyes flash, but he looks from his mother to me, and his hard expression softens, almost into guilt. "I can't just leave her."

A small smile crosses my face.

"Here." I toss him the keys to the cells. "You keep charge of these, okay?"

He nods. Bone sighs, gathers the weak woman in his arms, and lays her on the makeshift bed in the corner.

A few doors down, we come to another locked room. Bone aims

another kick, and this time, when the door flies open, we see a room full of missiles going all the way up to the incredibly tall ceiling. We tilt our heads back at the whole scene before us, the missiles looming over us like sleeping giants.

Bone ducks further into the room, me close behind him. He turns so I can see his lips as he speaks. "Lucky we caused a big commotion upstairs. Otherwise, this place would be crawling with soldiers."

"How is this possible?" I ask, circling as I stare at the ceiling. "These should be tearing through the roof right now."

"I'm pretty sure this room is an add-on to the school," Bone says, bending down beside one of the missiles. "They dug it out right next to the original building."

"How do you do that?"

"Very carefully," Bone grunts. "Gimme the virus."

I reach into my jacket and produce the canister. "Which one are you putting it in?"

Bone cocks his head and recites the characters identifying the missile he chose. "X-138. This'll wipe out nearly the entire Wood all by itself. Make sure that tech of yours knows which one to blow. Don't want him setting off a firecracker instead."

"How far away do we need to be?" I ignore the twinge in my gut.

Bone shrugs. "Doesn't matter. This missile has a waco exhaust system. The heat from the detonation gets funneled into vent shafts and dispersed back to the surface. There'll be a lot of smoke, but as long as you don't touch the casing, you'll be fine."

He undoes a latch and lets a small door on the side of the missile swing open. Inside is a tangle of wires and metal that make no sense to me, but Bone rubs his palms together like he's ready to dive in and eat the thing.

"You sure you know how to do this?" I ask.

He grins. "Sure thing, Fiver." He reaches out his hand, and I extend mine, but before his fingers can grasp the canister my father gave me, a crash sounds from the other side of the room. The canister drops to the floor with a muffled thump, and Bone's eyes fill with horror at the sight behind me.

Four soldiers have stormed into the room, and right behind them is Abraham Gallander himself, complete with a demented smile of greeting.

FIFTY-FOUR

THE SOLDIERS CARRY KNIVES INSTEAD OF GUNS—PRE-sumably because no one wants to be blown up if they can avoid it—which is the only reason we're not dead on the spot. But Gallander's sniggering face doesn't seem at all worried as he moves forward with long strides.

"Well, well, what could possibly have led you boys to this particular room? This was my best-kept secret."

"Cat's outta the bag, you might say," Bone grunts, his features hardened into an expression of stiff fury.

Gallander looks at him and his grin widens. "Tired of your freedom already, Bone?" he says, his voice grinding in my ear. "Your family must be, too."

Bone's jaw tightens, his face flushes red. His head tilts down and his eyebrows form a solid line across his forehead. "You touch any one of them, and I'll skin you alive."

Gallander chuckles. "That may be difficult to do with your insides strung up like party decorations." He cocks his head toward his soldiers, who are still poised and ready for a fight. My hands have slowly inched toward my belt, fingers brushing the knives holstered there. "I want Fiver alive. Kill the traitor," Gallander demands.

The soldiers rush forward like a flood of muddy water, splitting up and lifting their blades. I fling one of my own, but I misjudged the man's speed, and the knife flies harmlessly out behind him. Before I can see what happens to the second dagger I throw, I duck behind one of the tall missiles and press my back against it.

Bone's fear-filled eyes meet mine, and his hand tightens on the door of the missile's cavity. I'm sure we're thinking the same thing: *The canister. The virus.*" How long can Micah and the others hold the soldiers off upstairs?

Bone sets his jaw and surges forward toward the fallen canister just as one of Gallander's soldiers rounds the corner and plows his shoulder into him. The two men tumble downward, the soldier straddling Bone's torso. The soldier burns with rage, and I think the only thing that saved Bone from a knife in his back was his enemy's heated desire to see the look in his face when the blade hit its mark.

But Bone has his own anger to feed, and he bucks himself upward. Delivering a heavy punch to the chin, he rolls the man onto his back. The two continue their struggle, but the canister is still on the floor, not three meters from them.

Two feet step in front of it, a hand reaches down to grasp it between long fingers. The soldier darts his eyes from the canister to me and cracks a grin. "Looking for this?" He wiggles it at me as Bone heaves the bloodied soldier he's been grappling to his feet and shoves him at the other.

The second soldier grunts as the disoriented soldier crashes against him, and they tumble backward. I lunge forward, ready to grab the canister, but it clatters to the floor. The second soldier groans beneath the weight of the other one, and I scoop the canister up as Bone drives his blade into the second soldier's back.

I thrust the canister over to Bone. "Get it in the missile!" I shout. "I'll hold them off!"

He nods and takes the virus with one blood-stained hand. I turn back to the soldier struggling underneath the dead weight of his companion. He's not going anywhere.

Lukas's cry is like a bolt of lightning to my spine. My aim had been true on my second knife-throw, but even with one other soldier dead and another down, there was still one more left. And Gallander.

I dart around the missiles, searching for the source of Lukas's scream. Fear shoots through me as I find him in the grip of Gallander's last soldier, his fingers wrapped around Lukas's neck and pushing him up against the wall. Lukas pulls desperately at the fingers around his throat, and metal flashes as the soldier reaches for the knife at his belt with his free hand.

"No!" The sound bursts from my lungs, fear filling me. Lukas was supposed to be safe with his mother. Why is he here? I can't lose him again. I won't. I promised I would keep him alive, and I almost failed. I won't do it again.

The soldier lifts the knife, and Lukas goes pale at the sight of the blade. The hand plummets downward, but Lukas lifts his arm and blocks the hit, and suddenly the fear on his face evaporates like a raindrop in a campfire.

His eyes flare in fury. These are the people who took his mother. Who tortured and nearly killed her.

With his other arm, he reaches up and pries one of the soldier's fingers off his neck and yanks it backward. I don't hear the snap, but the finger sticks out at a strange angle with the soldier shouting in pain. Lukas is reaching for another finger as his attacker releases him and takes a wild, enraged swing with his knife.

Lukas lunges, but before I can reach him, another hand stretches out of the shadows and grips his shoulder. Blood freezes in my veins, and Lukas's face again drains of color as Gallander steps out from behind one of the missiles and yanks Lukas around to face him. The Commander offers one stiff smile before he plows his fist into Lukas's cheekbone hard enough to knock him off his feet.

"Fiver!" Bone's voice barely reaches my ears. I turn and see him struggling with the soldier I'd left him with, one hand holding the man off while the other desperately reaches for the opening in the missile. The canister is inside, connected to wires and tubes. Bone's face strains, veins protruding from his forehead as he struggles to bring his hand to the door.

The soldier grabs at Bone's neck and thrusts his hand forward. Bone freezes, his lips parting strangely. The soldier steps back, and I see the hilt protruding from Bone's chest.

A breath hitches in my throat. Pain and shock flare in Bone's eyes, but as the soldier's face breaks into a devilish grin of triumph, anger bursts through me like a gushing waterfall. I barely feel my feet hit the floor as they propel me forward. My knife slides easily into the soldier's back, and he collapses with a grunt. Bone's jaw clenches, even as he sways on his feet, and with one last surge of strength, he staggers forward, reaches up to the opening in the missile, and slams the door shut. There's a hiss and a puff of smoke, and a light blinks red.

Bone's eyes gloss over, and though he tries to remain upright, his legs buckle beneath him as he crashes to the floor. My insides seize, all the anger and betrayal I still held inside vanishing at the sight of his blood staining the front of his shirt.

I'm on my knees at his side, watching in horror as he tries to hold on to consciousness. The blade has missed his heart, but there's no doubt it caught a lung. His eyelids flutter, but he catches my gaze, then looks at the missile.

"It's in," he grunts, grimacing in pain. "It's ready to go." His hands paw at the walkie-talkie poking out of his pocket. Asher. We have to tell Asher to blow it.

I move to take the walkie-talkie from his pocket, but hands grip my arms and yank me up. I cry out and jerk against their hold; Bone lets out a weary sigh and his eyes close as they drag me further away from him. And the walkie-talkie.

Gallander's face looms in front of me, and his soldier shoves me to the Commander's feet. Gallander laughs. "Just can't beat me, can you?" He waves at his remaining soldier. "Go join the rest of the squadron and take care of the others."

The soldier nods obediently and jogs toward the door. I push myself to my feet and steel my resolve. We're running out of time. I have to get the missile's number to Asher, but Gallander watches my every movement. I'll never make it the three steps to Bone and get the walkie-talkie.

I can't just stand here.

Gallander pops his joints and stretches his muscles, assuring me of his power before I even move.

"Are you sure you want to start this battle with me, son?" The Commander's eyes narrow at me, shooting out all his potential in one glare. I'd seen that look on his face before, whenever he was about to slaughter someone.

I open my mouth, begging my voice not to shake. "Someone has to stop you." It's low, but there's no quiver.

Gallander laughs out a booming sound. "And who's that gonna be? You?" He flexes his biceps, the muscles straining against his uniform's shirt. "You're a good soldier, Fiver, I'll give you that, but you're no match for me."

In a flash, he shoots forward, his arm stretched out to catch my torso as he passes. I'm on the ground gasping for air before I even register his movement.

He looms over me, his fists balled. "I could kill you in less than a second," he growls.

With my hand pressed into my bruised chest, I pant, trying to pull air into my lungs as I struggle to prop myself up on one elbow. "Then . . . do it already," I say between breaths.

Gallander lets his lips stretch wide. "Not yet, Fiver," he says, crouching beside me. "I still need you. And your father. But once I get my serum, don't worry, I'll be more than happy to put you out of your misery."

Rage builds beneath my skin, my teeth grinding together. I consider Gallander's words for only a second before my fist flies forward, aiming straight for his face.

His hand catches it in midair, yanking my wrist to the side. I shout in pain and shock. Frustration rips through my veins; how can he move so fast?

"Don't even try," he growls at me, pulling my arm back to bring my body closer to his. Pain explodes through my face as he lands a punch to the side of my head. Black spots flash in my vision as he releases my hand. I slump to the floor and gasp for breath, struggling to clear my sight.

Once the spots begin to fade, a sole figure moves in the background behind Gallander. I blink, and Lukas's face comes into clearer focus. There's a giant purple bruise swelling out from his temple and going all the way down his cheek, but his eyes are hard as ice. He's looking right at Gallander.

I shake my head, but he only mimes talking into a walkie-talkie before he lunges. My heart drops like bullets in water. Gallander notices, but it's too late, and Lukas has his arms wrapped around the Commander's neck.

Gallander roars like a poked tiger, straightening his legs and reaching for Lukas, who's now hanging from his neck. His eyes are squeezed shut, his arms gripping the Commander with all his strength.

It won't take long for Gallander to throw him off, hurl him across the room like a wet towel. I turn onto my stomach, peering over to where Bone lays. Pushing with my feet, I half-crawl, half-slide to his side and reach for the little black box still in his pocket.

Hands trembling, refusing to consider if Lukas is still holding Gallander off, I mash the button and practically scream into the receiver.

"Asher! Number X-138! Number X-138! Blow it now!"

§

There's no time to pray my message got through, or even hope that someone is still alive upstairs. I start to repeat the instructions, but the walkie-talkie is ripped from my hand, and I whirl around to face the Commander. He squeezes the device in his giant fist, the plastic cracking beneath the pressure. Before I can blink, his other arm flies down, his hand gripping the front of my shirt. With an inhuman snarl, Gallander flings me aside, my shoulder cracking against the cement floor.

I shift, moving to face him before he can come at me again, but his eyes aren't on me. They're fixed on the missile. He steps toward it, tossing the mangled walkie-talkie to the floor. My stomach shrinks in horror. He's going to remove the canister with the virus. All he has to do is rip it out, and it will all be over. His hands reach for the small door in the side of the missile.

My shoulder aches, and my muscles protest, but a fierce cry wrenches from my throat as I force myself to my feet. With every ounce of strength left in me, I spring forward, propelling myself at the Commander's legs.

Gallander's hand is on the handle of the small door as my body crashes into his. His knees buckle, and we tumble together in a twisted mass, my fingers clutching at his uniform with an iron grip.

A low rumbling rises from beneath the floor. The room trembles around us, the deep growl from below growing louder. Sunlight bleeds in from above as the ceiling begins to retract with a grating sound.

Gallander gasps, wriggling in my hold. I clench him tighter, my arms shaking from the strain. His face flushes with anger as he tries to free himself from my grasp.

Smoke curls out from beneath the missile, its body rattling against the supports holding it upright. The ceiling has retracted fully, the full heat of the sun beating down on the room. Tears blur my eyes from the sting of the smoke, now billowing out from the missile freely.

Gallander gives a howl of frustration, his arm reaching back to plow his fist against my shoulder. Pain shoots through my body, but still I hang on. I hang on for Lukas. For Bone. For Atara. For Tomas. For my father.

The rumbling grows louder, the smoke hissing from the missile. Gallander's struggles renew, his legs thrashing, arms reaching. The fabric of his uniform tears in my hands. Panic surges through me as it rips even further. My fingers strain, fumbling to regain my grip, when Gallander's powerful fist gives a final blow to my knuckles. My hands give way, and the Commander pulls free.

As he surges forward, a feral scream tearing from his throat, the missile shoots from the floor in a blast of smoke. I turn away and cover my face with my arms, pulling my shirt over my mouth and nose.

Gallander's screams fill my ears along with the missile's rising thunder. I risk a peek over my shoulder. The room is engulfed in smoke, a trail of it lifting up and through the open ceiling. I let my body roll onto my back, relief flooding my chest as I close my eyes. It worked. Asher did it. We did it.

My relief lasts less than an instant as a hand clenches around my neck like a vise. I gasp for air, but barely half a breath makes it in as Gallander lifts me with one hand until my feet are barely grazing the floor. I choke, my throat closing at his grasp.

"You," he hisses through his teeth. The sound is like metal dragged across a gravel road, and it sends shock waves of fear through me. His eyes are more furious than I've ever seen.

"You will pay for this," he snarls. "Every single person you've ever known—I will hunt them down and burn them alive, and you'll watch every second of it!"

I can't breathe. Pulling on his arm does nothing, and when I reach for his fingers, he takes his other hand and yanks mine away. He rips the knife-belt from my waist as my lungs blister, screaming for air. I'm gagging and choking like Walker did all those years ago.

I know now that Gallander won't wait until his serum is finished; he'll crush the life from me right here and now.

There's no air, no relief for my lungs. I can feel the nothingness coming for me. *At least Gallander won't have me to experiment on any longer.* I think. *The virus will still work without me. He's too late. He can kill me, but it will still be too late . . .*

Darkness clouds my vision. It won't be long now. Soon I'll be—

—The sound of the gunshot seems far away, even for my ears. I force my cloudy eyes open as the iron grip loosens around my neck. Gallander's face comes into focus, the anger there now twisted with confusion. I don't understand, either, until he looks down and releases me entirely.

I collapse, heaving for air and choking. A red dot, tiny at first, spreads across Gallander's uniform, and he peers down at me with an overwhelming sense of disbelief as his hand clutches at the bloodstain.

"But . . ." he stammers, swaying on his feet. "But you can't. I . . . I was . . . so close, and . . ." His hands stretch out for me, but before I can muster the energy to dodge them, his eyes glaze over, and his legs collapse beneath him. His massive body tumbles down and doesn't move again, his lifeless eyes wide open on his infuriated face.

A figure moves behind him. My father. Pistol gripped tightly, finger still on the trigger. The gun, and his glare, are aimed at Gallander's head. Waiting for the Commander to move again. As if he can't believe the man could possibly be dead.

Even I expect him to rise from the floor, dust off his uniform, and pick up right where he left off. How could one bullet be enough to kill him?

"You okay, son?" my father asks. I can't speak, only nod, my hands rubbing at my sore neck.

The others. My pulse quickens, and I spin around, catching sight of Bone's body a few feet away. The faint rise and fall of his chest, even as blood pumps out of his wound.

I'm on my knees at his side in seconds, his eyelids fluttering open at my movement. I press the folds of his shirt against the wound, but he's lost too much blood. Even now, his face is white, red at the corners of his mouth.

He blinks, trying to focus on me.

"Fiver?" he croaks. It's a strained, burbling sound. He coughs and blood trickles down his chin. The sight nearly makes my heart burst out from my ribs. He inhales again, struggling now simply to breathe. "Did we win?"

His eyes flicker, and a crackling comes through the walkie-talkie. My head whirls around. Where is it? I can't pinpoint the sound, but as I turn, Lukas's battered face appears. His hand is outstretched, the mangled walkie-talkie resting in his palm. Blood is drying in a broad line from his nose to his lips; another gash on his forehead drips into his eyebrow. But the pain in his eyes is not from his wounds. He's seen too much death. Why does he have to endure more?

I hold the walkie-talkie close to my ear. "Repeat, repeat, we have a confirmed hit! A confirmed hit!" Asher. His voice rings out in relieved exhilaration, shouting praises to Elorai while victorious voices call out in the background.

Bone's pale lips stretch in the faintest of smiles. His hand clamps on mine, and I return his grin.

"Yeah, man, we won," I say. My voice catches, but he doesn't seem to notice. His brow creases with a serious, desperate look, and his grip tightens.

"Fiver," he gurgles, then coughs out more blood. My insides strain, threatening to break.

"Hey, take it easy," I tell him. "We're gonna get you out of here, okay?"

Bone shakes his head. He knows better. Why try to fool him if I can't even fool myself?

"Listen, Fiver," he tries again. "What I did . . . you gotta know I'm—"

"—Don't." Tears spill down my face. "It's okay."

But his eyes don't relent, his hand still clinging to mine. "I can't . . . make it up to you."

I squeeze his hand as if the pressure of my grasp could keep him alive. "You don't have to," I tell him. "It's finished. It's over."

His tears flow freely, streaking down his cheeks like water from a sieve. "Forgive me. Please."

My chest is torn to shreds. I can't breathe. Can't speak. I nod, wetness dripping from my face and onto our hands. I find my voice and force myself to say it: "Of course I do."

He lets his head loll back, his eyes closing in relief. "And Gallander's . . . dead?"

I nod again, letting a sorrowful laugh press out from my lungs. "Yeah, he is. He's not gonna make his serum. It's all over."

Bone lets his eyes flicker open again. He swallows painfully, each breath a ragged struggle. "Then . . . I'd say we did . . . pretty good today."

His grin widens, and I return it, the heartbreak overwhelming my chest. He regards me with one final satisfied smirk, and his eyes fall closed again. He heaves more air into his lungs, and I can barely hear the last words he says over the thudding inside my ribcage.

"Thank you . . . Joshua."

FIFTY-FIVE

SMOKE RISES IN WISPY TENDRILS FROM THE SCORCHED earth beneath my feet. Patches of flames still lick at the scraggly remnants of branches, grass, bushes, and bombed-out trees.

The Wood is gone.

I recognize nothing in this barren place. For miles, all I can see are ash and gaunt trees alongside craters where the bomb fragments made impacts several feet into the dirt. The leaves are gone. The streams are choked with debris. The animals are gone. My snares. My storage spaces. My home. All gone.

My father wanted to come with me, but I wouldn't let him. He argued the two of us together would make the task go twice as fast, but I promised I would get enough samples for him on my own. All I wanted was one last walk through the Wood I once called home.

I find the South Stream and follow it north along once-familiar pathways now completely destroyed and unrecognizable. The leather satchel thumps against my thigh as it always did, the strap in its comfortable position across my shoulder, ready to be filled with a variety of the day's findings. But there's only one thing I'm collecting today.

Twigs snap beneath my feet, my boots kicking up the devastated earth. I step over the charred remains of branches and broken trees, my eyes alert as always. But there is no movement. Nothing flitting from tree to tree. Nothing skirting beneath the bushes. Nothing splashing across the stream.

I kneel and sweep my hand across the ground, shoving aside the loose dirt and ash and crumbling, charred sticks until I get to the firm earth underneath. I pull a trowel and a small plastic container from inside my bag and scoop up enough soil to fill the container. Sealing it, I place it inside my satchel alongside the nine others like it.

Later, in the lab, my father will analyze the samples to confirm the soil is dead. That the unique compounds inside it have been destroyed, that no Vitmor will ever be able to grow here again. That no one will ever be able to recreate Gallander's serum.

My father is pacing beside the hovercab when I return. He stops when he sees me, his eyebrows lifting.

"You filled all of them?" he asks. I nod, pulling the satchel off and handing it to him. He peers inside and pulls out one of the containers. "All from different areas?"

I nod again, and he puts the container back inside. "Good," he says.

My gaze lingers on the remains of Endenbough Wood, and the tugging in my chest that I've been trying to ignore returns with full force. Some things will grow back, given enough time. But it will never be the same again.

My throat constricts at the thought of Inari. There was no sign of her anywhere.

My father lays a hand on my arm. "I'm sorry, son." His eyes overflow with sympathy, but there's pride there as well. My father is proud of me. I won't ever get used to that look.

"Now come on," he says, motioning toward the hovercab. "We've got a long way to go. Nathaniel said he wants to see you."

I gaze over my shoulder toward Boqua.

"Hang on." My ribcage tightens. "There's something I need to do first."

§

They're both blond.

Netta Deagan and her husband, Beamer—better known as Beams Deagan.

They're both surprised and wary when they open the door and find me on the other side. It takes everything I have to keep from turning tail and disappearing from this place.

The house is small and clean. I sit on the edge of the couch and try not to touch anything. Netta brings me a cup of something hot that tastes like bitter water, but I drink it anyway. She can tell just by looking at me that I have something to say that they're not going to like.

"Atara is dead."

No point in sugarcoating it. I watch their eyes refuse to believe me, but my own are welling with tears at what I have to say next.

"And I killed her."

Beams and Netta exchange pain-filled glances, but I don't stop. I can't stop. More words have never come from my mouth at once, and they tumble out like boulders careening downward in a rockslide. "Atara was the bravest person I ever knew, the strongest person I ever saw. She wouldn't let the Commanders fill her head with lies, and she was the only one who cared enough about me to plant a germ of doubt in my mind. She was brilliant and tenderhearted and beautiful, and I loved her."

And she's dead because of me.

By the time I'm finished, my face is soaked and my eyes sting, and I can barely form coherent words. When I peer up, Netta is buried in her husband's arms, her shoulders shaking. Beams holds her and looks to me, his features strained with grief.

"If it wasn't for her, I wouldn't be here." I barely manage the words.

I wait for them to throw me out. To scream and curse and damn me to every hell imaginable. It's the least I deserve.

But Beams gazes at his wife, and something passes between them I can't understand. He steps into the hallway behind her and opens a door, peering inside. A moment later, a small blond head appears.

My heart catches in my throat as the boy looks from me to Beams. Eyes the same vibrant blue. Piercing, just as hers were. Like knives in my chest. Beams leads him down the hallway toward me and stands behind the boy with his hands on his shoulders.

"This is our son, Alaric," Beams says. "He's eight years old. We found out that the Peacekeepers were on their way with his letter when word came out that Gallander had been killed." His voice cracks. "If it wasn't for you, *he* wouldn't be here."

Netta nods in agreement with her husband. When she speaks, her voice quavers, heavy with grief yet tinged with the slightest hint of hope. "If it wasn't for you, sooner or later, we *all* wouldn't be here." She exhales through her nose with a puff of air, then disentangles herself from her husband and crosses the five steps over to me.

She leans down and takes my head in her hands, one palm on each cheek, and holds my gaze, her face full of questions and pain. As our eyes lock together, I force mine to stay open, force myself to face what I've done. But then something very much like relief softens Netta's features, and her pupils grow wide with compassion. She pulls me to my feet and embraces me, her arms welcoming and her firm grip reassuring. She holds me there for several long moments as if I were some precious thing. For first time in fifteen years I feel a mother's love.

FIFTY-SIX

DEKKAN IS SLOWLY REBUILDING. GALLANDER'S FORCES barely left a stone unturned in their search, and I feel a prick of guilt: the city suffered because of me. My father and I tread through the littered streets, which are crowded with people. They shout back and forth as they replace a roof or patch up a fence or haul debris into large supply cabs. My father's spirits are lifted at the swell. He's out in the open again, not imprisoned by four walls filled with nothing but Vitmor, science equipment, and fear. Already his pale skin shows more color as the sunlight sinks into his pores.

The crowd has the opposite effect on me, but I ignore the unintelligible chatter and lead my father to Nathaniel's house. The building hasn't suffered as much damage as those on the main streets, but the front door has been kicked in, and it hangs crooked on bent and broken hinges. The grass has been uprooted, and what's left of the lawn is littered with trash and whatever the soldiers had hurled through the broken windows of the house. Kitchen plates and even a couple of chairs, their legs splintered, are scattered across the front yard.

I hear skittering from inside the house, but I can't make out the voices inside. My father smiles and picks up his pace. "Yes, it's us!" he calls.

Nathaniel appears in the doorway, his face breaking out into a large grin. He's seen my father several times since the Wood was destroyed, but each time he captures his brother in a warm embrace, as he does now.

"I thought you said you were fixing up this place," my father jokes.

Nathaniel raises his eyebrows. "You wouldn't mind chipping in, would you?"

"Fiver!" Lukas appears from behind the house, his eyes lighting up at the sight of me.

I let a smile peek through. "How's your mom?"

He glows. "She's out of bed almost four hours a day! Doc says if she keeps going at this rate, she'll be running marathons before the month is out." His face calms and grows serious. "Thanks, Fiver."

I start to reply, but his eyes light up again. "Did you tell him yet?" he asks his father. Nathaniel barely opens his mouth before Lukas is tugging on my arm. "Go on, look inside!"

"What is it?" I let him lead me onto the porch, and he motions to the door, bouncing from one foot to the other in excitement. I push on the door gingerly, afraid it will crash to the porch at the slightest touch. It swings open on lopsided hinges, but it remains upright, revealing the inside of the house.

And I see her.

At first, I think I must be seeing things. Her fur gleams, brushed and clean. Her eyes, brown and wide, catch sight of me, and her fluffy tail flies out from behind her as she lunges from the floor with an excited yip. My chest swells, bubbling over with unspeakable joy.

I've dropped to my knees, and she collides into my waiting arms, pushing me to the floor and covering my face with her lapping tongue. I hold her and press myself into her fur as her calming presence fills me.

I can't believe she's here, she's alive. She's alive.

Inari lets me hold her for long minutes, her tail flapping back and forth hard enough to hit me on either side of my body with each swing. She nuzzles her head at the side of my neck, with small whines pressing out from her throat. My tears soak into her fur before I realize the others are looking at me.

"How . . . how did you find her?" I choke out.

"She came here!" Lukas beams. "She must've followed my scent." He chuckles. "She was covered in mud and gunk, but I knew it was her!"

I look back at them and see in each of their eyes something I thought was gone a long time ago. Something I remember being in my parents' eyes as a young child, the same thing I saw in Atara's blue gaze. They are family, each one of them. We are family.

Suddenly the Wood seems like a small price to pay for this.

I turn to one side, and I'm surprised to find Micah and Jael watching me with Inari. "Aw, what a nice little reunion," Micah says. He gives a sarcastic grin, one arm draped across Jael's shoulder.

They've changed. The two of them have traded in their uniforms for jeans and T-shirts, and Jael sports a sparkling gemstone in her upper left ear. The traditional symbol of a girl betrothed.

My eyebrows lift. Jael blushes and looks at Micah, who smirks at me. "What?" he snorts. "Surprised?"

I shake my head. Micah and Jael slip out from between each other's arms, and Micah crosses his. "I thought we were supposed to have a meeting, Nathaniel," he says.

Nathaniel nods. "Did you hear anything from Nova?"

Micah scoffs. "I've heard enough out of her. Asher and Jakob can listen all they want. But I say Nova is a ticking time bomb. She wants those kids out—now."

"She thinks Gallander's death has paved the way for her," I say, and to my surprise, Micah nods in agreement.

Nathaniel purses his lips. "The war is still raging out there. Even with Gallander dead, those soldiers still believe in him. Even if the rebels manage to get them out by force, they'll never be able to bring them home."

Silence falls on the group. My father shoves his hands into his pockets and gives me the slightest grim smile. We both know what has to be done. Too many lives have been lost for nothing. The pang of Tomas's death still bleeds raw in Micah and Jael's eyes.

"The war has to end," I say, stepping forward. All eyes flit to me. "Gallander's army has to know the truth. The Boquan people have to know the truth."

Micah clearly approves, but Nathaniel squints in doubt. "They won't believe Lucians," he says.

"So we start with Gallander's secrets," I reply. "He kept that research facility from even the highest government officials. All the proof we need is in that school or in the soldiers we captured there."

"He's the one who started the war," Micah says. "He's bound to have evidence of the massacres he planned on Boqua."

"He's a traitor to his own people," Jael says. "If he could betray Lucia, what would have stopped him from betraying Boqua?"

I nod, my eyes sweeping over Nathaniel's face. "We have to expose the real reason for the war," I say. "With no war, there's no need for the soldiers. Boqua can have its children back."

Everyone watches Nathaniel for a response. He rubs his chin, stretching the skin beneath his lip. We wait.

He draws a deep breath. "Peace," he says, the blue of his eyes shining with hope. "This is the first chance in decades to bring peace to our countries. And it's all up to us."

EPILOGUE

WIND TUGS GENTLY AT MY HAIR, MY BANGS REACHING down to my eyebrows once again. I thread my fingers through the cool grass while Inari rests her head across my ankle and lets out contented sighs.

The hill is far outside of Dekkan and its noise. It overlooks a long, grassy meadow, and just beyond I can see the Wood. Over the last year, green has made its way back into that barren place, slowly but surely reclaiming the land again. Covering the scars.

The sun dips below the ragged trees, casting red and orange streaks across the darkening sky. My ears are open. I don't always wear the hearing aids Nathaniel gave me, but on nights like this, I often come up here to listen to the soft sounds of summer. The crickets chirp out their welcome of the night while the stars in the sky awaken and shine.

I didn't see many stars in Endenbough Wood.

Inari's ears twitch, but I've already heard the footsteps behind me. Lukas says nothing as he folds his legs beside me and sinks into the grass, tilting his head and looking at the sky.

"I wish all nights were like this one," he finally speaks, the words clear and precise.

One side of my mouth pulls itself up in a half smile. "Then you wouldn't appreciate them nearly as much."

He grins. "True."

He reaches out a hand to Inari, and she wags her tail as she swipes her tongue across his fingers. His smile broadens, and he scratches her head. His gaze reaches out past the meadow, following my line of sight to the Wood.

His smile fades. "Are you going to go back?" he asks in a whisper so low I can barely hear it, even with the hearing aids.

I take a breath. Feel it fill my lungs, let it out quick. Watching me with soft eyes, Inari pulls her head away from Lukas's touch.

Someday, the Wood will be whole again. The streams will clear. The trees will stand tall. The animals will return. Some part of me longs for it. Some part of me is dreaming of the day when I can again step into the embrace of the trees and disappear. But a larger, stronger part of me knows I would never be happy there again.

"My home is here," I tell Lukas, looking away from the spindly trees and into his waiting face. "Because my family is here."

His smile returns, and he settles back into his relaxed slouch, tempting Inari to come closer with affectionate pats.

"Dad's doing a pretty good job negotiating, don't you think?"

I nod, turning to the meadow. Who knew Nathaniel would make as good of a diplomat as he did an infiltrator. Traits I wouldn't necessarily want combined for such a job, but for now at least the senseless killing has paused while Boqua considers our evidence. Encouraged by the response Boqua has given to their requests, Nova and her followers finally braved daylight and made themselves public. The children haven't been freed from their duties yet, but their parents have been granted visits with them at regular intervals.

"Are you still in touch with Atara's parents?"

Atara. The name stabs as it always will.

"Not really," I whisper as I flinch inwardly. The look in their eyes as I recounted her final moments was enough to make me wish I had been in the Wood when the bomb hit. But I'd wanted them to know what she had done. That her bravery, the truth she never lost sight of, and everything she stirred within me were the reasons we were here today and free from Gallander.

Inari leaves Lukas's side and presses herself against me. She's sensed the change in me, a shift too subtle for Lukas to notice. Sweat building on my palms, heartbeat beginning to race. I breathe in deeply and reach for her soft fur. She gives my arm a gentle lick and settles onto the ground between Lukas and me.

"They have peace," I say. I take another deep breath. "Hopefully, others will, too."

Lukas catches my eye. "And you?"

I let my fingers brush through Inari's fur again, no longer feeling my heartbeat pound. Bone's face floats out from my memories, and I find I miss his sarcastic smirk. He made a mistake, but at least he died confident that we won.

I think of my father. He tells me he has nightmares sometimes, like I do. He'll be back in Gallander's lab, a room swarming with needles and rats, watching as I'm dragged away with shadowy hands.

My dreams aren't much different, but now we have each other again after so many years apart. We are a family again. We have a new family, together. We're different, all of us. Changed nearly beyond recognition, but enough of us remained to patch up the tears that divided us. Even Lukas and his father have begun to heal.

But me?

I take one last look out at the Wood and let out a long breath, lifting my lips in a grin. I turn to Lukas, his face patiently waiting.

"Yeah, Lukas," I tell him, watching his eyes sparkle. "Me too."

ACKNOWLEDGMENTS

I would like to thank:

God, for giving me the desire and passion for writing that brings me so much joy and fulfillment.

My parents, Glen and Donna Ritchie, for nurturing the love of stories that has led me to where I am now.

My sister, Kayla, who never doubted me.

Dr. Marcia Hurlow of Asbury University, who taught the one and only creative writing class I was ever able to take.

My amazing editor, Erika DeSimone, who has believed in this story from the day she first read it, and who has never once let me doubt myself. Without her wellspring of knowledge, insight, and brilliance, this book would never have gotten off the ground.

And all my friends who give me all the encouragement, advice, and support I could ask for.

ABOUT THE AUTHOR

JACY RITCHIE WAS BORN AND RAISED IN OHIO, SUR-rounded by trees and fields and horses. Her love for books started even before she could read, and once she discovered the local library, it only grew from there. She wrote her first complete novel in the sixth grade, using a number two pencil and a spiral-bound notebook. Writing has been her passion ever since.

She currently lives in Indianapolis, Indiana with a very destructive cat named Milo. When she's not writing, you can find her exploring the woods with her dog Hachi, playing one of her favorite videogames, or practicing jiu jitsu.